"Doesn't a fine lady know when a man's in love with her?" Morgan asked, his voice soft as velvet.

"How can you love me? You don't know me," she protested feebly.

"I know you in my heart and soul. Isobel De Lacy, for once in your life, admit the truth. You're not nearly as cold and distant as you pretend."

Inwardly she panicked, afraid and excited, yet at a loss for what she should say or do. When she raised her arms to push him away, he captured her wrists to pull her closer. The aura of heat from his body engulfed her as his arms went around her back.

"No," she protested one final time.

"Forget who and what you are. Come, let me make love to you."

Other *Leisure* books by Patricia Phillips:
THE ROSE OF RAVENSCRAG
THE CONSTANT FLAME
THE ROSE & THE FLAME
NIGHTINGALE

Bride of the Dragon

PATRICIA PHILLIPS

LEISURE BOOKS NEW YORK CITY

For Lady, Christie and Alice, my canine companions on my travels to another time and place.

A LEISURE BOOK®

January 1998

Published by

Dorchester Publishing Co., Inc.
276 Fifth Avenue
New York, NY 10001

ISBN 0-8439-4340-8

Printed in the United States of America.

Bride of the Dragon

Chapter One

1347, Stoneham Magna Castle, Herefordshire

Isobel De Lacy drew her cloak tight against the morning chill. From the castle battlements she had an unobstructed view of the surrounding countryside veiled in gold and tinged bronze and scarlet by the frosty autumn nights. When the sun finally rose above the trees, it set the valley afire. In the flood of light the castle's sandstone walls sparkled, Stoneham Magna's turreted splendor a sharp contrast to the distant backdrop of the Black Mountains of Wales hidden under a dawn shroud of mist.

Directly below the castle walls came the rising clamor of many voices, neighing horses and clanging armaments. The surrounding meadows were filled with knights and their retainers, who had assembled to compete in Stoneham Magna's grand tourney.

All week competitors had been gathering, and their colorfully striped tents splashed the green meadows like exotic blooms. Beside the river the tilt field stood ready, barriers in place, empty wooden stands waiting to give the spectators an unobstructed view of the lists. The striped canopy over the stands was bright with silken banners and flags flapping in the wind.

Hawkers and entertainers were already thronging the tilt ground, where merchants had been erecting their stalls since before dawn, eager to be ready for the first customers. Now the savory smells of meat pasties and burned sugar mingled with the acrid scent of horse and woodsmoke.

Isobel hugged herself in anticipation of today's excitement. The castle had not seen so much activity since her father brought home his new bride. When that lady died five years later, Isobel had not mourned her. In fact, had whining, sickly Phillippa never come into her life, she would not now be under the thumb of a stepbrother she barely knew.

Last spring her father had died while fighting in France. Phillippa's adult son, Lionel Hurley, lost no time in petitioning the king for control of Isobel's wardship, including the revenue from her dower lands. She supposed this latter prospect had been of greatest interest to him, for Lionel was always out of funds.

Isobel hurried indoors to get ready for the big day. As she wound down the twisting tower stairs, she wondered how Lionel had been able to finance a tournament, let alone one on such a grand scale. Even the king had been invited, but, to Lionel's disappointment, King Edward had more pressing obligations. All England celebrated with nonstop revels and tournaments the king's return from France following his victory at Crécy. Lionel probably hoped to improve his image by winning in the lists. Doubt had been cast on his courage in the field, and though he swore his enemies spread lies about him, Isobel was not convinced. In the short time she had known her stepbrother she had found him to be devious and untruthful. Merely the hint of cowardice tarnished a knight's honor, and Lionel was eager to repair the damage, whether he could afford a tourney or not.

In Stoneham Castle's great hall Lionel lounged in his chair, alone at the lord's table; the other knights were eager to be out on the field. He, however, could afford to bide his time. There were none who could best him in the lists, and he welcomed this upcoming challenge to publicly prove his worth. The huge purses he had offered as prizes had drawn many skilled competitors, most of whom were well known to him. His thin mouth curved in satisfaction as he reviewed the likely field of challengers. Because they were known to him, they presented little threat. The only competitor he feared, Bryan, lord of Meyric, lay abed recovering from wounds received in France. Lionel's cunning choice of October for this tournament was no accident.

He felt a stab of unease when he considered the remote possibility of being bested by an unknown challenger. Then he quickly drowned his misgivings in a deep swig of Gascon wine. He would defeat all comers and keep the prize money for himself.

He had to win—he had nowhere near the gold he had promised. Were he to use every penny of the entry fees and empty his own coffers to boot, he could not raise so vast an amount. But, as gambling was his lifeblood, Lionel considered the odds of this particular wager very good indeed.

He left the dais, striding across the hall; then he paused, catching his breath at the vision he saw gliding toward him. Great shafts of sunlight speared her satin and brocade garments, striking metallic glints from the fabric and crowning her with a halo of gold. He swallowed hard, his blood racing. By the rood—were he not already married, he would take the beauteous Isobel to wife, stepsister or nay. There were no blood ties between them, after all. Still, he need not wed the wench to have his pleasure with her—if she were willing . . .

''Dearest Isobel, you are a vision,'' he said, barely able to keep a husky note of arousal from his voice. Lionel held out his beringed hand, bringing her quickly from the rushes, where she had dropped him an obedient curtsy.

''My lord,'' she said, using the term politely and only at his insistence, for she thought of none other than her late father as lord of Stoneham Magna.

''Nay, sweeting, Lionel . . . brother,'' he suggested softly, licking his lips in anticipation as he gazed down on the white mounds of her breasts, delectably framed by a narrow band of sable.

Isobel could not mistake the desire flickering in his hazel eyes, and the discovery chilled her. Stiffly, she smiled as she took a step backward, disengaging her hand from his eager clasp.

A serving woman handed her a dish of honey-soaked bread, with a goblet of sweet wine to follow. Isobel quickly ate the food, eager to be part of the excitement beyond the walls.

''Isn't Maude ready yet?'' she asked when she did not see the rest of the family. She was still uncomfortably aware of the predatory gleam in Lionel's eye.

''Aye, probably,'' he agreed absently, reluctant to take his attention from this vision that brought the gloomy hall to life. He could feel his heart racing. Were King Edward not already wed, perchance even he would find this wench appealing, for she was surely glorious enough for a king. Then reality quickly squelched his schemes—Isobel De Lacy was too baseborn ever to be queen. But why not the king's mistress? Edward was the one man on earth he would not object to sharing this woman with, for, after all, Edward was king. Mayhap he could introduce Isobel at court.

His wife, Maude, his two small children, and their maids entered the hall amid a chorus of infant wails and rustling skirts. When Maude came to stand beside her sister-in-law, the contrast was painful.

Isobel had creamy skin and lustrous blue-black hair; her large eyes were a melting violet and so heavily lashed, her cheeks seemed smudged with charcoal. Though only of average height, Isobel was fully fleshed, firm, white and delectably shaped, with her small waist and full breasts. Even her beringed hands were dainty, her voice sweetly husky. . . .

Lionel shuddered at his own lascivious thoughts before courtesy made him turn to greet his wife.

"Welcome, dear one," he said mechanically, stepping back to avoid the sticky, reaching hands of Audrey, his infant daughter. Edward, his four-year-old son, bowed deeply to him, and Lionel was well pleased.

"Shouldn't we head for the field?" Maude asked in her high-pitched, nasal whine.

Tall, and thin as a flagpole, she hid no yielding treasures in her mulberry satin bodice. Maude was as flat as a board. Today her carroty hair was hidden under a wimple, which Lionel found an improvement; there was little she could do to conceal her dry, freckled skin and small brown eyes. Maude was definitely no beauty. But then, he had not married her for her looks. She was to bring him a great dowry, which, in reality, had fallen far short of his expectations. Lionel had never forgiven her for that.

"You look well in the new gown, sister," Maude said grudgingly, envious of Isobel's appearance. Her own gown of mulberry satin trimmed in braid had pearls sewn across the fabric; its long, hanging sleeves edged in fur and lined in yellow satin were very grand. It was a magnificent gown—yet beside her glowing sister-in-law, Maude felt as drab as a moorhen.

Isobel smiled in pleasure, a dimple appearing in her right cheek. To her chagrin, she had no matching dimple in the other cheek and she considered this discrepancy vastly disfiguring. High on her cheekbone there was a second flaw to her beauty, a black mole, present since childhood. Not versed in the ways of men, Isobel could not know that men considered such distinctive marks arresting.

She turned slowly to give Maude a better view of her new gown of lustrous magenta satin rippling over gold brocade. The long, hanging sleeves were lined in magenta, while the laced surcoat was trimmed with dark fur at the neckline. In the splendid gown she felt like a princess, which, Lionel had assured her, was exactly for whom this gown had been made. He had brought back both gowns as part of the spoils of war captured from the defeated French, giving Isobel the gift to help sweeten her mood before he told her it was he who now had charge over the castle. Worse than that, Lionel also had charge over her and her dower lands until she married. This favor had been quickly granted to him by a war-weary Edward. The king had more important matters to consider than the wardship of some unknown gentlewoman.

A dozen dresses would never make her accept Lionel as lord of Stoneham Magna Castle: that position belonged to someone with De Lacy blood, not this son of the dead Phillippa, sired by an obscure Irish baron. And even if he gave her a thousand dresses, he could never make her love him!

When Lionel had ordered Isobel to return from her remote manor of Ambrey, at first she thought he intended to betroth her. Later she realized he had merely wanted her off her fertile land so he could conduct matters there as he saw fit. Lately she had also realized that Lionel wanted her in a very different manner, and this knowledge made her flesh crawl. She could not dispute his right to take her income while she was his ward, but he had no right to anything else. Isobel was careful to keep her distance from Stoneham Magna's puppet lord.

When she requested to go to Ambrey Priory, where her great-aunt Blanche was prioress, Lionel had angrily refused. So, for the past five months, Isobel had smarted under his watchful eye and the austere measures he imposed on the household, effectively siphoning what he could from the castle coffers to pay for his own vices.

Lionel's squires were hovering impatiently in the background, anxious for their lord to commit to the field.

Maude quickly pecked her husband's cheek and wished him success.

"And you, sweet," Lionel hinted, stepping close to Isobel. "Will you not kiss me and wish me well?"

She smiled sweetly as she slipped a gauzy scarf from about her headdress. "I'll give you my favor to wear."

Lionel smiled too, but his expression was forced. He accepted the token and looped it about his fist before raising it to his lips, where he inhaled her perfume. The heady fragrance quickened his pulse. Watching Isobel above the folds of filmy gold, he asked huskily, "An I become today's champion, what favor will you grant me then, sweet Isobel?"

Again she smiled with studied sweetness. "Why, brother, I'll present you with the victor's laurels."

Abruptly Lionel spun on his heel and strode from the hall. Maude glanced sideways at her sister-in-law, aware that something untoward had just taken place, but not sure what it was. Tension always crackled between those two. Clearly there was no love lost on Isobel's part. . . . She was not sure what fueled her husband's moods, though she doubted it was brotherly love.

"Come, you two layabeds, we're missing the tourney."

Maude's young cousin, Brianna, raced inside the hall, blue skirts flying, her coiled red hair springing from its fret. "There are hundreds of handsome men just waiting to pay court to us and you're in here wasting time," she cried, seizing Isobel and dancing her about the room, their soft-soled shoes swishing through the rushes. "Come, Isobel, come. There are minstrels and mummers with dancing dogs."

Isobel allowed herself to be propelled forward until Maude was left behind, trying to hurry the maids and the children, complaining all the while that they were moving too fast for her to keep up. She also wanted them to ride instead of walk to the tilt field, as more befitted their station.

Maude's complaints were ignored as the two young women raced across the drawbridge and over the damp grass, laughing like village maids. Brianna always talked nonstop, commenting on everything she saw. She could not wait to experience the carnival atmosphere, which made the tilt ground as noisy as a fair, alive with entertainers and vendors raucously shouting their wares. As they passed they were accosted by pie and ale sellers, while marchpane figures and sugared comfits beckoned silently from gaily decorated stalls.

To have Brianna as her companion had been the only benefit Isobel had received from Lionel's unwanted tenure at the castle. And even that pleasure would soon be gone, for in the spring Brianna was to be wed. Her impending marriage had heightened her eagerness to be courted by all and sundry before it was too late. When a handsome man smiled at her, Brianna swung into action, fluttering her eyelashes and coquettishly lowering her lids. In minutes she would be openly flirting with him. The younger woman had the knack of knowing just what to say, as if she had been born with the gift, whereas Isobel often felt uncomfortable in a man's presence. Visiting knights to the castle either stared at her like dumbstuck fools, or treated her with a reverence worthy of the Blessed Mother.

As Lady Edith had died giving birth to her, Isobel had no mother to teach her the rules of courtship. The matter seemed to be conducted in such a silly fashion, she thought, with the man paying extravagant compliments and the woman simperingly accepting them. Why couldn't people just say what was in their hearts, instead of having to follow foolish rules?

Arnol De Lacy had raised his only child in the same

straightforward manner in which he conducted his own affairs. Isobel's confidence in her abilities was shattered when she went to be schooled by the nuns at Ambrey Priory, where her great-aunt was prioress. Aunt Blanche was dismayed by her unladylike manner and scolded her brother for thinking he could raise a girl child alone. It was she who advised him to take a wife, if only for the girl's sake. Isobel assumed ideal female behavior probably fell somewhere between her father's lax theories and the rigid ones of Aunt Blanche, for in her opinion, the prioress weighed too heavily on the side of piety, decorum and simpering obedience.

When she was finally allowed a suitor, she hoped courtship would no longer be a mystery. By that time she would be a dried-up spinster, for Lionel turned away any man who came to court her. Beyond a curtsy, and the polite exchange of greetings, Isobel was not allowed to speak to her would-be suitors. She was banished to her room while Lionel spoke on her behalf. Her most persistent admirer was Sir Rafe De Gascon. The young knight appeared pleasant, glimpsed as he was through the smoky shadows of the great hall.

Lionel kept her like a captive in her room. Since the day he had summoned her to Stoneham Magna Castle from her manor of Ambrey, life had been boring and restricted. Lionel's petty rules sorely tried Isobel's patience, for at Ambrey she had been her own mistress. Despite Aunt Blanche's schooling in womanly obedience, Isobel was hard-pressed to accept Lionel Hurley's command.

''Oh, look, Sir Rafe's staring at you,'' Brianna said with a squeak, clutching Isobel's arm. From their vantage point in the center box of the stands, they had a perfect view of the tilt ground and its contenders.

A young knight rode toward them. His head was bare and the light glinted on his sun-streaked brown hair. He stood in the stirrups to blow a kiss of greeting for the noble ladies, eliciting a delighted response from the female spectators.

"He's so handsome, and he's madly in love with you, Isobel." Brianna sighed dreamily, as she leaned her chin in her hands and gazed down on the assembling knights.

"Well, much good it'll do him," Isobel observed gloomily as she watched her stepbrother ride onto the field.

"Why? Don't you like him?"

"I don't know him. Lionel barely lets me see him before I'm whisked away. Sir Rafe looks well enough and I know he's spoken for me."

Brianna clasped her hands in delight at the idea of being courted by such a handsome knight. Pressing her clenched fists against her bosom, she practiced swooning in his strong arms. "Oh, I wish he wanted to be my husband. Sir William's old and he likely smells of ale." Here she giggled, giving Isobel a playful shove when she contradicted her description. "He wants me to give him babes. That's why he wants a young wife, because he needs an heir."

Isobel's attention wandered from Brianna's oft-repeated story about her future husband as she watched the splendidly caparisoned knights pacing their mounts back and forth, their horses' trappings gleaming in the sunshine. There were hundreds of strangers here today at Stoneham Magna. She had never seen so many people of such diverse shapes and sizes. If only every day could be this exciting. Later, when the first courses had been run, she and Brianna would walk around the tilt ground to watch the entertainers and shop at the stalls. Isobel had money in her hanging pocket to buy trinkets and sweetmeats; she planned to ignore Lionel's edict that they spend only what was strictly necessary.

Finally, when all was ready, the grand parade of knights began. The two women gasped at the splendid colors of the horses' trappings, admiring the elaborate embroidery and gold-fringed saddlecloths that swept the ground as they passed. Some of these visiting knights had such tall and fanciful helms surmounted by plumes and crests that they looked like giants in the saddle. Their horses were richly caparisoned in cloth of gold and silver, in red, green and lapis velvet, until they were hardly recognizable as fierce warhorses.

Splendid purple damask bordered with goldsmith's work adorned Lionel's mount as he led the parade about the tilt field, the knights' magnificent horses keeping a measured gait behind him. Three great emerald green plumes danced on Lionel's sparkling helm, making him appear very tall in the saddle. Behind him came his liveried retainers leading a pack of prize hunting dogs wearing gold and emerald collars.

The parade of mounted men moved slowly about the perimeter of the field, rich colors sparkling in the sunshine. Isobel enjoyed the spectacle so much, she would have liked it to continue without any need for the courses to be run, though she knew this grand parade was merely the preliminary to the real event, a strutting show of wealth and bravado intended to impress the spectators.

One of the champions paraded a leopard on a golden chain, and Isobel stared in wonder at the exotic wild creature, hissing and baring its teeth, tail angrily twitching. She had seen a leopard before only on coats of arms.

The entire field was a seething, glittering panoply of pennants and heraldic banners. Each knight could be identified by the coat of arms embroidered on his surcoat worn over a suit of plate armor. Lions rampant, unicorns and bears, even a few fire-breathing dragons were represented below. Then Isobel noticed Lionel's device and her fists clenched in anger. The gold Irish harp on a green ground that he had inherited from the Irish Hurleys had been quartered with the De Lacy's scarlet device with its silver ramparts! Isobel seethed in anger at his audacity in wearing an insignia to which he had no right. Lionel had been careful not to let her see this new coat of arms in advance, for he probably guessed she would give him a tongue-lashing for his thievery. Now, more than ever, she hoped someone would smash him into the dust and shatter his overbearing ego.

The last of the glittering participants slowly left the field, filing through the gates to the tent-dotted meadow. The trumpeters blew an extended fanfare before announcing the contestants' names and establishing the rules of combat. The tourney of Stoneham Magna had begun.

As the courses were run, Isobel was unpleasantly surprised by Lionel's skill in the lists. One after another of his opponents toppled from their saddles until he alone returned to offer further challenge.

Then, to Isobel's delight, as Lionel grew overconfident, he was finally toppled from the saddle by none other than Sir Rafe De Gascon! Isobel cheered loudly and long as Lionel's squires helped him up. His lance had splintered and now there would be a delay until it was either repaired or replaced.

Sir Rafe rode victorious about the field to the cheers of the crowd. Isobel stood to wave to him when he rode close to the stands, deliberately walking his mount to the rail so he could stand in the saddle and offer her his victor's lance.

Brianna squealed and clutched her arm. "Oh, Isobel, you're supposed to put a favor on the lance."

Regretting that she had already given her scarf to Lionel, Isobel ripped a circlet of pink flowers from the rail before her and fitted the wreath around the end of the lance. Solemnly Sir Rafe bowed to her from the saddle; raising his hand in acknowledgment, he backed slowly toward the middle of the field, holding the lance aloft to show he had earned the lady's favor. Much laughter and applause greeted the byplay, and with his raised gauntlet, Sir Rafe acknowledged the cheers.

Because he now wore his helm, Isobel could not see

Lionel's face, but she knew he could not have missed that chivalrous exchange, or her own eager role in it. The fact that she had honored his rival would make him livid. Isobel knew she would probably pay for her recklessness, but at the moment she was enjoying her newfound freedom.

She had seen Sir Rafe's face clearly when he rode close to the stands, and she found him handsome indeed. When he had stood in the saddle, he had looked up at her so ardently, she could not help being flattered by his undisguised admiration. Why could she not be courted by him? She was almost past marriageable age—three years older than Brianna, who had been betrothed since childhood.

While she stayed unmarried Lionel enjoyed the fruits of her land; when she married, the property would become her husband's. Feeling as if a great light were going on in her brain, Isobel suddenly understood Lionel's reluctance to see her courted. The fruits of Ambrey's fertile fields were too good to surrender. Now she was even more determined to petition for his acceptance of Sir Rafe's suit. This way at least she would have a say in choosing her husband instead of having to accept some terrible old winebag chosen for her by her loving stepbrother.

The courses were again resumed. Isobel's hopes for Lionel's defeat were dashed when, on the first charge, Sir Rafe's lance splintered and he fell from the saddle. Triumphant, Lionel virtually crowed as he galloped past the stands, gripping his mount like grim death, but staying in the saddle.

Finally tiring of the monotony of thundering hooves and splintering lances and the even more monotonous crowing of the victor, Isobel and Brianna left the stands to walk about the tilt grounds.

Within minutes Isobel had bought a glittering silver-and-purple-striped ribbon to match her Sunday gown; then they each bought a marchpane favor shaped like a castle and frosted with boiled pink icing.

Brianna lingered to chat with the various stall holders. Even though she was not socially experienced, instinct told Isobel these young men were not suitable companions for Brianna. Though her friend pouted in disappointment after Isobel pointed this out, she accepted Isobel's ruling. She knew the men were baseborn, but she found their rough-hewn looks attractive, and their openmouthed admiration was most satisfying to her ego.

On the tilt ground they passed parties of foreign knights, some wearing a device of stars and scimitars. Their dark, swarthy skin and coal black beards convinced Brianna they were all dangerous infidels. Isobel recognized Welsh and Irish voices in the crowd, having heard these accents from visitors to the priory. All her life she had been told the savage Welsh lurked in their mist-locked mountains awaiting an opportunity to swoop down and murder the self-respecting Herefordshire folk. Now that she had seen them face-to-face, Isobel was vastly disppointed to learn that these knights and their retainers were indistinguishable from the rest. She had half expected them to be cutthroats brandishing knives in their teeth and threatening to carry off unprotected maidens.

Several troupes of brightly dressed tumblers leaped about the grounds, slipping in between the spectators to fall at the girls' feet. Isobel clapped enthusiastically as the men virtually tied themselves in knots, sitting twisted like a Chinese puzzle. After much hesitation she threw them one of her precious coins as a reward for such a skilled performance.

Brianna had already skipped away to watch the dancing dogs, which wore ruffs about their necks and had strings of colored bells jingling from their harnesses. Soon tiring of the dancing dogs, Brianna raced away to watch the fire-eater, dragging Isobel with her. From there they moved to the magician and gasped in awe at his mystifying tricks. Finally tiring of the excitement and the hot press of the crowd, the two women bought barley-sugar sticks to revive themselves. Brianna also bought a wooden toy of a crude painted figure that leaped and turned somersaults each time the handles were squeezed, which afforded her much entertainment.

Isobel saw Lionel's men walking about the tilt ground, and they politely touched their forelocks in deference to the noblewomen. She wondered if they had orders to spy on her. Then she shrugged away the thought. It did not matter if they did, for she would have already done what she wanted long before they could make their reports.

Isobel and Brianna shared a refreshing cup of cider before climbing back into the stands to watch the rest of the tournament.

During their absence several feats of arms had been fought between lesser contenders, the coveted prizes of saddles and bridles now being carried away by the winners. To Isobel's amazement, she found Lionel was still the champion. She could hardly believe it as the marshals reeled off the wins and losses for each noble contestant, the announcements preceded by heraldic fanfares.

Lionel had even taken off his helm so the crowd could see his face as he rode around the field, basking in the spectators' adulation. Now the field was opened to anyone who wanted to challenge the champion. As several parties of knights had been late arrivals, they had competed among themselves. The victor of those contests now emerged, a sinister figure clad in black armor and riding a big black warhorse. It was he who challenged Lionel for the championship.

Isobel heard Lionel sneeringly telling Maude about this upcoming bout. He was convinced that in a matter of moments this stranger would be wallowing in the mud.

"You're so brave, husband. I never doubted you'd win," Maude gushed, basking in Lionel's reflected glory. As Maude spoke to him, Lionel's attention drifted elsewhere. He watched Isobel, waiting for a crumb of admiration from her.

Finally out of patience, Lionel prompted, "And you, love, have you not watched all my triumphs?"

"Yes, and I was surprised by your skill," Isobel admitted honestly. "I was also surprised by your new emblem," she added, pointedly staring at his surcoat. "You've no right to the De Lacy arms. That coat of arms doesn't belong to you."

Lionel shrugged, though his face had tightened. "How so? It's mine now. I'm wearing it, am I not?"

With that he stalked away without another word, clanking down the stands to the field.

"You shouldn't have upset him. You'll make him lose," Maude snapped, her face pinched with disapproval.

"Good," Isobel muttered to herself, looking daggers at her sister-in-law.

Meanwhile, two knights were fighting on foot below, swinging maces and crashing to the ground, which by now was nothing but churned mud after the day's events. Both men were finally laid out and had to be carried off the field.

Now it was Lionel's turn to face the black knight. A stir rippled over the stands as people craned forward for a better look at this challenger. Both men already wore their heavy black jousting helms, which allowed only a narrow slit through which to see. No one wanted any further delay, for the afternoon was growing chill as the sun slipped lower in the sky.

The heralds sounded a rousing fanfare. This was the signal for the jugglers and mummers, who had been on the field entertaining the crowd, to scatter to safety through the gates. This done, the contenders for the upcoming bout were announced. A second fanfare was blown and it was announced that the Dragon Knight challenged Lord Hurley to three courses, to be followed by a feat of arms.

Thinking "the Dragon Knight" a very strange name, Isobel also leaned forward for a better look at this mysterious stranger. The man's torn surcoat depicted a fierce, fire-breathing dragon in glittering gold against a black ground. She wondered if he was a Welsh knight, for they often used the dragon as their emblem. This knight's horse was also starkly caparisoned in black that was narrowly edged in gold. The man's somber choice of color gave him a very menacing appearance.

A hush descended as, losing no time, the two knights dropped their lances to the proffering position and spurred their horses forward. The galloping men met with a crash and their lances splintered simultaneously. A surprised roar came from the crowd. People clapped and stamped their feet against the wooden stands at this unexpected outcome. Though both knights had been rocked in their saddles, both still sat their mounts and were able to canter back to their respective places.

Isobel could hear Maude's wails behind her as she grew afraid her husband would be injured. Fresh ripples of excitement stirred the spectators as they realized this unknown knight was going to be a worthy contender.

The jugglers ran out onto the field to entertain the crowd until the next course was set.

This contest consisted of three courses, and the second course was now to be run. Once again a hush descended over the crowd as the knights took up their positions. The lances tipped, dropped, and then came the thundering charge—this time both knights clattered noisily from their saddles, bouncing and clanging over the ground. Neither man appeared to be seriously hurt as their squires helped them up.

The fall had shaken both men, and they withdrew from the field to briefly rest in their brightly colored pavilions before continuing with the bout.

The buzz of excitement mounted as spectators placed heavy wagers on their favorite, hard-pressed to decide which of these two excellent contenders would be triumphant.

Inside a gloomy tent Lionel's squire held cold cloths against his master's bruises, attempting to minister to him, despite his lord's seething rage.

Cursing violently, Lionel had pounded his gauntleted fist against the wooden fence before leaving the field. *That bastard should have been laid out by now!* Two passes should have been ample to decide the winner. Today's splendid performance in the lists had fully restored his honor. Until this accursed Welshman appeared, none had been able to best him. He could not lose now, not when the money was within his grasp.

As soon as he'd seen that dragon insignia, his stomach had plunged. He recalled hearing about some Welshman who wandered the continent accepting and winning all challenges. Dressed all in black, a glittering gold dragon on his breast, this mysterious Dragon Knight struck fear in the hearts of all who encountered him. Who in God's name would have thought the bastard would come here? On top of that, the stranger had been late. If only he had barred him from entering the lists, as some would have done. Now, because of his own generosity, he was risking defeat.

Lionel ran his hand across his sweating brow, shoving aside his servants with their cloths, having matters of far more importance on his mind than a few bruises. There was only one thing left to do. It would be tricky to pull it off, but he had no other choice.

Lionel signaled his master armorer and, in an undertone, he growled, "Bring me the reserve lance."

The man understood.

Though from a distance this lance appeared blunt, as was the rule, all would not be as it seemed. He'd learned this clever trick from an old champion and had saved it to use on just such a desperate occasion as this. When he made that final pass, his lance would be buried deep in the Welshman's chest, long before anyone suspected aught was amiss. Accidents happened in the lists, and though such a thing was not common, it was not unheard of.

Ready, Lionel clanked out of his tent. His retinue followed and he remounted his horse, preparing to run the final course.

This time the heralds blew their most elaborate fanfare before announcing that this final pass would decide the champion of the day. And Sir Lionel Hurley, convinced of victory, had wagered his entire winnings on this single pass.

To his amazement, Lionel saw the Welshman shake his head when the terms were read, indicating he did not accept them. Livid, Lionel demanded to know the meaning of his action.

The tourney's marshals conferred with the challenger.

"My lord, the Dragon Knight wishes to state that if this course is not conclusive, he will give combat on foot as previously written."

Lionel smiled, his thin mouth sly. Was that all? He could well afford to grant him that. After all, how could this Welshman know what surprises lay in store for him? A doomed man should be granted his dying wish.

Briskly Lionel nodded agreement, and the message was duly conveyed. Already the sun was beginning to sink in the sky and the breeze was freshening. It was high time the day's events were over. Again that confounded bastard shook his head. Lionel could hardly believe it. His face was flushed with anger. This time the stranger wanted the weapons of hand-to-hand combat decided. Lionel held up his hand for silence as the crowd grew noisy.

"Tell the bastard we'll fight to the death, an he so wishes, with whatever weapons he chooses," he growled in an undertone to the chief marshal, eager to have this contest settled before someone discovered his trickery. "In fact, tell him I'll wager my castle on the outcome of the bout," he added with smug confidence.

When that message was relayed, the unusually high

stakes brought a buzz of comment from the stands as the spectators marveled at Lord Lionel Hurley's reckless assurance.

This time the Dragon Knight finally nodded his agreement of the terms.

Lionel smiled grimly as he pictured the knife-edged lance smashing through his opponent's breastplate. He was so sure of winning, he could have promised his opponent the moon with similar confidence.

His impatience mounting, Lionel clattered to the start, where he took up his position. The sinking sun suffused the sky with orange, and fingers of purple shadow crept slowly across the ground.

The heralds blew a final fanfare.

The knights' helms were secured, their visors snapped shut. Shoulders hunched, heads bent, the combatants heaved their lances upward, tips tilted into the proffering position to indicate their readiness to charge. The light from the setting sun struck fire off their armor as they galloped forward. As the horses thundered over the field, the twenty-foot lances dropped into the strike position.

A great wail came from the stands as Lionel's lance fell short, impacting the ground, where it quivered harmlessly as the black-armored Dragon Knight thundered by untouched. Lionel had been momentarily distracted by the glaring sun, which had thrown off his timing. In the split second after Lionel knew the lance would drop too low, the Dragon Knight chose not to strike his opponent, apparently aware he had already won this course by default and wanting to spare his opponent injury.

Though the crowd's roars of approval were deafening, the Dragon Knight's chivalry was not well received by Lionel. He was enraged to think that not only had he failed, but that failure had elicited sympathy from his opponent.

Angrily, he shouted for the other man to face him in

hand-to-hand combat, loudly accusing him of faulting the course.

Tension mounted in the stands. Even the jugglers and mummers had ceased their foolishness, crowding close to watch the outcome of this competition, which had fast become a grudge match. The men's jousting helms were replaced by lighter helms offering better visibility. Feats of arms were always eagerly anticipated, for in these men fought for blood and often to the death.

Isobel's heart thudded uncomfortably as the two knights sized each other up on the muddy field below. It was not that she was afraid Lionel would be wounded; her fear stemmed from his reckless wager. What if he lost this bout? This unknown Dragon Knight would become owner of Stoneham Magna! The castle had been in the De Lacy family for generations, and though Isobel preferred her manor of Ambrey, she was incensed to think a foolish braggart like Lionel could throw away her future children's birthright. She clung desperately to the hope that Lionel would win, for if he lost, she might not have a roof over her head by morning.

The combatants circled each other, wielding their maces; next they switched to the swords chained at their waists. Back and forth they fought, stumbling, staggering with weariness, even falling, but always getting up to resume the fight.

Everything began to blur. In shock Isobel could see that Lionel was getting the worst of it. Clenching her hands until the knuckles showed white, she tried to tune out Maude's piteous sobs. Even Brianna was pale and silent.

A roar went up from the crowd as Lionel finally drew blood. The blow was cleverly aimed through a weak point in the other man's armor; now a sticky residue trickled down the black plate. Buoyed by his victory, Lionel closed in for the kill. He had already decided to give no quarter to this man, who, truth to tell, would surely not expect it. This had become a fight to the death.

Lionel skidded in the mud as he tried to fit his sword point through an opening in the other man's plate. The Welshman turned just as the sword connected, jamming it between the metal plates and wrenching it from Lionel's grasp. Lionel's sword, already unhooked from his belt, clanked harmlessly against the other man's armor and was kicked out of reach. Appalled by this unexpected turn of events, Lionel scrabbled for the dagger at his belt, drew it, and leaped into a crouch as the Dragon Knight came on.

Surprised by the ferocity of his opponent's assault, Lionel faltered, his footing insecure. He slipped on the mud and went down. In a flash the other man was on top of him. The dagger was whisked from his grasp and flew in a gleaming arc to the ground.

Mingled gasps, groans and cheers echoed from the stands as Lionel lay spread-eagled on the mud with the other knight kneeling on top of him. Still flailing his arms and legs, Lionel could not throw the other man off. Finding the vulnerable chink where his helm joined his plate, the Welshman pressed his dagger point against Lionel's throat.

Cheers came from the crowd, and a slow, bloodthirsty chant for Lionel's death began. Isobel knew Lionel was not popular, but she could not tell if the spectators were more influenced by the gore of the moment, or if their personal feelings drove them to demand his death. The choice belonged to the Dragon Knight, for Lionel refused to yield. Only the coup de grâce remained.

Cold steel quivered against Lionel's throat as he muttered Hail Marys and commended his soul to heaven. The Welshman had already pried up his visor, and Lionel was staring up into the man's eyes, for he too had opened his visor for air. Those glittering, inhuman eyes shone icy pale against his dark face. Lionel shuddered, but he refused to beg for his life.

Though in fact it lasted only a few moments, this stand-off seemed to the crowd to have gone on for hours. Near hysteria erupted in the stands when the Dragon Knight unexpectedly withdrew his dagger, sheathed it, and sprang to his feet. Stepping back, he raised his hands in the air to show he held no weapon.

A collective gasp of amazement was followed by stunned silence. Slowly the crowd's mood changed, their bloodlust sapped. Now cheers for the Dragon Knight's overwhelming chivalry filled the air as they applauded his generous gift of life to Lord Lionel Hurley.

Chapter Two

''What will become of us now?'' Maude wailed, wringing her hands, her freckled face tearstained and woebegone. In unison her maids wailed with her, until Isobel longed to slap them all.

''You surely don't expect me to take this lying down,'' she retorted, her anger barely controlled. These past hours Maude's tears had grated on her nerves. Beside her Brianna was uncharacteristically quiet. She squeezed Isobel's arm in comfort.

''Don't be angry, Isobel. Likely when Lionel's paid off the prize money, this Dragon Knight will leave us in peace. What would he want with this place?''

What indeed? Isobel glanced to where the men were gathering around the lord's table. Because of the unexpected outcome of today's tourney, Lionel had banished the women to the solar and placed an armed guard on the stair. Isobel was sure this was to keep her out of the way, for she doubted Maude would question his behavior. He knew she would demand the answer to a dozen questions:

Whether he held title to Stoneham from her father, or the king? If he had been granted ownership of the land, or if he was merely castellan?

Lionel provided a meal for the more important knights at the tourney, reserving a place of honor for the victor. This evening many of their guests limped, or walked stiffly; others were swathed in bandages as they slowly made their way through the great hall.

There was a stir at the far end of the hall as the victorious Dragon Knight entered the room, still wearing his black armor. Heads turned as he passed, everyone being eager to see the champion. His hair looked as black as his armor as he strode confidently through the hall, broad shouldered and commanding, his men walking close behind him.

Isobel could not see the knight's face from here, but by his movements and the ferocity of today's fight, she assumed him to be young, though his sinewed strength told her he was no lad.

As she watched him take his place with the others, her heart thumped uncomfortably. She might be looking at Stoneham's new master. The high table was too far away for her to hear what was being said, or even to see the men's faces clearly through the gloom. Lionel's hearty laughter pealed out and she marveled at his ability to laugh after the outcome of today's contest. Surely he was not expecting to weasel out of his debt. Isobel even wondered if Lionel knew how close he had come to dying. And she very much doubted he had the courtesy to have thanked the other man for sparing his life. Damn him! Had she been her father's son instead of his daughter, Lionel would never have taken charge. It would be she down there supping with the men instead of being shut away with these simpering fools.

A soldier poked his head inside the solar and curtly told Isobel his lord had ordered that she not keep looking down into the hall, or she would be sent to her bedchamber.

Seething with resentment, she went to the hearth and took up her embroidery, stabbing her fingers in her anger and spotting the linen with blood.

"If Lionel's fool enough to have lost the castle, I swear he'll pay," she vowed mutinously, and for once Maude did not argue with her.

The goblets were refilled. Lionel lounged back in his great carved chair, sizing up the Dragon Knight. He was not as old as Lionel had expected, not having the grizzled appearance of a battered warrior. Welsh—he had already guessed that much, and the man's nationality was confirmed when he spoke. Lionel sorted through a dozen possibilities in his mind, wondering how best to extricate himself from his predicament. Clearly the man had competed for the money. And therein lay the crux of his problem—he did not have gold enough to make good his offer.

The crackling sides of beef and haunches of venison were consumed in relative silence, washed down with copious quantities of wine and ale. The seriousness of Lionel's wager hung like a pall over the diners. It was uncommon for a man to wager his son's birthright on the running of a course. Some among them had even begun to question Lionel Hurley's sanity.

Even before the first dishes were cleared away, today's champion was impatient to get down to business. "Thank you for the meal, my lord. If it please you, I'll take my winnings and be on the road," said the Dragon Knight, pushing aside his trencher.

Lionel tried to remain expressionless. "As you wish, though that might prove difficult, Sir—What shall I call you? 'Dragon' doesn't seem appropriate." Lionel flashed him an ingratiating smile as he beckoned to a server to refill his guest's goblet.

"I'm used to being called Dragon. In my own land I'm known as Morgan of Nels."

Lionel repeated the name to himself; this was the first time he had heard the Dragon Knight's name. Unfortunately, the style of his title sounded important. His heart sank.

"Nels . . . I've never heard of that. Is it a fiefdom?"

The other man smiled. "An ancient Welsh princedom, my lord."

It grew worse. Lionel gulped down more wine. He had hoped this Welshman was some landless knight who could be fobbed off with ready gold and empty promises. The man's assurance and his apparent position made him much more difficult to dismiss. Besides, there were far too many witnesses to his wager. Already some of the men lounging at the table were watching him curiously, as if they awaited some spectacle. He already knew he was not well liked, and today that sentiment had been glaringly apparent. Uneasily he realized the other diners were aware of his shaky finances and were waiting to see him disgraced. A surge of hatred for his fellow knights went through him. Lionel sat straighter in his chair and glanced uneasily toward the stairs leading up to the solar, where a soldier stood guard. At least his stepsister was not here to further complicate matters. He would deal with that problem at a later time.

He drank more wine and shifted position in his chair.

"Lord Morgan, surely you realize I don't keep such a large sum in my coffers. It will take time to raise what you are owed."

The Welshman was not pleased. His dark brows drew together threateningly and Lionel gulped, his hands growing clammy.

"How much time are we talking about?"

"A few . . . weeks," Lionel allowed vaguely.

"I've not got a few weeks. As I'm a reasonable man, I'll take a portion with me and return later for the rest."

"I've less than a hundred gold pieces to hand."

Morgan of Nels leaned across the table.

"I was warned it might be difficult to get what was owed me. This castle alone is worth ten times that and more, my lord Hurley. And, if I recall the terms of your final wager, it is mine for the taking."

Lionel drew in his breath, aware that the others leaned closer to hear what was being said. From the start he had been aware of knowing glances being exchanged between the Welshman and these other knights. Damn them, they had the audacity to suggest he would try to avoid his obligation. Lionel was consumed with rage because his fellow knights had gone behind his back in support of this foreigner.

"What use have you for an unimportant English castle miles from your lands? Perhaps you'd agree to my paying a forfeit instead? Surely you'd rather have gold."

The Welshman smiled, displaying even, white teeth against his sun-darkened face. "That I would, my lord, yet if you're already hard-pressed to pay my winnings, how can you pay enough forfeit to cover the value of a castle?"

Lionel's face was stony as guffaws of laughter greeted his question.

"Aye, Hurley, answer that, if you can?" challenged a familiar voice.

To Lionel's rage he saw that it was Rafe De Gascon who led the mocking chorus. He glared at the young knight, trying to think of a clever answer. His mind was a void. He drank more wine and grew aware of sweat trickling down his face.

"This is a matter to be settled between Morgan of Nels and myself," he snarled, striking the table with his clenched fist. "Would you mock and taunt while your belly's still filled with my provender?"

At least De Gascon had the good grace to look ashamed. One by one the others moved away, some to throw dice, others to attend to their mounts in the stables. The Dragon Knight and a half dozen of his men remained at the table.

"The others warned me I'd have trouble claiming my just reward," said the Welshman, his voice rich with humor. "By God, it looks as if they were right."

Lionel blanched, his discomfort growing. There was little point in trying to bluff his way through this. He had been given a chance to absolve himself of a foolhardy wager, made because he never dreamed he could lose.

"Rest assured, you'll get what you are owed, plus a forfeit for the value of the castle. Surely that will satisfy."

"It will."

"I'll give you what I can today."

"Which is only a fraction of what I'm owed. We'll draw up a note for the remainder. Having an Englishman as debtor will be a new experience for me."

Though Lionel gave him a sickly smile, he felt no humor. The party of Welshmen, however, seemed to find the idea most amusing after Morgan of Nels translated what he had said. Lionel waited for their laughter to subside. "Agreed," he said, his voice cracking on the word. Lionel had already sent for a clerk.

"As a hundred gold pieces is not nearly enough, what else can you give me? I'm owed twenty times that, not counting the forfeit for the castle."

"Maybe fifty more gold pieces, a few bits of jewelry, several splendid hunting hounds—" Lionel halted his recital, but the Welshman nodded for him to continue. "Some saddles, bridles, fine Arabian horses, plate, bolts of cloth."

"Wagons to carry it?"

"Yes, that too, if you wish," Lionel agreed stiffly. This damned foreigner was bankrupting him and thoroughly enjoying the sport. How Lionel hated him; he itched to strike him, but dared not with his henchmen beside him. Instead he drank more wine and then wondered at the wisdom of his act, for it was likely his light-headedness was not all due to rage. Mayhap he should have touched not a drop in order to keep a cool, clear head, yet he had needed extra courage to face this man.

"Wagons, horses, saddles, plate, hunting dogs—poor substitutes for cash, but I'll accept them nonetheless. What else?"

"More?" Lionel croaked and then forced a sickly smile as several heads turned at the lower tables, attracted by his anguished tone. Damn them all! How they were enjoying this. He knew that if he did not pay this Welshman generously, did not uphold the deed they signed, the others would trample the name of Hurley in the dust. Many of these men had long-standing scores to settle with him. Without honor, he would be nothing, maybe even forced into exile. . . .

Desperately Lionel looked around the shabby hall. What more was there? Had he a grand palace like royal Edward, he could have quickly satisfied this man's puny wants; as it was, the entire castle of Stoneham was not worth much.

"There's nothing left besides the castle. Would you take that from my son? Have you sons, Lord Morgan?"

"None that I claim."

Lionel noticed a serving woman standing in the shadows, full of breast, with flowing golden hair. He beckoned to her as a brilliant idea crossed his mind. The wench came at his bidding, casting admiring glances at the famous Dragon Knight, coyly lowering her lashes as she refilled his cup.

"What say I give you a woman?" Lionel suggested, leaning forward, his hands clasped inches from the strong, sun-browned hands of his rival. "Look around the hall. Pick any you want and she's yours."

"I've little use for a wench," the Dragon Knight said dismissively.

Lionel drew back his hand, his brain already churning

with new possibilities. "Then a lad . . . I've several pretty pages," he suggested slyly, beckoning to a lounging youth.

Morgan of Nels chuckled. "Nay, lads aren't my preference. I meant, as we're traveling men, a woman would hamper us."

"I've nothing else to offer." The clerk was at his elbow, already writing what Lionel had reluctantly dictated.

The Welshman turned about in his seat to glance around the hall, scanning the available offering and finding it wanting. "Any woman?" he asked at last, reading the paper the clerk had written.

Lionel was disappointed. He had hoped the other man could not read.

"Any woman on the manor of Stoneham Magna is yours for the asking. I realize you've not seen all of them, but surely there's someone who'll please. A man without sons is in dire need of a woman."

The Welshman carefully read the terms of their agreement, pointing out a discrepancy to the clerk and waiting while it was corrected. "There was one of great beauty who took my eye," he said finally.

"Ah, I knew it! Which one?" Lionel asked, cheered that the signing was at hand, that the man was going to agree to the modest amount he had stated.

"Add to that the horses, dogs, plate, saddles, cloth, all you promised, my lord, just in case you later have a memory lapse."

Lionel's face darkened when the other man again hinted at his dishonesty. "I'm a man of my word. Name your price, Welshman."

"Good—then double that figure. It's not enough to buy the castle outbuildings. And give me the black-haired wench who sat in the center stands. She wore gold and rosy silk, by far the prettiest woman there."

Lionel was so busy overseeing what the clerk wrote, he was listening with only half an ear. Damn him, the Welshman was going to have it all in writing before he signed. Everything he owned of value would soon be going out the door. And on top of that, now the Dragon Knight was demanding a wench to boot. Some black-haired woman in gold and rose . . . Lionel's head snapped up, realization dawning icy and sobering.

''Black-haired woman,'' he croaked, his breath choking in his throat. ''Nay, not her . . . I meant a serving wench.''

''You said any wench on your manor, my lord,'' the Welshman reminded, a veiled threat in his voice. ''As I recall, you owe your life to me.''

Heads again turned to look at him, and Lionel knew he was doomed. ''But she's no common wench,'' he protested feebly, ''she's my stepsister, Isobel. You can't take her.''

''Why? Is she already betrothed?''

Lionel shook his head. Now he regretted turning down De Gascon's suit. Had he agreed to it, at least he would have been spared this trap. ''No, but not my stepsister.''

''Why? Is your stepsister too good for me . . . is that what you're saying?''

The Welshman half rose in his seat and leaned across the table, his fists clenched. Lionel grew deathly afraid of the expression on his face, reminded of this man's strength and skill at arms.

''Nay, it's just that . . . well, I didn't mean . . . I . . . Oh, very well,'' he finally agreed, his voice choking. ''But she will settle the debt entirely.''

''Write it into the agreement and I'll sign.''

Lionel was aware of the blood pounding through his head as he helplessly watched the clerk write that the Lady Isobel De Lacy was to be betrothed to Lord Morgan of Nels to conclude their agreement.

''She has no dower lands,'' Lionel said, in a desperate attempt to dissuade him.

The other man shrugged. ''I've land enough for both

of us,'' he dismissed quickly. ''Her beauty can be her dower.''

Rain pattered against the stonework, and a loose shutter creaked in the wind. Isobel lay awake in the early hours of the morning filled with unease. She had been wakened by a disturbing dream, which might not have been a dream, after all, she realized, as she saw that her clothes chest was gone. Ever since she'd come to Stoneham that chest had been in the corner. All those scraping, bumping sounds, the flitting shadows, were not a dream after all! The outcome of this evening's gambling and drinking, she could only guess. Earlier her spirits had lifted when she thought she heard the Dragon Knight leaving. There was such a commotion as wagons were loaded, accompanied by neighing horses and barking dogs. The unholy racket continued for some time before weariness finally overtook her and she drifted to sleep.

Isobel had taken great comfort from the understanding that if the tourney's victor were leaving, he was not to become the new owner of Stoneham Magna. Now she began to wonder if that truly had been the case. Why would her clothes chest have been moved so stealthily in the night? Another curious development filled her with dread: when she rang for the maid, no one answered her summons, almost as if she were alone in the tower. Even the fire had been allowed to burn low.

Last night after she was escorted to her room, Lionel had sent up her supper. Neither Maude nor Brianna had come to say good night. Was she being punished for challenging Lionel's right to the De Lacy arms?

A strong gust of wind tore open a loose shutter, bringing a spatter of rain inside the room. Isobel slid from her warm bed and securely fastened the wooden shutter. Campfires flickered in the predawn darkness, revealing that at least some of the tourney's competitors still camped nearby.

The uncertainty of not knowing what had happened last night was driving her mad. She decided to go downstairs to find out what was going on.

Isobel dressed in a plain blue wool gown and pulled on her fur-lined boots, for the castle's stone corridors could be cold as a tomb. Fortunately the missing clothes chest contained only her better clothing, or she would have had to go downstairs in her night rail. She had just taken her cloak from its hook on the wall, when she heard steps on the stairs.

Isobel stepped away from the door as it opened to admit Lionel. She was at once suspicious of her stepbrother's unexpected visit in the wee hours of the morning. He had never come to her room alone. Recalling his often lecherous, hungry gaze, she kept her distance, instinctively clutching her cloak to shield her body as he quietly closed the door.

"Good morrow, Isobel dear," Lionel said, his tone oily and insincere.

The warning flags went up. "What do you want with me at this hour, Lionel . . . dearest?"

"Just to talk. Come, sit here beside the hearth. Why haven't they mended the fire?"

"I assume because you gave them orders not to."

He frowned at her. Isobel was not going to make this easy.

"And where's my clothes chest?"

"Clothes chest?" Lionel repeated innocently, making a great show of looking around the room.

"Oh, enough—I'm no half-wit. Do we still have a roof over our heads?"

"Have no fear; we're still in possession of Stoneham. . . . Now sit, Isobel; there's no need to stand."

She perched uncomfortably on the edge of the bench before the hearth while Lionel drew up a padded stool to the warmth of the dying fire.

"You'll be pleased to hear all debts have been settled to the Dragon Knight's satisfaction."

"Making that final wager was the most foolish, boastful thing you've ever done. Were the man not honorable, you wouldn't be here to tell about it. You've no right to gamble with my castle! As for your clever new coat of arms, I'll take up that issue with the college of heralds. Firstly, you've no charter—"

"Oh, for God's sake, shut up," he snarled, all pretense dropping away. "The arms are done now. No one but you objected to the styling."

Isobel's eyes flashed. "No one but *me* has any right to object, my lad. Those arms are mine! They are the badge of the De Lacy family."

"Don't call me *my lad*, like some scruffy pot boy. Sit down and hear me out. Your precious castle's safe—at least I've done that much."

"Am I supposed to thank you for it?" she demanded, clenching her fists in the folds of her cloak.

As he looked at her, some of Lionel's anger softened. Even when she flared with temper she was beautiful . . . and so very desirable. Now that damned Welshman had possession of her. But not for long. He would see to that.

"Listen carefully, Isobel. We've not much time."

"I thought you said the castle's safe."

"It is. This concerns another matter. In a way, you've had a big part in saving the day."

"How can that be when I've been locked up here?"

"Because I acted in your stead . . . as is my right."

Her suspicion growing by the minute, Isobel leaned forward to demand, "What have you done? Come on, spit it out, Lionel. What arrangements have you made on my behalf?"

Lionel cleared his throat and then swallowed uncomfortably. One might think the wench's eyes spit fire, so evil was her glare at him. Were he of a superstitious bent, he might think she had supernatural powers.

"In order to save Stoneham Magna, you're taking a journey."

"Where?"

"You're going to Wales with the Dragon Knight."

"What!" Incredulous, she stared at him, hardly able to believe what she was hearing.

"To cinch our agreement I had to let him think that he's betrothed to you."

Isobel sprang to her feet, and Lionel gripped her wrists to keep her from hitting him. "How dare you! I won't go anywhere. You can't make me go with this man. I'm not a bond servant."

"You're my ward. If I see fit to betroth you to this knight, then so be it! You've no recourse under the law."

"You've betrothed me to a stranger? Some barbaric Welshman? I can't believe it."

"Oh, calm down. It's only on paper, you little fool. I've got a plan—"

"Oh, spare us any more of your plans. I suppose you planned to cheat and win the tourney and keep all the money for yourself. And what happened to that plan?"

Lionel blanched, amazed that she had come so close to the truth. "Things didn't go as intended. I apologize for putting you in this position. God knows, Isobel, the last thing I want is to send you into some other man's arms," he said, his voice softening as he reached for her hand.

She glared at him, aware that at least in this he spoke the truth. "What if I won't go?"

"Then the contract is invalid. And the Dragon Knight owns Stoneham Magna. I've nothing more of any worth left to give. As it is, he's near bankrupted me with his demands. It'll take years to recover from this."

"He's only asking for what he was promised when he entered the tourney," Isobel reminded him tartly. "Promised by you only because you thought you'd never have to pay it out." When he flushed and looked down at the rushes, she knew she was right. The sheer lunacy of his scheme was hard to believe.

"It would have worked—but for him. There's little use in arguing now about what could have been. The Welshman's milked me dry to pay his winnings. On top of that, I added a hefty forfeit to keep him from taking the castle. I'd hoped he'd just take the gold on hand and go back to Wales and not bother us again."

"He would have if you'd paid him what you owe."

"That wasn't possible. Anyway, as part payment of our debt, I offered him a woman from the manor. How was I to know he'd choose you? I couldn't back out—there were too many witnesses."

Isobel looked witheringly at him, seeing Lionel as he really was, devoid of all his puffed-up pride. This pitiful worm of a man had enslaved her to pay his losses.

"I'll tell him I'm a free woman and he must choose one of the maids. He seems to be a reasonable man; he'll understand. You must not have explained it to him," she said confidently, turning toward the door.

"No! It's *you* he wants. It's written in the contract. Now, just sit down and hear me out. I've got a plan."

"Another? Pray God this one works better than the last."

"We let him leave with you and then, on the road, I overtake him and kidnap you. He'll be none the wiser. You'll be back home in a couple of days."

"A couple of days! A couple of hours and he can take me ten times over. Have you a second plan to restore my virginity so I'll be marriage material for another creditor?"

Lionel refused to face her. "Just tell him you've taken a vow of chastity—anything to stall for time," he mumbled uncomfortably, still not meeting her gaze.

"I'll tell him nothing of the sort, because I'm not going."

"You'll go if I have to bind and gag you. You've no

choice. I'll let you take your gelding and the yellow hounds."

"I can't. My bitch is too close to whelping."

"Well, she's going to stay here, but you can take the others."

"I can't leave her."

"I promise she'll be cared for."

"Yes, I suppose in that I can trust you. After all, her pups will be prize hounds and you can sell them for a handsome profit," she said bitterly.

"If you go quietly, it'll be better for all concerned. You don't have to pretend to love the man—you don't even have to speak to him. I'll ambush him on the way to his next tourney. They're only bound for Hereford. That's a stone's throw from here."

"Don't you think he'll be suspicious? Won't he come back to demand his right?"

"No. There are a dozen robbers on the highway, some having larger bands than mine. He'll have no idea I had a part in it. This way I can also take back the goods he's squeezed out of me. In all, I think we're going to come out of this quite well, sister—that's if you do as you are told."

Chapter Three

The cavalcade of men and wagons crossed the drawbridge in the driving rain and turned to follow the sluggish stream that formed Stoneham Castle's moat.

Isobel rode in the middle of the soldiers, looking straight ahead, though she could see little through the blur of her tears. She was wearing a fur-lined cloak, fur-lined gloves and boots, yet still she felt numb with cold. This morning's journey seemed so unreal, she half expected to wake in her own bed to find it was all a terrible dream.

Most of her belongings had been packed in the wagon rattling along behind her: her clothes, her padded chair, her embroidery frame and two wooden cages to hold her yapping dogs. She rode her fine gelding, Spartan, who was putting on quite a show as he pranced along, head tossing, hooves lifting high, the bells on his harness jingling in time to the clopping hooves. To the casual observer she appeared to be a fine lady traveling in state. At the head of her armed escort rode her betrothed—the famed Dragon Knight!

Despite Lionel's assurances that this was merely a sham to placate the Welshman and that she would soon be back at Stoneham Magna, Isobel had a terrible sinking feeling of finality about this journey. Pray God her stepbrother's plan would not go awry. He seemed not so clever about his schemes as he supposed. She must remember to act afraid when they were set upon on the road, for she could not let these men suspect that her abduction was planned.

What if the robbers were really robbers and not Lionel's men in disguise? That idea was too terrible to contemplate. Uneasily Isobel admitted she was at the mercy of fate.

Isobel looked back at the small fortress of Stoneham Magna, the movement jarring free tears that mingled with raindrops on her face. No one stood on the battlements to wave good-bye and the lack of concern made her feel lonely and abandoned. She had thought that at least Brianna would have come out to see her off. Probably Lionel had forbidden it. What if this was all part of his scheme to be rid of her? What if he had no intention of coming to her rescue, if in truth she was to become this stranger's bride?

That frightening thought made her shudder and she sat straighter in the saddle, not wanting the men to think she was afraid. After all, she was a noblewoman of ancient blood, the last of the proud De Lacys: it would take more than this to cow her. Defiantly Isobel looked at the men riding on either side of her, but they kept staring straight ahead. They had not treated her cruelly, merely with indifference. Possibly these common men ignored her out of self-preservation, for it might not be wise to be overly familiar with the Dragon's betrothed.

When she again considered the possibility of becoming this Welshman's wife, a chill of dread crept along her spine. She did not even know his name, or what he looked like. When she heard him speaking to his men, his voice sounded pleasant, though she had not understood anything he said. She had not realized she would not understand his language, and yet surely he spoke English, or how else could Lionel have negotiated with him?

The rain increased and Isobel hunched down miserably inside her cloak, the weather reflecting her mood. She rode out unloved into a world of strangers, bound for a foreign land—then she remembered they only rode to Hereford. A wry smile tugged at the corners of her mouth when she realized how melodramatic she was being. However slowly they traveled, it could not take more than a couple of days to reach Hereford. And somewhere between here and there lay her salvation.

Around noon the party halted at a roadside inn, and Isobel was grateful to be out of the rain. A welcome fire blazed in the stone hearth of the inn's low-beamed common room. The landlord soon had trestles set up to accommodate the Dragon's large party. The inn's other travelers kept to themselves at the far side of the room. Though they did not speak English, two of the Dragon's soldiers indicated to Isobel that hers was the seat closest to the hearth.

"Allow me, my lady."

Isobel swallowed uneasily as she glanced up to find a bulky figure standing beside her in a rain-sodden cloak. There was little to be seen of the Dragon Knight, for his hood was pulled down over his face to keep out the rain. Silver rivers ran down his cheeks and splashed on the table when he leaned forward to assist her with her cloak.

Suddenly he threw back his hood to reveal gleaming black hair plastered against his brow in rain-sodden curls. As he leaned forward, the firelight burnished his face, and she saw that he was not as old as she had supposed, though his heavy black brows and smooth olive complexion gave him a foreign appearance.

Isobel was pleasantly surprised when he knelt to pull off her boots. Thankfully she stretched her feet in their wet silk hose to the warm fire. He still crouched at her feet and he rocked back on his heels and looked up at her, his pale eyes gleaming a startling, silvery blue against his suntanned skin. Isobel had expected his eyes to be brown, like those of the dark-haired knights she had seen at the tourney. So admiring was his gaze, she smiled against her will and he grinned back, showing very white teeth against cleanly chiseled lips.

"Thank you, my lord. It's good to be inside where it's warm and dry," she said politely.

"If the weather's too wet for you, we could lodge here till it clears," he suggested, his rich voice bearing a lilting accent that made his speech hard to understand.

"Oh, no," Isobel hurriedly replied. They must not delay, nor should they take lodging, for then he might try to bed her. She had already wondered what excuse she would use if, at the end of the day, he expected to share her bed. As they were merely betrothed and he seemed not to be an ill-mannered churl, she hoped he did not have designs on her maidenhead.

"That's good, for we'd not intended to break our journey."

He stood then, an expression of relief on his face. Taking off his own wet cloak, he draped it over the back of the settle, where it steamed in the heat from the fire. Beneath the cloak he wore a dark, padded jerkin and a russet hide shirt laced at the neck. A thick bandage on his left arm reminded her he had been wounded in yesterday's tourney. Without his sinister black armor, this fearful Dragon Knight was no more formidable than any other man. Isobel's unease lessened at the discovery. He continued to be solicitous of her welfare, piling her trencher with roast meat and gravy and filling her tankard to the brim with warm mulled ale.

While she ate and drank, Isobel watched him covertly, for once she was settled with her meal and her comfort was assured, he had left her to her own devices. Now he sat with his men studying a map and conversing in his own tongue.

She drained her tankard and emptied her trencher, feeling pleasantly revived. In different circumstances, she mused, as she relaxed in the warmth, she might not have minded being betrothed to this man. Critically she studied the Welsh knight, finding him fully as handsome as Sir Rafe De Gascon. With his firm-jawed, strong-nosed profile and smooth olive complexion, he was quite the most handsome man she had ever seen. Even his unusually pale eyes added to his arresting appearance, until Isobel could not keep her eyes off him. Was she tipsy? In alarm she wondered if the warmth she felt, this softening mood and the unusual stirring in her blood were due to the ale. Another tankard and she would be inviting the man's kisses! The preposterous idea made her giggle.

At that point he glanced up, appearing surprised to find that she watched him. And he smiled. Soon he had left his men and slid along the bench to her side.

"Have you supped well, my lady?"

"Yes, thank you, my lord. I'm most comfortable," Isobel said carefully, finding that her voice was unusually husky. She sat straighter, leaning back against the settle. Dear God, could he tell she was tipsy?

He was looking closely at her, seemingly fascinated by her appearance. His close scrutiny brought fresh color to her cheeks, and she looked away from his penetrating gaze.

"Is your name Isobel?" he asked her softly.

"Yes . . . Isobel De Lacy."

"It's a pretty name. One I've not heard often."

"It's French."

"Are you French?"

"No, English, but my mother fancied the name. And what shall I call you, sir?" she ventured, when the silence stretched on while he continued to look at her.

"I'm Morgan of Nels."

Morgan! Somehow she had assumed his name to be Dragon, but that was a foolish assumption, for the dragon was merely his armorial device. "And I've not heard that name often before," she said, feeling she had to say something in reply.

He smiled. "It's Welsh. You'll have to learn to speak my tongue, but there's plenty of time for that. I'll get you a maid as soon as I'm able. It's not respectable for a noble lady to travel without women. I told your brother as much, but he insisted no maid could be spared."

Not surprising. Isobel felt a flurry of anger over Lionel's behavior, but then it was quickly gone. Here, in this warm inn room, it seemed as if Lionel had ceased to exist, as if those Welsh soldiers were gone also, leaving only her and Morgan of Nels alone in the fireglow. He held her in thrall by the power of his pale, dazzling gaze. Isobel found herself looking at his mouth, noting the darkish pigment of his finely chiseled lips, the prickle of black beard sprouting along his jaw. How broad and hard were his shoulders, and his arms were so heavily muscled they bulged beneath his hide shirt, but she already knew that, or how else could he have wielded a sword so expertly, or driven the lance . . . ?

Isobel put her hand to her brow, feeling light-headed as the room began to spin.

"What's wrong? Are you ill?"

His voice came from a great distance. His face swam giddily before her, and Isobel felt as if she were melting. Strong hands gripped her shoulders, holding her upright when she began to slip sideways on the settle.

"Too much ale, I think," she whispered as he slipped her cloak about her shoulders. What followed grew increasingly hazy: Isobel was aware he was putting on her boots, that she was standing, moving, though none of it seemed to be under her own power.

Before she realized it, they stood outside in the gray afternoon, where rays of gunmetal light speared the clouds and glimmered on puddles collected on the cobbles.

"This fresh air will soon revive you."

His voice still seemed to come from a distance, but at least the sound of it assured her she had not been abandoned. Against her will, Isobel was propelled around the innyard, which was gradually coming into focus. The heated fog in her brain dissipated until she felt chilled, and she shivered as the wind flowed inside her damp cloak.

"Feeling better?"

Isobel nodded, though she was shamefaced. How foolish she felt. She should have known about the ill effects of drinking so much ale. "I don't usually do this," she apologized.

"You'd not eaten for hours and the ale was good. It'll pass."

Inside the wagon she could hear her dogs yelping in joy at the sound of her voice. He heard them too and, aware that she was concerned for their welfare, he took her to see the dogs. Isobel's heart lifted when she saw their beloved furry faces and heard the wild thumps of greeting as their tails struck the sides of their wooden cages.

The dogs had been given food and water; even Spartan, her gelding, had been rubbed down and was enjoying a feed bag of oats. She thanked the Welsh knight for making sure her animals were well cared for. To her surprise Isobel saw that the dogs in the second wagon were from Lionel's prized hunting pack, while in the stables stood the two Arabian horses he had bought last month from a neighboring lord. For once Lionel spoke the truth when he complained he had been bled dry to pay off this debt.

"We're old friends," she explained after she had affectionately greeted the horses and the hounds, aware the Welshman watched her. He had also fondled the beasts, and she could see by the animals' reaction to his touch that they trusted him. And, because she valued an animal's judgment of character, Isobel decided she too could trust Morgan of Nels.

In midafternoon a makeshift bed was prepared for her in one of the wagons. Though she would never have asked him for the consideration, she was thankful for this Welsh knight's thoughtfulness. She was already sore from the long hours spent in the saddle, not having ridden so far since she had left Ambrey. There were blankets and a thick wolf robe to keep her warm, and a goose-down pillow for her head.

The rock and sway of the wagon, combined with the rhythm of the horse's hooves quickly lulled her to sleep. Isobel dreamed of Morgan of Nels, a strange, disturbing dream wherein he pressed her against his body and she eagerly sought his mouth.

It was already dark when she woke, and she was glad of the darkness, for her face flamed to recall the intimate nature of her dream. Isobel was surprised to find they were still on the move, for travelers generally put up at dusk. When she poked her head out of the wagon, all she could see were trees and empty blackness. The rain had stopped. A cold wind buffeted her face and she gladly returned to the warm fur robe. By the slant of the wagon bed she knew they were traveling uphill—sharply uphill, she realized when she had to clutch the sides of the wagon to keep from sliding out the end. She had not realized the road to Hereford was so steep.

As she lay drowsily in the darkness, Isobel could hear men calling to each other, sometimes even bursting into song. During these past few hours they seemed to have come to life. She wanted to ask when they intended to stop for the night, but knew it was useless. Only their leader appeared to speak English.

Finally they stopped. Isobel lay dozing in the warmth until the abrupt cessation of movement roused her. Soon she heard voices and crunching footsteps approaching the wagon. When the canvas lifted, Isobel saw that the

Dragon Knight himself had come to rouse her. He held a lantern aloft, shedding a pool of light inside the wagon.

"Did you sleep well?" he asked as he helped her down. When she hooked her foot on the wagon's wooden siding he quickly took her weight against him to keep her from falling.

"It was heavenly—I feel quite refreshed."

A dark mass of buildings huddled in the background. The men and horses milled about in what must be a very large innyard, cobbled and rimmed with stables. They were unpacking the wagons.

"Are we already in Hereford?" Isobel asked in surprise, looking about curiously at the unfamiliar surroundings and wondering what had happened to Lionel's plan to ambush them on the way here.

"Hereford?" Morgan asked in surprise as he guided her over the uneven cobbles. "Why do you ask that? We're already home . . . at Llyswen."

"What!" Isobel felt as if someone had thumped her on the chest, making her heart lurch before it began a frenzied beat. "Where did you say we are?" she croaked, the words sticking in her throat.

"Llyswen." He repeated the name slowly, amused by her shocked expression. "My home. Why did you think we were going to Hereford?"

She clasped her hands tight to stop their trembling, fighting for breath over the roaring in her ears. Lionel had played her false after all! "My brother . . . said you were to compete at a tourney there," she finally mumbled, seized with panic at the discovery of her abandonment.

"Ah, well, yes, I believe I did say that. I had every intention of competing, only my circumstances changed. We'd far too much baggage to drag to a tourney. Besides, I've your comfort to consider now, Isobel."

Her heart pounded in her chest and her legs trembled, making it hard to walk as he guided her over the courtyard. Light gleamed off a body of water, and she assumed this rambling dwelling had a moat. She had a swift impression of painted timber and great slabs of white rock glittering in the lantern light before they stepped inside an arched entryway.

"Your home . . . in Wales?" she asked, resisting the urge to panic.

"Yes. Oh, don't be afraid." He chuckled as he looked at her stricken face. "I know you English suppose this whole country to be a barbaric, warlike place, but I assure you, we're safe here. Llyswen is my stronghold, in the very heart of my lands. I suppose you'd call it 'White Palace.' Come inside to the warmth. No one's expecting a fine lady, but we'll soon remedy that."

Isobel stumbled over the threshold, almost too shocked to take it all in. What would happen to her now? Did Lionel wait on the Hereford road prepared to spring his latest plan? Oh, damn him for his bungling stupidity, for his perpetual gambling. . . .

A woman stepped forward and curtsied, glancing from her master to the woman in traveling clothes.

"Nerys, have them prepare a room for Lady Isobel. She'll be living with us. Where's Blodwen?"

The servant shrugged. "Lady Blodwen's been gone for hours."

He muttered beneath his breath and his brows drew together in anger. Then, shrugging aside his emotion, Morgan gave instructions to several servants, who were staring wide-eyed at this woman their master had brought back from England.

Isobel glanced around the dark-paneled room where firelight cast dancing flames across the woodwork. At their lord's command, servants piled more wood on the fire until the blaze leaped far up the blackened chimney. The resulting golden light revealed low ceilings of whitewashed plasterwork that were decorated in red, blue and gold leaf. Belying the splendid ceiling, the room's furnishings were plain. Carved benches and a trestle stood beneath the shuttered windows, while before the hearth were two wool-padded stools and a tall cupboard beside the inglenook.

After an uncomfortable silence Morgan said, "You seem ill at ease. Did you not know you were coming to Wales?"

He was puzzled as he watched Isobel huddle over the fire, her hands clasped in a death grip until her knuckles showed white.

"No. I understood you were bound for Hereford."

"Does it matter?"

She did not answer. The dreadful finality of her plight was a crushing blow. No one would be able to rescue her from the heart of his territory. The awful truth that this plain Welsh manor had become her home was too hard to accept. Here she would be surrounded by people who could not understand what she said, making this man her only link to the rest of the world.

All the growing warmth she had felt toward handsome Morgan of Nels had evaporated. He had become the enemy—the man who would imprison her in this wild land and never let her see her beloved Ambrey again. So homesick did she feel, even the sight of shabby old Stoneham Magna Castle would be welcome. Isobel blinked back tears, not wanting him to see her cry and learn her weakness.

"I'll treat you honorably. I assured your brother as much. As soon as we're able, we'll be wed."

"I don't want to be wed," Isobel snapped, glaring defiantly at him. Oh, why had she thought him so handsome? It was the ale, of course, she quickly reminded herself. Tonight his face looked hard and drawn, the black stubble on his chin giving him a ruffianly air.

"You've little choice. A dowerless woman takes what she can get."

"Dowerless! Where did you get that idea?"

"Your brother told me—presumably to dissuade me

from choosing you, but, as I told him, I've land enough for both of us."

Eyes flashing, Isobel stood, trying to stop her legs from shaking with anger. She hated the fact that he was head and shoulders taller than she. "I am not dowerless," she corrected with a defiant lift of her chin. "I have a rich manor. My stepbrother only wanted my wardship so he could keep the revenues from it. Stoneham Magna Castle also rightfully belongs to me. He'd no right to wager it. Lionel's just the son of my father's second wife—he's no blood relation of mine. The king granted him my wardship, but that doesn't give him the right to treat me like a chattel."

"You came with me willingly," Morgan reminded her, surprised by her outburst. "By that I assumed you were resigned to the situation."

"Resigned," Isobel repeated, fuming. She moved back when he stepped closer.

Curious servants crowded the doorway, understanding the emotion, if not the words, of their argument. It was scant comfort to know they could not understand what was being said in this very public discussion. Should she reveal Lionel's trickery? Should she tell this proud Welshman she'd had no intention of ever becoming his wife?

The silence stretched on.

"Well," he prompted, tiring of the situation, "say your piece."

Isobel took a deep breath, and, as she stepped closer, she clenched her hands in the folds of her cloak.

"I'm neither resigned to living in Wales, nor to becoming your wife. So, if you've any chivalry, you'll take me home as soon as you're able."

How starchily formal those words sounded, especially considering how much raw emotion they hid. Isobel could tell he was angry; one glance at his stony face revealed that. His heavy brows drew together while his mouth formed a thin, hard line above a jaw set like granite. She swallowed and waited.

"You want to go home?" he repeated in disbelief, towering over her and making Isobel feel small as a child.

"Yes."

"But you were part payment made to me by your brother—an unorthodox settlement, I agree, but a settlement nonetheless. I have it in writing, lady, with both our names plainly writ, sealed by your brother's seal."

Isobel took a deep breath, knowing there was nothing left but to tell him the truth.

"My lord of Nels, that paper was never intended to be binding. I came with you only to save the castle. Lionel promised to rescue me, that I'd never really have to go through with this. I wasn't supposed to come to Wales. That was why I never objected. Don't you understand? There isn't any betrothal."

Surprise, anger, even hurt registered on his face as the full meaning of her words sank in.

"Aye, I understand well enough—Lord Hurley's played me false from the start. He probably never had the prize he offered."

Isobel nodded, feeling ashamed, though it was not her doing. "You ruined his plans by winning. Until the early hours of this morning, I didn't know I was part of what he'd promised you. By then it was too late. He said if I refused to go with you, he'd have me bound and gagged. Lionel's goal was to get you away from Stoneham Magna as soon as possible."

"What did he plan to do next?"

"He was going to rob you on the Hereford road, and abduct me."

"By God—that means he'd have taken back everything he gave me."

Stunned by her revelation, he was silent for a few minutes before he finally began to chuckle at the audacity of the scheme. "All in all, Lord Hurley's cleverer than I gave him credit for."

"How can you laugh?" she cried, clenching her fists in anger. "When are you going to take me home?"

The humor left his face. "When I have time, lady. I promise, you won't be treated ill. I wish you'd told me sooner about your brother's trickery—preferably before we left England."

"When you have time? Pray tell when that will be?"

He shrugged noncommittally, and the forbidding expression on his face chilled her. It was as if a cold wind had swept through the room: gone was the warmth, the pleasure, the admiration. She suddenly felt excluded from his life.

"I've many pressing matters to deal with here. When next I travel to England, I promise you'll go with me. Until then, you must bide your time. You're not a prisoner. You're free to ride about the countryside. And you have your dogs. I'll even find a woman who speaks your tongue to wait on you. That way you won't feel isolated."

"But winter's coming on!"

"There's a tourney at Christmastide in Shrewsbury. Perchance I'll go to that," he offered casually as he went to the door, scattering the watching servants into the shadows.

"Christmas! Oh, why hurry? The weather will be far pleasanter come spring . . . or summer," Isobel exploded in rage, made furious by his nonchalance.

Morgan's mouth twitched, but his expression remained stern. "You make an excellent point, lady. Now, if you'll excuse me, I'm weary from traveling. Nerys will show you to your room."

In stony silence Isobel allowed the woman to help her undress and bathe before the sluggish new fire in her chamber. She shivered until her teeth chattered, for the room was damp and had not been used lately. Servant girls put clean linen on the narrow bed and thrust a warming pan filled with glowing coals under the covers to dispel the chill. While they worked they kept casting furtive glances at her, staring as if she had three heads. Had they never seen a noblewoman before? Isobel thought in irritation.

But then, she considered, as she lay shivering between sheets that still felt damp, despite the warming coals, there was little about Llyswen or Morgan of Nels that did not irritate her. Though in all fairness, she must admit, he had been an innocent party in this deception. The real villain here was Lionel, damn him! If he were in this room, she would have flown at him and tried to scratch out his eyes. Sometimes her stepbrother called her a cat; tonight she could have lived up to his insult. Lionel was fortunate he lounged in the comparative comfort of Stoneham Magna instead of here in this damp, windy backwater in a remote corner of the kingdom.

Though she had considered herself too angry, too dispirited for sleep, Isobel soon drifted off. When she woke in the night, at first she did not know where she was. As she remembered, she finally gave in to tears. No need for bravery now. As long as she was tucked away here, no one would know, or care, how many tears she shed.

Chapter Four

For several days Isobel kept to her room with only her dogs for company. Her embroidery frame and silks, her clothes chests and her padded chair, all made this room seem familiar. True to his word, the Lord of Nels even produced a woman who spoke passable English to wait on her. The wench had learned the language while married to an Englishman who had served with Lord Morgan's company of archers.

Mali was no beauty, having a thin, sharp face and sandy hair, yet she seemed pleasant enough and eager to please. As a widow living off her brother's charity in the neighboring village, she was grateful for this position. Attentive to her new mistress's wants, Mali spoke sharply to the other servants if they did not show enough respect for Lady Isobel.

At least Isobel had the soft, affectionate licks of her dogs to show her she was not wholly abandoned, and their company did much to lift her spirits. Isobel had chosen to bring the young dogs, Sybil and Hector, with her. These powerful hunting dogs had been bred by one of her father's former huntsmen. Suited to either field or hall, the large brown-and-yellow-dappled dogs were eagerly sought by neighboring landowners. Bluebell, her favorite, was due to whelp any day, and Isobel fretted about her welfare. It had been painful to leave her behind. Because Lionel hoped to present a perfect specimen of the new breed to the king, she was sure he would take care of Bluebell while she whelped. Afterward, she could only guess what treatment the animal would receive, especially if the poor dog failed to produce a gift suitable for royal Edward.

Sitting in this isolated room, Isobel had many hours to reflect on her situation and to decry her lot as a woman. Somewhat ashamed of her weakness, Isobel recalled the gallons of tears she had shed, centering most of her blame on the men in her life. On her father for marrying Phillippa in the first place, on Lionel for his treachery, and on this Welsh knight for keeping her here when she so badly wanted to go home.

Today, when she woke, Isobel decided that the moaning and the wailing were over. She would no longer skulk in her room like some wounded animal. After all, she was a De Lacy, and though of late she had overlooked that fact, today her resolve for change was strong. She would go down to the hall and break her fast with the family. Mali said only the lord's sister, Blodwen, lived here, though other relatives often visited.

When she found a receptive ear in her new lady, Mali had eagerly gossiped about the family; she had also gossiped about her lord's women. This discovery enraged Isobel even further, though her emotion made little sense. She did not intend to become his wife, yet the idea that he still dallied with other women filled her with anger.

When she saw her lady's black mood, Mali diplomatically switched to a story about how Lady Blodwen acted more like a man than a woman, and how Lord Morgan's father had purportedly sired dozens of children in the surrounding valleys, some of whom were now impatient to share what they considered their rightful inheritance.

Morgan's mother was Siân, hereditary lady of Nels, who was descended from fierce warrior princes. Dark like her son, with flashing black eyes, Siân was as brave as any man. Here Isobel wondered aloud about Morgan's strangely hypnotic pale blue eyes. Mali laughed and told her that this feature he had inherited from his father, handsome Owen the Rhymer, harpist, singer and poet, with eyes like the winter sky and hair pale as primroses. Lady Blodwen had inherited her father's pale hair; Lord Morgan only the color of his eyes. Owen even played and sang for the king, but he yearned for his Welsh homeland and left the royal court. Here he lived out his days, playing the harp, singing, writing poetry and stealing every man's wife or daughter. Hereabouts anyone with pale eyes and yellow hair wondered if he was descended from Owen.

Lady Siân's father, Caradog, was a great warrior prince known as the Dragon of Nels; her warlike nature she had inherited from him and bestowed upon each of her children. Love of arms served Lord Morgan well, but made Lady Blodwen a misfit in a woman's world.

Though Isobel found this information interesting, she jealously wondered about the women who had captured Morgan's interest. Mali swiftly assured her the women were in his past, though Isobel supposed her reassurances were made to spare her feelings. It was likely Morgan had made a conquest within hours of their arrival. It should not have mattered, but it did. Anger, and an emotion she refused to admit was jealousy, surged through her. Mali told her his favorites' names were Lawri and Modlen, and she wondered which one he had turned to for comfort after the lonely nights away from home. Almost as bad as knowing their names, was the knowledge that both women were blond, so Isobel surmised that his ideal beauty had golden hair. Self-consciously she touched her own lustrous black locks.

If the truth were known, those two were probably his illegitimate sisters, she thought angrily as she later brooded on her discovery, picturing the unknown women. What a tribe of primitive savages these Welsh were. She could not wait to go home to England. Somehow voicing that sentiment, even to herself, made her feel comforted.

Later, when she entered the great hall, Isobel found those same primitive savages sitting politely at the table breaking their fast. This was not the room with the decorated ceiling, but a huge, cavernous place where many soldiers were eating at trestles, and the smoky rafters housed pigeons and cobwebs.

Head held high, Isobel marched toward the lord's table set on a dais reached by three steps at the far end of the hall. She did not look from side to side, though the audible stir from the men told her she had not gone unnoticed.

Morgan was sitting at the table with a woman with flowing silver-gilt hair who wore what appeared to be a man's padded jerkin. This must be Blodwen.

The Lord of Nels looked up, sensing something unusual taking place in the hall. When he saw Isobel standing before him, a smile of genuine pleasure crossed his face.

Isobel was unprepared for her own reaction as her heart lurched before beginning a frenzied beat when he took her hand in welcome. She had been so angry with this Welsh lord, she had almost forgotten how handsome he was, or how broad were his shoulders, or how his thick hair sprang into curls and waves about the collar of his doublet, dark and glossy as a raven's wing. She was startled by the pale, intense gleam of his eyes, showing even here in the hall's uncertain light, which filtered through arrow slits and was supplemented by torches belching smoke and soot. He also had the ability to hold her spellbound with his gaze, until she was forced to look away and break the spell.

"Isobel . . . good morning. How pleased I am you decided to join us," he said in his musical speech. "Blodwen—this is Isobel."

Blodwen half rose from her chair and nodded in greeting, though her expression was not welcoming. Isobel wondered why they all seemed so hostile and suspicious. At least his sister could understand English, for it was that language that Morgan used.

A chair was brought, and Isobel sat stiffly on the edge of the seat. The servant had placed her chair on Morgan's right hand, as was fitting for his bride. He must not have told them they were not to be wed.

The soft brown bread and honey stuck in her throat, and Isobel found the sliced meat as appetizing as paper. Ale was brought and, mindful of her last experience with the drink, she barely sipped from her cup.

Once the polite repertoire of questions about how she had rested, if she liked her room, and was her maid satisfactory, had been exhausted, brother and sister lapsed into Welsh.

After a few minutes, Morgan turned back to Isobel to ask if the lad he had sent to exercise her dogs had handled the animals well, and she agreed that he had. That was the extent of their exchange. Though the meal had taken less than a half hour, Isobel felt as if it had already dragged on all morning.

Blodwen's face was hard and angular, and Isobel found the frank gaze from the other woman's pale eyes to be disconcerting. Had she not had that cloak of shimmering hair, Isobel would have mistaken her for a boy.

Finally Blodwen excused herself and strode off through the hall, clad like a man in dark doublet, boots and hose. She was tall and rangy with large, strong hands; if her hair was hidden, from the back no one would have guessed she was a woman.

Morgan noticed Isobel's gaze following his sister and he laughingly commented, "You'll never catch our Blodwen sewing a fine seam. She's more likely to be shooting a bow, or caring for the hawks. I'm afraid she's the older brother I never had."

"She doesn't like me," Isobel remarked peevishly. The minute the statement was made, she could have ripped out her tongue for making her sound so petty and childish.

"Blodwen doesn't know you. Besides, she probably sees you as a rival. You remind her of all the things she's not . . . dainty, womanly, beautiful."

Isobel swallowed, overwhelmed by his unexpected compliments. The fluttering in her stomach was a new experience. Anxious to regain her composure, she asked him sharply, "Have you decided when we'll go back to England?"

Morgan shook his head. "Not yet. Would you like to go for a ride? I've a couple of hours to spare."

Isobel hesitated. She should say no; she did not care to ride with him, especially after he had just dismissed her inquiry so shortly. She should—but she could not bring herself to do it. How she longed to be outside in the fresh air, to see open spaces after her self-imposed confinement.

"Yes, I'd like that," she blurted out before she could change her mind.

"Good. Meet me in the yard in half an hour. Bring the dogs if you like. They'll enjoy an outing."

He nodded, stood, and strode away, leaving Isobel feeling abandoned and unimportant. Why did this man have the ability to send her heart soaring one minute, and plunging the next? He never failed to arouse her to anger—or maybe it wasn't anger, she considered, aware of the heat in her face. Surely those few sips of ale were not enough to have again changed her perception of the dark-haired Welshman.

Within the half hour, Isobel stood waiting in the courtyard in her pine green riding habit, soft leather boots, and leather gauntlets to protect her hands from the reins.

Though this was an ordinary wool garment, Mali had gone into raptures over the fine quality of the wool, which had come from France as another of Lionel's peace offerings. A padded, rolled hat draped with lilac gauze covered Isobel's black hair, with streamers of gauze floating down her back as she walked. Her white leather gloves were embroidered with violets.

Here he came. Nervously she twisted her riding crop while she waited, rewarded by his swift intake of breath when he saw her standing in a patch of pale sunlight.

"Ah, lady, you're dressed too fine for a gallop through this country. You should be riding with the royal court," he complimented huskily, raising her hand to his lips in a very gentlemanly greeting.

Isobel closed her eyes as the heat of his mouth touched her flesh, having the absurd desire to lean in to him, to allow him to take her weight against his body as he had done when she caught her foot on the wagon bed.

"Thank you, my lord," she said, suddenly finding her voice as she swallowed the emotion rising in her throat.

Today he wore a dark blue doublet, the color making his hair seem even blacker. He was clean shaven, with no dark stubble marring the hard outline of his jaw. So perfect was his bone structure that he might have been chiseled from marble, she mused contentedly, until she caught the treacherous nature of her thoughts and thrust them from her mind as she turned to follow him.

Morgan of Nels was so strong and broad shouldered, Isobel felt as delicate as a flower beside him. Never before had she felt this small and overwhelmed when in a man's company, for she had always considered herself a strong woman able to pull a bow, use a hunting knife, or ride as well as any man. Morgan of Nels made her highly aware of her femininity.

Yelping and barking, her two dogs burst outside, joyfully leaping about, virtually dragging their young handler off his feet. Even Spartan whickered loudly in pleasure when he saw his mistress, and Isobel felt a warm surge of emotion that started in her toes and curled all the way to her throat. These three animals shared a bond of love with her. Yet she was not sure if her feelings were solely in response to the animals' affection, for, when this Welsh lord knelt, cupping his hands for her to mount, she flushed and was overwhelmed by the bolt of energy that shot between them.

Isobel looked down at him, finding his face in shadow, his pale eyes gleaming through the duskiness. Captured by his intent gaze, she looked at him for what seemed an eternity, reluctant to break the contact. Uncomfortable, she finally broke the spell, feeling very young and foolish. With his help she mounted Spartan and fought hard to regain her sanity.

He quickly mounted his own horse, and they were soon headed for the narrow bridge spanning Llyswen's sluggish moat, the dogs yapping at the horses' heels.

Seemingly endless open country spread before them, the rolling terrain broken in places with tangles of gorse and rusting bracken. Morgan led the way uphill along a narrow sheep track, until they reached the summit. From here Isobel could see England's patchwork fields dappled by sun and shade, laced by belts of autumn-brown trees and girded by a ribbon of sparkling water.

"It's hazy today, but on a clear day you can see the sea," he said at her elbow. "Your home's over there to the east."

Her home! A great wave of homesickness beset her at the thought of home. That close! How easy it would be to ride back to England, yet she was not familiar with the terrain and was unsure how to negotiate the woods and moors safely. Did robbers lurk in the trees as she had been warned, bloodthirsty cutthroats who lay in wait for unsuspecting travelers?

"If that's England, then this has to be Wales behind us," she said, turning to survey the craggy landscape. She swallowed her dangerous emotion, afraid he would interpret her thoughts and decide to keep her under guard.

"As far as you can see and beyond the mountains," he said, pointing to black-shadowed peaks on the horizon, their summits disappearing in cloud. "There are mighty castles in the north . . . all controlled by English barons!"

"If the English own so much of Wales, why have you been allowed to keep your land?"

He grinned at her question. He turned his horse's head back downhill. "Because, lady, my father knew whose bed to warm. In return for my father's keeping their wives content, the ruling lords were lenient with him. He seemed such a harmless poet come to entertain their guests. Between my father's gentle methods and my grandfather's sword, we've kept most of our ancient princedom intact. We're far enough inside Wales for the land to be undesirable to the Marcher lords, and remote enough to make conquest unappealing to the rest, though I've covetous Welsh neighbors, like Rhodri of the Mount. This land's scrubby and poor, not the lush farmland you're used to. We graze sheep and scrawny cattle, and my farms produce poor crops scratched from an unwilling soil."

Not convinced this tale was the entire truth, Isobel smiled. "That might be so, but you're still like a prince hereabouts, aren't you?"

"Yes, though a penniless one. Why do you think I keep risking my neck at tournaments for a purse of gold? It's not just for the fight, though I admit I'm skilled with weapons. So far my luck's held out. I need gold to be able to keep my men in the field, to help the people on my land, just to feed my household. I don't know any other way to get it. Once I sold my men to the English king, but I won't do that again. He's not generous with his wages and he shamed my men. They were berated for killing the French as they'd been trained to do. King Edward thinks common men haven't the right to kill nobles, even when they're French. He prefers they pay a ransom to swell his coffers. My men threw their lives away in France for nothing.''

Isobel heard the bitterness in his voice. His judgment of the king was no surprise, for when she'd met Edward in Hereford, though outwardly he was the perfect warrior king, she did not trust him. Lionel curried favor with Edward, but then, she did not trust Lionel either. Likely they were birds of a feather.

''It's never wise to trust kings or courtiers.''

''That's a true observation if I ever heard one. Your brother's Edward's man, is he not?''

''My stepbrother would be Edward's right hand if he would allow it. Lionel's ambition is boundless.''

As they crossed the open moor, the salt-laden wind whipped at her gauzy scarf, sending it streaming behind her like a banner. Long ago the dogs had fallen back to hunt for rabbits in the scrubby gorse. Before them stretched heavy woodland, and here Morgan reined in.

''This is far enough for today. Tomorrow we'll go in another direction. I'll race you back.''

Laughing in surprise at his challenge, Isobel set spurs to her mount and shot ahead. In minutes Morgan had outstripped her, but surprisingly, today she did not mind defeat. It was exhilarating to ride with the wind whipping her face, breathing the scent of bracken and heather and listening to the screeching birds overhead. Before them a hawk circled, finally dropping like a stone to the bracken, while in the distance a herd of feral goats moved up the hillside. So lonely did this wild land appear, it was as if no other living soul inhabited it.

On their return journey they rode in companionable silence. On the last stretch of road the dogs joined them, panting alongside the horses, tongues lolling and faces bright.

''If you'd like, I'll arrange a hunt to keep them fit,'' Morgan suggested before he whistled for the dogs to follow as they crested the final hill.

Before them, centered in the upland meadow and circled by a mountain stream, lay the fortress of Llyswen. In the bright sunlight, Isobel finally saw his stronghold. To her surprise she found it looked more like a walled town than a single dwelling. Timberwork overhung the stone walls, partly ringed by crenellated outer defenses. Conical towers of different heights jutted above the gables, aflutter with flags and pennants.

"It looks like a fantasy castle," she exclaimed in delight, as she reined in beside him. "Is it called a castle, or is it a manor house?"

Morgan chuckled at her question. "I don't know. The Dragon of Nels needed a fortress, but my father wanted a house to rival the ones he'd seen in England. He built one atop the old castle. Do you think it ugly?"

"No . . . but you must admit, there's probably no other like it."

"Not in the length and breadth of either England or Wales. I've also made my mark here," he confided with a grin as he clicked to his horse to move forward down the slope.

"One winter I sheltered some foreign craftsmen. In payment for their lodging, they painted murals and worked stone. The ceiling of the room you saw the night you arrived is their work. When I've more time, I'll show you the rest. There's also a lake and a waterfall. We have wild creatures abounding, with boar and deer in the forests. You'll like it here once you get used to things. I'd like you to help me decide how best to use some bolts of blue cloth I won in part payment at a tourney. I promise you, someday Llyswen will be known as the most unusual dwelling in the land."

"I think it must be that already," Isobel said with a smile, her violet eyes sparkling with laughter. "I'll give my suggestions after I've seen the cloth, if you wish."

"Oh, lady, I do wish, most sincerely," he replied huskily, his eyes fixed on her face. His accompanying expression made her heart flutter and she looked away in confusion.

Time was passing far too quickly, for they were soon riding into the cobbled yard, where waiting grooms took the horses.

When the lord of Nels helped her from the saddle, Isobel found that time passed quickest of all. She had just begun to enjoy the warmth of his hands, thrilling to his touch, when she found herself set down on the cobbles. His face looked strained, and when he absently touched his arm, she remembered the wound he'd received at the Stoneham tourney.

"Does your arm still hurt?" she asked him softly, unexpectedly moved by the thought of his pain.

"It throbs and likely needs redressing, but it's a very minor wound," he said dismissively. Despite his words, she could tell her concern for his well-being pleased him.

As they headed for the studded door she automatically whistled for her dogs, who lagged behind with the horses. Her ability to whistle surprised him, but he did not remark on it as he held open the door for her.

As she passed, Isobel brushed his wool doublet, not expecting the warmth of his body to engulf her like a cloud. Taken by surprise, she glanced up at his face, wondering if he, too, was as startlingly aware of her nearness. His expression was unfathomable. As if they were frozen in time, their gazes locked. His head dipped slightly and she fancied he leaned toward her. A bolt of emotion shot through her body. Isobel swallowed, unconsciously licking her lips as she gazed up at him, awaiting his kiss. His hand felt warm on her shoulder as he gently turned her toward him. Isobel breathed in the scent of wind and moorland on his skin. Mentally she acquiesced, not debating the wisdom of her action, knowing only that her heart thundered and her legs grew weak. The palms of her hands felt sticky; her breath tangled in her chest and she could not speak. . . .

"My lord!" A soldier emerged from the shadows, his manner and speech agitated. This unexpected outburst shattered her fantasy and Isobel drew back, ashamed of her own abandon.

In rapid Welsh the soldier relayed his message. When the man was finished, Morgan's face was grim, and he quickly issued orders, which the man hurried to obey.

"Rhodri of the Mount, one of those Welsh enemies I mentioned, has set fire to some farms and stolen our cattle. I'm going after them."

"But you're wounded," she protested quickly.

He shook his head, suppressing a smile. "Nay, I told you it's just a scratch, not enough to keep the Dragon of Nels from retaliating. Swift punishment is the only way to keep what's mine. Why don't you go up to the solar? It's pleasanter there than in your room."

At that point Lady Blodwen appeared dressed for battle, a helmet hiding her hair. A sword clanked at her waist and daggers gleamed in her belt. She wore a man's boiled leather jack and had gleaming prick spurs on her tall leather boots.

"Come on, brother, stop dallying. Isobel can entertain herself. They're getting away."

Morgan slid his arm about Blodwen's shoulder as they strode off. More like two brothers, Isobel thought, seeing the mutual love of combat in those two disimilar faces, alike only in their pale, penetrating eyes. She was surprised Blodwen did not cut her hair like a man; then she could ride to tourneys with Morgan.

Isobel was not sure why she felt such anger toward his sister. Blodwen had dismissed her so shortly, she felt shut out. Was that the reason for her anger, or was it because Blodwen was part of the pressing business that shattered her fantasy? Against her will, Isobel's pulse quickened as she considered what would have happened had they not been interrupted.

Later, while exchanging her riding habit for a green

wool gown, Isobel worked to convince herself it was fortunate they had been disturbed, or by now he would consider her just another conquest. After all, she was a De Lacy, not some panting village wench. De Lacys always conducted themselves with pride and never forgot their ancient heritage, or so she had always been taught. Were it not for Lionel, she would not have been in this position in the first place. Oh, she would make him pay dearly for this humiliating fiasco when she got back to Stoneham.

Feeling stronger now, able to turn aside those weak, feminine impulses aroused by Morgan's nearness, Isobel marched toward the solar.

The room over the Great Hall surprised Isobel, for so grand a room seemed out of place in the old castle. This must have been another example of the foreign craftsmen's work exchanged for their keep during that long-ago winter.

A brightly colored biblical scene covered one wall. Vines climbed up the opposite wall, their tangled branches stretching over the ceiling where a great, fire-breathing dragon was depicted. Isobel assumed it was made in tribute to the lord of Nels' heraldic dragon. Though this dragon was well done and very lifelike, she found it somewhat unnerving to have such a fierce creature hovering overhead.

A deep, recessed window overlooked the surrounding countryside. Blue sky seemed to stretch endlessly over the wild landscape until it was eventually swallowed by the dark, forbidding mountains shadowing the horizon.

A cheerful fire was blazing in the hooded fireplace, which also had the dragon insignia chiseled in the masonry. Before the hearth stood an inviting padded settle flanked by tapestry-covered stools and a pair of carved chests. Isobel was pleased to find candelabras in use here instead of the foul smoking torches lighting the hall below.

Mali brought Isobel's embroidery and she sat contentedly before the hearth, working the altar cloth, which was to be a gift for Aunt Blanche. While she sewed, she relived these past hours spent in the company of the handsome Welsh knight. Though she had resolved to put pride and family before her own feelings, Isobel could not help regretting how quickly the time had passed when they were together. It seemed only a few minutes between departure and return. She was surprised she had not been afraid to ride alone with him. Though it was disloyal, she had to admit she no longer disliked the man. In fact, her feelings were quite the opposite. And it had definitely not been dislike she felt when he stood close to her in the doorway. Time and her heart had both stood still. Thank heaven that soldier had broken the spell!

Isobel paused in her stitching, aware she was not being honest. She was not glad they had been interrupted; in fact she was bitterly disappointed that such a tremulous moment had been destroyed. She had hovered on the brink of insanity, spellbound by his nearness, held captive by the dictates of her heart.

Purposely Isobel drove away that soft, yielding emotion threatening her self-control. It was high time she went home to Stoneham Magna while she still had a few of her wits. First Lionel would get a piece of her mind, and then she would petition the magistrates for the return of her lands and the dissolution of her wardship, asking for Sir Rafe De Gascon's help if necessary. Surely he would be only too eager to thwart Lionel's greedy plans, for if they married, her land would become his.

Married! That idea no longer appealed to her. It seemed odd that she had ever considered marrying the young knight to strike a blow for her freedom from Lionel's odious control. In fact, she did not want to marry anyone. Someday, after she had resettled her manor and Lionel had been ousted from control of her affairs, she would have a husband. Until then she had no desire to exchange one master for another.

Yet, as she stared into the dancing flames, trying to picture that time, all she could see were the heather-clad Welsh uplands with birds calling overhead, the scent of sea and bracken in the wind, and Morgan of Nels beside her.

Isobel's afternoon meal was brought up to the solar and the fire was kept mended. It was dark before she heard a commotion coming from the hall below. And she knew the soldiers had returned.

Eagerly Isobel looked around the half-open door, straining for a glimpse of that familiar figure that set her heart racing. Slowly the soldiers filed inside the smoky hall, but she did not see Morgan. She kept back in the shadows, not wanting to be seen. Morgan would send for her soon; she did not want to seem too eager. Here came Blodwen, carrying her helmet under her arm, silvery hair disheveled as she laughingly recounted some tale.

Servants followed the soldiers, carrying linen and basins of water to clean their wounds. Isobel could see bloodstains on many men's clothing. Despite their injuries, the generally high spirits of the soldiers assured her they had been victorious.

She still did not see Morgan, and she wondered if she should go down now or wait for him to send for her. Deciding it was more proper to wait, Isobel went back to the hearth to resume her sewing.

Sometime later she jerked awake, realizing she had dozed. The general buzz of activity below had quietened and she was puzzled that Morgan had not sent for her.

To her further dismay, when she looked into the hall, only a couple of torches still burned. The soldiers were already stretched out on the rushes, bedded down for the night. A great wave of disappointment washed over her. Why hadn't Morgan sent for her? After that emotion-charged incident today, she had assumed she would be very much in his thoughts. Had the love of battle blocked out all else?

She felt betrayed as she wondered uneasily if that mounting emotion she attributed to him had only been in her imagination. Then again, he could have been wounded and unable to send for her. But surely his men were too high-spirited for their lord to have been hurt.

Though from here the room appeared deserted, she moved into the doorway for a better view of the lord's table. It was a jumble of dishes and half-eaten food—then her heart leaped as she saw someone sitting in the shadows. Even though it was gloomy, she could not mistake that dark-haired, broad-shouldered figure. Morgan was waiting for her to join him!

Her heart leaping with excitement, Isobel eagerly stepped forward, chiding herself for holding back. Then she heard a woman's laughter. An icy hand gripped her heart as she watched a woman approach the table carrying a bowl and linen. He had been wounded after all!

As the hateful tableau unfolded, Isobel noticed that Morgan seemed too cheerful to be in pain; he lifted his wineglass to toast the woman. Isobel's stomach lurched as she saw the curtain of yellow hair spilling over the wench's shoulders and guessed who she must be. The russet gown she wore molded her ample hips and thighs; her waist looked so narrow, Morgan's hands could easily span it. Which one was this—Lowri or Modlen?

Isobel's heart thundered so hard, it threatened to tear apart her chest, and she felt faint as a spiral of nausea rose from her belly. She knew she should look away, but sick fascination kept her watching as the wench slid onto Morgan's knee and plunged her hands into his thick hair, tilting back his head, the better to kiss him. Nay, not just kiss him—she devoured his mouth with her own. It was so painful to watch, Isobel felt faint, and she clutched the doorjamb to keep from falling.

Eventually the old bandage was changed to the accompaniment of much giggling, kissing and fondling. Voicing his thanks, Morgan fed the wench sweetmeats, and with each bite she kissed his fingers, turning the simple pastime into an erotic interlude.

Face set like stone, Isobel turned away, unwilling to watch any more. She stalked to the hearth to get her embroidery.

But when she returned to the door, an icy "Good night" on her lips, they were gone. Servants were clearing the littered table. It took little imagination to guess what Morgan did now, or why he had left the hall in such a hurry.

Drawing herself to her full height, Isobel clutched her embroidery against her body like a shield and stiffly descended the stairs. Beyond a casual glance, no one paid any attention to her.

Damn him for his treachery! Damn all men! Isobel fumed, winding through the cold passages, her face wet with tears. She had taken a sputtering torch off the wall to light her way, as none of the servants came to help her. They probably felt safe ignoring her, expecting their lord to be occupied for the rest of the night.

Isobel flung open the door to her room, waking Mali, who sat dozing beside the hearth. One murderous glance from her mistress warned the servant to keep her questions to herself.

It was far into the night before Isobel finally felt drowsy. She had alternately fumed and cried, feeling angry, hurt and betrayed. But out of her pain had come a plan. She had not been forceful enough with this Lord of Nels. Tomorrow she would demand to be taken home. Lately he seemed always to be too busy to discuss the matter. Likely he intended to keep her here. She was valuable chattel to him, paid as part settlement of a debt. The handsome Welshman even had a paper to prove his purchase.

Whenever she considered her own foolishness, she

cringed. How could she have thought his warm smile and apparent interest meant anything special? She had read so much into his attentions. Fortunately she had learned the truth before she gave in to feelings she had not yet managed to overcome. Though at first she had not considered it so, she now saw how fortunate she had been to have caught him with that wench before she made a complete fool of herself. So far her emotional commitment to him was minor.

But the painful throb of unshed tears, the ache in her heart, told her she had not been in time. It was already far too late for wisdom.

Chapter Five

For over three days Isobel had simmered in mounting anger, waiting for Morgan to make himself available to her. She was always told the Lord of Nels was too busy to speak to her. It was hard to believe he was still fobbing her off with excuses. His very reluctance to meet with her told her he was well aware what she wanted to discuss. This morning she would confront him, convenient or not.

"I demand to go home," Isobel said when she found him breaking his fast in the hall.

"What?"

"I said, 'I demand to go home,' " she repeated clearly. He had heard well enough, though he was conveniently pretending to be deaf, all the more to aggravate her.

"It's not your place to demand anything of me," he said at last, his jaw set.

Isobel plunged on recklessly, too angry and hurt for caution. "You promised to take me home, yet every time I ask when that will be, it is never the right time. In fact lately you always pretend to have pressing matters to attend to. The truth is, I'm tired of your excuses, my Lord of Nels.''

''Well, today, I have a new one for you—the weather's about to turn stormy. If you've a fancy to become a drowned rat—''

''I've a fancy to go home—wet or dry, makes no difference to me.''

Boldly she held his gaze, tense with anger. Today she saw no yielding in his wintery stare. She gradually became aware that her angry tone was turning heads throughout the hall. She did not want his people to witness another quarrel between them; with this in mind, Isobel made an effort to swallow her anger. At least Blodwen was not here.

Morgan motioned to the empty chair beside him, and Isobel walked around the table and sat down. She did not want to sup with him, nor even to sit beside him. She wanted to go home.

''You must have patience, lady. Surely I've provided well for your comfort—what more can you want?''

''To go home.''

Her eyes flashed in anger at his stubborn attitude. She could not believe he was continuing with his meal, as if she spoke of inconsequential matters.

''You keep putting me off—the truth is, you have no intention of honoring your word, do you?''

''Today—no.''

She drew in her breath, afraid of what she might say if she continued. Her hand itched to pick up the porringer and pour it over his head. Instead, after treating him to a fierce glare, she calmly left the dais. The curious glances she received from the assembled men merely hastened her exit. Down the familiar corridors she marched, heading for her distant chamber. Oh, how she hated him! He had no intention of relinquishing what he considered to be his. Why had she trusted and believed him? All along he had been playing her false.

Within the hour Morgan left with his men, riding hard to the west; the riders were booted and spurred and wore leather jacks and helmets. At least today it seemed he did have important business. Maybe it was the same pressing matter that had occupied him these days past. Then, aware of her softening mood, Isobel hardened her heart. Nothing short of a massacre could keep him too busy to at least help plan her return to England!

She determined to waste no more time feeling sorry for herself. If he would not take her home, then she would go by herself. She had ridden out each day, familiarizing herself with the surrounding country. She need only keep the mountains at her back to be headed in the right direction.

Beyond a few items in her saddlebags, she could take nothing without causing suspicion. She longed to take her dogs, but was afraid they could not keep up all the way home to Stoneham. And once she had committed herself to flight, she dared not tarry, for she would risk capture. It was a painful decision to leave the dogs behind, for she would have liked their companionship and protection on the journey.

Her mouth was set in a bitter line as she pulled on her fur-lined cloak and gauntlets. What little money and jewelry she owned, she wrapped in an oilskin pouch. A few toiletries, her silver-handled hunting knife and sheath, spare wool stockings and shift—the saddlebags were full.

As no one had ever objected to her riding outside the walls, she did not expect to be stopped. This time the Lord of Nels's generosity would serve her well.

Sybil and Hector were kenneled near the stables with the other dogs. When she went to say good-bye to them, the dogs thought they were going on an outing and they yelped with joy. Isobel hugged their muscular necks, burying her face in their soft fur. Puzzled by her unusual behavior, the dogs licked the tears from her cheeks as they tried to console her.

Presently Isobel was clattering over the bridge and out into open country. Excitement swirled inside her as she contemplated leaving this place far behind, envisioning herself riding up to Stoneham Castle to surprise them all. Warily she glanced at the threatening sky. Damn him, he was probably right about the rain too.

Clucking to Spartan, she picked up speed and was soon cantering along the sheep track. The farther she got from Llyswen, the faster she rode. Isobel fastened the neck of her cloak, trying to keep out the cold wind that crept inside her clothing.

It seemed as if she had already been riding for hours when she came to the forest. Dense woodland stretched to the horizon. Was this where they had turned back? All woods looked alike. There was no one to ask for directions, and even if there were, it was doubtful they would understand her.

The road home went through the forest. Here the trees were so tall, they shut out the sun, leaving all in a greenish, murky twilight. After Isobel had been riding for a while she gradually grew accustomed to the unnatural light. Wild creatures rustled through the undergrowth and birds called an alarm as she passed.

Ahead a sudden bolt of lightning seared across a clearing in the trees. Spartan reared in fright. Isobel was barely able to hang on to her seat and it took her utmost effort to calm the terrified horse. Across the clearing she raced, forcing him to move, though he tossed his head and whickered in fear as a second flash of lightning ripped the sky asunder. Muttering a prayer for her safety, Isobel plunged back into the trees on the other side.

These were gnarled, ancient trees, their trunks covered in moss and lichen, with toadstools growing around their bases. The forest grew sparser, and now Isobel could see how black the sky had become even as the first drops of rain spattered the browning leaves. She hunched inside her cloak as the deluge began in earnest, wondering if she should turn back to shelter in the denser trees. Here the narrow paths meandered in all directions and she was not sure she still followed the same path. Deciding to plunge ahead through the slanting rain, Isobel did not know if it was late in the day, or if the sky was dark only because of the storm.

Spartan screamed in terror as lightning again cut a jagged swath across the sky. Thunder rolled and lightning struck again. She had to find shelter before the horse bolted in terror. Through the trees she could see a shed, though the driving rain made it hard to see anything. It was a lean-to for fodder, and she headed for it, fighting to control her terrified mount.

A fodder shed meant habitation nearby. At first she toyed with the idea of asking for shelter, thinking she could offer money for her lodging, yet alone as she was, if the strangers were villains they would rob her and leave her for dead. Far better to wait out the storm here.

She was soaked to the skin and her boots squelched as she struggled to get the frightened horse inside the shelter. Finally Isobel was out of the rain. She wrung out her clothing as best she could and made herself comfortable on a mound of hay. The lightning still flashed and thunder rolled in the distance, but the center of the storm was already moving away.

Eventually the rain slackened. It was then that she heard approaching hoofbeats. Listening intently, she determined it to be a single rider. Pulling Spartan as far back into the shed as possible, she hoped the stranger did not also intend to shelter here.

Just to be on the safe side, Isobel got her knife from the saddlebag. It was pitch dark in the shed. She tried to pierce the darkness as the hoofbeats came closer. She prayed Spartan would not make any sound to betray them. When the approaching horse snorted loudly close at hand, she knew the rider was coming here.

In a panic Isobel considered hiding under the straw, but

the horse would still be here and his saddle betrayed the fact that he had a rider. Nervously clutching the knife, she waited, prepared to defend herself if need be.

Even darker than the vast forest, a large bulk loomed before her, accompanied by the strong smell of horse. Then she heard the rider dismount, heavy boots squelching in the sodden forest mast.

"Isobel."

She stiffened in shock as she heard the harsh voice. And her breath choked in her throat. Morgan of Nels had come after her!

He had already found the horse, and Spartan whickered in greeting, the animal's disloyalty greatly annoying her.

"I know you're here," Morgan growled, reaching out.

She dodged his arms, shrinking against the wooden shed, trying to become one with the wall. Though she considered it, she did not slash him with the knife. In a moment he had found her, and she was yanked forward.

"Damn it, Isobel, why are you doing this?" he growled impatiently.

"I'm sheltering from the storm," she said, fighting his imprisoning grasp until he let her go.

Though at first she had thought to leap into the saddle, she now discovered he had hold of Spartan's reins. Her other idea of bolting into the trees to escape him also evaporated as he stood squarely in the way, blocking her escape.

"Thank God I found you. I'd almost given up hope."

She fumed inwardly at being captured, disdaining to speak to him. But that idea she also abandoned as her anger bubbled over. "Why did you bother? Or didn't you want one of your possessions to escape?" she snapped, shaking off his detaining arm.

"You could have been killed. There are bogs and robbers . . . it was a damned fool thing to do. What did you intend?"

"To go home. As you won't take me, I'm going by myself."

"You don't even know the way."

"I've come this far."

"You've no idea where you are, do you? Go on, admit it."

Though he was right, she was reluctant to agree. "No," she admitted finally in a small voice. "But I've kept the mountains to my back, so I know I'm headed in the right direction."

Isobel could not believe her ears: he was actually chuckling!

"Oh, *cariad, cariad*," he said softly as he gently caressed her face. "You're a fiery one and no mistake. But you're miles from the border. You could have ridden day and night and ended up where you started from."

She swallowed, not wanting to accept that he was right again, but aware it was probably true. She was cold and weary; these dense trees hid all manner of danger, and this past hour she had tensed at every sound.

"Let's go where there's a fire to dry ourselves."

His voice was soft, soothing, persuasive. She shook her head. "No," she said.

"You can't stay here. If not for yourself, consider the beast. He's sodden and full of burrs. He needs a rubdown and a bag of oats. Come, you've made your point."

"Made my point! Do you think this was just to make a point?" she cried, trying to pull free, but he held her fast.

"Whatever it was for, I'm too wet and cold to stand here debating it. Get in the saddle of your own accord, or I'll put you there."

Bristling at his command, aware of the growing edge to his voice as his patience waned, she still refused to obey. Pulling herself to her full height, Isobel stood defiant while trying to ignore the cold trickles of water inching down her back.

Morgan gave her no further time to argue. Suddenly Isobel was swept off her feet and jarringly deposited in the saddle.

"Stop fighting! Have sense, or you'll do yourself or the beast some injury," he said with a snarl when she tried to jump down.

Sullen, Isobel finally gave in. Her teeth chattered with cold and she felt guilty for treating poor Spartan so badly. She allowed herself to be led from the forage shed and through the trees. Spartan's reins were looped about Morgan's wrist, as he led her like a child. Isobel fumed at the indignity of it, but even she had to admit she had given him little choice and she was far too cold and tired for argument.

Through the trees appeared a cottage with firelight flickering through its unglazed windows.

"This is where I intended to stay until first light," Morgan said, swinging from the saddle. He helped her down. "I'd given up finding you, when I remembered the shed. I'm glad I did. You're safe now."

She did not say she was glad also, merely looked stonily at him as he helped her from the saddle. Once she was on solid ground, Isobel moved away from him, making a great show of smoothing her clothes, though they were so sodden, the action made little difference.

A lad emerged from the cottage, and by his smile she could see he was pleased his lord had found her. They spoke in Welsh and the lad nodded and led the horses to a building in the rear.

"Iestyn will see to your horse. He's my squire. A good, loyal lad."

Again she said nothing, but she could not suppress a shudder of pleasure as they entered the cottage and were met by the warmth from the fire. Isobel's hair dripped, and her cloak and the skirts of her wool habit were wrapped soggily about her legs. Water still squelched in her boots and trickled coldly down her back.

Outside, stirred by the rising wind, the dripping trees gave the illusion it still rained. Morgan lit a candle and stuck it in a dish; it was not white beeswax, only a poor tallow dip that smoked and gave off a rancid odor. This low-ceilinged cottage was primitive, but at least it was dry.

Isobel crouched before the hearth, holding out her hands to the blaze. Behind her she was aware of him opening cupboards and banging utensils. They had not spoken since entering the cottage and the silence grew uncomfortable. She was not sure what to say to him; whenever she pictured him with his hands on that wench's breasts, her anger was rekindled. Even though she knew she was being unreasonable, she could not let go of that feeling of betrayal.

"Are you hungry?"

He offered her a hunk of bread spread with a dark paste. Pride told her to refuse; hunger bade her accept.

"Thank you," she said stiffly. The salted meat paste tasted surprisingly good. Next he handed her a horn beaker of flat ale to rinse away the saltiness.

"Take off your wet clothes. This shirt's dry, and though not fashionable, it's large enough to preserve your modesty."

Startled by his suggestion, she saw that he had a man's shirt draped over his arm. He was also offering her a rough towel.

Isobel glanced about the single room, seeing no curtain or screen for privacy. She backed away from him, finding his presence overwhelmingly threatening in this small space.

"I'm going for more firewood," he said, providing her an opportunity to undress in private.

He went back outside and she could hear him speaking to his squire. Thankfully Isobel stripped off her wet clothing, shivering in pleasure as the fire's warmth embraced her cold body. While she toweled dry, she kept an eye on the door, making sure it stayed closed. This shirt was so big it reached to her ankles.

When Morgan came back indoors Isobel was sitting on a stool before the fire, holding her sodden hair to the blaze.

"Ah, feeling better now, are you?" he asked as she smiled tentatively at him. He dumped an armload of dry wood beside the hearth. When he threw a couple of logs on the fire, a shower of sparks shot up the sooty chimney and sprayed from the hearth, making Isobel jump back.

"I've some things I'd like from my saddlebags."

"No sooner said than done, lady. I'm one step ahead of you." Morgan dragged the leather bags inside. "Save your clothes for another day—you look charming in old Tomas's Sunday shirt."

Uneasily Isobel recognized the telltale warmth creeping into his voice and she swallowed uncomfortably. She did not want to charm him, especially now that he had betrayed her trust.

"It isn't my intention to be charming, my lord, merely to be dry," she announced stiffly, aware of his admiring glance.

Morgan put the bags beside her. The leather was soaked, and Isobel fumbled with the wet straps, reluctant to ask for his help. Finally she worked open the buckles and took out her hairbrush. Spreading her hair before the heat, she brushed it into a silky cape around her shoulders. So absorbed was she in her task that when he came back to the hearth she was surprised to find he had taken off his wet shirt and doublet. Stripped to the waist as he was, she could not fail to notice his powerful, muscled body. However immodest her scrutiny was, she could not keep her eyes off him. Her gaze moved across his bare chest matted with dark hair, to his broad, muscular shoulders where the smooth skin glowed bronze in the firelight. He was stacking logs beside the hearth, and each movement made the muscles ripple under his skin. Though he still wore his boots and hose held in place by a wide leather belt, the wet fabric molded to his buttocks, revealing every sinew, until he might as well have been naked. And the garment was probably just as revealing elsewhere, Isobel concluded uncomfortably as she quickly averted her gaze.

It had become much too hot beside the hearth and she pushed back her stool into the middle of the room.

"You can have the benefit of the fire for a while," she offered, her voice sounding strangled and distant.

He nodded his thanks. He crouched before the flames, toweling his hair before he carelessly combed it back in place with his fingers.

"Want more to eat?" he asked, as he stood with his back to the hearth, drying his steaming clothing.

"All right," she agreed, trying not to look at him in his current state of undress. As she had thought, the frontal view was equally as revealing, and her cheeks were hot when she looked away. She was becoming highly aware of their compromising position here alone in the forest, though he seemed unconcerned with propriety.

Swallowing a mouthful of bread, she finally asked him, "Are we to spend the night here?"

"Of course. You surely don't expect to ride home at this hour."

"There's only one room."

"Aye, and one bed, which I'll either give you, or share with you, whichever you prefer."

"Share with me?" she croaked in shock.

He chuckled. "Fully clothed, keeping to my own side, if that will ease your concern."

Her anger was sparked by the growing amusement she heard in his voice. "This isn't some jest, my lord."

Morgan nodded gravely. "To be sure, my lady, you're right. Forgive me. Yet, as you are to be my wife—albeit only on paper—I thought sharing a bed wouldn't be a problem."

"Your wife?" she said with an indignant gasp. "How can you still say that after all I've told you? That document's not binding. Lionel tricked you."

"So you said."

"Then why do you persist in calling me your wife?" she demanded, jumping to her feet, and then backing away as he moved toward her.

"I persist, lady, because I want it to be so with all my heart," he answered gruffly.

His unexpected words echoed with each heartbeat, pounding through her veins with the flowing blood until his voice was all around her. He wanted her to be his wife! He did not think of her merely as chattel, a possession; he considered her a person. Stunned by the revelation, she stared at him in surprise. Then recalling his betrayal, she deliberately hardened her heart against him.

"Why? You can't be that desperate for a wife to choose an unwilling woman. Or is it that you're reluctant to give up on a bargain?"

"Nay, Isobel De Lacy, I don't count you as much of a bargain," he said with a growl, his expression changing until he looked hard and determined. "I've damned near ridden across the county after you, getting soaked to the skin, and for my pains I get no thanks, only a sharp, vicious tongue."

"What did you expect—that I'd leap into your arms like those wanton sluts you're used to handling?"

Oh, how she wanted to lash out at him, to punish him for wounding her so. Isobel was breathing hard, having difficulty getting her words out. He stood so close he made her highly uncomfortable.

"Had we not been disturbed that day, I think you'd have come readily to my arms," he reminded her, "though I'd not have called you wanton for it."

Isobel snorted, regretting her past foolishness. "Well, be that as it may, it won't happen again," she declared, annoyed that he knew how close she had been to succumbing to his advances. Steeling herself not to weaken, Isobel stood her ground, holding her hairbrush defensively between them.

"Why can't you admit the truth?" he asked quietly.

"The truth—and what is that? Surely you have no need of me when you've already got your bedwoman. And I'm sure you can find some decent peasant wench to bear your brats. I'm not your wife, Morgan of Nels, nor will I ever be! I'm a De Lacy and I have my pride. We're not sold like slaves to satisfy a debt. Likely you're not used to dealing with noblewomen, only servant girls."

His mouth twitched with humor as he shook his head. "Oh, lady, don't be too sure. I've not spent my life in a monastery."

The implication behind his words made her flush. The bed was less than a foot away. Though it was merely a straw pallet covered by a blanket, it looked clean. She would retreat there to escape him while she was still able.

"I'll go to bed now. You can sleep over there by the hearth," she suggested in her best noblewoman's tone.

"Is that so?" he said with a menacing growl.

Isobel had already turned her back on him and she stopped, the hair rising on the back of her neck—they were almost touching, so close she could feel the heat from his body.

"Yes. Good night," she continued in a tight voice.

Isobel was suddenly spun about. His hands bit through the linen shirt as he gripped her shoulders, giving her a shake. "I'm no serving churl to be so dismissed," he snarled, his face hard and angry.

She could not meet his gaze, looking instead at the fresh weal on his arm, still red but healing. Another puckered scar ran from his shoulder into the hair on his chest, and a thin line crossed his belly and disappeared inside his hose. She swallowed, averting her gaze as she mentally pictured where that weal ended.

"Well," he said, "I'm waiting."

"Forgive me, I didn't intend to treat you like a servant," she said in a small voice, finding this apology hard to make.

Then suddenly he smiled at her; the change was so unexpected her stomach pitched. Swallowing uneasily, Isobel tried to slip out of his grasp.

"Don't be so hasty to leave. First I'll have my say. If at the end of it you still feel the same, so be it."

"There's nothing you can say," she protested, her voice quavering. Oh, how she wished he would stop looking at her in that manner. She kept having to remind herself of the wench on his lap, how disloyal he had been. . . .

"You're wrong, *cariad,* I've much to say." His voice was husky with emotion.

"Before you start, I have to tell you that I saw you in the hall with the yellow-haired wench," Isobel blurted out, desperate to forestall any romantic speech that might leave her vulnerable. "You were kissing and fondling her."

"And what was wrong with that? I've known Lawri many years and we've been good friends."

"Friends?" she spat, her flashing eyes black in the firelight. "You looked like far more than friends."

"Sometimes, yes, we have been," he agreed, releasing her shoulder. He lifted a handful of black hair off her brow. "But, lady, you never wanted that part of me. You've always kept your distance."

She glared at him, moving her head away from his invading hand. "How dare you flirt with her whilst I watched?"

"Firstly, I didn't know you watched, and secondly, I didn't know you cared. But now that I see you were jealous, I'm sorry you were hurt by what you saw."

"I wasn't jealous," she insisted, refusing to thank him for his apology. How dare he suggest she was jealous! And the apology seemed not much of one at that. Fighting for composure, she stonily met his gaze. He traced his finger over the dark mole on her cheek.

"Don't—it's ugly."

"Nay, not ugly—unique. This too." He touched a place on her cheek. Though she was not now smiling and he could not see the dimple, he knew its location by heart.

"Don't!"

"Listen to me, Isobel. Lawri means nothing to me. No woman means anything to me—except you. Don't you think I wished it was you I kissed . . . and touched?"

Isobel gasped as, just for a second, he suited his actions to his words and his fingers brushed her breast. To her horror she felt her nipples tighten. "No," she cried, trying to get away from him. Her heels met the resistance of the pallet and she quickly steadied herself, regaining her balance.

"Doesn't a fine lady know when a man's in love with her?" he asked next, his voice soft as velvet.

"How can you love me? You don't know me," she protested feebly.

"I know you in my heart and soul. Isobel De Lacy, for once in your life, admit the truth. You're not nearly as cold and distant as you pretend."

Inwardly she panicked, afraid and excited, yet at a loss for what she should say or do. When she raised her arms to push him away, he captured her wrists to pull her closer. The aura of heat from his body engulfed her as his arms went around her back.

"No," she protested one final time.

"Forget who and what you are. Come, let me make love to you," he whispered, drawing her closer.

Isobel cried out in alarm as she felt herself falling. Morgan took her down with him until they landed on the blanket-covered pallet.

His supporting arms drew her against the hard, sinewy strength of his body until panic was replaced by a totally different emotion. Isobel had never felt this way before.

As his mouth closed over hers, his lips hot, firm and fragrant, soaring excitement possessed her.

"Say you don't still hate me, *cariad*. At least give me that satisfaction," he whispered, kissing her brow and stroking the black mesh of hair tangled between them.

Isobel's first inclination was to fight against his embrace, to preserve her chastity at all costs. But emotion soon drowned out conscience as blood thundered wildly through her veins.

"I don't hate you," she finally admitted, nestling against his warmth. "I suppose I never really did."

She felt his mouth curve into a smile against her brow. Gently he kissed her cheek, his kisses following the line of her jaw. "You don't know how glad I am to hear that."

"I think you're deceiving me. . . . I suspect you've always known."

"Aye, I have," he admitted with a grin, "only I was waiting for you to know it too."

"We shouldn't be here like this," she protested at last, finally regaining her wits.

"Why not? Don't you like it?"

The old Isobel De Lacy would have lied, but the newly awakened Isobel could not. "Very much," she admitted truthfully, smiling as she stirred in his embrace. "You're also right that I was jealous when I saw you kissing that wench. Only then I thought I hated you for it."

"I'm sorry about that, sweetheart. I'll never hurt you again, I promise," he whispered, his breath fanning her cheek. "Now, no more about hurt, or pride, or family—there's just the two of us and the night is ours."

The unspoken promise behind his words made Isobel's heart skip a beat. She wanted to tread that forbidden path and discover the secrets he invited her to share. If she allowed it, this fierce, proud Welsh lord would become her lover. He was so unlike all she was used to, the idea should have repelled her, but in truth she ached to have it so.

To her surprise, Isobel discovered it did not matter that she had never learned to flirt. Morgan did not act as if this was to be a chaste courting game; his arousing kisses spoke of hot-blooded passion. She shivered in delight as he caressed her neck and shoulders before moving down her back, where the heat from his hands molded the curving length of her hip and thigh.

"Is it true . . . you really love me?" she asked, hardly able to believe it could be so.

"I really love you. . . . Oh, Isobel, sweet, are you blind? I've been drawn to you from the first moment I saw you sitting in the stands beside that carrot-haired wench. Though I didn't have your favor, I imagined it was for you I fought," he admitted softly.

His revelation amazed her; she could not credit that so feared a contestant would have held her image softly in his heart. "You looked so threatening and sinister in your black armor. I never dreamed I'd ever be in your arms, or wanting you to—" Embarrassed by her frank thoughts, she looked away from his probing gaze.

"Don't be shy with me, *cariad*. I want to be your lover, your husband, your slave."

Isobel's face flamed at his husky vow and she hid her blush against his warm, hard shoulder.

His hands were gentle as he lifted her head, forcing her to look at him, his expression tender. Morgan was the most handsome man in the world, made even more appealing now that his eyes shone with love for her. Isobel realized this was what she had longed for. This was the man she had been waiting for all her life. She trembled beneath his tender kisses, aware he was holding his passion in check, not wanting to frighten her.

"And I want you always to love me," she whispered.

"That's an easy request to fill." He took her hand and laid it against his brow. "Here you are loved . . . and here." Now he moved her small white hand down to press against his chest. Isobel shivered as she felt the thunder of his heart beneath her hand. Now Morgan moved her hand down across his belly until he molded her fingers around the swelling lifting his hose. ''And here most of all,'' he whispered, holding his hand over hers, wanting to make her fully aware of his desire for her.

Isobel trembled with emotion as she learned how much he wanted her. She was not ignorant of the workings of a man's body, but that knowledge had not prepared her for the steel hardness, the size, or the throbbing heat of him. Once she would have been afraid of the discovery, but tonight it only fueled her desire.

Morgan kissed her face, his breath fanning her skin, his firm lips burning a trail of kisses along her neck and across her shoulders. Isobel shuddered in pleasure as the moist heat of his mouth penetrated the shirt fabric, aware that these caresses were only a promise of what was to come.

Made bolder by the intimacy they had shared, she stroked his face, tracing the outline of his thick brows and fierce profile, delighting in the hard touch of his features under her fingertips. His mouth felt hot and firm as she gently outlined his lips, and Morgan kissed her fingers, sending shivers along her spine.

''None of this seems real,'' she confided at last, stroking his hard shoulders, tangling her fingers in the thick mat of hair on his chest. She followed the length of the puckered scar, wondering how and where he had been wounded.

''No, it's like a wonderful dream—one I've dreamed many times since first I saw you.''

''Really?''

He chuckled. ''You amaze me. For such a beauty, you've so little faith in your appeal. No man worthy of the name could fail to be aroused by you. I still can't believe my good fortune.''

''So I'm not such a bad bargain after all, then?''

''Nay, the best I ever made.''

Pleasant though this time of mutual discovery had been, Morgan's blood boiled and his body throbbed with passion. Eager to hasten the proceedings, he kissed her harder. He touched her breasts, tentatively at first, then cupping the eager flesh before gently flicking her engorged nipples with his thumbs. His unexpected action made her gasp as a hot stab of pleasure shot through her belly until it grew into a burning ache between her legs. When Morgan pulled open the fastenings of her shirt, no longer satisfied with his chaste exploration, Isobel eagerly assisted him.

The shirt fell down about her waist. So beautiful was she, Morgan caught his breath. Isobel looked like a wonderful pagan deity, with her black hair fanning about her shoulders in a damp cloak, her white, unblemished skin bronzed by firelight. Her full, heavy breasts were dark tipped and uptilted, offering themselves to him. He groaned with desire as he took the satin-smooth flesh in his hands, molding those perfect globes until she quivered beneath his touch. He bent his dark head to her breast, breathing in the perfume of her body, filling his nostrils with her scent. Morgan fastened his mouth about the erect bud of her nipple, slowly laving his tongue around its edge, drawing on her until she cried aloud in ecstasy, clasped his head against her, and shuddered at his tormenting caress.

Isobel made him stop, for she felt that if he continued, she would lose control, though of what she did not know. Choked by sobs of pleasure, she clasped him to her, pressing her breasts against his bare chest, feeling his dark, crinkling hair rasping against her nipples. Isobel wanted to arouse him further. No longer afraid, or protective of her chastity, she had abandoned herself to his lovemaking.

Morgan thrust down the linen shirt past the curving globes of her buttocks, until Isobel finally kicked it aside. Now she was naked before him. No man had ever seen her body before. Eager for her lover's approval, Isobel was excited by his arousal, by the smoldering passion in his face and by the way his hands shook as he molded the delectable curve of her hips and slid his hands along her thighs. Just as she was about to give herself up to delight, he stopped. Isobel gasped in disappointment, thinking she would go insane if he did not touch her soon. She throbbed with longing to feel his hands on the most secret part of her body, to have him bring her to even greater heights of passion.

Gently Morgan explored the silky black bush at the base of her belly; then he parted her thighs, seeking and finding the moist portal of delight.

As he touched the core of her passion, the fire in Isobel's blood accelerated. His further caresses as he rubbed and stroked her sensitive flesh made her cry out in pleasure. She was breathing hard; muscles she had not known she possessed were clamping inside her. In a flash of insight, she suddenly realized she wanted to feel him inside her. She was yearning for that most intimate caress. Her eyes widened in shocked surprise as she understood this secret of lovemaking.

As Morgan held her, he pushed down his clothing so that she could caress unhindered the pulsing brand he had kept hidden from her, and which, as yet, she had only tentatively explored. Shudders of passion beset Isobel as she clasped the gift. She marveled at the throbbing strength of his smooth flesh, at its fiery heat, surprised to feel the tracery of blood vessels beneath her touch. Her exploration was thorough, from his crinkling pubic hair to the moist tip where the skin was velvet smooth and highly sensitive. So much was she enjoying her task that, Morgan was forced to halt the pleasure. Eager for further intimacy, Isobel eased his throbbing length between her thighs. As the fiery brand rubbed against the sensitive font of her passion, the pleasurable sensation made her gasp. She stroked his neck and shoulders, slipping her hands into his curling black hair, sinking her fingers into its thickness. She could not get enough of his hard, arousing body. Isobel tongued his dark nipples, imitating what he had done to her, and Morgan voiced his pleasure before he halted the delight.

"Oh, Isobel, much as I love what you're doing, you must stop," he pleaded huskily.

At first his agonized whisper puzzled her, but Morgan gave her little time to dwell on the puzzle as he fastened his hot mouth over hers, probing her lips apart. Surprised, but not resisting this strange kiss, Isobel felt the sudden hot stab of his tongue, as Morgan imitated what he longed to do to her body. Eagerly she opened her mouth wider and moved her tongue against his, flicking, darting, sucking. Morgan's hands were no longer gentle on her breasts as he felt their weight, and his swollen manhood thrust demandingly against her thigh. With a groan of defeat he rolled her to her back and spread her legs as he introduced the throbbing tip of his manhood to that hot, moist chamber. All the while he whispered endearments to her in Welsh. Though Isobel could not understand his husky words, she basked in his heated caresses, aware that his arms trembled as he tried to control his passion. When he thrust, his mouth was over hers, absorbing her surprised cry as her maidenhead broke.

Isobel's eyes flew open in surprise at the sharp pain threatening to spoil her pleasure. She asked him to stop, but he no longer heard. As her discomfort lessened, she became aware of a mounting heat in her belly. Those inner contractions had a purpose now as she felt him slide deeper inside her, until his hot strength consumed her body. Slowly he began to move, aware her pain was fading. Isobel no longer analyzed what was happening to her, merely allowed her body to float free in a hot world of unexpected pleasure. Shuddering, trembling, she cried out as she vainly tried to control the mounting sensation. Morgan moved rhythmically inside her, his manhood swelling until she thought she would burst with heat, swept toward a crest over which she had no power.

When Isobel asked him to slow down, the more to enjoy this unexpected pleasure, he remained deaf to her pleas. He was driven by a primitive power that soon ensnared her until she no longer asked him to slow down, but urged him to move faster.

Into a firestorm of light and dark she sped, until she unexpectedly reached a climax, taken completely by surprise as pleasure rocked her body. Helpless tears poured from her eyes and ran into her hair and ears. Clutching him, she held on to Morgan's strength, needing comfort in that free-floating darkness, hardly able to believe such a feeling of total involvement could be real. Gently she floated back to earth with his strong arms around her, his hot mouth against hers. Isobel was a little afraid to come back into the present, aware she would never be the same; this man's love had changed her forever.

"Oh, Isobel, sweet, how much I love you," he whispered thickly, aware enough now to speak to her in English.

"I never thought it would be like that," she whispered in awe, her lips soft and bruised.

"Nor I."

They lay in each other's arms, bringing mutual comfort in the aftermath of passion. Isobel felt safe and cherished, so thoroughly loved, she almost believed they were the only two people alive in this forested, rain-drenched world. She watched firelight dancing across the beamed roof and heard the dripping trees outside, her awareness of sight and sound blunted by this otherworldly feeling she hoped would never stop.

Chapter Six

Blodwen cursed beneath her breath as she watched three riders emerge from the mist. He had found the Engishwoman after all. She had hoped the silly creature had ridden into a bog or been set upon by thieves. She turned and marched back inside the tower.

"Welcome home," she greeted, as Morgan led his bride-to-be inside the hall. "All safe and sound, I see."

"Don't sound so disappointed," Morgan snapped, eyes narrowing as he beheld the hostility in his sister's face. His hand went protectively to Isobel's shoulder.

This frosty reception quickly dampened Isobel's enthusiasm for being back at Llyswen. Blodwen had never made any bones about disliking her, though today that emotion seemed closer to hatred. She swallowed uneasily, comforting herself with the reminder that it was Morgan, not his sister, who ruled the land.

"Will you sup?" Blodwen asked next in English, ignoring her brother's warning frown.

"Yes, but first I'd like to wash and change my

clothes,'' Isobel replied with forced civility.

Morgan sent for Mali to assist her mistress.

''You could at least pretend to like her for my sake,'' he began, barely waiting until Isobel was out of the room before he rounded on Blodwen.

''Why? Will that make it so?''

''No, but I'll remind you to mind your manners. Isobel will soon be lady of Llyswen—and of Nels.''

The reminder stung. Blodwen looked stonily at her brother's set face. She had hoped he would come to his senses and send the woman packing. Now that seemed unlikely. When she looked closely at him, he shifted his gaze, almost as if he did not want her to see some truth revealed in his eyes. Then her heart plunged to her belly as she realized it was already too late. Just as surely as if she had been there, she knew what had taken place during last night's storm.

''You bedded her!'' Blodwen accused, grabbing his arm when he would have walked away. ''Don't lie to me.''

''Aye, I did. But don't forget—she is my betrothed.''

''Ha, betrothed . . . on what authority, a piece of parchment filled with English chicken scratch? There are a dozen good Welsh women only too eager to be your wife. Why must you choose this silly little partridge in her fancy clothes?''

''Don't ever let me hear you call her that again,'' Morgan snarled, his hand a vise on Blodwen's arm.

His grip hurt, but she would not flinch. Instead she stared him down: two hard, unyielding faces; two pairs of winter-bleak eyes glazed with anger.

''*I* am lady of Nels.''

''Only until I marry,'' he reminded, letting go of her arm.

Blodwen stepped back. ''If it weren't for lack of a male organ, I'd be *lord* of Nels,'' she stated bitterly.

"True, but you do lack it, and firstborn daughters don't inherit."

"Our mother did."

"Because she had no surviving brother. Besides, we live in different times. The men wouldn't follow a woman now, so don't get any dangerous ideas," he warned, eyes narrowed, hardly able to believe they were having this conversation. "You will accept Isobel as my wife and the lady of Nels, or you will leave Llyswen."

Though she immediately regretted it, Blodwen could not keep from gasping at his shocking statement. In a matter of weeks her whole life had been turned upside down. From sharing the rule of this vast land, she had been relegated to spinster sister. And now she was being threatened with expulsion if she refused to bow to this foreign woman—expulsion from the land that was just as much her birthright as his.

"By God, you're your father's son, all right," she said with a snarl, sidestepping him when he would have grabbed her arm. "From all accounts, handsome Owen would sacrifice anything in exchange for his pleasure between a woman's legs. Doubtless, if not for our mother, neither of us would have aught to argue about."

"I don't want to argue with you, Blodwen," Morgan began with a sigh. "Besides, Owen the Rhymer wasn't the pleasure-loving fool he pretended. He played a part in holding on to Llyswen. I don't want to turn you out. I want you here, beside me, just the way it's always been. We're the same flesh and blood."

The earnestness in his face melted a little of the ice encasing her heart. Blodwen forced a smile. "You're my brother and I love you, yet it pains me to see you turned soft, bewitched by some foreign wench."

"Nothing will change between us because I marry Isobel," he promised, flashing her a tentative smile.

They gripped hands to mark their truce, and Blodwen had to be content with that.

* * *

Isobel waited in the courtyard while the last bags and boxes were heaved aboard the wagons. Now Morgan's huge warhorse, Bryn, was loaded into a cart. The animal's enormous hooves thundered across the boards and his snorts of displeasure echoed round the yard. The black destrier would not be ridden on the journey; his strength must be kept in reserve for the upcoming tournament.

As it was not practical to take her dogs to the Shrewsbury Christmas tourney, Isobel had bidden them good-bye one last time, steeling her heart against their whimpering and doleful expressions. Even now their piteous wails added to the general noise of departure.

The rising wind rustled through the dead leaves of the beeches overhanging the stables. Isobel took a deep, invigorating breath of sharp December air. Though Llyswen was Morgan's beloved home, she was not sorry to be leaving it. She had grown fond of the wild, craggy countryside; the manor house was a different story. An undercurrent of hostility prevailed, due, she was sure, to Blodwen's influence. Only Morgan, and her maid, Mali, acted as if she belonged here. The others treated her like an unwelcome guest. Careful now not to appear openly hostile, Blodwen maintained a strained civility toward her, and made Isobel feel almost as uncomfortable as when she had shown her anger.

And though Morgan assured her Blodwen would get used to the idea of his taking a wife, Isobel was not convinced. Whenever his sister was present, she sensed danger. She did not expect an assassin's dagger; it was more a subtly malevolent undercurrent.

Though it was hard, Isobel had to admit that not all the jealousy was on Blodwen's part. Isobel resented being excluded from all discussions about governing the land. It was not only because brother and sister usually spoke Welsh that she felt left out; it was because no one seemed to expect her to have any part in the conversation, as if she were merely a pretty child without the wit to understand more serious matters.

Just then she heard Morgan's voice as he strode into the yard, and Isobel shivered in pleasurable anticipation, contemplating having him all to herself. These past weeks had been a time of awakened passion, and though in their shared bedchamber Morgan made passionate love to her until her body sang with joy, she realized she did not know him very well. Beyond their intense physical bond, they had shared little. He always seemed to be riding about his land, or training his men. Christmas in Shrewsbury would be theirs alone.

When Morgan came toward her, his smile warm and welcoming, Isobel felt as if the sun had shone on this gloomy day. How she longed to embrace him, but ever aware of the watching soldiers, she contented herself with a handclasp.

"Come on, sweet, mount up. The day's already half over."

He led her gelding forward, saddled for the journey.

Weak with longing for his embrace, Isobel shivered as his hands encircled her waist when he swept her into the saddle. Solicitously he arranged her fur-lined cloak about her legs. Morgan smiled up at her and, ignoring the others, held out his arms. Isobel leaned down to kiss him, finding his mouth firm and hot. Deep emotion sped between them, and she felt light-headed. Fleetingly she touched his crisp hair, his nose, his brow, before he pressed her fingers to his lips in parting. Those lingering kisses made her shiver again in pleasure before Morgan stepped back, no longer just her lover but once again lord of the land.

The cavalcade of men, wagons and horses finally clattered across the lowered bridge and turned toward the highway.

Blodwen stood at the door waving good-bye. Isobel doubted the woman was sorry to see her leave, though by her unsmiling face she appeared genuinely saddened by the prospect of her brother's absence at Christmas. Morgan had asked Blodwen to come with them to Shrewsbury, but she'd declined, saying she would feel out of place. Even the offer of new garments befitting her station would not sway her.

Several other parties of knights joined them along the way as they traveled over open moorland and wooded hillside. On this main route to England, inns were plentiful, yet at this time of year they were crowded with travelers heading to nearby towns for the Christmas festivities.

As they drew closer to Shrewsbury, they passed many parties of knights loaded down with baggage and armor, their snorting destriers likewise held in reserve for the tourney. Many of the knights were accompanied by finely dressed ladies who giggled and chattered like magpies, greatly excited by the prospect of celebrating Christmas in Shrewsbury.

To Isobel's dismay, these women stared at Morgan in open admiration. Her jealousy flared when she correctly interpreted the invitation in their faces; in fact, so brazen were they, she wondered if these truly were ladies, or merely high-priced strumpets traveling with the knights. She also was ogled. Being unused to such rude stares from men who made little effort to conceal their thoughts, Isobel felt her cheeks flush. Not sure how she was supposed to react, she averted her gaze, trying to ignore their inviting smiles and sly winks.

Far from the idyllic interlude she had anticipated, the journey to Shrewsbury was a big disappointment. She never once shared a room with Morgan, and their time alone was hurried and stolen. Space at the inns was at a premium, so she was forced to sleep in a communal room with other lady travelers, or she and Mali were squashed into quarters no bigger than a cupboard. After first making sure she was provided for, Morgan stayed in the stables with his men, taking turns to keep watch over their horses.

Thieves abounded on the highways, and innkeepers were often in league with robbers who waited in the shadows.

After seemingly endless, jouncing days in the saddle, they finally reached their destination just before dusk, halting outside Shrewsbury's city gate. To the west the sun sank into the winding river encircling the city, bronze rays burnishing the masonry and setting the dark water aflame.

They waited to be admitted, jostled back and forth by a clamoring throng of travelers equally anxious to be safely inside the city before the gates were closed for the night. An equal number of people seemed just as eager to leave Shrewsbury for the same reason. It was almost impossible to be heard above the uproar of bleating livestock, rattling wagons and impatient tradesmen. The sheer press of beasts and humanity panicked Isobel's gelding, and she had to battle to keep him in check.

Slowly the pushing, malodorous throng moved along, bringing them through the gates and into Shrewsbury's cobbled streets.

The winding, crowded streets were lined with tall buildings whose painted, gilded facades reflected the sun's dying rays. Isobel stared about in wonder at the splendor of the buildings, wishing they had arrived earlier on this short winter day so she could have seen more before dark.

The first street they had entered was broad, yet once they turned off the main road, moving sharply uphill, their way narrowed. Here overhanging buildings virtually met across the cobbled street, and they had to press close together just to pass along this narrow thoroughfare. Above their heads each house's succeeding story thrust farther into the street, blocking light and air.

They were headed for the Falcon, where Morgan had made prior arrangements to stay. It was fortunate he had made advance plans, for this inn was also filled to overflowing; many travelers were forced to sleep under their wagons or in the stables with their beasts.

Isobel had not expected the city to be so crowded. This must be an important tournament to draw so many competitors. There was also a Christmas goose fair, and sundry other entertainments taking place at the same time. It was so exciting, she could hardly wait to go exploring, though Morgan had warned her she must never go out without an escort, for danger could lurk where she least expected it.

One recurring thought dampened her pleasure. If men traveled from across England to compete in the tournament, it could mean Lionel would be here also. Her stomach pitched at the idea.

Their room at the Falcon was tucked beneath the eaves. Overlooking the street was a dormer window covered by painted wooden shutters and an oilcloth cover. The huge bed almost filled the paneled room. Upon inspection she found clean bedsheets miraculously free of vermin.

A few minutes later a bath arrived, carried by panting, sweating lads who had manhandled the unwieldly metal bath to the inn's top floor. A stream of servants followed, bringing jugs of hot water, towels and fresh logs for the hearth. Isobel was delighted by Morgan's thoughtfulness. How could he have known a hot bath was just what she longed for to soothe her weary limbs? How blissful it would feel to soak in the water and wash away the grime of travel. Isobel poured scent from her precious glass flagon into the water and inhaled the delightful fragrance. Carefully she unwrapped a treasured bar of fine milled French soap, hoarded like a precious gem.

A tray of food and wine arrived next, saving her from having to go down to the crowded common room to sup. Before departing, the young lad mended the fire and pushed the bath closer to the hearth, draping the towels to air before the blaze.

She waited until the water had cooled enough for bathing, but when the temperature was right, Isobel was disappointed that Morgan still had not come. Several times she looked into the gloomy corridor as steps sounded, but it was always someone else passing the door. She had hoped he would come upstairs to join her, and then their bath would have been a shared sensual pleasure. As it was, she would have to bathe before the water grew cold.

Isobel lay back in the bath, pouring a flagon of water over her hair to rinse away the soapsuds. Her soap smelled deliciously of musk roses, scenting the water with a delightful aroma. She imagined she lay in a warm bed of rose petals. How heavenly it was to lie here drowsing before the fire. There was but one pleasure missing. Where could Morgan be? She had laid a fur-edged crimson velvet bedrobe across the foot of the bed. As their evening meal was already here there was no need to dress at all, she thought with a smile.

When the water was chilling a knock came at the door, and two red-faced serving women arrived, puffing and panting, as they hauled steaming containers to warm the bath. Isobel extravagantly emptied the last of her flagon in the water and lay back to enjoy the scented warmth.

Morgan quaffed the rest of his wine and put down the cup, preparing to leave. Lord Deganwy lifted the decanter to refill his glass.

"Nay, I must to bed. The serious jousting starts tomorrow. Would you have me dead on my feet from lack of sleep?" he asked, joking easily with the other man. Yet all the while he was picturing Isobel alone in their room waiting for him. Isobel, firm flesh glowing pink from her bath, her soft, delectable curves warm, perfumed, and so inviting . . .

Morgan cleared his throat, shifting uncomfortably on the settle. Such a stirring picture had sprung to mind, he must steel himself against betraying his thoughts.

"We'll be allies in the melee, your men and mine," said Lord Deganwy, his open countenance drawn with fatigue. "Have you looked the field over?"

"No, it was dark before we reached the inn. I'll look it over at first light, get a bearing of the land and plot a strategy," Morgan said, feeling it was now safe to get up without shaming himself. "Till tomorrow."

The men clasped hands and Morgan refused a parting cup of wine. Then he was finally out the door and hurrying along the narrow corridor, up small twisting flights of stairs, round bends, heading for the inn's top floor, which overhung narrow Swan Lane. He had drunk enough, yet not too much, for his steps were still steady; the wine imparted a feeling of well-being without its accompanying stupor. No thanks to Deganwy and his brimming bumpers. So many old friends all insisting on sharing a drink while they renewed acquaintance, pledging loyalty as they chose sides for the grand melee on the morrow between black knights and white. They were already two days into the tourney. The lesser competitors had been eliminated, leaving the foremost contenders to compete for the big prize money.

Morgan pushed open the door to their room, finding it lit by the glow from the hearth, suffused in welcoming golden light. A large metal bath stood before the fire, and there lay his precious Isobel, having slid down in the water, her black hair spread around her shoulders and fanning out over the bath's sides. Only the top curve of her firm white breasts peeked above the water. His mind's eye quickly supplied the complete picture and his breathing grew shallow.

He shut the door quietly behind him and she did not stir. For a few minutes he stood there, admiring her, reluctant to break the spell. Never had he felt this way about a woman. They were a necessity of a man's life, yet in truth, there had been few who held his attention for long. In his heart of hearts he always dreamed of finding the perfect woman, his ideas fueled by romantic tales of star-crossed lovers, an ever-popular subject of minstrel and troubador.

Now he had given his heart to Isobel, and in a way Morgan was sorry. When he entered the lists, or risked life and limb in a melee at some far-flung tournament, he would always fear dying and leaving her.

Unaccountably his throat needed clearing, and the sound startled her awake. She did not start in alarm, merely inclined her head slightly and cocked one eyelid open.

"So, you're finally here," she said, her voice husky with sleep. "Where were you? Not servicing a passel of whores, I hope."

He grinned. "And if I were, why should it matter, lady? You don't own me."

"Ah, that's where you're wrong. I own every inch of you and refuse to share with another. If I as much as catch a wench's hand on you, I'll scratch out your eyes."

"Rest assured, that part of me's kept safe just for you."

"Aye, hoarded like gold ever since we left Llyswen," she remarked tartly, sitting up and swishing her damp hair off her face. "I swear, I've not seen or touched your most treasured possession since we took to the road."

"What do you mean, my most treasured possession—surely it is you who're my most treasured possession," he joked, ducking as she splashed water at him. "The delay was innocent, just reacquainting myself with old companions . . . all male, my love, I swear. Tomorrow we'll be allies in the melee."

"A melee . . . what's that?"

"A mock battle."

"Battle," Isobel said in a shocked squeak. "You could be hurt."

"I hope not, but yes, that's a possibility."

Sobered by the news, she peered up. "I wouldn't like that," she said in a small voice.

"Remember . . . the Dragon Knight is invincible."

"If only that were so."

"This is the way I earn our money."

''I know.''

Isobel stretched out her hand to him, but he did not come forward. Instead Morgan pitched his cloak across the bed and began to unfasten his doublet.

''Is there warmth left in the water?''

''A little, but you'd best hurry.''

''Will you soap my back?''

''With my best French soap.''

''Heaven, I'll smell like a whore's backside.''

''How do you know what a whore's backside smells like?'' she challenged sharply.

''I can assure you, most probably don't smell nearly as pleasant as your soap.'' He laughed and pitched his clothing on the bed.

Isobel stood up, water streaming down her body, and Morgan paused in the act of unlacing his hose, mesmerized by the perfection of her form.

''You'd best hurry,'' she reminded, smiling at him, her pulse quickened by the smoldering desire in his face.

''Aye,'' he agreed huskily, ''I'd better while I'm still in the mood to bathe.''

He grunted as he stepped into the cool water, and Isobel set aside his hand when he reached out to fondle her body. She swathed a towel about herself, soaking up the trickling water. Then she ordered him down in the water while she lathered his hair until the soapsuds ran down his neck and shoulders. With a contented sigh he lay back and allowed her to scrub him; he stood obediently when commanded. Isobel licked her lips as she contemplated soaping the rest of his body. It was almost more than she could do, to maintain her composure as she admired his hard, sinewed body. Washing his back and shoulders had been arousing enough, but now, as she reached up, sliding her hands across his chest, touching the puckered weal of his scar and running her fingers through his crinkling chest hair, she knew in a moment she would move lower, to his taut belly and beyond. Her imagination was almost her undoing. Her hand slid so easily across his soapy flesh and she shivered in pleasure at the touch. He could not hide his growing arousal, and his flesh pulsed in her hand as she soaped.

Morgan opened his eyes when she stopped. Though it had been difficult to endure, he had greatly enjoyed the pleasurable sensation of her soapy fingers sliding over the length of his flesh. He was aware she had fought valiantly to wash and not titillate. It had been a losing battle.

"I've never enjoyed a bath so much," he whispered huskily as his hand strayed beneath her towel. Gently he traced the damp flesh of Isobel's inner thigh, tangling his fingers in the silky bush of dark hair. "Come, sweet," he invited, "am I not clean enough?"

Isobel tipped a final jug of rinse water over him, and the firelight turned the cascading water to liquid gold as it streamed down his body. Her breath caught in admiration as she looked at him, magnificently, terribly male. So overpowering did he seem in this small room, she was almost afraid of his strength. Then he gently stroked her face, his fingers tender against her cheek, and the flicker of fear passed. Morgan was her lover, and his sheer power was tempered by his love for her. This man did not seek to bend her to his will, but cherished her instead.

"I love you," she said softly, "for ever and ever."

"That's all I ask from life," he vowed sincerely.

His arms slid about her as he enfolded her against him. The towel between them absorbed some of the water from his wet skin. Isobel took one of the warming towels from the chest and slipped it around his back, rubbing the fabric back and forth to dry him. She had dropped her own wet towel on the rushes, and Morgan wrapped her in the warm fabric, encircling them flesh to flesh inside the cocoon.

It was barely a stride to the bed, and he leaned back against its frame, taking her weight on top of him. As she settled over him, he slid the thrusting heat of his organ between her legs so that Isobel shuddered in pleasure each time his throbbing flesh slipped against her body's sensitive core. So delicious did the contact feel, she gasped aloud in pleasure. Morgan moved her lazily back and forth along the length of his flesh, drawing out the pleasurable sensation until she had to fight down a swift surge of desire.

Growing more urgent, Isobel locked her arms around his neck, struggling to keep his mouth welded against hers. Morgan's lips opened and his tongue plunged deep inside her mouth. Morgan kicked aside the towel and pulled Isobel with him, struggling under the mound of sheets and blankets, pulling the covers over them to ward off the room's chill.

Next the feather pillows went under her head. Isobel lay back expectantly, positioning him over her, her legs spread. She kneaded his back, urging, cajoling, threatening all manner of doom if he did not make love to her this instant.

Morgan's mouth was like fire as their lips seared together, bodies moving automatically. Arms locked tight around him, Isobel moaned as the searing heat of his body plunged deep inside her. She cried out in delight, and grasped his shoulders as she thrust her hips higher.

Morgan moved at his own pace, deaf to her instruction. It no longer mattered, for she had gone beyond redemption, cresting a wave of passion that rocked the very depths of her being. For so long she had yearned for his lovemaking. Now, her emotion was almost as intense as that first time, yet it was so much better, for she understood the passion of his body and the demands of her own.

The heady, swirling intoxication of lovemaking filled the room as she became emotionally in tune with the man in her arms, giving and taking, seeking and bestowing all the passion of which she was capable. Mutually cresting the wave, they slowly descended to earth in the warm darkness after midnight, blissfully spent and secure in their love.

Morgan and Isobel dozed in each other's arms, waking to make love again. This time their lovemaking was less frenzied, but just as satisfying in its own way. Hungry after their exertions in the wee hours, they ate their cold supper, feeding each other tidbits and sharing a goblet of wine. Morgan heaped more logs on the fire before padding back to bed.

Lying drowsily in each other's arms, they watched the garish shadows moving over the walls and ceiling as the logs roared, crackling and sparking up the sooty chimney. A blast of winter wind rattled the shutters and moaned in the chimney as they held each other safe, shutting out the cold loneliness of the December night. No other place existed beyond this firelit room. Content in their embrace, sated with passion and secure in their love, they would have no regrets if life ended now, for they could truly say they were happy.

Chapter Seven

The tilt ground outside the city walls buzzed with activity. Armorers abounded, here to repair and sharpen the contestants' weapons and batter-dented armor back into shape. Colored bunting decked rows of wooden stalls selling all manner of goods, from food to singing birds. Entertainers and cutpurses mingled with the crowds thronging the open fairground.

Goodwives, townsmen, 'prentice boys and whores had all come out to enjoy the festivities, gaping at the performing dogs, the mummers and the tumblers vying for their attention with fire-eaters and sword swallowers. Even a huge shaggy bear was presented for their enjoyment, the animal turning slowly in a shambling dance.

Isobel, however, did not feel the intense excitement she had known as she anticipated the Stoneham tourney, for she was too worried about Morgan's safety to enjoy the courses. Sitting crushed in the rickety stands among the other women, being elbowed and stepped on, she found little to enjoy. To Isobel's horror, after the first two courses, Morgan was unseated, and her heart sank when he lay on the ground for what seemed an eternity before his squires had him up and moving.

Most of all she dreaded the approaching melee, today's most spectacular event. The buzz of excitement mounted in the stands as the time drew near. The crowd roared approval as each champion thundered forth, until the field swarmed with men and horses, banners fluttering in the brisk wind. Gasps greeted the arrival on the field of the fearsome Dragon Knight clad in his customary black, the gold dragon insignia glinting on his surcoat. Morgan's men also wore black, only their banner adding a touch of color.

Lord Deganwy with his retainers followed Morgan. They were joined by two other knights leading out their own bands of soldiers. They formed a rank to one side of the mock battleground, their pennants black to indicate today's allegiance. Morgan's men took the center position on the field, Deganwy on his right, Martyn of Merioneth on his left; the other knight's men brought up the rear. Their opponents carried white pennants. These white knights were not as threatening in their white surcoats; their leader's horse was caparisoned in cloth of silver with strings of silver bells jingling from the harness.

Eager bets were being placed on all sides over the outcome of the main event.

Though all day Isobel had looked for the Hurley standard, or the new combination of arms Lionel sported, she had been surprised to find neither. Surely he would not pass up an opportunity to excel, unless the competition here was too fierce for him.

The gates sealing off the field clanged shut following the hasty exit of the sundry entertainers. Now an expectant hush descended on the crowd. Stomach in knots, Isobel clenched her hands in her lap, knuckles whitening. She could see her gold silk scarf fluttering from Morgan's lance.

Trumpets sounded. The tournament marshals announced the contestants' names and titles, their words blowing away in the chill wind. As usual Morgan was introduced as the Dragon Knight, with no identifying place name or title.

The acrid smell of horse and hot grease from frying pasties drifted from the outfield; somewhere close at hand a vendor shouted his wares. All around her the crowd had grown expectantly quiet as the opposing sides maneuvered into position on the field.

The marshals surveyed the field one last time, making sure all was set and that the opposing ranks were evenly matched. Trumpets sounded a fanfare, and the foremost knights positioned their lances in readiness. Then, at a signal, spurs were set into the destriers' flanks and the thundering horde rode forth, covering the distance between opposing sides in the blink of an eye. They met with a terrible crash of steel. Men shouted, horses whinnied, and the crowd cheered.

Isobel closed her eyes, unable to watch the slaughter, picturing her beloved being trampled beneath those mighty hooves. Cries of dismay sounded around her, quickly followed by shouts of triumph. At last she could stand it no longer and she had to look, all the while chiding herself for her terrible cowardice. What she saw made her gasp in horror. This was an actual battle! Blood dripped from man and horse. A half dozen men were already laid out on the churned ground, while several riderless and injured horses careened around the field, screaming in pain and fright. In the midst of the clanging engagement still taking place in the middle of the field, she could see Morgan's distinctive black armor. And she let out a shuddering sigh of relief to discover he was still in the saddle.

The fight raged on, with the opponents battering, shouting, giving and taking ground until, a few minutes later, the victor was declared. Surrendering to preserve both life and limb, the defeated white knights would forfeit their horses and equipment and pay their captors a ransom.

The Dragon Knight, flanked by Deganwy and Merioneth, moved forward toward the stands. Their visors pushed back, the three knights stood in their stirrups, acknowledging the cheers of the crowd.

Nausea rose bitter in her throat as Isobel stumbled blindly from the stands, hurrying down to the field to make sure Morgan was not hurt.

The melee was over. The wounded were being carried off the field. Squires staggered past, bearing their masters on stretchers, taking their bloodied, groaning charges to their own pavilions, where they would have their wounds dressed. Not all the men groaned, and Isobel was horrified to see that several were so still and white, she was sure they must be dead.

The black knights rode around the perimeter of the field one final time to the roars of the crowd. Then they left the arena. At the same time the tumblers and jugglers came on the field at the other end, anxious to divert the crowd's attention from the less pleasant sight of injured men and horses and the need to clear debris from the field before the contests could continue.

The black knights were not without casualties. To her own damnation, she was sure, Isobel thanked the Blessed Mother that it was not Morgan whose shoulder drooped low and whose head gushed blood, or who had to be carried from his horse because his leg was crushed. Though the battered Welsh soldiers had many slashes and bruises, they appeared not to be seriously hurt. One man's helmet had been crushed by a mace, and he yelped in pain as his comrades tried to pry it off. Even Martyn of Merioneth was injured after losing his helm in the fray, and blood ran into his eyes from a gash above his brow.

Morgan's black pavilion flying the dragon banner stood waiting. The tent was equipped with basins and cloths, flasks of pain-killing brews and bowls of soothing salves and unguents, all ready beside the champion's pallet.

Morgan groaned as his squires helped him out of the saddle. He limped toward her.

"You're hurt!" Isobel cried accusingly, rushing to him.

"Aye, some bastard tried to shatter my kneecap," he growled, anxious to get out of his plate and assess the damage. "Nay, sweet, don't cry, it's not that bad. We won the purse, and we'll have ransoms to divide. All in all, today went well."

She said nothing, biting her lip to keep back bitter words of condemnation. If this was considered a day of victory and success, she would hate to see a bad day.

Sweat trickled down Morgan's face, making white rivers in the blood and grime. Isobel was unprepared for the sight of him looking so battered. In the past she had not known the mysterious black-clad knight, so his wounds mattered little to her, his great triumph overshadowing all. It was not so today. Tears filled her eyes as she saw his swollen, grazed flesh and heard him groan and wince when they stripped off his plate armor.

"I thought this was a mock battle," she remarked acidly while she tried to sponge his swollen knee with ice water.

"It was—no one died, did they?"

"Some of them looked dead to me."

"Nay, a loss of blood and courage, that's all. They'll be better tomorrow. You mustn't fret so, sweetheart. Did men not get injured where you are from?"

"Yes, but I didn't love them," she admitted, stepping back to allow his squires to minister to their lord. They were far more familiar with treating battle injuries than she.

The broken armor had gouged his flesh, and the resulting swelling from the injury had driven the metal into the swollen leg. When his squires had finished cleaning the wound, they slathered on an unguent of primrose leaves and sallow willow, before tightly binding his knee.

Morgan grinned at her. "There, good as new. Come, sweet, the afternoon's late and we need to collect our winnings."

Several hours later, in the gathering dusk, their party climbed uphill toward the Falcon, the men singing in their own language, elated by today's victory. The pavilion, armor and weapons had been packed away; Bryn, Morgan's warhorse, was banished to his cart. Morgan had decided not to compete in the tourney's final day, allowing his leg time to heal before the next big event.

Isobel was deep in thought as they rode through the chilly streets. A few snowflakes drifted past to settle on her face, melting from the warmth of her cheek. She had been considering the future. How did other knights' wives cope with the constant prospect of their husbands' being injured? Seeing Morgan in pain, knowing today's outcome could have had far more serious consequences, had cast a pall on her happiness. Perhaps, when she had wrested her holdings from Lionel, she could persuade Morgan to abandon this dangerous profession. He could use the money from her fertile land to pay his soldiers. Surely there would be enough. Or was his need for money only part of the reason he competed? She had seen the intense enjoyment in his face as he practiced at the quintain, or trained with his men.

She turned to look at him but could see little in the shadows. His nose and brow formed a dark line under his cap; his cloak was bunched about his neck to keep out the chill. They passed beneath a lamp standard spanning the narrow street outside the Bull and Bear. Just then Morgan turned to look at her. He smiled, and Isobel's heart bumped and thudded with excitement. Oh, what a fool she was to love a fighting man.

"Our feast will be waiting for us when we get in," he said, maneuvering his horse closer to hers until their knees almost touched as they moved along the narrow street.

Morgan brushed snowflakes off her shoulder, his hand gentle.

"A feast?"

"Aye, to celebrate my victory."

"But how could you know you'd win when we left this morning?" she asked, a puzzled frown on her face.

"Because I always win," he said, voicing supreme confidence.

Her heart plunged. His words confirmed what she'd already suspected: Morgan's skill on the field was as much a part of his identity as his speech, or the color of his hair. And she sighed, masking her defeat with a smile. She could never ask him to abandon something he loved to do just because she was afraid he would be hurt. To ask him to give up competing in the joust would be like emasculating him.

The following morning traces of snow lingered in crevices and edged the roof tiles; driven by the wind, it twined sparkling ribbons around steps and foundations. Though the air was still cold and crisp, the sun was already breaking through the banked gray clouds.

Though Morgan did not let Isobel know, it was a painful struggle to mount his horse. Once in the saddle, he was able to rest his injured leg against the animal's broad side, the warmth from the horse's body helping to soothe the hurt. Walking was another matter. He would face that challenge when he must.

Because there was still one more day of competition at the tournament, the goose fair was not as crowded as they had expected. The scrubby ground was lined with row after row of stalls. Geese could be heard cackling for a full five minutes before they reached the fairground: here Shrewsbury housewives would buy their Christmas geese, much haggling and shouting accompanying the transactions. The sacrificial victims often tried to escape, and there were frequent chases of cackling, waddling geese hotly pursued by red-faced 'prentice lads.

Because it was cold, Isobel wore her heavy wool traveling gown of Lincoln green under her fur-lined cloak. Morgan also wore dark green, and she was pleased that they were similarly dressed. Just like brother and sister, he had teased her when she laid out the green garments, remarking with pleasure over their matching raiment.

"Then we're a very unholy brother and sister," she reminded him tartly.

"Oh, I assure you, there are many of those about," he added with a wicked grin.

While they laughed and jested she had pretended not to notice the fresh lines pain etched in his face as he hobbled downstairs. By now she knew Morgan well enough not to question the wisdom of going to the goose fair. His mind was made up and nothing short of divine intervention would change it.

A party of six men rode with them, the others staying behind at the inn to guard the horses and baggage. During the night someone had been tampering with their bridles, and the Welshmen were on heightened alert for thieves.

Morgan reined in at the edge of the fairground, barely able to make himself heard over the din of cackling geese, rough-voiced stall holders and the housewives' constant chatter. A straggling procession of itinerant musicians threading their way through the crowd only added to the racket.

"Would you go ahead with Mihangel, sweet, whilst I look up an old armorer. Only he can rivet to my liking."

Isobel agreed after he assured her he would join her in a few minutes. Mihangel, one of his lieutenants, and two other men, dismounted to accompany her.

Though he was in need of an armorer, Morgan wanted to buy a few minutes' time to survey the fairgrounds, making sure all was to his satisfaction. Morgan narrowed his eyes against the sunlight streaming between the clouds. Soldiers and armored men were a common sight in Shrewsbury, especially when a tournament was being held; however, Iestyn told him the man caught tampering with their saddlery was so clad, and that was not a common sight, for it revealed him not as an ordinary thief, but a man in some lord's employ. Did a jealous rival from yesterday's tourney seek revenge? Or was it someone from his past who intended to even the score? It could even be someone connected to Lord Hurley, for he must still be smarting over the failure of his plan to recapture his goods.

The men sat astride their mounts looking over the crowd and seeing nothing amiss. No damage had been done last night. The horses weren't lame, no baggage was stolen; in fact, the man had done him a favor, for now he was alert for any sign of trouble. Though all that was true, Iestyn's discovery still made him uneasy. Ever since they'd arrived in Shrewsbury he had felt misgivings. Then he had assumed his unease came from an anticipated confrontation with Isobel's brother. It was a relief when Lord Hurley was nowhere to be seen. Yet still the feeling lingered.

He signaled to his men and they rode quickly to the armorer's tent, where he had brought several pieces to be worked on. The man assured him everything would be ready by the end of the day.

A few minutes later Morgan spotted Isobel in the crowd, accompanied by Mihangel.

Taking a sudden gamble, he decided to dismount. Iestyn, alarmed, leaped to his lord's aid. Between them, with his face purposely turned away from Isobel, Morgan came out of the saddle. Sweat beaded on his brow with the effort. Though he hated the indignity of it, he acepted the thick, knotted stick Iestyn handed him to aid in walking.

"Oh, you're feeling better," Isobel cried in surprise, innocently unaware of the effort this simple act had taken. "Only walk for a little while lest you tire."

Teeth gritted, Morgan nodded, looking away toward a nearby stall crowded with singing birds in gilded cages, colored ribbons and baskets of silken flowers. That would take her attention from his disability.

"See, likely there's something there you'd fancy."

Isobel stepped forward, her face lighting expectantly. She drew him after her by the hand, slowing her pace until he had adjusted to walking with the stick. Yes, indeed, this stall was crowded with wonderful goods. The first thing that caught her eye was a sumptuous hood of scarlet brocade. The hood was lined with beautiful cream-colored fur, thick and silky soft, with black spots circled in yellow. She plunged her hand into the fur, marveling at its softness. It was light as down.

"How much?" she asked the merchant, who seemed to be somewhat distressed. At first he tried to snatch the hood away, all the while glancing about the sparse crowd as if he searched for someone.

"Not for sale," he mumbled, still trying to take it back.

Isobel held on. Eyes flashing, she challenged, "If it's not for sale, why is it in full view on your stall?"

"A . . . a mistake, lady."

"Everything's for sale. How much?" Morgan growled, tiring of the charade. His knee felt like fire, and the pain did not improve his disposition. It was all he could do to stand there, let alone haggle for an hour.

"Oh, no, my lord, I beg you. Not now. Come back later," the man pleaded, eyes darting about the shoppers at the nearby stalls.

Morgan also glanced about, finding the man's actions exceedingly odd. It was as if he were looking for someone. "Is the hood already sold to someone else?" he asked.

"Nay, just come back this afternoon," the man repeated.

"We can't come back. We'll take it now."

Isobel tugged at the red hood, and the man's grasp

slackened as Morgan produced a bag of coins. This seemed to be a strange transaction. "What fur is it?" she asked the man curiously.

"I don't know the name . . . some beast from distant lands, maybe even from the holy land," the man mumbled, eyes shifting from the hood to the money.

He obviously didn't know. Again Isobel stroked the lustrous fur. Oh, if only she could have a cloak lined in this beautiful fur! She doubted even Queen Phillippa would have such luxury.

Coins clinked on the wooden board and rolled amid the silver ribbons. Morgan was growing anxious to leave. Not only did his leg hurt, but this transaction made him all the more uneasy. He had even begun to wonder if a trap were being laid. If the ambush was not yet in place, then that would explain the man's insistence that they come back this afternoon.

The stallholder hastily counted the coins, bit the gold to make sure it was genuine, and then thrust it in his purse. The hood finally exchanged hands, and Isobel was ecstatic with her purchase. All the while the merchant glanced about uneasily, still watching the crowd.

"Something tells me we shouldn't tarry here," Morgan said, nodding to Iestyn to bring up the horses.

Isobel was disappointed, though she shared his unease. It was probably for the best. While Morgan struggled into the saddle with Iestyn's help, out of the corner of her eye she noticed a band of men in huntsmen's green watching them from the shadow of an apothecary stall. Heads together, these men appeared displeased when they saw that she and Morgan were preparing to leave. Behind her, Isobel was also aware that the stall holder had slipped away, leaving his apprentice in charge as he melted into the shadows as if trying to avoid detection.

Their mounted party walked from the narrow lane between the stalls, ignoring shouted pleas to examine fine goods and sample delicious food and drink. Once out in the open, Morgan felt more at ease and he slowed the pace, even allowing the horses to stop to crop the scrubby grass. The green-clad huntsmen had watched their departure, but made no attempt to stop them.

"Likely the hood is stolen, or he's already been paid for it," Morgan said, wanting to soothe Isobel's fears. That explanation seemed too simplistic, yet he hated to spoil her special outing. "Why don't we go to the jeweler's stall? He has his own guard there."

They turned about and headed to the edge of the fairground, where a small tent and several wooden stalls stood apart from the rest. A huge mastiff with a spiked collar was on guard before the stall; two other large dogs waited behind the table with their master. The display of jewelry sparkled in the sunshine. Much of this was only gilt, set out to attract attention. In the back of the stall were the genuine pieces.

The old jeweler and his dogs were well known to Morgan, for he had seen the man many times in Hereford, Chepstow and Ludlow, as he plied his trade along the border.

"Well, Daniel Jacks, how are you this fine morning?" he hailed, reining in before the stall.

"Is it my lord Morgan? What a pleasure! You're here for the tourney?" asked the old man, pushing back his straggling white hair as he shuffled around the table to greet them.

"Aye, but I won what I wanted yesterday. Today's my lady's day to buy trinkets. What do you have to show her?"

"Your lady . . . well, that is a welcome addition since last we met. And so beautiful too. Welcome, welcome, lady."

Isobel smiled, extending her hand in greeting to the jeweler.

"Fine brooches and rings, or maybe a pretty pendant

to grace that lovely neck?'' suggested Daniel Jacks, smiling in pleasure as he surveyed her beauty.

Isobel was helped from the saddle, but Morgan decided to stay put, not deeming it wise to attempt to dismount in full view of both Isobel and the jeweler.

A tray of his best merchandise was produced for her inspection. The sparkling assortment of pendants, rings and brooches dazzled her eyes. A gold medallion on a slender chain caught Isobel's glance. The medallion's face bore an enameled oval with a single rose inlaid with rubies. There was also a handsome filigree brooch next to it, so appropriate for Christmastide with its green- and red-jeweled spray of holly. These two pieces were her favorites. She had not asked their price, or even if Morgan wanted to buy them for her. Tentatively Isobel held out her selection to him.

Morgan examined the pieces, turning them over to study the hallmark. Then he asked, ''Are you sure this is all you want? He may have other things to catch your fancy.''

''This is more than enough.'' Isobel was not anxious to discuss finances in such a public place, but she had to ask, ''Are they too dear? If so, I can put them back.''

''No.'' Morgan shook his head, surprised she would even suggest such a thing. He leaned down from the saddle, speaking to the jeweler in an undertone. Finally a bargain was struck and more gold changed hands.

Isobel watched this transaction uneasily. This was not what Morgan should be risking life and limb to buy. When she was back in the saddle, the jewelry tucked safely inside her purse, she decided she would have to caution him about his extravagance. At this rate, when they finally got back to Llyswen, he'd have barely enough money left for winter fodder.

They waved good-bye to the jeweler and trekked across the scrubby fairground. Pulling her mount close to his, Isobel said, ''You mustn't keep buying me gifts, sweetheart. The money you earned is to outfit your men, for saddles and weapons—you mustn't risk your life just to give me presents."

There was a puzzled frown on his brow as he asked, "Don't you like gifts?"

"Yes, of course. I love them. But I also love for you not to be hurt. The more money you spend on me, the more tournaments you'll have to enter to get money for expenses."

Morgan considered what she had said, greatly surprised by her statement. Women, in his experience, counted gifts as an important part of the male-female relationship. He had always prided himself on knowing a lot about women, but now Isobel was proving him wrong.

"I give you gifts to show how much I love you," he explained, not really understanding her reasoning.

"Yes, I know, and they're beautiful, but every sovereign spent on a gift for me, is a sovereign you have to earn. Besides, every night and day you show me how much you care. To have you safe beside me means more than all the gifts in the world."

She reached out to clasp his hand, feeling the warmth of his fingers through his leather gauntlet. They exchanged tender smiles and continued to ride in silence.

Not only was Isobel more beautiful and more passionate than any other woman he had met before, Morgan thought, she was truly unlike all others in character. She was a treasure beyond compare.

He smiled to himself as he considered that flowery epithet, culled from a minstrel's lay. It was fortunate he kept such thoughts to himself, for had his fellow knights even suspected the depth of his feeling for Isobel, they would conclude he had taken one too many blows to the head. Even he had to agree, love had scrambled his wits. It was a delirious state of being, but a dangerous state for a professional soldier. Love had made him more cautious on the field. And too much caution was sometimes mistaken for cowardice.

Chapter Eight

"If I live to be a hundred I'll still not understand you, *cariad,*" Morgan whispered to Isobel as they stood beside the horses in the Falcon's yard.

"You know women always pride themselves on being mysterious," she reminded him, reaching up to kiss his cold cheek.

They waited for his men to come out to take the horses. To Morgan's annoyance no one appeared, so he sent Iestyn to find out the reason.

Iestyn returned with a baffled expression on his pale face. He thrust his way through the inn's common room, which was already filling up with diners eager for their noon meal.

"My lord, no one's there."

"What do you mean, no one's there?"

"They've gone."

"Everything . . . the horses? The baggage?"

"No. And that's the strangest part of it. Things are as we left them, but no one's on guard."

Though Isobel could not translate the Welsh, by Morgan's expression she knew something must be very wrong.

"What's happened?"

"I wish I knew. Iestyn says no one's in the stables. Help me up, lad. I'll go see for myself."

As their meal had not yet arrived, Isobel went with him, taking his arm on one side, while Iestyn supported the other.

Morgan limped to the stables. Just as Iestyn had said, everything was as they'd left it, with the exception of his men. It was as if they had been spirited away. When the other men began to mutter among themselves about it being witchcraft, Morgan told them to be quiet.

"There has to be some explanation. You two stay and guard the horses. We don't want to take any more chances. As it is, it's a miracle we've not been robbed. I'll see if anyone at the inn knows where they've gone."

Though Isobel wanted to go with him, Morgan suggested she go inside to eat the meal that was now waiting on the table. He knew there must be an explanation to the puzzle, but after this morning's strange exchange at the fairground, he was not sure he was going to like it.

After questioning the servants, he pieced together an improbable tale. Apparently one of the men had received a message from his sister that she'd been robbed on the road to Shrewsbury. Morgan couldn't believe all his men had gone to help her. Damn them for their blind family loyalty. To think they'd left everything unguarded in this city teeming with thieves.

Morgan rubbed his brow, wondering what to do next.

He did not have to wait long. A few minutes after he sat down beside Isobel to eat his meal, he saw the landlord pointing him out to a lad in a flat 'prentice cap.

His stomach pitched as he wondered what had befallen his men. Was he to find them with their throats slit in some alley behind the shambles?

The boy doffed his cap. "I've a message for Lord Morgan of Nels," he said, his voice quavering.

"I am he."

"My lord, your men need your help."

"Where are they?"

"On the Ludlow road."

"Dear God, what are they doing on their way to Ludlow?" Morgan growled. "Is that all?"

"Yes, my lord."

"Who sent you?"

"A man by the cathedral gave me a sovereign to bring the message."

"Was he a Welshman? How was he dressed?"

"In a dark cloak, but he wasn't Welsh. Reckon they all must've been out hunting together," the lad added helpfully.

"Yes, that's right. Here, take this for your pains, and thank you, lad."

Morgan pressed a coin into the boy's rough hand. He and Isobel exchanged glances as the 'prentice backed away from the table, setting his cap on his carroty head before heading outside.

So the messenger was a huntsman! One of those men from the goose fair. Isobel's stomach sank as she made the connection. A sinister thread was drawing together those seemingly unrelated events.

Morgan also pondered the news. The more he thought about the story, the less sense it made. His guards had apparently abandoned their post to rescue a maiden in distress. Though at first he had not thought about it, when he mentally counted the horses, none were missing. So, without horses, how had the men gotten to the Ludlow road? The message had to have been delivered by someone who spoke Welsh, for his men could not read and did not understand enough English to have made sense of message in English.

"Someone's gone to a lot of trouble to spring this

trap,'' he said, washing down dry rye bread with a swig of wine. ''And I intend to find out what game they're playing.''

''You're going to Ludlow?''

''Only as far along the road as I must . . . and not alone. If I find the men there, all well and good. But I can think of several enemies who may be plotting against me.''

''You think it's someone from the tourney?''

''Possibly. Yet someone Welsh-speaking who knows Will's sister's name sounds more like an enemy from my side of the border. Don't worry, sweet, I'll be back before bedtime.''

Morgan smiled reassuringly at her, reaching out to look at the pendant around her neck, the ruby rose glinting against her dark green bodice.

''Do you like it?'' Isobel asked, seeing his smile.

''Yes, but I like you far better, my Christmas rose. Now, promise you won't fret. It might be safer if you stay inside the inn till I get back. I'll leave Mihangel and his nephews to guard you.''

Within the half hour Isobel watched them ride out of the innyard, armed and wearing helmets and leather jacks. Though Mihangel did as he was bid without question, it was clear he would rather have been in the heat of the action alongside his comrades on the Ludlow road.

Later Mali told her the messenger had come while she was washing her lady's linens in a tub in the yard. Though she did not see him, she heard him speak. By his accent she thought him to be a Merioneth man, and she had assumed he was in Lord Martyn's employ. The men went with him in his cart.

Isobel found the news disturbing. Martyn of Merioneth was Morgan's comrade in arms, so he surely had nothing to fear from one of Martyn's men. Nonetheless, she wished he had heard what Mali had to say. With typical male disregard for a woman's word, Morgan had questioned only men at the inn.

The light faded as the winter afternoon drew to a close. The two women had sewn beside the window until it grew too gloomy to see. Mihangel's nephews had gone down to the stable to attend the horses, leaving him on guard outside the door.

A light supper was sent upstairs on a tray: a jug of good wine, fresh bread and a platter of sliced meat. There were rice cakes and gingerbread to follow. Unused as she was to such fine fare, Mali stuffed herself, eating all Isobel did not want. Before long, she was snoring beside the hearth.

Isobel wanted to be awake when Morgan returned, yet she found it increasingly hard to keep her eyes open in this gloomy room. She took some food to Mihangel, who intended to sleep outside her door tonight. Though he drank only a little wine, saying he must stay alert, he was grateful for the food. Now that the platters were empty, Isobel was sorry she had not eaten more, as her stomach repeatedly growled in protest.

Some time later a bump against the door startled her. Isobel realized she must have been dozing and was jerked awake by the sound. It must be Morgan returning. She had no idea what time it was, though by now the inn was quiet, suggesting that most guests had already retired for the night. Mali still slept beside the hearth.

The door creaked and groaned when she opened it to look down the narrow corridor, dimly lit by a flickering rushlight at the bend of the stairs. She almost fell over the dark bulge of Mihangel sleeping against the door. It was so icy out here, she was sure he must be cold, for he was wrapped only in his cloak and lying on the bare floorboards. There was an extra blanket in the chest and she went back to get it.

He slept so deeply and quietly that when she spread the blanket over him, he never stirred. As she tucked the coarse blanket around his shoulders, her fingers suddenly felt wet and sticky, and by the weak rushlight she saw darkness on her hands.

Inside the candelit room Isobel stifled a cry of shock when she saw that the dark stain was blood. Almost afraid to touch Mihangel again, she forced herself to go back to see how badly he was hurt. After she pulled aside his cloak, she could see that his throat had been slit.

Horrified by the discovery, Isobel backed against the wall, wanting to stay away from the dead man. A scream of fright died in her throat as a suffocating hand suddenly clamped over her mouth. Managing to break free for an instant, she screamed for Mali to help, but the woman never stirred beside the fire. Huge, dark shadows crowded inside the room. First the men extinguished the candles; then, grabbing Isobel's cloak, they threw it over her head to muffle her cries. Isobel could not see their faces, nor did she hear them speak. The whole operation was carried out in virtual silence.

Once again she tried to shout for help, fighting her abductors with all her strength, kicking, twisting, desperate to be free. The man's big hand crushed so hard, Isobel thought her lips would be bitten through, while her throat felt as if it would burst from the force of her mute cries. She was dragged, still kicking and punching, into the corridor. Several times her head banged the plaster wall, and when she stumbled on the stair she bounced down several treads before she was yanked back onto her feet. Why didn't someone help her? Who were these men? And where were they taking her? She felt cold steel press against her back when her abductor pulled her against his chest as he wrestled her outside into the yard. These men were soldiers, but in whose employ?

For an instant Isobel broke free and let out a piercing scream. Her defiance was met with a torrent of curses before she was finally cuffed into giddy submission by a man's bruising fist.

When she came to, she was tied across a saddlebow,

thumping and bumping along the highway in the black winter night.

Driven by the brisk north wind, grains of sleet stung Lionel's face. He drew his cloak tighter under his chin to keep out the cold. And he waited. Damn him, in all things that bastard did the unexpected. He should have come along the highway hours ago.

"My lord, someone approaches."

"At last!"

Wheeling about, Lionel spurred his horse to a nearby thicket, crashing through the undergrowth just in time as the first rider rounded the bend. Two men waited behind on the highway, the one apparently fallen from his horse, the other kneeling beside him, wringing his hands in grief.

Lionel's thin mouth curled in anticipation of what would take place next. *Yes, that's right. Slow down, debate what to do.* He virtually rubbed his hands in glee. Now the leader of the small group was dismounting, though he was taking a hell of a time about it. Likely a painful reminder from yesterday's tourney. Just as expected, he was going to offer his assistance.

The two Welshmen he'd positioned on the road knew what to do. Lionel's archers, hidden behind the brush, had their bows trained on them; one false move and they would be food for the crows. So confident was he of success, Lionel clucked to his horse as he maneuvered toward the edge of the thicket, prepared to ride triumphantly into the open and declare the upstart Welshman his captive.

A shout! The tableau before him changed in an instant. *The fools! The loyal fools!* Arrows whistled to their marks, and with cries of pain the decoys fell, mortally wounded. Too late! Their treachery had already warned the Welshman. *Oh, damn, damn them to hell. . . .*

Lionel galloped forth, shouting to his men. No need for stealth now. Who would have thought the fools would sacrifice their own lives to save their lord? Shouting until he thought his lungs would burst, Lionel tried to rally his startled men.

"Surround them . . . go to it . . . now, you fools!"

The Welshman was already back in the saddle and within a hairbreadth of escaping. The road here was narrow, the banks steep: the very reason he had chosen this spot for the ambush. There was no escape, if only his own men would act promptly.

Separated from his comrades, Morgan drew his sword, slashing wickedly at an opponent who was closing in. The man went down with a bloodcurdling scream. Others tried to catch Morgan's bridle. Though he fought furiously and almost managed to get away, the overwhelming odds were against him. More armed men came out of the thickets to block the road in either direction, capturing Morgan's men with him.

"Give ground, my lord of Nels. You're outnumbered."

Morgan dashed stinging sweat from his eyes and licked blood from a gashed lip. Angrily he turned to face the soldiers' leader, finding something unpleasantly familiar about that voice.

"Lord Hurley . . . to what do I owe the pleasure?" he ground out as he recognized the rider.

"I understand you were victorious at yesterday's tourney. May I offer my congratulations," said Lionel formally, managing a tight smile, though it pained him to do so. He had wanted to compete, had to steel himself not to throw caution to the wind and, in disguise, challenge all comers. Well, he almost had to steel himself against it, he admitted, with an unusual burst of honesty. The competition was too fierce, and the swift execution of this plan was more important.

"Thank you. I'd expected to meet you there. Were the odds in Shrewsbury not to your liking?"

Lionel drew in his breath. The devil mocked him! See how he leaned forward in the saddle, an insolent grin on his face.

"Tie them up. I didn't come this far to make idle chat. It'll be dark soon and we need to be on the road."

With that Lionel wheeled about, aware of snickers from his own ranks, quickly stifled. If he but knew which man mocked him, he'd have his hide. Mastering his anger, he forced a smile. He could afford to be generous. Today he had the upper hand.

The night was black and freezing by the time they reached camp several miles across country from the steep-banked road. Tonight they were using barns and outbuildings, for which Lionel had sourly paid the landowner an inflated rent, aware he would not find any more convenient place than this. He intended to make up for it. A few contraband chickens would find their way into his stewpots tonight, and anything else they found useful to help even the score.

Their arrival was greeted by a handful of men, securing the camp until their lord's return.

The captives were soon bound and taken away. The Welsh lord was separated from his men, though a slender lad, who was probably his squire, fought like a wildcat to stay with his master.

"Treat Iestyn well, or you'll be sorry," Morgan threatened as soon as they removed his gag.

Lionel raised his brows.

"He won't come to any harm if he does as he's told. Your concern's touching. Is your relationship so intimate you can't bear to be parted for one night?" Lionel sneered. He took a quick step backward when the other man glared at him fiercely.

Aware he was being goaded, Morgan chose to ignore the slur. Just as he had once suspected, Lionel Hurley was responsible for these mysterious happenings of late.

"You're probably wondering why I brought you here."

Morgan nodded. His leg burned and felt so weak he wondered how much longer he could stand on it. All the while he glanced about the shed for a means of escape.

Only one entrance and that guarded. They had already taken his weapons and his jack—his helmet as well.

"You needn't think to escape," Lionel snapped, correctly interpreting his thoughts. "When the time's right you'll be set free. Despite what you think about me, I'm a generous man."

"I never think about you. Life's too full to waste time and energy on things so inconsequential," Morgan drawled, deliberately irritating his captor and enjoying every minute of it.

Lionel clenched his fists, refusing to lose his temper. "Tonight you stay here. Tomorrow I'll let you go."

"What senseless game are you playing? I've little worth stealing unless you're resorting to horse thievery these days."

Morgan made a sudden move and the guards leaped forward. Now he stood pinioned between them.

Lionel smiled a tight, mirthless smile. "Insult me all you want, Welshman, but I promise you, I will have the last laugh."

After a night of fitful sleep, Morgan woke to a cold, gray dawn. His guards brought him meat and bread and a cup of ale. During the night he had heard horse's hooves. He had indulged in the fantasy that his men had managed to free themselves and were coming to rescue him. He soon learned that was not the case.

The gunmetal sky already glimmered gold in the east as he was led outside. They took him to the barn, where his men had been kept under guard. To his surprise he found Lionel Hurley waiting for him, already dressed for travel.

"See, your men aren't harmed, including that special lad you favor," he added slyly, disappointed when the Welshman failed to react to his barb. Lionel hurried on. "I've a surprise for you. This morning you're free to go back to Wales. We'll even escort you to the border."

"I can't. I have to return to Shrewsbury."

"There's no reason for that. Everything's been brought here to save you the trouble."

To Morgan's amazement, when he looked around the area he saw Bryn's traveling cart, where the big destrier could be heard snorting and banging the boards, chafing over the inactivity. The wagon of armaments waited beside the barn, though that vehicle looked not as full as he remembered, suggesting that his captor had exacted a toll for his trouble. Even the horses left behind at the inn were here, tethered safe and sound, with Isobel's gelding cropping grass beside the wall. So surprised was he, Morgan could not completely hide his reaction from the other man.

Lionel Hurley laughed as he strode confidently forward. "There, you see, just as I said, all here. I will take payment of a couple of your best beasts. After all, board and lodging for so many doesn't come cheap." He flicked an imaginary piece of fluff from his immaculate tawny doublet, consciously preening before his captive, who stood disheveled, with a day's growth of black stubble on his jaw.

"You seem to have gone to much trouble for your entertainment—I hope it was worth it."

"Oh, I assure you, it was well worth it."

The two men looked at each other, loathing plain in their faces. Morgan had purposely not asked about Isobel, though he had looked around, hoping to see her waiting in the shadows. Lord Hurley was so fond of tricks and plots, he could not think the last act had already been played out.

"Why don't you ask me about her?" Lionel prompted at last, unable to keep his final triumph to himself a moment longer. "I know you must be wondering. She's not been harmed, I'll tell you that much."

Morgan drew in his breath and he lurched forward, his eyes blazing. "By God, if you've hurt her . . . where is she?"

"Not here," Lionel said, relishing this moment and not anxious to be done with it. "She's safe. Where she belongs—in England."

"You bastard! Why have you taken her? Do you ask a ransom?"

"You ask too many questions. Go home. We'll give you safe passage."

"I won't leave her here. At least let me see her."

"I've told you she's not here."

"Where then?"

Morgan's fists clenched at his sides and he longed to sink his knuckles into Hurley's face. What game was the villain playing now?

He could not give up Isobel. Whatever was at stake, he would gladly sacrifice it to get her back.

"Somewhere in England; you don't need to know more. Don't you understand—she's no longer part of your life. Go back to Wales and be thankful you're free."

"She's my betrothed."

"No. She's never really been that. And it's her choice to come home."

"Never! She wouldn't willingly leave me. If you don't let me see her, how do I know you really have her?"

Lionel sat astride his big chestnut looking down on the other man. Understandably the Dragon Knight was sorry to let Isobel slip away; she was part of his prize, after all, and no man wanted to relinquish his possessions without a fight.

Mouth curving in a sly smile, Lionel reached inside his doublet and pulled out an object. "Here, maybe this will answer your question. Perhaps you recognize this, Welshman."

Stunned, Morgan looked down at the glinting piece of jewelry Lionel dropped in his outstretched hand—the ruby rose pendant he had bought Isobel yesterday.

"Isobel wants you to have it back. Perchance you can

give it to one of your other women. She has no need of it now.''

Pain welled up inside him. Now Morgan knew without a doubt Hurley had captured Isobel. He crushed the jewelry in his palm, fighting back his emotion.

''What is it you want from me?'' he ground out at last, his voice tight.

''I want you to go home quietly and leave us in peace.''

With that, Lionel pressed his knees into his horse's sides, moving the animal forward. Pretending not to be interested in the Welshman's reaction to his news, he stole a glance at him out of the corner of his eye, surprised to see the stunned expression on the man's face. Now he was glad he had added that final, cruel dig. Though in truth he had not yet spoken to Isobel, doubtless those would be her sentiments. His men had brought him the trinket just in case he needed some evidence to convince the Welshman he meant business. It had been perfect. Lionel shook his head in amazement. He could not believe the fool actually thought Isobel chose to be with him. The Dragon Knight's reputation had gone to his head. Likely he imagined every wench in Christendom panted for him.

There was such continuing resistance on the Welshman's part, Lionel finally had to threaten his squire's life to make him cooperate. At last the cursed Welshman was back in the saddle and headed in the right direction, with his men and baggage carts rumbling along behind him. Lionel still smarted over not being able to repossess what he had been forced to pay the man. Unfortunately most of his treasures were hidden too far across the border for him ever to get them back. He would have to be content with what he had. And, after all, he had the most valuable prize—Isobel would be warming the royal bed before spring was out. Royal Edward would be most appreciative of his gift, rewarding him generously for his favor.

The black shadow of the Welsh mountains loomed forbiddingly on the horizon. Bare-branched birch and mountain ash lined the roads as they headed west. Under close guard, Morgan rode in silence, forming plan after plan and discarding them as soon as they were made. He was sure it was not one of his own men who had betrayed him. Those two lads Hurley had used on the highway to trick him had had little choice but to obey. They had given their lives to save him. His throat tightened when he considered the depth of their loyalty. Faithful unto death. He would tell their wives they had died bravely—that would be scant comfort to them on cold winter nights, he thought bitterly, letting his gaze roam over the bleak countryside, alert for a chance to elude his escort.

They would not let him ride with his men. Morgan realized his safety relied as much on his men's cooperation, as did theirs on his. For what it was worth Hurley had given his word that once they reached the border, he would let them go in peace.

Morgan's mind teemed with escape plans, with plans for revenge; it was filled with everything but what he truly wanted to think about. And that he could not trust himself to dwell on. Where was Isobel? She was Hurley's sister, so he surely would not treat her cruelly, yet with this slippery nobleman one could be sure of very little.

As he rode, those hurtful words—*She wants you to have it back. You can give it to one of your other women*—formed a litany in time to the hoofbeats. Yet, he reminded himself, he did not know she had really said them. He refused to believe she had. But as the miles slipped away, he could not shut out the nagging doubts that chipped away his resolve. Faced with the chance to go home, had Isobel abandoned him? She'd always longed to go back to England. He also knew she was jealous of the other women in his past. There was also her conflict with Blodwen, whose hostility made her feel unwelcome at Llyswen. Isobel was a noblewoman with jewels and rich clothing. What need had she of a paltry trinket from Daniel Jacks's stall?

So low did Morgan feel, he might have shed tears over the loss of his love if he had been alone.

The afternoon drew to a close and cookfires were started, dark smoke from many chimneys curling into the leaden sky. As they rode past, Morgan was freshly reminded of the hearths of home. There was the smell of rain in the wind, and he felt a longing for Wales.

Finally the English road ended in that boggy, scrubby no-man's-land between the two countries. Here Lord Hurley drew rein, signaling to his men to let their captives cross peacefully into Wales. Even though the Welshman had given his word not to retaliate, Lionel was not going to turn his back on him until he was safe in the distance.

Morgan galloped to the head of the column, ordering his men to follow. They formed ranks and rode in the direction of Llyswen. Once he turned around to see the English lord still sitting there motionless, his troops grouped around him.

The Welsh soldiers were ecstatic over being given their freedom, for when they were captured and disarmed, they had considered their lives forfeit.

As the miles slipped away, Morgan made plans in earnest, vowing that, though it might take the rest of his life, he would find Isobel. He did not believe she had willingly left him. Their love was too deeply passionate to be cast aside that easily. If Isobel truly did not want him, he would hear it from her own lips, not secondhand from Lionel Hurley.

Chapter Nine

A piercing draft came through the window where Isobel huddled in her fur-lined cloak, watching the distant horizon. The silver-edged cloud bank promised snow. Eyes straining against the dimming light as the sun sank to its death in a molten ball, she finally turned away. He would not come now. Maybe tomorrow.

She huddled over the meager fire, warming her frozen hands. This most northerly tower of Stoneham Magna had become her home. She had been given no explanation of why she had been brought here against her will. No one came to visit her. For a while bitter tears had been her constant companion, but now even they were dry. It was as if her heart had died. The only thing that lifted her spirits was the hope that Morgan would soon rescue her. She had such faith in him, and she knew he would come for her if he could. If he still lived! The chilling thought that he might not have come because he was dead speared her heart.

"My lady." A wan face peered around the door. It was

the maid, Jenny, who brought her spartan meals.

"Yes, Jenny, come in. Has Lord Hurley come home yet?"

"Not yet." The girl shook her head and closed the door behind her. "They say 'e'll come soon."

Isobel accepted the news without comment. Jenny had been telling her the same thing every day. She could not understand why she was a prisoner. She had also wondered why no one came to visit until she learned that Brianna had already gone to join her future husband and that Maude was too close to her lying-in to venture up the tower stairs. Isobel was grateful for the note of welcome Maude had sent. In her current circumstances a welcome note was something to be grateful for, some assurance that the rest of the world knew she was still alive. Isobel smoothed out the crumpled parchment to read Maude's greetings for the hundredth time.

Jenny mended the fire and raked the faltering logs to a blaze. The wood was usually damp and it smoked. Isobel picked halfheartedly at the coarse rye bread and spooned up the pottage of greens, which as usual was lukewarm. Was this boring existence to be her future? Every time she tried to go downstairs, Lionel's soldiers led her back to her room.

"Jenny, if I have to stay here much longer, I swear, I'll go mad," she said, breaking the heavy silence.

"Oh, no, my lady, don't say that. There be good reason for it, you can be sure. Mayhap some danger's out there that his lordship's protecting you from."

Jenny's faith in Lionel was unfounded. But she was new here and could be forgiven for her misconception. To her surprise Isobel learned Lionel had sent food and medicine to Jenny's parents in their final days. It was to repay that kindness that the girl had come to the castle intending to serve Lord Hurley's family.

"You're a sweet girl, Jenny, but misled."

Isobel took the blankets off the bed and wrapped them around her shoulders to keep out the cold.

"Is that snow?"

A flurry blew by the window on the gusting wind, illuminated a moment by the light from a cresset burning on the battlements.

Jenny smiled as she marched to the door to retrieve a pot she had left outside. "See, fresh goose grease for your window," she announced triumphantly. "This'll keep out the snow."

Isobel thanked her, choosing not to add that it would also keep out light and air. Methodically Jenny painted a thick coating of grease on both sides of the linen window cover. Then she pushed the frame into place and secured it. Next she fastened the shutter over that, considerably reducing the wind's cold blast.

"Thank you, Jenny, for being my friend," Isobel said, squeezing the girl's hand. "Can't I persuade you to get a message to my lord?"

Jenny disentangled her hand and backed away. She already knew "my lord" referred not to Lord Hurley, but to the mysterious Welshman to whom Lady Isobel had been given. Though she had grown to love her lady, her loyalty still lay with the master. Sadly she shook her head.

"Don't keep asking me that. You know I can't. But I did bring something for you."

Like a magician producing a magic apple, Jenny whipped out a plaited cross from her pocket. "Here, Lady Isobel, I brought you Saint Bridget's cross for protection. No harm will come to you as long as you have this. I plaited it myself . . . and none of the rushes was cut with iron, just pure steel to keep in the luck."

Touched by the girl's thoughtfulness, Isobel accepted the cross. She knew the villagers harvested rushes for these traditional crosses on Saint Bridget's Day, January 31, plaiting the tokens to protect the owner from evil throughout the coming year.

"Thank you, Jenny. I'd no idea it was already February. Up here all the days run together. Has Candlemas passed?"

"Yes. When I asked them to let you come down to mass, they wouldn't without the master's permission. It's well into February now, lady. Not much sign of spring yet, though I did see some catkins on the hazel by the smithy," Jenny added as an afterthought. "That's promising news, eh? Flowers'll be out afore you know it."

Already February. Isobel considered this alarming news. She had been locked up here for over a month. At first she was even unaware this was Stoneham because they drugged her with poppy brew. What a relief to discover she was in familiar surroundings and had not been kidnapped by dangerous strangers. However that euphoria soon passed. Isobel had decided now that she would probably die from neglect and inactivity instead. Some days she ached with such boredom and loneliness, she thought she would have welcomed a knife to end the monotony. Such unholy thoughts of suicide quickly sent her to her knees to seek forgiveness.

She examined the neatly plaited cross, smiling again as she thought about Jenny's thoughtfulness. She must not blame the girl because she wouldn't disobey her orders. To Jenny, Lionel virtually wore a halo.

Morning dawned dark and cold. An icy wind blew flurries of snow against the stone coping. Through the window, which she had opened for air, the fields were spread with a thin white icing, and the leaden moat had frozen into runnels of gray and white. An unexpected movement on the horizon caught her attention. Isobel blinked and rubbed her eyes, then stared into the distance, afraid she had imagined that black line moving closer.

With a thundering heart she dared to hope—it was Morgan coming to rescue her at last! Tears of joy trickled down her cheeks. All along she had known he would come; she had just not expected it to take this long. For a better view she stood on a stool and leaned on the stone embrasure. The icy wind blew her hair around her shoulders and buffeted her face as she strained to see him.

By now the column of riders had moved into the lower meadow. They were soldiers; she could see the glint of their steel breastplates. Eyes slitted against the cold wind, she searched their flapping pennants for the distinctive Welsh dragon, but she did not see it. Instead, as the riders came closer, her heart sank when she identified the green Hurley standard with its golden harp. And there, carried alongside it, flapped the quartered arms of De Lacy. Lionel was coming home.

For the next few hours Isobel stewed in ignorance, hearing faint sounds of renewed activity echoing through the castle, though up here in this isolated tower it was like being in another world. By now she had swallowed her disappointment. Lionel was home and she could at least get some answers to her questions. She put on her cloak and marched outside, only to be brought back by a pugnacious ruffian with bad breath who cursed her when she demanded to be taken to his lord.

Finally steps sounded outside the door and she was surprised to hear women's voices chatting and laughing. Not deemed fit to be presented to his lordship in her current state, she was to be bathed and dressed. Though Isobel welcomed a bath and a change of clothing, she resented having it done to please Lionel.

An hour later she was ready. Her hair had been brushed and braided with a length of silver gilt ribbon entwined with strands of pearls. To her surprise Isobel found her clothes here, or at least the trunks she had taken with her to Shrewsbury.

Isobel selected a gown of lapis velvet bordered in scarlet brocade. It was a fine gown, yet one she had never really liked. It seemed fitting that she should wear it today for Lionel—a man she had never really liked. The comparison made her giggle. Blessed Mother, she was fast becoming a half-wit, making so much of a silly play on words. She had been cooped up in the tower far too long.

They brought her a headdress she had not seen before, of silver gilt with jeweled cauls and fluttering blue draperies. Gasping in delight over her splendid appearance, her handmaidens dutifully backed to the door. When Isobel tried to follow they told her she must wait to be sent for.

Fuming, Isobel paced the floor for what seemed like hours. It felt good to be moving, for her legs were stiff from cold and inactivity. She doubted she could even mount a horse, let alone run. In the future she must take care to exercise to keep her limbs supple. Morgan would not be helped by having to rescue a semi-invalid.

Presently she was sent for by two soldiers who came to tell her Lord Hurley was waiting for her. Marched out between them, Isobel likened herself to some important royal captive being led to an audience with the king. That was also vastly amusing, and she stifled giggles as she dwelled on the notion.

It was not to the great hall she was taken, but to a small audience chamber luxuriously outfitted to imitate a room in the royal palace. Either Lionel was eager to show off his new furnishings, or what he had to say was of a private nature. Or even— Her stomach pitched uneasily as she wondered if he intended a romantic tryst. She shuddered to recall the thinly disguised lust she had often seen in his face. But she quickly dismissed that possibility. Had it been so, Lionel would have summoned her to his bedchamber.

Lionel was waiting for her beside the hearth, posing with one arm resting on the stone mantel, the better to display the drape of his fluted marigold velvet gown with its hanging sleeves edged in black fur. The gown fastened up to the neck with jeweled buttons. His boots of peacock blue suede had long, pointed toes decorated with silver bells.

Isobel stood in the doorway looking at him, aware her stepbrother was specially dressed for the occasion.

Lionel smiled, beckoning impatiently for her to come inside the room.

"Sweet sister, welcome, welcome." He signaled to the guards to leave. Lionel moved languidly from the mantel and came to take her hand in greeting.

Though Isobel's first inclination was to snatch her hand away, she knew no information would be forthcoming if she antagonized him.

"Am I welcome? So far I've been treated like an unpleasant and dangerous relation, stuffed away in that cold tower room and kept under guard. What silly game are you playing now, Lionel?" she demanded, finding it impossible to remain pleasant now that they were finally face-to-face. She longed to slap him, to scratch out his eyes for his treachery.

"Tish, tish," he drawled, aping a man he greatly admired at court. "You're acting the shrew, Isobel. Where's that sweetness I remember?"

"Frozen to death in that icehouse you call a bedchamber," she snapped, going to the side table where there was wine and cakes. Without waiting to be invited, she picked up a couple of honey-crusted cakes, delighting in the unaccustomed luxury.

"Do help yourself," Lionel said, straightening up and discarding his lazy, languid manner. It did not really fit his character anyway. He much preferred to be a man of action. He would leave such ennui to Rofe de Monde, who had perfected the art.

Striding forward, Lionel poured himself a glass of wine, watching Isobel sipping wine before polishing off the cakes. Though she still possessed amazing beauty, those smooth, perfectly tinted cheeks he had so admired looked peaked. Her face had also developed a pinched sharpness he did not like. Perhaps his orders for her austere diet had been too strict. He made a mental note to fatten her up.

Edward much preferred women with flesh on their bones.

Lionel indicated a pair of blue padded chairs before the hearth. "Shall we sit?"

"Aye, the fire's welcome. My hearth would shame a pauper."

Her tongue had also acquired an unpleasant edge to it during her confinement, or mayhap he had forgotten how uncordial their dealings had been in the past.

"Are you not glad to be home?" he asked, thinking to bring her around. "I kept my promise to you."

"Promise?" she repeated, puzzled. "What promise did you ever keep to me?"

"I told you I'd bring you back to Stoneham, that you needn't stay in Wales," he reminded her, slightly annoyed that she should have forgotten.

Isobel snorted in displeasure. "Oh, that! You mean you really meant it? It wasn't just said to send me quietly on my way?"

"Of course I meant it. How was I to know the bastard would go back on his word and cross the border instead? I damned well froze my tail off waiting for you. I was there, lady, just as I said I'd be. It was *you* who broke the agreement."

"Me! What choice had I in the matter? All the arrangements were yours. Now, talking about arrangements, what exactly is your purpose in bringing me here to Stoneham?"

"Curb that bitchy tongue. Men don't like shrews," he reprimanded her sharply, taking an instant dislike to her attitude.

"The only man who matters to me hasn't objected," she said tartly. She went back to the table and took the last cake.

"What man is that?" Lionel asked, surprised by her statement.

"The lord of Nels. Have you forgotten you sold me to him?"

"You know it was only a temporary arrangement, born out of necessity. I never really expected you to go through with it."

"Well, you waited long enough to remedy the matter."

"It couldn't be helped. If you knew how hard I planned this entire— You ungrateful bitch! I risked my life to bring you back to Stoneham."

"Well, you can risk it again to take me home to Wales. Your ruffians manhandled me like some kitchen slut and killed an innocent man. Why didn't you tell me they were your men instead of letting me think I was being kidnapped by an enemy? Or didn't you think it mattered?"

"I didn't expect you to be hurt. Besides, if you'd drunk the wine and eaten the food I sent, none of that would have been necessary. You'd have simply wakened in your own bed here at Stoneham. As it was, you spoiled everything. Fighting and screaming, so I was told. If you behave like a kitchen slut, expect to be treated like one."

Isobel clenched her fist, virtually hissing at him in her anger. "How dare you! You self-important fool. Well, your silly plan backfired. It didn't dawn on you that I didn't want to be rescued? I was perfectly happy with him. He's my lord and I love him. Is that plain enough for you?"

Speechless, Lionel stared at her, silently opening and closing his mouth. Had she not been so angry, Isobel would have found his shock amusing.

"What?" he croaked at last, finding his voice.

"I love him! He's the man I intend to marry."

"You're mad!"

"I've never been more sane."

"What are you saying?" Angry color flooded Lionel's face, and his lips tightened in rage. "You've taken the Welshman as your lover?"

"Did you think he'd let me stay virgin for three months?" she challenged, beginning to enjoy this exchange.

"He raped you! Damn him! I'll have his heart for this," Lionel cried, driving his fist against the wooden bench.

"He didn't rape me. Don't you understand—I love him. And I will marry him. You see, however unwitting on your part, this is one scheme that wasn't a disaster after all," she said, venturing a smile.

Instead of softening at her words, Lionel became even angrier. "No! That's not possible. I'll not waste you on some ignorant Welshman. None of it was meant to be real. You knew the betrothal was a farce. We agreed to it."

"We also agreed you'd bring me home in three days, not three months. It's far too late now for your plan. Best discard it and take me back to him."

They glared at each other, tension mounting between them. Lionel was so enraged, he found it hard to breathe. Though in truth he had not expected the bastard to leave her virgin, he had never expected this. He had intended to gloss over that unfortunate flaw. Edward would be so hot for her, it would make him careless. He would never notice if they substituted chicken blood for nature's virgin stain. . . .

"It's not possible," he ground out. "I've other plans for you."

"I won't be part of any more of your plans."

They glared at each other, eyes hard, faces set.

Lionel sat down heavily, for he had jumped to his feet, longing to strike her out of sheer rage. But he did not. He must not risk scarring her face; unblemished, she was still a prize offering.

"You little fool! You've no idea what you could have," he said at last. "Think—do you want to spend your life with some wild chieftain on a mountaintop? Or would you rather lead a life of luxury?"

"What luxury? Barely subsisting so you can deck yourself as fine as the king himself?" Isobel countered, jumping to her feet. "Are you going to let me go by myself, or will you take me back? Tell me what you intend.''

''I intend for you to do as you're told. You've always been a willful wench. You haven't changed.''

''And what am I being told to do this time—marry some old windbag to whom you owe money? Is this how I'm to get my life of luxury?''

''You're a beauty beyond compare.''

She looked stonily at him, not swayed by his compliments.

''If you won't take me back to him, then let me go home to Ambrey.''

''No!''

''Will you keep me here under guard forever?''

''We're going to court, you stupid wench. There you'll have gowns fit for a queen. How would you like a cloak like the hood you bought at the Shrewsbury fair? Lined with fur costing a king's ransom?''

Isobel stared at him, shocked by his knowledge. ''You knew about the hood?'' she blurted. But of course he knew. It had been his men disguised as huntsmen who had watched their every move. Likely his spies had made full reports to him from the minute they arrived in the city.

''Had all gone according to plan we'd have taken you at the fair. But that fool vendor ruined everything by his greed. No matter, he'll never live to spend his gold,'' Lionel threatened. ''Damn it, Isobel, if you do as you're bid, neither of us will ever want for anything again. Forget the Welshman. All men are alike underneath, one's just as good as the next. The only difference is in their wealth. And the man I want you to accept is wealthy beyond compare, powerful beyond compare—he'll make both our dreams come true.''

She was staring at him now, a light beginning to dawn. ''And what man is this?'' she asked suspiciously.

''Edward.''

''The king!''

''Aye, the king.''

''No!''

''He'll treat you well. He has an eye for beauty, Isobel. None of his women can compare to you. I know he's not as young as you might like, but he's still in his prime. And by God, even if he were in his dotage, think what he can give us.''

She did not trust herself with words. Today Lionel had shown his true colors. ''Is this your new profession, pimping for Edward Plantagenet?''

''He doesn't know. It's our secret.''

''Then our secret it'll remain. The answer's no.''

Lionel hissed in anger, clenching and unclenching his fists. ''You stupid little bitch! After all I've done to get you here—you'll do as you're told, or I'll have you beaten. We'll see how defiant you are then.''

''I won't. I did as I was told the last time and it did not please you. Let me go back to the man you gave me, for he's my choice.''

Lionel shook his head in disbelief. ''If you think that Welshman cares a jot for you, you're a bigger fool than I thought. Compliments and gifts are easily given. You don't see him here trying to rescue you, do you? Obviously he doesn't care enough to bother. . . .'' Lionel stopped, afraid he had already said too much. Her stubborn refusal to cooperate called for a drastic change of plans.

''Likely he's not rescuing me because he's also your prisoner,'' she challenged angrily. ''Is that it? Is he your prisoner too?''

''You're not a prisoner. You're in your own home.''

''Answer me. Is Morgan your prisoner?''

Lionel looked down and sighed. ''Ah, you're too clever for me, sister. Yes—and a prisoner he'll stay until you agree to my plan.''

Isobel jumped to her feet, eyes flashing as she looked

down at him. She longed to take the wine decanter and crash it over his head.

"You'd better hope Edward lives a long time, because you'll have to wait till he's in his dotage to carry out your plan."

"Very well, if that's your choice. Remember, the Welshman will also grow old. For him an English prison is the most severe punishment this side of death. I'll happily tell him it's your choice that he languishes there in the darkness."

Tears spilled from her eyes at his cruel reminder. No longer able to keep her emotion in check, Isobel slid to the rushes. For Morgan to be in prison would be like death for him. Exiled from his beloved country, never able to ride or practice arms again.

"Oh, no, Lionel, have pity. For him that will be like dying."

Lionel looked down on her, crumpled at his feet, head bowed, crystalline tears coursing down her pale cheeks. His glance flicked over her shapely body, over her lustrous black hair beneath the silver gilt fret, which he longed to take off, to release that perfumed mass and sink his hands into it. . . . He swallowed, checking the surge of desire that was almost his undoing.

"Remember, you hold his fate in your hands. Agree to come to court with me, and I'll release the Welshman today. It's that simple."

Lionel took her hand, steeling himself not to drag her into his arms as he gently pulled her to her feet.

"I can't," Isobel whispered, licking tears from her lips.

"It's your choice. Go back to your room and think on it a while. If you change your mind, have the guard send for me."

Lionel turned his back on her. Isobel stood there, blinded by tears, hating him more than she had ever thought possible.

With the utmost control, Lionel opened the door and called for the guards. It was still possible to take her. At the moment she was so soft and vulnerable, he was sure she would bargain with her body for the Welshman's life. The very idea brought blood leaping to his loins, and Lionel was grateful for his long, concealing gown. Patience, he reminded himself. After Edward had rewarded them well, after he had tired of Isobel, she would still be beautiful. Then he would have her. Cheered by the thought, Lionel stepped aside as the guards came into the room and he ordered them to take Lady Isobel back to the tower.

Like a wraith Isobel paced the small tower room, wrestling with her dilemma. If she agreed to Lionel's plan he would set Morgan free. Yet how her lover would despise her for the decision. He hated royal Edward. It would be the ultimate defeat to lose her to the English king.

Days passed. The snow cover melted and the grass turned green. Jenny told her there were primroses in the woods, and she could hear the birds twittering about their nest building. How Morgan must pine to be free. Her heart twisted with grief as she considered his pain, made worse because it was in her power to end it. But in agreeing, she doomed their love. Though Lionel had not come to see her, by now she was sure his patience must be wearing thin.

April ushered in warming showers, and Isobel sat by the hour gazing through the window at the unfolding countryside, pining to be free. She watched the birches turn from light green to emerald and the hedgerows sprout.

Suddenly, one day, Lionel's patience came to an end.

Isobel was lying on her bed, dozing, dreaming of happier times, when the door crashed open and there he stood, face dark with anger.

Slamming the door, he marched to the bed. "I'm not prepared to await your pleasure any longer. Agree to go to court, or the Welshman dies."

Isobel cried out in shock. "No . . . oh, Lionel, no. I beg you, don't hurt him."

"Then you must agree to my plan, or I give the order."

"I . . ." Isobel could not speak and wiped tears from her eyes. "Even if I agree, what assurance do I have you won't kill him anyway?"

Lionel dropped to his knees beside the bed. She was so close to yielding, he was stunned. He had not dreamed it would be this easy. True, she had had much time alone to reconsider, but this was working beyond his wildest imaginings.

"Isobel, dear heart, agree to come to court with me," he said softly, taking her hand, which trembled in his like a frightened bird. "If I promise to release the Welshman unharmed, will you agree?"

Lionel reached inside his doublet and pulled forth a gold reliquary on a slender chain. "I swear to you on this," he said, holding it out to her. "A piece of the true cross. May I be damned for all eternity if I break such a vow."

She hesitated, still wondering if she could trust him. Even to someone like Lionel, a vow sworn on a sacred relic would be upheld. "If I agree to go to court with you, you'll let him go unharmed?"

"Not just to court . . . now, don't try to trick me," he said with a snarl. "I've wasted enough precious time waiting for you to come to your senses. You must swear to become Edward's mistress in exchange for the Welshman's life."

For some time she hesitated, wrestling with the decision, yet in her heart knowing she had no other choice. To save Morgan's life she would sleep with the devil.

"I agree."

"Swear it."

Isobel placed her hand on the gold reliquary, gone cold now in this chill room. She was glad. She would not have liked to touch it still warm from Lionel's body.

"I swear to become Edward's mistress in exchange for

Morgan's life . . . and his freedom,'' she added, just to make sure.

Solemnly Lionel put his hand on the relic. ''In exchange for your vow, I swear I'll cause no harm to the Welshman.''

It was done.

Isobel saw the triumphant light in his hazel eyes. And she felt as if she had just signed her own death warrant in exchange for Morgan's freedom.

The following day Isobel dared to hope. With Morgan free, would he slip into the castle to rescue her? She pictured herself riding with him on his great black horse, going home to Wales. It was such a wonderful dream that she dwelled on it, taking much comfort from the picture.

In late afternoon Lionel came to her room, all smiles and ingratiating manner. He brought with him a cup of wine, two rabbit pasties and a perfect, fragrant orange.

''You won't regret this,'' he said as he handed her the reward. ''Your Welshman's already safe across the border.''

Stunned by the news, at first Isobel tried not to react.

''He's already gone home?'' she whispered.

''Of course, that's what we agreed to.''

Yes, it was exactly what she'd agreed to. She could find no words, for she had begun to rely so heavily on her fantasy, it had become reality. She had even pictured Morgan running up the stairs with drawn sword as he declared his undying love for her as in some minstrel's fanciful tale.

''You're sure he's really gone?'' she asked in a tight voice.

''Positive. I watched him ride across the border myself. He's gone for good, Isobel. Forget him.''

Tears trickled down her cheeks and she hung her head in grief. ''Thank God he's safe,'' she whispered at last.

''Oh, you were expecting him to come to see you. . . .

Oh, dear, sweet sister,'' Lionel said with hypocrisy. ''My heart aches for you. That scoundrel never gave you a second thought. He was over the border like a hare, never stopped galloping till he reached the mountains. He's not worthy of your affection. Don't waste tears on him.''

So weak, so heartbroken did she feel, Isobel even allowed Lionel to take her against his chest to offer comfort. He rested her head against his shoulder, where she wept into his fine velvet doublet.

Lionel looked over her bowed head to the open window where the sky stretched blue with fleecy clouds scudding across the broad expanse. Her pain was hard to endure, for he really wanted to comfort her with the heat of his body instead of this brotherly charade. It surprised him that she was so heartbroken over the loss of the Welshman. He winced in pain as he reviewed this perfect opportunity he was letting slip by. He grudgingly consoled himself with the reminder that his sacrifice was made for king and country.

Isobel finally drew away and wiped her tears.

''Don't cry, sweet. So much awaits you. One day you'll laugh to think you ever hesitated to claim the good fortune that is yours.''

She wasn't listening. She looked through the window also, staring at those same fleecy clouds as she pictured Morgan galloping home. He would never know the sacrifice she had made to buy his freedom.

''You're sure he safely crossed the border? I have your word?''

''Be assured, he's safe across the border,'' Lionel said. ''I watched him ride far into the distance.''

She smiled wanly, apparently pleased by his assurances.

Lionel looked away, still stirred by her grief. He chose not to tell her it had been in December when he had watched the Welshman gallop back to Wales. That truth would remain his secret.

Chapter Ten

The summer of 1348 was unusually dismal, even for England. Rain poured down day and night. Oats, wheat, hay and straw rotted in the fields. The wet weather drove people indoors, where they huddled around their smoking hearths trying to stay dry.

During the spring and early summer, Isobel was fitted for a new wardrobe of elaborate gowns, with which Lionel hoped to transform his sister into a vision to entice the king. Seamstresses sewed frantically to complete the wardrobe in time. The clothes were finally ready. Yards of azure and emerald brocade, wine velvet and red and gold satin had become slender, low-necked columns shimmering in the light. Fur-trimmed surcoats and silver and gold buckram headdresses complemented the gowns, making Isobel look sumptuous as a princess. Now, all that remained of the luxurious bolts of fabric brought by wagon from Bristol was the massive debt, a sum Lionel's creditors were growing impatient to settle.

Though Isobel was thrilled with her new wardrobe,

when she considered the purpose behind the clothes, her joy evaporated. Lionel even had an embroidered velvet harness and saddle made for her gelding, Spartan, which he'd brought from Shrewsbury. The wagons had been buffed, the horses freshly shod, the trunks were packed, all was in readiness for their momentous journey. The only thing lacking was the cooperation of the heavens. Rain sluiced down the battlements in buckets as nature continued to defy Lionel's dearest wish.

Isobel helped sew new green draperies for the solar, and when she tired of sewing, she sang for the others, accompanying herself on the lute. Some days she was allowed to ride into the countryside under the watchful eye of Lionel's guard; she also visited the villagers, bringing medicines for their many ailments. She attended mass. She did anything and everything to block out her thoughts of *him*. Oh, the effort she put into that endeavor. Now she no longer wondered every day if Morgan would come to rescue her. Though she rarely accepted what Lionel told her, sadly she decided that this time his account had been the truth. Lonely weeks had quickly become months as Morgan stayed safe across the Welsh border, probably thanking his lucky stars for Lord Hurley's generosity. Did he ever think about her? Surely he could not dismiss their passionate lovemaking, those vows of undying love they had sworn. . . .

Angrily Isobel shook her head, trying to destroy the vision of Morgan that came so clearly to mind, undimmed by time.

She got up and busied herself returning linens to the chest. Though she did not enjoy running Lionel's household, Maude was still too weak after giving birth to adequately function as lady of the castle. Isobel's new responsibilities helped occupy her time, though they did little to fill her mind.

So long had they been waiting to embark on their journey to court, she even wondered if that event would ever take place. Lionel still refused to give back Ambrey, bleeding her estate dry to finance his latest grand venture. Isobel had already decided that if she ever had the king's ear, she would petition him to return her lands and dissolve the wardship. Lionel would not be expecting her to turn the royal acquaintance to her own advantage.

They had gathered in the solar as usual, this room being warmer and more cheerful than the great hall, where moisture seeped between the stonework and dripped from the rafters.

"By the rood, is it to rain all summer?" Lionel growled, staring through the window at the dismal scene beyond.

"Maybe it's an omen," Isobel offered, needling him.

Maude smiled at her suggestion. "Likely it means you're meant to stay here, husband, instead of traipsing around the land," she offered hopefully.

"If you can't say anything more intelligent than that, you'd best go back to your bedchamber," Lionel said with a snarl, turning a venomous look on her. After her difficult confinement and delivery, he found Maude even more unappealing than usual. Her freckles stood out like pocks on her parchment pale face, while her carroty locks straggled lifelessly from under her veil. Unfortunately the babe was another useless girl, puny and red haired, promising neither health nor beauty.

Maude fought back tears as she blindly gathered her needlework and did as her husband suggested.

While not overly fond of her sister-in-law, Isobel considered Lionel's treatment of Maude unforgivable.

"Don't be such a bastard to her," she snapped, "after what she's just been through to give you another child."

"A useless girl!"

"Well, take heart, in fifteen years you might be able to prostitute her to one of Edward's sons."

Lionel glared at her, but he refrained from comment, turning back to the window. Some time later he exclaimed in excitement. ''I do believe . . . yes, the saints be praised . . . look!''

Isobel turned toward the window, wondering what spectacle could bring such animation to his voice. ''What? I don't see anything.''

''Look, you ninny—there.'' He caught her by the shoulder and turned her to face the west. ''See, over there above the trees. Look at the sky. See that light?''

''It's the sun, Lionel—have you forgotten what it looks like?''

Exasperated, he pushed her from him. ''Oh, God, are all women idiots?''

''Only those forced to stay here with you.''

''Your sharp tongue will be your downfall, Isobel De Lacy. I'm not surprised the Welshman couldn't wait to be rid of you. You'd best keep silent in Edward's company, at least until he's given us what we deserve.''

Tears pricked Isobel's eyes at Lionel's cruel reminder. If the king gave you what you deserve, we'd all be better off, she thought silently.

Pleased that he had wounded her and put her back in her place, Lionel smirked triumphantly as he sauntered over to her chair.

''Sunshine means the rains are over. Now we can begin our journey.''

His words sent Isobel's heart plunging to her stomach. Though she had known it was too much to hope, she had prayed that momentous journey would never take place. Then she would not have to become Edward's mistress after all. Never had she hated sunshine so much.

''We'll leave in the morning—if it doesn't rain.''

Several times during the night Isobel strained to hear the blessed sound of rain against the stone. All stayed quiet. She knew she was doomed.

The party prepared to depart the following day. A company of soldiers would escort them to the royal manor.

Grooms, valets and maids comprised the remainder of their party.

Lionel smugly surveyed the cavalcade forming in the bailey. It was sufficiently impressive without being too ostentatious, he decided, though he'd have been more at ease if Milo of Bristol was not breathing down his neck, impatient for his money. Thank God the cloth merchant had been paid, for he employed a band of thugs to extract payment from laggardly debtors. He hoped he had convinced Milo to be patient a little longer, promising the moneylender the sum with interest once King Edward had given him a generous reward.

Maude wept to see them go. And Isobel came close to joining her as she mounted her gelding, decked splendidly in his new harness, jingling with every step. The summer was already well advanced, and Maude pleaded with Lionel to stay, saying that now they would be caught by the autumn rains.

Lionel countered that there was little difference between summer and autumn rain. He had already waited too long. By now Edward could have found another light of love and not be as open to Lionel's offer of a beauty beyond compare. Besides that, he was no longer sure which manor, or palace, the king currently inhabited, for surely during these intervening months he had moved from place to place. Lionel sourly surveyed the heavens, where clouds were already gathering on the horizon. Was there ever a man so cursed by fortune? he thought. Likely there would be a fresh downpour and his new hat and doublet would be ruined before they reached Hereford.

The threatened downpour held off until they were closer to Gloucester, but there it soaked the travelers.

Isobel did not care about the shower, apart from the discomfort of damp clothing and rain blowing in her face. It was as if her heart had turned to stone as she moved dully through the days.

While they waited to sup at the Gloucester Arms, she

saw a man who from the back looked like Morgan. The shock robbed her of breath and sent her heart racing. When he turned around, she saw he was a stranger. How many lies she had told herself trying to convince her wayward heart she did not care, she did not love him, that in fact she hated him for his indifference, for his neglect and for his cruelty in abandoning her to her fate. All meaningless in that breathtaking moment. Pain twisted deep in her heart as she was forced to admit the truth. Yes, it was true, she hated him—but she loved him also. Today she did not know which emotion caused her the most pain.

The riding party cantered noisily into the forecourt of the manor house, where grooms were waiting to take their horses. Refreshments had been set out on long tables beneath the shielding sycamores. The lords and ladies moved in a laughing throng to quench their thirst.

Isobel held back, not eager to join them. She did not know these people and they seemed uninterested in knowing her. Lionel was still with the king, putting a falcon through its paces to demonstrate the fine gift he had brought his king. He was trying to sweeten Edward's mood, for so far the king had not been as forthcoming as Lionel had expected.

Usually Lionel orchestrated her every move, leading Isobel around like a pretty puppet, telling her to whom she should speak and who was not worthy of her notice. The courtiers' way of life was not to her taste. Like gypsies, they were always on the move, always forced to be charming, and laughing as they moved through a nonstop round of entertainment. Once she became used to the guests' sumptuous clothes and elevated status, these glittering gatherings no longer impressed her. Courtiers were not like real people, for everything they did was dependent on the king's current mood. They laughed when Edward laughed; if he felt melancholy, they were melancholy too. Once someone was out of the royal favor, he or she simply ceased to exist.

Life at court was a lonely, boring charade, and she wanted to go home.

Isobel allowed a groom to help her from the saddle. After yesterday's ride it had been Edward the king who served as her groom, startling her with this unexpected intimacy. During their time at court, she had exchanged no more than a half dozen words with Edward. Unfortunately, instead of discouraging his attentions, her seeming indifference merely fanned the flames. Isobel wondered what else she could do to dissuade the king from his pursuit, for though Edward always treated her like a lady, she could not ignore the predatory gleam in his eye.

England's king was a commanding man in his late thirties, and though he was only of medium height, his noble bearing made him seem far taller. In armor he looked every inch the warrior king. His auburn hair was still thick, his eye keen. Isobel could not even fault him for his treatment of his wife, for Phillippa of Hainault was afforded every respect. As king he was not expected to be faithful to his queen; neither Edward's father, nor his grandfather, nor any king before him had considered that a desirable virtue. Kings married for power and conquest. Therefore it was not expected that they should love their wives, and they were expected to take mistresses by the score wherever and whenever they fancied.

Aware of this reality from the beginning, Isobel had still hoped her aloof indifference would chill Edward's ardor. She had been wrong. By keeping away from the courtiers as much as possible, she had intrigued him.

Sometimes when she sat beside the window in whichever manor they currently lodged, Isobel wistfully gazed at the open countryside and ached to be free. These flower-filled gardens and tapestry-hung rooms of Edward's nobles had become luxurious prisons from which she longed to escape. How she envied the birds soaring into the clouds, free to go where they pleased, while she must spend her days in servitude assumed for love of a man who had forgotten her existence.

Rain constantly drenched the land as the soggy summer wore on. And still the round of lavish entertainments continued as Edward moved from place to place in search of amusement. This life was so unreal, every morning Isobel fully expected to wake and discover it had all been an unpleasant dream.

Lionel rapped on her door, and then, as usual, entered without waiting for permission.

Though at first he had been angry over Isobel's indifference to royal Edward, once Lionel saw the magic it was working on the king, he gleefully congratulated her on her brilliant strategy. Unfortunately, by now the royal patience was strained. Just this morning Edward had spoken to him about the matter.

"I'm not as young as I'd like. We've neither of us a lifetime ahead. Mayhap it's time for the ice queen to thaw, eh?"

Then Edward had fixed him with his penetrating gaze, making Lionel's knees turn to water. They were this close—dear God, he couldn't risk losing everything now.

"Isobel, how long do you intend to play your foolish game?"

She stared at him, hardly able to believe what she was hearing. Though she knew that at first Lionel had been angry when she did not encourage the king, his manner swiftly changed when he saw how well her coolness was working. Not once had he accused her of trying to get out of her obligation, though she was sure it was just a matter of time before he came to that conclusion.

"What foolish game? You told me it worked well. Are we to play a new game now?"

"Edward's getting impatient. Let him kiss your lips, touch your breasts, anything to keep his attention. We're too close to risk losing everything we've worked for."

His words sent her heart hammering uncomfortably. So the day of reckoning was finally at hand. She should have guessed yesterday when the king handed her from the saddle, his hands lingering on her waist, that Edward was closing in for the kill.

"Why must we change things? It's worked so far."

"You swore an oath," Lionel said with a snarl. "Whatever suggestion he makes, be it walking in the garden, dancing, or—" here he paused, the rest implied—"you'll do as you're told. I swear, if you destroy my plans, I'll have you flogged. And don't sit on the fringe of Phillippa's ladies acting like a nun. We both know you're no nun. It's only poor deluded Edward who thinks you're virgin, hence his patience so far."

"How do you intend to explain the lie of that?" she asked curiously, desperate to think of a way out of her dilemma and finding none.

"We'll use a trick as old as time. Being virgin is not a requisite for the royal bed but unfortunately, as I told him you were still intact, in your case it is. Given his mounting impatience and randy look, perchance we should make all the arrangements just in case. He could send for you tonight, so dress well—the gold satin with the embroidered surcoat should be suitable. We're riding over to Garston Manor this afternoon. It's close to Havering Bower. We'll stay there for the week. There'll be jousting, and I'm expected to compete. By the way, Edward wants to wear your favor in the lists."

Isobel's hands shook as she dressed for the evening's banquet. Already a desperate plan was forming in her mind. It was her only hope of staying out of Edward's bed. The king assumed that her reluctance came from virginal modesty, apparently believing that once he had wooed her, she would come to him willingly. Her plan hinged on Edward's not wanting a reluctant woman in his bed. Though on the surface he appeared charming and easygoing, she had heard that he had a vicious temper. Her gamble was that once he learned of the blackmail Lionel had used to bring her to his arms, the famous Plantagenet temper would be aroused. She was also guessing that Edward's vanity would not let him bed a woman who had come to him solely to save her lover's life.

This elaborate gown was trimmed with bands of sable around the hem, and the cloth-of-gold hanging sleeves were fur edged also. The heavy satin and brocade weighed down her shoulders, making her tired before she ever left her chamber.

The prospect of this evening's probable conclusion robbed Isobel of an appetite for the king's upcoming banquet. Garston Manor lay just over the treetops from the royal manor of Havering. It took only a short ride through the sodden countryside to bring them into the woodland surrounding the mellow stone dwelling, which tonight was ablaze with light and reverberating with music and laughter.

On their arrival servants ushered them indoors with the other sumptuously clad guests. The manor house's huge hammer-beamed hall was filled to capacity with bejeweled men and women, their chat and laughter virtually ringing the rafters.

This was the most splendid event Isobel had ever attended. When not isolated in her room, her time was usually spent riding with the queen's attendants. Once she had hunted with the king's party, though that day she did not think he noticed her. The other two banquets she had attended were given by lesser nobles anxious to impress the king. It had been easy to escape the noise and stifling heat by walking outside in the drizzle, drinking in the rain-drenched air and wishing herself a thousand miles away. For one insane moment she had even contemplated stealing a horse and galloping to freedom. It was at that point, almost as if the man had read her mind, that Lionel's guard appeared and told her it was time to go back.

Instinctively Isobel knew tonight there would be no slipping outside for a blessed few minutes' quiet, for on this auspicious occasion Lionel was sure to keep her under close scrutiny.

So far neither the king nor his queen had joined their guests, and Isobel clung to the hope that perhaps tonight they were indisposed. A few minutes later she knew her fate was sealed when a servant stopped her and bowed.

"Lady Isobel De Lacy?" he asked.

Gulping in surprise, she stammered, "Yes . . . yes . . . I . . . am she."

Desperately she glanced about for Lionel, who at this moment seemed to have deserted her. Would this be the royal summons?

"I have a gift for you, my lady, from the king."

With a thumping heart Isobel accepted the gift and went to a window embrasure out of the press of people to examine the small sandalwood chest. When she pressed the clasp, the lid opened to reveal a jeweled necklace sparkling amid folds of black velvet. Isobel gasped in surprise, aware that this was a very valuable gift. With a sinking heart she also understood its significance: this emerald necklace winking green fire was a signal that Edward's patience had come to an end.

Though a servant offered her wine and pasties from a silver tray, Isobel could not eat, for her stomach was in knots and she felt sick. Until the last she had held out hope that she need not betray her love for Morgan. This lavish gift told her Edward expected her to share his bed, and there was little comfort in the uneasy reminder that one could not refuse the king. She must hope her feeble plan worked, gambling that Edward's own nature would be her salvation. If it were not, then she must honor the vow she had sworn on those holy relics.

Observing the servant's attentions, Lionel thrust his way through the noisy throng, eager to reach Isobel's side. He snatched the chest from her, looked inside and then gasped, greatly impressed. His face broke into a triumphant smile. "I was right. This is the night," he said with a chuckle. "Soon all our dreams will come true."

Lionel tried to quell his rising emotion. Excitement, yes, but there was jealousy also. Certainly he was pleased Edward was ready to take the bait . . . but he was also devastated. Whenever he pictured Edward bedding Isobel, his jealousy blazed white hot. He had made the supreme sacrifice for his king, and though Edward was still his friend, Lionel had not been rewarded as generously as he had expected. In fact, Edward had been slow to reward him at all. Lionel was also alarmed to discover that the king's small circle of confidants had little room for another. He longed to become part of that inner circle and enjoy the power and wealth that came with belonging. Unfortunately, during his long absence from court, the budding friendship he had eagerly cultivated with Edward had cooled to lukewarm.

"This necklace looks too valuable."

"Nonsense, it just shows how highly he esteems your charms. I'd better keep it for you."

Isobel saw a look of greed flash across his face and she held on to her gift. "No. The king will expect me to wear it."

Lionel paused, his fingers closing about the glittering emeralds. "Yes, of course, you're right," he agreed reluctantly. He wanted that necklace in part payment for his trouble, yet he knew that when Edward saw it around her slender neck it would merely heighten his interest. When he saw that lozenge-shaped drop nestling in the hollow between those creamy breasts . . .

Lionel turned away while he fought to regain his composure. In a strained voice he said, "You're far cleverer than I gave you credit for. Here, let me fasten that for you."

The lingering touch of his hot hands against her neck was so distasteful, Isobel stiffened. When his touch blossomed into a caress, she pulled away, forcing Lionel to snap the clasp and move his hands.

It was all Lionel could do to keep from burying his mouth in the delectable nape of her neck. He must keep reminding himself that this sacrifice was for his king—the one man he had imagined he would not object to sharing her with. Now that the time was upon him, he was shocked to discover he had been deluding himself.

From the minstrels' gallery the first chords were struck for a lively tune to signal the beginning of the dance. Eagerly the guests formed a wide circle, the ladies giggling as their escorts flirted outrageously with them.

Isobel held back, not anxious to have to fend off unwanted admirers. Tonight Lionel did not push her forward, for he wanted her accessible to Edward as soon as he appeared. Where was he? Damn him, keeping them in suspense like this.

"My lady."

It was the same liveried servant. Isobel swallowed and turned to him. Did he bring her another gift?

"Yes."

"Please follow me."

It was as if a great, thundering blow struck her chest, setting her heart pounding with distress. When Lionel stepped forward to accompany her, however, the man shook his head.

"His grace only requested the lady, my lord," he explained apologetically.

Lionel immediately understood, and the two men exchanged knowing winks. Isobel felt trapped and vastly humiliated. It did not matter that her rendezvous was with Edward Plantagenet; she still felt tawdry and soiled. Swallowing the growing lump in her throat, she held up her head and stepped out briskly to follow the servant. She had no need to look at Lionel to know his gloating expression of triumph.

Fresh rushes crackled beneath her soft-soled velvet slippers as she followed the man through deserted corridors, their way lit by a page carrying a torch. That was two servants and Lionel who knew about her disgrace—and Edward, of course.

Up short flights of steps, around a bend; then the page stopped before a closed door and knocked sharply, and Isobel heard a man's voice bid him enter. The door swung open and the servant gently pushed her forward before he quietly closed the door.

Isobel stood in the candlelit bedchamber, her throat dry. Could the king have her executed for refusing to do as he said? The thought flitted through her mind and was gone. Reminding herself that this assignation with Edward was not by her own choice, she pictured the gold reliquary on which she had sworn that sacred vow in exchange for Morgan's life. Despite Morgan's apparent disregard for her, she was here because she loved him more than she loved herself. Tonight she would be the sacrificial maiden—well, hardly that, she thought with a hysterical laugh. Only Edward considered her a maiden. Belatedly she wondered how she would fare once he discovered that was also a lie. But she must remember, it was not her lie—that one belonged to Lionel.

"You laugh, lady. Does that mean you're happy to be here?"

Isobel gulped in surprise as the king emerged unexpectedly from behind long brocade draperies. He spoke to her in court French and she replied in the same language, grateful she had been well schooled, for at Ambrey everyone spoke English.

"Your Grace."

Remembering her manners, she curtsied to him, staying down on the rushes, her skirts spreading about her like golden rose petals. It seemed an eternity before he crossed the room and gently raised her to her feet.

The king's mouth was firm as he kissed her hand, turning her palm. "I've been eagerly waiting for this moment,

Lady Isobel,'' he said, his voice turning husky.

Forcing her gaze to meet his, Isobel saw that his eyes appeared dark in the gloom, yet even in this light she could see desire burning in their depths. Edward reached out to finger her emerald necklace. Smiling his approval, he followed the rope of gleaming stones until they disappeared in the hollow between her breasts.

''Do you like my gift?''

''It's very beautiful, Your Grace.''

Isobel tried not to stiffen when his exploring finger outlined the twin mounds of her breasts partially revealed over her fur-edged bodice.

''Not nearly as beautiful as you. I swear, you're a vision,'' he said sincerely. ''By far the most delectable creature there's ever been at court.''

''Thank you, Your Grace.''

''No, not 'Your Grace' . . . you must call me Edward. Say it.''

''Thank you—Edward.''

''That's much better.'' He smiled and drew her closer. ''Do I frighten you?''

''Yes,'' she agreed honestly.

''You mustn't be afraid of me. I'm kind and gentle . . . I can be very loving, especially with beautiful women. After tonight you won't be afraid of me, will you?''

''No, Your G— Edward.''

''Come, there's wine on the table. Why, your hands are like ice! I trust not every part of your body is so cold.'' He chuckled as he drew her toward the blazing hearth. ''Warm yourself and I'll bring you wine.''

Edward continued chuckling to himself while he poured two goblets of wine. Isobel accepted the wine, gulping more quickly than was prudent in an effort to find much-needed courage. Now that she was alone with him, she grew faint hearted each time she reminded herself this was no ordinary man—this was England's king.

The king smiled at Isobel over his gold-rimmed Mur-

ano goblet, studying her in the flickering firelight.

"I've been waiting all my life for a night like tonight," he confided at last. Quaffing his own wine, Edward took Isobel's empty goblet and put both on the side table.

Nervously Isobel wondered what would happen next as the king came back to her. With an elegant, beringed finger he touched the mole high on her cheek, then traced her brow, her nose. Lazily he followed the column of her neck, and then gently molded her swelling bodice. From there he explored her waist and hips, those ample curves seeming to invite his caress beneath the cold, slippery satin.

To her surprise, Isobel suddenly found herself trapped in a close embrace. As the King tightened his arms about her, he whispered endearments, calling her *cherie*, his voice muffled by the buzzing in her head. It was so long since she had been held in a man's arms, so long since someone had whispered endearments, that tears of longing pricked her eyes and hovered on her lashes. Her emotion was not a reaction of pleasure at the royal caress, merely an expression of longing for all she had known and lost.

Edward drew her toward the high bed, which until now had been merely a curtained bulk in the corner. A footed brazier glowed beside the bed, bathing the crimson hangings in rosy light. Isobel could see the royal crest on the mounded gold, scarlet and blue velvet covers, finding it an unwelcome reminder of the power of the man before her. In his long bedrobe of blue velvet embroidered in gold, Edward could have been an ordinary nobleman; it was her misfortune that he wore the crown.

"What about your guests, Edward?" she blurted out suddenly, surprising them both with her unexpected question.

"Guests?" he repeated, pausing, his arm about her shoulder. "They're downstairs dancing and making merry. Later I'll feed them right royally. What more can they expect?"

"The royal presence," she said, emboldened by wine.

"Oh, that—well, they'll have that when I've drunk my fill of you. You're probably wondering why I sent for you so early in the evening."

She nodded, not because she cared, but because she wanted to postpone the moment of truth to give herself time to think.

"Because, sweet child, I couldn't bear to wait for you a moment longer."

Isobel smiled, thinking it wise not to displease the king. As he spoke, Edward fumbled with the lacings of her gown.

"God's blood, must we call a maid? No . . . I've undone enough gowns in my time. I won't be defeated."

His words were slurred, and Isobel wondered if he was tipsy, or if he was just overcome with desire. She did not help him as she would have helped a welcome lover. When Edward pressed against her she was repelled by the hard reminder of his growing arousal. With a triumphant cry he finally pulled loose the surcoat's silken lacings, and the garment slid to the rushes. Conquering her gown came next, and he set to eagerly as he tried to undo those lacings, his hands shaking with desire.

"Why don't you help me, you witch?"

She listened carefully and was sure he said witch, not bitch, so she was assured of his continued good humor.

"Because, Your Grace, I thought this was something you'd take pleasure in doing yourself."

He merely grunted his reply, concentrating on his task. Isobel realized she had delayed too long. Licking her lips in preparation for her speech, she realized Edward was watching her. Alarmed when she saw his knowing smile, she realized he interpreted her gesture as a silent invitation. Encouraged, Edward grasped her and welded her to his body. Though Isobel struggled, she found she was trapped by his superior strength as he molded her against his writhing hips. His mouth was hot and demanding. The movement opened his bedrobe, and Isobel saw he was naked underneath. Shutting her eyes, she turned away from the sight of his swollen flesh.

"You mustn't be afraid of him," the king whispered, chuckling at her modesty. "He's most kind to pretty ladies and he promises to be gentle. Come, feel how hard he is for you."

When she tried to hold back, the king grasped her fingers and molded them around his hard organ. Trying not to show revulsion at the unwanted touch of his throbbing flesh, she could not keep from tightening her lips against his eager, invading kisses.

Edward pushed her down on the bed and Isobel thrust at him, holding her hands on his shoulders to keep him off her. His bedgown gaped open, revealing his body gleaming white in the gloom.

"Please, Your Grace, first hear me out."

Edward blinked, surprised by the change in her tone.

"This isn't the time for talking, wench," he protested jovially, but his hand stopped kneading her breasts. "What is it?"

"It isn't my choice to be here. It's all Lionel's doing," she began, trying to hold his attention as his gaze strayed back to her breasts, half exposed by her unfastened gown.

"I know that. Few women ever seek me out, least of all young virgins," he dismissed. Then he bent his head to her swelling breasts, his hot, wet tongue dipping between the curves to taste their scented warmth.

"Edward, listen to me," she said, raising her voice, her head buzzing from the effect of that goblet of wine on an empty stomach. She grasped his head and held his face between her hands, forcing him to hear her out.

The king blinked in surprise at her boldness, and his mouth curved with pleasure. The ice maiden was coming to life.

"Lionel made me come to you. I already have a lover."

"What?" Edward blinked, slightly befuddled by wine and desire.

"My lover's a Welsh knight. Lionel threatened to kill him if I didn't agree to be your mistress. To save Morgan's life, I swore an oath on holy relics—"

"What are you saying?" Edward pulled back, startled by her unexpected revelation. "A lover . . . you're virgin! Your brother swore it to me."

"He lied. He knew it wasn't so because it was he who sold me to the knight to settle a debt. Only Lionel didn't expect me to fall in love with him. Oh, Your Grace, I was so afraid he'd kill Morgan if I didn't agree. I never wanted to deceive you," she added in growing alarm as Edward's face darkened.

Angrily Edward knotted the sash of his bedgown about his waist in a belated effort to cover his nakedness.

"How dare you! Have you forgotten—I am the king!"

"Please, Your Grace, forgive me. That's why I couldn't refuse your summons, because you are the king. Have mercy. I swear what I tell you is true. I trusted that once you knew I wasn't here willingly, you'd—"

The king bounced off the bed. He drew himself up to his full height as he angrily demanded, "Are you saying you don't want me?"

"Because I love another man," she whispered tearfully. "We are pledged to each other."

Edward's nostrils flared in anger. He glared at her. She was weeping now, her unlaced gown slipping off her creamy shoulders, her lustrous black hair spilling from its fastening. She angered him, but he still wanted her. Desire had made him let down his guard, until he completely forgot he was the king and became just plain Edward instead, vastly desirous of the woman in his arms. He became a lover instead of a king, thereby compromising the dignity of the throne. This woman had been allowed to see the royal person stripped of all regalia, needy and vulnerable as any ordinary man.

"You deceived me!"

"I'm sorry, Your Grace. I didn't intend to make you angry."

"I'm more than angry—I'm enraged to think you plotted to deceive me! Lionel's greed and ambition will be his downfall."

All his softness, his cajoling good humor, had flown. Edward's brows drew together in a grim line and his mouth was hard and thin.

"Please say you understand," she pleaded through her tears. Fear gripped her when she wondered what punishment the king would impose. He stood before her, his face threateningly grim, while he contemplated retribution for her crime. "Were I free to love, I'd consider it an honor to serve you," Isobel said, adding this white lie in an attempt to soothe his injured pride. Almost instantly Edward's face softened.

"Would you, wench? Your loyalty to your lover is admirable. Few women could deny a king's favor to honor such vows."

"Yes, Your Grace," she whispered, head hanging in shame, tears dripping from her chin. If he only knew her lover had abandoned her. But it would not serve her purpose to reveal the whole truth.

After what seemed an eternity, Edward stepped forward and clumsily patted her head. "There, there, stop crying. There's no need for it. No harm's been done. Dress yourself and go down to the banquet. I'll deal with Lionel later."

With that, Edward turned on his heel and without a backward glance strode into his dressing room. From somewhere nearby she heard a bell clang and assumed the king had rung for a servant to escort her back to the hall.

Springing into action, Isobel slid off the bed and quickly tried to relace her gown and surcoat. The king's hot, sweating hands had wrinkled the fabric, and her attempts to smooth out the creases failed. Her hair was falling from its pins and she clumsily rebound it and speared the untidy mass with bone pins to keep it in place. Her headdress wouldn't fit properly over her hair, but she fastened it as best she could, finishing just as the outer door opened.

Drawing herself up to her full height, she stood proudly, hoping no one would notice her tearstained cheeks. Isobel acknowledged the servant standing in the doorway, indicating with a nod that she was ready to leave. Well versed in court etiquette, the man remained indifferent to her appearance, though she was sure he must be curious about the reason she was leaving so soon. He would probably assume her tearstains were the aftermath of her lost virginity.

Holding her head high, Isobel tried to act as if nothing were amiss as she followed the servant back to the hall, where the banquet had already begun. Everyone was seated at the tables listening to the entertainers while they awaited the king. Isobel hung back. She did not know where she should sit, or even if she should sit. Prepared for her late arrival, however, the servant discreetly led her behind the seated guests to an empty place at the end of the table adjacent to the royal dais.

Her trenchermate was a young gallant in blue velvet, and he turned an appreciative smile on her, surprised at his good fortune in being given so beauteous a table companion. Several nearby women giggled and gossiped, heads together, before staring curiously at her. Isobel's cheeks burned when she realized everyone knew about Edward's interest in her. They had even guessed the reason behind the king's delay. She was so ashamed, she wanted to sink through the floor. The fact that she had not succumbed to the king's demands was immaterial. Everyone in the room assumed they were now lovers and judged her accordingly. Her reputation had been destroyed by gossip.

Wine was being offered around the tables; the food was

withheld awaiting the king's arrival. Though Isobel probably should have refused, she accepted a goblet of Gascon wine, letting the heavy scarlet liquid bathe her lips and tongue before it burned a fiery passage down her raw throat. Her eyes were sore with weeping and her throat ached. She could not recall a time when she had felt more miserable amid so much laughter and gaiety.

A troupe of scantily clad dancing girls swept past the table, pink fabric fluttering, affording stolen glimpses of thigh and breast, much to the gentlemen's enjoyment. A flurry of movement at the far end of the hall signaled the arrival of the royal party. With sinking stomach, she tried to dispel her unpleasant memories of Edward Plantagenet as she stood with the other guests to greet the king and queen.

Edward looked every inch the king as he walked briskly inside the hall. Dressed in gold brocade with black fur trimmings, aglitter with gold and jewels, he bore little resemblance to the lusty Edward she had known. On his head he wore a plumed black velvet cap pinned with a jeweled clasp, and around his neck hung heavy jeweled chains. Not once did he look in Isobel's direction as he moved across the room to his seat at the high table. No one seemed to find his attitude unusual, so she assumed this was how Edward's lights of love were treated when he was in his wife's company. Queen Phillippa walked beside him, dressed in silver and brown brocade, looking plump as a peahen beside her vigorous spouse.

Many knowing glances came Isobel's way. Now even the young man beside her, after being enlightened by his neighbor to the right, viewed her in a different light. He was obviously impressed to have been given such an important trenchermate.

Thoroughly miserable, Isobel fought tears as she stared down at her hands. It made her feel sick to look at Edward and remember the taste of his mouth, his demanding caress and that unwelcome intimacy he had forced upon her.

She had noticed Lionel signaling to her across the room, anxious to know how she had fared. But she purposely ignored him. He would not dare leave his place until the meal was over. Until then she was safe. After that she did not know what would happen. She had been promised a flogging for refusing to cooperate: her punishment for betraying his deception to the king would be far more serious. Surprisingly, she was not afraid of the punishment. Nothing about tonight seemed real. After another cup of wine Isobel even began to enjoy the mellow state of acceptance that was creeping over her. The king, her stepbrother, even her own shame, receded into the past. Nothing mattered. There was no reality beyond the soft buzzing in her head, the chat of the guests and above all the sweet, plaintive song of lute and harp soaring in the background.

That tune! Isobel sat up, shaking off some of her comforting oblivion. It sounded sad and far away, yet so very familiar. Perchance it was a current court favorite she had heard at another gathering.

Looking over the heads of her tablemates, she saw a band of minstrels moving around the room. Five men, or were there only four? Her eyes blurred and she could not be sure. Their song sounded sweet as an angel's chorus, high and low voices blending into a familiar, plaintive melody.

The procession of elaborate dishes had already begun; the king's arrival had been the signal to bring out the food. The kitchen staff paraded around the room to display the succulent fare. Curls of steam eddied from a crackling boar's head, borne aloft by the fat cook. A silver platter bearing a peacock, resplendent with its iridescent tail feathers, was followed by stuffed capons swimming in purple sauce, haunches of roast venison and dishes of gleaming jellied sturgeon. A string of serving lads followed, carrying tureens of fragrant pottages, pounded meat pastes, loaves of bread, fruit flummeries and almond milk molds tinted pink with sandalwood.

So many people were moving around the room that Isobel could no longer see the minstrels in their hooded Lincoln green tunics. She wished the parade of dishes were over, because she wanted a better look at the men. There was something strangely familiar about the taller minstrel; his manner of walking and the sight of his broad-shouldered frame tugged at her memory. The lead singer's strong, clear tenor floated about the rafters. The spine-tingling quality of his voice brought a temporary hush to the room as the diners ceased their chat to listen, enraptured by his song.

When the verse was over, the others joined him in the chorus. Their small harps, flutes and pipes picked out a popular tune, and from the fretted minstrels' gallery the royal musicians took up the melody. Soon all around her were singing the jolly round, and even the king's rich, tuneful voice could be heard joining in the chorus.

The dancing girls sped back inside the hall, weaving and bobbing to the lively music, holding ribboned garlands of field flowers aloft. When the combined entertainment came to an end, the flower garlands were sent sailing over the heads of the guests. Laughing, Isobel's trenchermate stood to catch one and it partially came asunder over their food, as he presented it to her.

Isobel smiled her thanks, praising him for his efforts. Taking the unwinding cornflowers, poppies and daisies, she twined them back together. These flowers of the cornfields reminded her of past freedom and tears of loneliness began to trickle down her nose. Again the minstrels played that familiar tune, sounding slightly different this time, for the singer's voice was deeper and richer than that of the young tenor. Harp strings rippled, the music trickling like ice water down her spine. The song's words were muffled inside her head and she fancied they weren't even English, or French. Could they be singing in Welsh?

Did these talented minstrels know *his* tongue?

Doubly cruel, the memories twisted deeper as she suddenly recalled where she had heard that tune. The reminder made her catch her breath. It has sounded so familiar because it was the plaintive Welsh ballad sung by Morgan's homesick men, all their sadness and longing expressed in its sweet melody.

Tears and wine combined to blur her vision, until the band of minstrels doubled and tripled. In the background Isobel heard the king call out for more; he clapped enthusiastically until the minstrels moved forward to stand directly before the royal table.

Though everything was watery and indistinct, she saw the men bow to their sovereign. This music had only added to her painful memories of *his* embrace. Would the torment never end? she thought miserably. Through tears she watched the taller minstrel step forward and make a sweeping bow before the king. Smoke from the torches wreathed about his body, making him appear wraithlike and insubstantial.

The king requested "The Ballad of King Arthur," it being one of his boyhood favorites. The popular ballad was begun, the tenor taking up the first narrative verse. The ode droned on. Isobel soon stopped listening and set about mutilating one of the large white daisies from her garland, dropping the petals on the gravy-soaked plank that formed the bottom of her trencher.

At last it was over; she could tell because of the thunderous applause. Once again the minstrels were free to play their own distinctive music and they began to sing another Welsh song, voices raised in unison. Backing from the royal dais, the group moved slowly away, singing as they went. Isobel stared at the blurring image, listening to those Welsh words. As they passed her table, the tall minstrel glanced up. They were not close, for he was still in the center of the hall, but close enough that she gasped at what she saw. The chill sweeping over her chased away even the mellow warmth left by the wine. What a cruel jest! In this half light, the man looked like Morgan.

Blinded by tears, Isobel stumbled to her feet. Swaying slightly, she stood there trying to get her bearings. She felt that if she did not leave, she would be sick all over the king's fine banquet table. Sweat trickled from her brow and she felt alternately hot and cold. Heads turned as she stumbled back, finding the rush-strewn floor lower than she had expected, then suddenly higher, like the rolling deck of a ship.

Isobel leaned against the cold wall. She could feel Lionel's eyes boring into her back. It was as if he actually spoke to her. He half rose to follow her, but Lionel was seated directly under Edward's gaze and dared not leave. Isobel doubted that his concern was out of genuine distress over her health; it was more likely anger that she was slipping away from Edward's notice so early in the evening.

A servant stepped forward to help her through an arch to the passage that ran alongside the hall, well out of the path of tables, servers and guests. Here, amid the half-gnawed bones and lurking hounds, the picked-over fowl carcasses and empty goblets, Isobel crouched on a wooden stool, holding her head and trying to still its rolling throb.

A hot tide of nausea rose in her throat. Abruptly she stood, aware she must get outside. Only this time strong arms caught her and held her up when she would have faltered. Her feet seemed too high off the floor, which tonight was a maze of uneven flags perilously hidden beneath the rushes.

"I thought you'd learned your lesson about strong drink, lady."

Through the confusion in her brain she heard the man's amused voice, sounding so much like *his*, she sobbed, her breath catching in her chest. Would all this longing and hurting never end?

"Come with me. This way. Let's get out in the fresh air."

Urged by that soothing voice, she allowed the strange man to lead her outside. It did not matter that she did not know him. He wasn't real. None of this was really happening. Morgan was in Wales. The illusion was born out of a combination of wine, heat and noise . . . mingled with the pain of the terrible wound in her heart that refused to heal.

Chapter Eleven

Sunshine crept across the wall, until it finally shone upon her face. Isobel flung up her arm to block the light. Her head pounded and felt far too big for her body. Carefully, slowly, she rose, but a wave of dizziness overcame her and she fell back down with a groan. Last night she had drunk too much wine, and this morning she was suffering the consequences.

She should have known she could not down three goblets of wine on an empty stomach without some effect. And what an effect it had been! Imagining that some nameless minstrel was Morgan. And the man who helped her outside into the fresh air sounded so much like him, she was sure she called him by that name. A combination of too much wine and that nostalgic Welsh music had swept her back into the past, rekindling memories both pleasant and painful. In the bright morning light the entire night was like a bad dream.

Now that she looked around this small room, hardly bigger than a cupboard, Isobel was ashamed to admit she had no idea where she was. This was not her room at Garston Manor. She did not think she had drunk so much that they had moved on without her knowledge. No, they were still at Havering, for beyond the window she could see bright waving pennants, and the roar of the crowd told her the royal tournament had already begun.

Beside her narrow bed was a bell, and she rang it.

The door opened at once and a young maid tripped eagerly over the threshold, dropping a quick curtsy. "Are you ready now for me to dress you, lady?"

It was then Isobel realized that she wore only her shift, which meant someone must have undressed her, for she doubted she had been capable of managing that task herself. Her gold gown was nowhere to be seen.

"Where am I?" she asked, just to make sure, even though she thought she knew the answer.

"Havering Bower, lady."

"Why am I here?"

The maid smiled and dropped her gaze. "The king asked for you to be lodged here . . . after you were taken ill."

Isobel smiled ruefully. Yes, that was a delicate way of putting it. Her stomach pitched uneasily at the reminder of Edward's continued concern, though by it he had spared her a confrontation with Lionel. That unpleasant event could be postponed until after the joust. She suspected Edward was also leaving her stepbrother's chastisement until later, so as not to cloud today's entertainment, for Lionel was to compete and Edward enjoyed a worthy opponent. Though it was only a short reprieve, Isobel was grateful.

"Am I expected to attend the joust?"

"Oh, yes, lady. I'm waiting to dress you. The other knights and ladies are already there. There's to be jugglers and tumblers and all the waving flags and handsome knights," the girl rhapsodized, her hands clasped and her round face alight.

"And you're to accompany me?"

"Yes, lady."

"Then we'd best get started without further delay."

"Your brother sent some clothes from Garston."

So Lionel still orchestrated her life. That news alone told her the king had not revealed what he knew.

For today's festivities Lionel had chosen a close-fitting gown of lapis satin with cloth-of-silver trimmings. Grudgingly Isobel admitted it was a flattering choice. But then, Lionel was still anxious to present her at her best for Edward's enjoyment.

Isobel smiled grimly when she considered what would happen once the king and his errant courtier held their private meeting. Lionel would likely have apoplexy when he learned she had betrayed him.

While she dressed, Isobel also recalled that she had intended to ask the king to restore Ambrey to her, though last night she had given no thought to the matter. A golden opportunity thrown away, she thought in annoyance, as she held out her arms, twisting and bending so that the girl could lace her into her gown.

Isobel was finding sober reality not nearly as comforting as her cloudy, wine-sotted haze. Yet reality never gave her a headache like the one she suffered this morning. Aware that her lady was feeling unwell, the maid offered her a chilled herbal drink guaranteed to soothe the worst headache. Isobel thanked her and prayed the remedy worked.

The colorful jousting ground at Havering was a bobbing maze of flags and mounted knights. When Isobel surveyed the armored contestants, a quiver of hope shot through her. Would Morgan be here? Then her mouth tightened and she set her jaw against the treacherous thought. What did it matter if he was? He cared so little for her, he had not even bothered to write. She knew he was able to write, and there was no danger in sending a letter. Let him stay safe across the border. She had no use for a faithless lover. Only when wine softened her backbone did she ache for him, until she yearned after some nameless minstrel because he reminded her of her lost love, and she shivered at the sound of a voice in the darkness because it sounded like his. Sober, she would not care if he paraded in front of her!

But Isobel knew that was a lie. She could not keep from looking across the sea of banners, searching for a Welsh dragon. She saw none. The discovery made her both glad and disappointed at the same time.

Two other noble ladies shared a wooden bench with her in the corner of the bunting-decked stands. After they had politely inquired about her home and praised her gown, they left Isobel in peace.

She was grateful for their reticence. She sat there barely hearing the cheers of the crowd and the slapping of the wet flags, as she considered her bleak future.

It had rained during the night, but this morning a pale sun struggled out from behind the clouds, bathing the spectators in primrose light. This rare event elicited murmurs of approval. Sunny days this summer had been few and far between. And now, so close to autumn, there was little hope of recapturing the lost season.

Because of the frequent rains, the field was soft. When the horses wheeled, great showers of mud were thrown up. A contest took place below, but Isobel did not know the contestants. Out of the corner of her eye, she saw the royal banners as King Edward rode toward the field. Each time she saw him, a shudder crept along her spine. It would take some time for last night's unpleasant memories to fade. Likewise, she supposed, when the king saw her, he would remember that aborted intimacy between them. The knowledge that he had revealed his need to her and she had seen his nakedness would bring him such discomfort, she assumed that reminder alone would be enough to banish her from court. Likely once Lionel had been raked over the coals, they would leave that same day. Then the twists and turns of her life would follow some new direction, which she felt safe in assuming would also not be to her benefit.

The young maid, whose name was Mags, climbed up the wooden stands to bring her a cup of watered wine and a hot meat pasty. Isobel wanted to refuse the food, but she accepted it because she knew the girl had gone to the trouble of trying to please her. After she forced down the first few bites, it became less effort to eat.

Mags beamed with pleasure, urging her to finish the last crumb. The maid watched her from under the fringe of her pale lashes, waiting until she was finished to say, "Lady, I've a message for you."

Isobel leaned closer, straining to hear what Mags was saying above the marshal's strident announcement of the next contestants. Finally they abandoned all speech until after the heralds had blown their fanfares and the knights had thundered onto the field to the enthusiastic cheers of the crowd. Once the furor had abated, she nodded for Mags to continue.

"A handsome squire gave me this for you," Mags whispered, giggling in her excitement. " 'Tis a love token from his master."

Uneasily Isobel held out her hand. She could not imagine which knight would approach her thus.

Mags placed a folded piece of fabric with a hard center in her palm, folding her fingers around it and pressing them closed so no one else would see.

"His master says he'll meet you behind the ale seller's tent in the outer field." Mags looked sideways at Isobel, a note of expectancy in her voice.

Crushing the hard wad in her hand, Isobel smiled at the maid. The prospect of an illicit tryst had Mags all in a dither, for now she grasped her arm, leaning closer, forgetting her station in the excitement of the moment.

"Go on, open it!"

The linen strip was wound tight about a hard, oval object. Isobel unwrapped the bundle, concealing it in the folds of her surcoat. Mags craned over her arm, eager to see what secret it held. The maid gasped with delight at what was revealed inside the dingy linen.

Stunned, Isobel stared at the ruby rose pendant winking in the light. This was the gift Morgan had bought her last Christmas in Shrewsbury. The jewelry had been wrenched from her neck by her abductors on that frightening winter night. Did it come from Lionel, for it was his soldiers who had taken it from her? Was this just another of his inventive ways to get her attention? Or did she dare hope . . . ?

"Who gave this to you?" she asked, barely able to find breath to speak.

"A squire . . . his master's sore in love with you, lady."

"What name . . . did he say?"

Mags shook her head. "I can take you to him."

Still Isobel hesitated, afraid of what she would learn, afraid she could not endure so great a disappointment if the man was a stranger.

From the field below the crowd roared as Edward rode forth amid much fanfare and trumpeting. He was arrayed in fine armor, the royal arms emblazoned on his surcoat. His destrier had a sweeping saddlecloth of gold. Giant plumes waved atop his fanciful jousting helm with the lions rampant, making him a splendid kingly figure. Then a fluttering pink drapery dangling from his arm caught her attention. Tied about his plate was a trailing scarf suspiciously like the silk organza scarf she had left in her trunk at Garston. Anger and nausea made her stomach heave. Lionel must have sent her favor to the king, pretending it came from her, a good-luck token to ensure his victory in today's joust. How dare he do that without her permission! By this act Edward would conclude that she was still interested in becoming his mistress.

Clenching her fist, Isobel stood abruptly. Now she

hoped that sending this pendant had been another of Lionel's silly schemes, for she was eager to confront him. Oh, yes, this morning she was more than ready for Lionel! The words virtually burst from her tongue, impatient to be out.

"Take me to him," she said, grasping Mags's arm.

Roars of applause came from the stands. Obviously the royal joust was proceeding well. Isobel barely noticed the milling crowd as she rehearsed what she would say to Lionel. She also kept thrusting away that niggling hope that possibly, just possibly, this mysterious suitor would be Morgan. Yes, and it could be a dozen other men, for who knew what had happened to her pendant once it had been stolen. Maybe one of Lionel's soldiers had taken it. Whoever this man proved to be, she need not even speak to him if she did not choose to. And her precious gift had been returned, though she was no longer sure she really wanted it back, for with it came painful memories.

A crowd milled about the ale seller's tent, and the two women pushed their way through the throng. The smell of spilled ale was strong.

"Well," Isobel said, her heart pounding with emotion as she looked about. She did not see Lionel; nor did she see Morgan.

"He said here, behind the tent," Mags said, glancing about, "but I can't see him."

Sweating contestants and loud-voiced vendors alike were hoisting flagons of ale, then pushing their way forward as they yelled for refills. Isobel and Mags moved deeper into the shadows, stepping over ropes and iron pegs, to stay out of the throng.

"He must have lost his courage," Isobel said sharply, disappointment over this anticlimax making her irritable. "Come, we'll go back."

They had already turned about when a man in a boiled-leather jack stepped from the shadows.

"Have you so little faith, *cariad*?" he asked, his voice low and throbbing with emotion.

The color drained from Isobel's face. She gasped, her hands flying to her throat. From the deep purple shadows stepped an apparition, one so often conjured in her mind, she was not even sure he was real. Yet, when she glanced at Mags and saw her eyes widen, she knew the maid had seen him too.

"Morgan!" The name was somewhere between a sigh and a gasp, the speaking of it so painful, her throat ached.

"Here, wench, go buy yourself a trinket," Morgan said, his voice gruff as he pressed a coin into the maid's hand.

Mags gasped her thanks, glanced at her lady for permission, and then sped away to shop at the stalls crowding the fence.

"Morgan," Isobel repeated, hardly able to believe this was really happening. "Am I dreaming?"

His hand came up to encircle her arm. "Nay, but if you are, what matter, for I'm sharing it with you," he said, drawing her closer. He gazed intently into her face, his own features obscured by shadow. "God in heaven, it's been so long . . . so long."

Too many people watched for them to embrace openly. They gazed at each other, their mutual longing conveyed in that look. The noisy crowd, the clamor of the joust, faded away, until they were riding far from here, free as the wind sweeping off the mountains. They were together and nothing would ever part them again.

Isobel was the first to break the spell. She blinked and vigorously shook her head to clear her vision. Last night had not been a drunken illusion, after all. Her muddled brain had not created Morgan's image—he really was at Havering Bower!

"You were the minstrel?"

He flashed her that familiar grin and she nearly swooned as memories flooded back.

"And the man who took me from the hall?"

"Right again."

"But how?"

"Oh, sweet, that's a story you've not time to hear." He paused, then cleared his throat. "Just answer one question—do you still want me?"

Her common sense told her to consider his disregard, those months when she had heard not one word from him—but her heart would not listen. "Do you need to ask?" she said, trying to swallow the building lump in her throat.

Morgan smiled and let out a shuddering sigh of relief. "We've not much time. Likely your brother's spies are watching. Go behind the stands. Iestyn will be waiting with a horse."

Then he was gone.

Isobel blinked, wondering if this meeting had really taken place. There was no sign of him, for he had melted into the crowd. Just as Morgan had suspected, she saw a man detach himself from the crowd around the ale seller's tent, and head toward the infield and the knights' pavilions. Though to the casual observer he appeared to be an ordinary peasant, Isobel recognized him as Rodes, one of Lionel's men.

Her heart pounded so hard she thought it would leap from her chest. She could not believe she was this close to freedom. All she need do was walk back to the stands and she could be with Morgan again. It was that simple! So joyous did the prospect make her, she tried to convince herself it did not matter that Morgan had abandoned her for almost a year, that he had made no attempt to see her. . . .

Isobel stopped, standing her ground against the buffeting crowd. It did matter. It mattered a lot. But this was not the time to take issue over it. Today she would cast her lot with him, for that was where her heart lay. Once they were free of Lionel's tentacles, she would give Morgan a chance to explain himself.

Her expression a little grimmer, Isobel slowed her steps, resisting the urge to run. She even paused to admire a caged singing bird. She must not arouse suspicion. Any minute she expected to feel a hand on her shoulder as Lionel's men surrounded her. Yet maybe she worried needlessly. She doubted Rodes could tell Morgan's identity in the shadows. All he would know was that she had met a man, and that his master must be informed.

Those final painful yards seemed to take forever. Clashing steel echoed from the field and the crowd roared, enjoying the contest. What a wonderful stroke of luck! Isobel saw it was the Hurley standard bobbing around the perimeter of the field. For a while at least Lionel would be far too busy to listen to his spy. She almost sang for joy.

There, in the shadows behind the stands, beyond courting couples and drunken revelers, waited a slender lad holding a saddled horse. It was Spartan in his new velvet bridle and gold-fringed saddlecloth! The lad saw her and nodded, but did not speak. The gelding sidestepped and tossed his head in greeting. Isobel prayed he would not begin whickering as he sometimes did when he considered he had been neglected, thereby drawing attention to them. Quickly she stepped up to the horse and rubbed his muzzle. Then she took his bridle, all the time whispering soothing words to him. No one seemed to notice her, being too absorbed in their own affairs.

Iestyn knelt, cupping his hands to help her mount. Then she was up in the saddle, overlooking the Havering tilt ground. Iestyn led the gelding away toward the contestants' pavilions. Isobel's heart was pounding, for any minute she expected to be stopped. Miraculously, they left the stands without incident.

Amid the confusion of the knight's pavilions, Iestyn led her down a narrow path between the silken tents. There, in a clearing, stood a party of horsemen. When at first Isobel did not see Morgan, she held back, wondering if this was another trap. Then, to her relief, she saw him striding between the tents, leading his big black stallion.

Morgan merely nodded to her, glancing around to make sure they were not being followed. He leaped into the saddle; then, catching Spartan's bridle, he brought him forward until they were riding side by side. His men formed a rank behind them and they trotted smartly off the field, skirting the last of the tents. Only a lad hammering a piece of armor noticed them as they passed, and he touched his forelock to the departing knight's party.

Any minute now Isobel expected to see soldiers bursting off the field in hot pursuit. Through the gates they went and onto the road. Keeping up a smart pace, they didn't slow down until they skirted the heavy woodland of Havering Park. Only then did Morgan slow the pace, reining in beneath the shelter of the elms overhanging the roadway.

"If you can keep up the pace, I'd like to put a few more miles between us and Havering Bower before dusk," he said to Isobel. For a moment his hand lingered on her cheek. Then, as if catching himself, Morgan took away his hand and stepped back.

Puzzled by his changed manner, Isobel wondered what could be wrong. It was not her imagination: a barrier had gone up between them.

"I can keep up. Are we to ride all night?"

"No. There's an abbey where I've lodged before. We're headed there."

A wineskin was passed about, and each man took a couple of swallows to slake his thirst before they went back on the road. Though they rode briskly, Isobel could not keep her mind on the journey. What was wrong with Morgan? Why was he suddenly so distant? For those first few wonderful minutes beside the ale seller's tent she had felt so close to him, as if they had never been apart. Now everything was different.

Before the afternoon was over it began to rain, a light,

cold drizzle, which the wind drove into their faces as they rode west. When the golden stone walls of Alton Abbey came into view, it was a welcome sight. Lionel's men had not followed them.

The travelers were welcomed at the open abbey gate by the guestmaster, Brother Cherton, who ushered them inside a common room where a welcome fire was blazing. Morgan and Isobel were shown to a table beside the hearth, while the soldiers went to a trestle under the window.

When it began to rain Morgan had given Isobel his cloak, for clad only in her satin gown she would have been soaked. Now she saw how wet he was. His padded jambeson was black with rain, and his sodden hose clung to his muscular thighs; even his rough leather boots had big dark patches where the rain had soaked in.

"Here, give me the cloak. It'll dry over the settle whilst we sup," he said tersely, taking the wet cloak and spreading it over the back of the settle.

Abbey servants brought them steaming bowls of fish stew and loaves of fresh-baked bread, dotted with pieces of toasted hazelnut. There was also a bowl of mixed fresh fruit and a platter of dried figs and dates. The home-brewed beer had been mulled and warmed at the hearth. Though not an extravagant meal, the welcome food was hot and tasty. Everyone set to with a will. While she ate, Isobel puzzled over how she should approach Morgan to smooth over the rift that had sprung up between them.

"Are we to spend the night here?" she asked him, when he was finished eating.

"Yes. You'll have a room. I'll sleep with the men."

The harshness of his voice surprised her. Though she supposed it would not be in good taste openly to share a bedchamber in an abbey, she had still hoped they would. The chill deepened around her heart.

Morgan left the table to speak with his men. As they always conversed in Welsh, Isobel could not understand what they said. Now most of the soldiers got up to tend the horses, while Iestyn and two others remained. They spread out a map on the table and studied the terrain.

"Isobel, can you show us the quickest way to your manor?" Morgan asked, bringing the map over to her.

She scanned the crude drawing until she spotted several landmarks that enabled her to pinpoint her lands lying between Shrewsbury and Hereford. She showed him the shortest route to Ambrey, her heart leaping in excitement at the prospect of seeing her home again.

"You're going to come to Ambrey with me?"

"No. You're going to Ambrey where you'll be safe. I must go home."

"Why?"

"There's a fight brewing. A messenger came while we were at Havering. My enemies are building up their strength, that can mean only one thing. They plan an attack on Llyswen. There's even the chance we've been betrayed from within. I can't know how bad things are till I get there."

"I want to come with you."

"No . . . it's not safe for you. They could be waiting in ambush," he added, glancing away. "While you're at Ambrey you can decide what you want to do."

"Decide—I already know—" she stopped. He wasn't listening. His dark brows had drawn together over the bridge of his nose in a fierce, manacing scowl. Abruptly he marched from the room with the rest of his men, taking the map with him.

Isobel sat there in the flickering firelight, all her pain and disappointment flooding over her. Tears throbbed with each heartbeat, welling to her eyes and spilling down her cheeks. This wonderful time she had anticipated between them was not happening. And she didn't know why. What had gone wrong?

When Morgan returned, he was alone. He glanced at

her and saw the silver trickles on her face. His mouth hardened.

"Tears? Who are those for? Do you already miss your royal lover?"

Now she knew the source of his anger. Morgan had heard the gossip. "You're wrong. I have no royal lover."

"Oh, don't lie to me," he said with a snarl. "Let me tell you what I heard when I asked about you. 'Do you mean King Edward's new whore?' they asked. 'Nay,' said I, 'the Lady Isobel. She's no man's whore.' And they laughed at me and called me a Welsh fool! For that very night you were in his bedchamber. While I ached and yearned after you, you were with him! That royal whoreson! God knows, lady, if you'd wanted to cuckold me, couldn't you have found a worthier man?"

Fighting tears, Isobel stared at him in disbelief as she heard all the rage and pain in his voice. "Do you always believe the gossip you hear?"

"No—not unless it comes at me from all sides. Even today, on the tilt ground, after I left you, they were pointing and laughing, saying you were his new whore. Men said he wore your favor in the lists. Do you deny that?"

She hung her head. "He wore my favor, but it was none of my doing. Lionel gave it to him."

Morgan snorted in disbelief and looked away. Though he tried to set his heart against her, her tears and quivering mouth tugged at his heartstrings.

Isobel wiped her eyes. His anger suddenly incensed her. How dare he accuse her of faithlessness, after he had deserted her and left her to her fate? "And what if I had taken Edward for my lover, would it have mattered to you? Safe across the border, you gave little thought to my welfare all these months. My dearest brother has kept me prisoner. But you wouldn't know that, because you didn't care enough to find out. And let me tell you, Morgan of Nels, your safety was bought with my honor."

He turned to her, taken aback by the anger blazing in

her face and her bitter accusations. "What nonsense are you talking?"

"Lionel's men captured me in Shrewsbury at the same time they imprisoned you. My vow set you free. If I hadn't agreed to become Edward's mistress, you'd have been killed. That, my dearest Morgan, is the depth of my regard for you. I faced punishment if I disobeyed Lionel. While I was being groomed to impress the king, you didn't care enough even to send me a note to let me know you still lived. I haven't taken Edward as my lover, though if I had, you've no cause to question it. You abandoned me and my heart was broken. Up till the last I believed in you, that you'd come to set me free."

Morgan was staring at her, hardly comprehending what she was saying. "That's not true," he protested, his voice cracking. "I swear it. When was this bargain struck?" he asked, his voice harsh with anger. " 'Tis all news to me."

"Of course it's news to you. Though I'm surprised Lionel didn't tell you about it just to rub salt in your wounds."

"All Lionel told me was that you didn't want me. That you'd given back my gift with the suggestion I give it to another of my women."

Isobel gasped in shock at the bold lie. How like Lionel!

"That's not true. How could you believe it?"

"I didn't want to. I decided I would believe it only when I heard it from your lips . . . until I came to Havering Bower. There I saw you decked out like a princess, moving with the court. Then I heard the stories and the foul jests. Last night they laughed and said you were sick only from too much of Edward's probing."

"Stop it!" Isobel cried as she jumped up from the table and went to the unshuttered window. She stood looking out over the windswept gardens where lanterns cast wavering shadows across the gravel paths.

"I was sick from too much wine . . . and shame. Edward never bedded me."

"You expect me to believe that?"

"Believe what you will. It's the truth."

"Tell me that he didn't kiss and fondle you, for they say also that your clothing was all askew and your hair mussed . . . that you were the reason he was late to the banquet. Don't try to deceive me, Isobel. Minstrels always hear the latest, most titillating gossip."

She hung her head in shame. In all honesty she could deny none of these charges.

"You've gone very quiet."

"Because I've nothing left to say. Edward is the king."

Those condemning words hung heavy in the room, where the only sounds were the crackling fire and the distant notes of evensong.

For some time they did not speak, each locked in misery and hurt. A discreet throat-clearing at the door alerted them to Brother Cherton's arrival. He glanced from one to the other, aware all was not well between them, but it was not his place to interfere.

"The room is ready for the lady."

"Yes, she's tired. Good night, Isobel. We'll be on the road early tomorrow, so try to get some sleep."

Like strangers they parted. Isobel followed the servant who led the way to the guest chambers. The girl was to assist her to bed, and she had already turned back the bedcovers and placed a warming pan inside to take away the damp.

Isobel felt numb. She was tired, but it was not traveling that brought about such bone weariness. Morgan's unexpected anger and her own ragged emotions were responsible for her exhaustion. She had never anticipated what she would say to him when he heard the wild tales circulating around the court, though she would not have expected him to believe the gossip so wholeheartedly. His pride had been sorely wounded; his jealousy and anger aroused by the thought of Edward touching her. She did not know if he believed she had slept with the king. That really didn't matter. What had taken place seemed to have been enough to condemn her. Always stubborn and pigheaded, Morgan probably felt that his honor had been tarnished. Men never understood that a woman sometimes had little choice in such circumstances. Had she resisted Edward's advances too strongly, she might have found herself cooling her heels in some royal dungeon.

It was the total injustice of it all that hurt the most. She had given in to Lionel's demands to save Morgan's life! And so full of rage and jealousy had he been, he'd never even thanked her for her sacrifice. He was a jealous, pigheaded ingrate!

Anger made her stiff and uncooperative, though the servant girl tried valiantly to help her bathe and brush her hair. Arriving without any baggage had complicated matters. The girl offered her a clean brush, a face flannel and soap. Realizing she was being a pigheaded ingrate herself, Isobel smiled at the servant and thanked her for her trouble.

When the girl had gone she lay alone in bed between smooth linen sheets, listening to a fountain tinkling outside the window and night birds calling from the trees. Never, in her wildest imagination, could she have thought this dreamed-of escape would have ended like this. She was to be banished again, though this time to more pleasant surroundings at Ambrey. Going home was another trial to face, for under Lionel's control she had no idea in what condition she would find her lands. *Men! A pox on them all!*

Angrily she thumped her pillow and turned on her stomach, pressing her face into its smooth coolness. She would not yearn for Morgan, or rob herself of much-needed sleep in angry thoughts about Lionel and Edward Plantagenet. She supposed men were as their creator made them, though she would probably never understand their code of behavior. She wanted to hate Morgan; in fact she had sometimes thought she did during those lonely months when he had abandoned her. Even though tonight he was unjustly angry with her, had virtually cast her aside, blaming her for her fate, she still ached for the love and passion they'd shared in days gone by when he had loved her.

Chapter Twelve

Gloomy morning light slanted through the stained-glass windows set deep in the chapel's stone wall. Morgan knelt at the altar rail, shifting his stiff knees on the padded velvet kneeler. He gazed up at the tortured figure of Christ on the cross, flanked by flickering points of light from the burning tapers beside the altar. While he puzzled over what to do, he unconsciously rasped the dark growth of beard on his chin; then he wearily laid his head on his folded arms.

He had been awake half the night wrestling with his emotions, pride, jealousy and love all warring in his head. Would he risk losing her because of his own jealousy? The reason she had given him for being at court made sense. Lionel had always tried to manipulate her for his own purposes. And kings did what they pleased. To have resisted either man would have been pointless. Yet whenever he pictured her in Edward's arms, pain twisted through him. She'd told him Edward was not her lover. Why couldn't he accept that? Whether the king had bedded her was immaterial—that she had not given her heart to him was what truly mattered, though it was a hard truth for him to admit. During the months he'd searched for her, moving back and forth across England, he had never doubted her love. Why now, when they were together again, did he doubt her?

For much of the year he had neglected his own lands, making only brief visits there during which he attempted to govern, almost resenting time taken from his odyssey. Searching for his lost love had become his life. And now he had found her. Where was the joy? The pleasure?

Stubborn pride and trampled honor were standing firmly in the way of his happiness. By refusing to accept her story, by making accusations, Morgan knew he had wounded her. There was little enough time for them to be together, for almost as soon as they arrived at Ambrey he must be back on the road to Wales. Why then was he being such a stubborn fool?

Morgan had tried to pray for wisdom, but the words would not come. Possibly because in his heart he already knew what he must do. He had to accept what she told him and open his heart to her.

Wearily he got up, his legs stiff. His boots were still wet from the day before, and they creaked as he walked across the stone-flagged aisle to the back of the chapel. A sea of candles flickered here, brightening the gloom. He had lit many of them himself. He stopped to light one final candle. The orange flame shot forth vigorously, burning bright. He liked to think it was an omen, the flame a symbol of their love. He offered a brief prayer for help, thanking his Lord in advance for the aid he was convinced he would receive.

The sky was heavy as Morgan walked out of the chapel. His men knelt bareheaded on the ground while a priest blessed them, asking divine protection for their upcoming journey. A lad, swinging a censer, scuffled along in the wake of the priest's flowing vestments as he moved swiftly along the rank.

Morgan stood, head bowed, in the shadows, making his own responses to the familiar prayers. He was in need of much divine aid. He had no idea what waited for him at Llyswen. A recent messenger had suggested that his sister could be joining with Rhodri of the Mount to overthrow his rule. A distant relative who had always coveted Llyswen, Rhodri generated great respect and some fear, for he practiced the old religion and supposedly possessed supernatural power, calling upon the forces of darkness to work his will. Morgan did not know how much truth there was to that story, but he knew Rhodri was a formidable enemy. He found it hard to accept that Blodwen, however angry she might become, would betray him. Ever since he'd brought home a bride there had been bad blood between them, yet surely she would not let jealousy over Isobel . . .

Something made him glance toward an archway leading into the abbey herb garden. Isobel! There she was. His heart lurched when he saw her. Her dark hair was looped and braided neatly on either side of her head, her fluttering veils dry and fresh pressed. But she was not wearing his cloak, and the discovery made him uneasy. Would she brave the chill rather than wear a garment belonging to him?

Morgan knew he could not delay the inevitable any longer. Squaring his shoulders, he strode toward the herb garden. Pausing in the archway, he stood watching her as she bent to pluck sweet-smelling herbs to fill a silver pomander dangling from her wrist. A dark-robed brother walked beside her, offering advice. She smiled at him, but Morgan saw her face was sad. The reminder that he was the likely cause of her pain was not comforting.

"Isobel."

She stopped, her face blanching. Dear God, did he make her quail as did the other men in her life?

"Yes. Are we ready to leave?"

She did not look directly at him, rather looked out across the neat cushions of lavender, thyme and marjoram.

Impatiently, Morgan signaled to the brother to leave them alone.

"Not quite," he said, clearing his throat, for his voice sounded gruff and he did not want to hurt her again. "Come over to the bench. I want to tell you something."

Obediently she walked with him to a stone bench under the espaliered medlars on the south wall. She sat, equally obediently, holding the fragrant herbs. And she waited.

"Sweetheart . . . I'm sorry," he began, touching her hand. She did not respond.

At first Isobel was not sure she had heard what he said. Finally she looked up, braving his anger and condemnation, though at first she had not wanted to face it. Instead she saw his blue eyes shining with remorse.

"Sorry . . . for what?"

"For being such a pigheaded bastard. I don't care what happened between you and the king. I know you'd little choice in the matter. All I care about is that you love me . . . that we love each other . . . like before." Tense, Morgan leaned forward, awaiting her answer.

Isobel considered his words. The fragrance of the aromatic herbs in her lap drifted up to her, their scent released by the warmth of her hands. In the background she could hear the monks singing; much closer came the clang of pots and pans in the kitchen. At one time she would not have hesitated to respond, but that was before this past year of abandonment, before his jealousy and angry accusations.

"Why did you forsake me?" she asked at last, surprising herself by her calm tone.

"I never forsook you, whatever your brother may have said. And also he lied when he said he would spare my life in exchange for your promise. I was back in Wales just days after Christmas."

"Weren't you his prisoner?"

"Overnight. He made a bargain with me also. I had to leave England without delay to save my squire's life. He followed me to the border and made sure I was safe across. I swear I'm telling you true, Isobel. I didn't want to believe you'd rejected me, but I couldn't know the truth until I'd heard it from you."

"You say you were looking for me?"

"Aye, rumors had you first across the channel, then at Hurley's estate in Ireland. My information came from competitors at tourneys, or from wandering minstrels, or peddlers. Oh, sweetheart, had I only known you were at Stoneham. I neglected my own lands to search for you."

He took her hand, removing the green sprigs of herbs and laying them on the bench. Silently beseeching, Morgan could think of no other argument to convince her.

"Why didn't you write?"

"Where? Every time I thought I knew where you were, I sent a message, but none were of any use. Why didn't you send word to Llyswen?"

Mutely she shook her head. Because at first she had not found a servant who would carry a letter, and later, when she might have done so, in the face of his rejection, pride had kept her silent.

"We've both been foolish, but none of it matters now—we've found each other again."

The warmth in his voice made his argument so persuasive. Yet part of her still held back.

"My lord." It was Brother Cherton walking along the gravel path accompanied by two ladies. "Do you pass close to Monnow Park on your journey?"

Morgan tore himself away from Isobel, feigning an interest in the brother's question that he did not feel, for in truth the interruption could not have been more unwelcome. "Is it near Monmouth? We'll pass within twenty miles of there."

The older of the two ladies stepped forward, rubbing

her hands together as she gave him a most ingratiating smile. By her clothing she revealed her station as minor nobility, for though of good quality, her russet gown was worn and unfashionable.

"Oh, indeed, that will be most helpful. I don't know what to do now that my brother's taken ill. Two women cannot travel that far by themselves. I'm afraid I can't pay for your services. Could we impose upon your protection on our journey, my lord? 'Twould be a most charitable, Christian gesture."

It would also slow them down. Morgan hesitated. He needed to get to Wales without delay—but first they must get to Ambrey. He also needed to keep ahead of any pursuit launched by either Hurley or the king. Maybe one extra day would not make that much difference. . . .

"How many in your party, lady?"

"Three servants, besides my sister and myself. Perchance maidservants will be a welcome addition, for I see your lady travels without one."

Isobel heard the curiosity behind that statement. Admittedly, it would appear strange for a lady of her station to be traveling alone with a party of soldiers.

"Why, yes, a maid would be most welcome. We, too, met with a mishap, and my baggage wagons were lost. Unfortunately, we're heading home with all speed. Our pace will probably be too hard on you," Isobel added, swallowing past her white lie.

"Oh, no, if you're kind enough to help us, we can force ourselves to it. We're also in a hurry. Our sister's to wed and we'll miss the wedding if we don't leave today."

Isobel turned to Morgan. She could see he was not pleased by the imposition of two lady travelers. Brother Cherton smiled hopefully in the background, waiting for his decision.

Morgan knew it would be wiser to refuse their request, yet that would be difficult, especially after the abbot had waived payment for last night's lodging. "Very well," he agreed reluctantly. He swung away from the women without a second glance. "We leave within the hour, ladies," he reminded them as he strode away.

To her surprise, Isobel felt great relief, aware that she had just been granted more time to consider his story and decide if it was true.

"We're so grateful. A thousand blessings on you. I'm Lady Alyce, and this is my sister, Lady Roscilla."

"And I'm Lady Isobel," she said, smiling at the two fluttering, middle-aged women. Her heart lightened at the prospect of feminine company.

"Oh, you've also got a pomander from Brother Andrew," cried Roscilla, seeing the silver-fretted ball dangling from a ribbon on Isobel's wrist. " 'Tis very wise. Brother Andrew says there could be plague abroad this summer. This tansy's so pungent, it's bound to protect us. I've also added a little vervain to keep away the spirits," Roscilla confided, holding up a bone pomander.

"Plague . . . is your brother . . . ?"

"Oh, no, my dear, it's not the plague," said Alyce, laughing a trifle too gaily, for she did not really know what ailed Roger. "Just a weak chest, that's all."

"We heard yesterday poor little Princess Joan died on her way to meet her bridegroom," Roscilla added, relishing the gossip. "Fancy, and she was young, poor dear. Of course, that happened far away—somewhere in France, I believe."

Isobel, newly arrived from court, had not yet heard that story. Perchance it had not reached Havering before she left. News of any outbreak of plague was always cause for concern.

"Aye, pray God we're protected," she added, glancing questioningly at Brother Cherton. She was still wondering if the woman's brother had the plague. The monk, interpreting her unspoken question, shook his head to reassure her. She had heard that this latest epidemic sweeping the continent was more virulent than usual. Sense told her it was only a matter of time before it came to England.

Heavy summer foliage formed a backdrop to their journey as the travelers wended their way through the heart of England. Poppies and cornflowers swayed amid the stubble of the stripped cornfields. Crows glided over sickled fields, and flocks of lapwings searched among the stalks for grain. This year had provided a terrible harvest, with the ground so sodden crops had rotted in the fields. The yield was slim, forecasting a lean and bitter winter.

On dry days mist hung beneath the trees, not burning off until noon. On rainy days mist and rain blended into a soggy gray blanket. Already the first subtle tinge of autumn was apparent in the landscape as bracken began to rust and golden leaves speckled the lush green trees. Morgan's men were anxious to be home, for their own harvesting needed to be done and there were none to cut their fields. After seeing this dismal English harvest they were much concerned about their own crops.

The presence of Alyce and Roscilla was both a blessing and a curse. Isobel found they were a welcome buffer between Morgan and herself. But their incessant chatter made her head ache. The two women commented on everything they passed, and when the passing scene did not provide enough fodder for their tongues, they drew on their own vast store of experiences, until her head spun. She did not blame Morgan for his occasional glowering silence when he was forced to stay in earshot of those rambling tales.

Finally, thankfully, they reached the outer boundaries of Monnow Park, a small manor perched on the brow of a hill on the Hereford road. With a heartfelt sigh of relief, Morgan personally escorted his female charges to their sister's door. And his smile was genuine when he bade them good-bye.

Isobel waited below on the road with the men. Her

gelding lazily flicked his tail as flies buzzed around him, and Isobel listened with pleasure to birds twittering in the hedgerows. Today was a rare sunny day. The warmth on her back was pleasantly relaxing. She knew if they pressed on, today they should reach Ambrey. And she already knew what she was going to say to him when they arrived. These hours on the road had given her time to decide what was most important—holding on to her hurt and nursing her resentment, or accepting his words at face value and saying, "Let's begin again."

"Ready?" Morgan asked, moving quietly alongside her.

So deep in thought had she been, Isobel blinked in surprise to see him back so quickly. The relief in his face was apparent.

"Safely delivered?"

"Yes, thank God. I'll surely get my reward in heaven for this act of Christian charity. Those two women never shut up. They would try the patience of a saint."

Laughing at him, Isobel urged her gelding forward, eagerly leading the way home to Ambrey.

As they rode north and familiar landmarks began to appear, the sight of them made her stomach flutter with excitement. She could see that the surrounding fields had been harvested, though she supposed the perpetual rains had ruined the crop.

Isobel took the riders on a shortcut through sparse woodland before plunging into dense acres of ancient oak and sycamore; here the shade was heavy and the familiar coo of wood pigeons vibrated through the trees.

They suddenly came out of the trees at the crest of a low hill, and there she drew rein to survey the countryside. Morgan signaled his men to stop. Riding to her side, he saw they were looking down on a golden stone-and-timber dwelling nestled in lush parkland. *Ambrey!*

As she studied her manor Isobel grew uneasy at the air of shabbiness pervading the house and outbuildings. The stone wall shielding them from the highway had fallen down in places. As she had suspected, her manor had not fared well under Lionel's stewardship. Rage built inside her at the unwelcome discovery, adding one more reason to despise her stepbrother.

Morgan ganced at her set mouth, aware that all was not well.

"Is it not as you expected?"

"It's not as I left it," she replied sharply. Plunging forward, she quickly picked up speed on the downslope, heading for the east drive.

The clattering hooves of unexpected guests brought the household to life.

At her appearance in their midst, the servants emerged wide eyed into the sunlit courtyard, overjoyed to have their mistress home again. Weeping and laughter greeted her, though the servants cast fearful glances in Morgan's direction. A stranger, accompanied by a troupe of men-at-arms clad in leather jacks and helmets, made them uneasy. Isobel finally assured her people there was no need to fear Morgan.

Beckoning to him, she bade him ride forward. He had stayed back with his men, allowing her to greet her servants in private. At his approach the crowd around Isobel's horse respectfully moved backward. This knight on the big black horse should be afforded all respect.

"I want you to meet Lord Morgan of Nels—he is to be my husband," she announced in a strong, clear voice.

Morgan caught his breath at her words, taken by surprise. Then a slow smile of pleasure spread over his face to erase lines of worry and tension. Isobel had just given him her answer.

When the greetings were over, Isobel rattled off a list of orders that made his head spin. The cooks and scullions were instructed to prepare a feast, the maids to ready rooms and the grooms to care for their horses. Lastly she reprimanded the gardeners for allowing her lovely gardens to deteriorate into a tangled jungle.

This done, she beckoned Morgan to follow her under an arch leading out into the grounds for a swift tour of her manor.

The stone-and-timber manor house was built three stories high around a central courtyard. Portions of crenellated masonry revealed that Ambrey was a former stronghold inside whose tumbledown walls had been built a pleasant dwelling. One tower was still intact, and a massive wall cast its somber shadow across the court. A row of outbuildings leaned against the great stone wall, sheltered beneath its bulk. Here smiths hammered, and the squawks of fowl and grunts of pigs accompanied the hammering.

Beyond the house stretched many acres of tillage. A prosperous village nestled in the fold of a low hill. Close in were a flock of sheep, and a placid herd of black-and-white cattle grazed the buttercup-sprinkled meadows. Silver streams ran over the rolling landscape threading through wood and meadow, before feeding into a fish pond sparkling in the sun. On the south side of the house was a large walled garden that was Isobel's pride and joy.

They dismounted at the garden's entrance, tethering their horses to the iron gate.

To her dismay, Isobel saw how badly her gardens had been neglected. She suspected all manpower had been directed to more lucrative work than tending roses and herbaceous borders. When she had seen the parkland untidy with fallen limbs and tangled weeds, she had suspected as much.

Yet some of the beauty remained unspoiled. The curtain of fragrant white roses with pink centers still climbed over the house's south wall, gnarled branches stretching across the masonry like sinewed arms. Inside the garden wisteria drooped over the walls, and the espaliered fruit trees bore their crop against the sunny stone.

Morgan saw how neglected were her gardens, and, knowing Isobel, he was aware that she was already making plans to remedy the situation. Apparently Lionel had given little thought to anything but bleeding the manor for money to finance his latest scheme. Now that she was home, Isobel intended to put matters right. He smiled affectionately at her, recognizing that determined expression he knew so well.

When they had looked over the garden, Isobel led him to her favorite place, a bench beneath a weeping ornamental tree, the like of which he had never seen before. Here a stream meandered over mossy rocks, and yellow waterlilies floated in the pond's murky water. Ripples broke the surface as an orange fish leaped from the shallows before disappearing under dark green leaves.

"Well—do you like it?" she asked him at last, half afraid he would not enjoy her manor's tame beauty, for it was the complete opposite of his own country's wild scenery.

"I think Ambrey's lovely—a perfect reflection of its mistress," Morgan said carefully, aware that his answer was most important to her. He perched on the edge of the bench, his booted legs stretched out before him. He felt uncomfortable here, dirty and travel weary, with a growth of black beard. All this feminine color and softness made him feel shabby and out of place.

"I always dreamed of showing Ambrey to you someday," she confided, leaning back against the sun-warmed stone with a contented sigh. "I really can't believe I'm actually doing it. I'd thought you'd never come here." She stretched against the stone. "Next we'll see the stables and the kennels. Perchance you'll find them more exciting than my flower garden," she teased, giving him a playful push, aware that he was not at ease.

"I'll tell you what would excite me far more," he said, stroking her hand, captured in his own. "First a bath, a change of clothes, a good meal and . . ."

He didn't finish the sentence; there was no need. She looked down at his olive-skinned hands, trying to find words that wouldn't spoil the mood. The silence grew.

Misinterpreting her silence, Morgan growled. "For God's sake, Isobel, what more must I say? I thought after your announcement, things between us were right again."

"They are."

"Then why do you sit here like a stranger?"

She turned to him, seeing his face shadowed by the overhanging tree. In this half light, with his black, week-old beard, he looked dark as a Moor. Morgan was highly desirable, mysterious—and hers. Gently she took his hand and turned it over, finding his palms callused from holding the reins. Isobel pressed her lips against his palm.

"I want it to be right between us. Let's begin again, sweetheart, like new lovers," she whispered, a catch in her voice.

His arms came around her and she sobbed deep in her throat at the longed-for embrace. His arms locked, pressing her face against the hard warmth of his shoulder. She was aware of his heart thundering under his stiff leather jack.

"Isobel . . . I swear, I love you more than life itself."

She smiled in pleasure, feeling treasured and safe in his arms. "Come then, let's go inside. Tomorrow's soon enough to see the stables. First we'll bathe. Then, if the cooks have our meal, we'll sup. And then . . ."

He smiled at her unspoken suggestion, kissing her brow. "Then we're going to make love like no two people have ever done before. Oh, sweetheart, I've ached for you for so long, I don't know if I can wait through all those niceties."

For just a moment Isobel was tempted to let him make love to her here, but she was also aware that the gardeners she had put to work were close by. She could hear clipping and scratching rakes. It would not do for them to find their lady lying outside with her lover like some serving wench.

"It'll be all the more enjoyable for the wait," she promised him breathlessly, kissing his face as she fought down her own passion.

Morgan grasped her head in his hands, and his thumbs grazed her cheeks as he kissed her mouth. Not content with so chaste a kiss, slowly he parted her lips and his tongue sought hers, all the heat and passion promised by that intimate kiss making her legs grow weak. Isobel leaned hard against him.

He held her close, protecting and cherishing her, silently promising that nothing would ever come between them again.

The moon shone bright as day inside her bedchamber, splashing the paneled walls with silver. Isobel gazed through the unshuttered windows at the shadowed lawns where black shrubbery stood sentinel over the fish pond, all molten with moonbeams. The bright moon rode the clouds like a galleon, tossing wind-stirred patterns across the grass. Everything was so beautiful! Perpetual rain this summer had allowed little moonlight. Tonight, as if it purposely smiled down on them, the full moon shone in all its glory.

"I think the moon's shining just for us," she whispered as Morgan came to stand beside her at the window, his arm warm about her shoulders.

"I told you this is a very special occasion," he reminded, chuckling as he fitted her against him. His shirt hung unfastened and she leaned back against his bare chest. "Each night, when you look at that moon, you'll know I'm looking at it too," he said, momentarily saddened to realize he would be back on the road tomorrow. Tonight was all they would have together.

Isobel buried her face against his chest, shivering in delight as his black, crinkling hair tickled her skin. "Must you remind me of that?"

"Sorry. I forgot myself," he whispered remorsefully into her hair, breathing its sweet perfume. In all honesty, there had been times when he had wondered if he would ever hold Isobel again. "I missed you so much. . . . Welcome home, *cariad*," he whispered, his voice throbbing with emotion.

Isobel turned her face up to his and their lips met. At first his kiss was gentle, but it promised passion. The hot taste of his mouth ignited the fire in her blood, making her long to blend her body with his and become one. Morgan stroked her shoulders, warm through her thin shift, trying to prolong the moment, to remember each caress and endearment and carry it with him in the lonely months ahead.

"You never said whether you enjoyed your supper," she said, stroking his face before slipping her hands into his crisp, black hair. "That was very remiss of you, especially since we stripped the larder to provide it."

Morgan smiled, turning her about to face the window so that the moon shone full upon her. "I enjoyed it immensely. And my bath was also wonderful—though I'd have preferred to share it with you."

Isobel pulled a face at his mock reprimand. "Think how much nicer our time together will be because of your sacrifice."

"Oh, lady, I don't intend to sacrifice much longer," he said darkly. As he spoke, Morgan unfastened her shift, slipping the fabric off her shoulders to expose her magnificent breasts. Her flesh gleamed silver in the bright moonlight, and he shuddered with desire at the arousing picture.

Aware how much he desired her, for the insistence of his body probed against her buttocks, Isobel proudly thrust her breasts forward, making them even more pronounced. Tantalized beyond reason, Morgan groaned. Unable to keep his hands off her, he eagerly cupped her breasts, trying to be gentle, though his blood boiled with desire. Encircling her nipples with his thumbs, he brought the dark buds erect. When Isobel tried to turn toward him, he kept her prisoner. He trailed kisses down her neck, his mouth hot and passionate, until she was beset by shudders of passion, terribly aroused by his nearness. Isobel moaned, aching to press their bodies together.

So insistant did she become, Morgan could not hold out against her protests and he slackened his embrace, allowing her to turn in his arms. Their bodies welded together, throbbing with desire, eager mouths opening, seeking, devouring, drinking in each other.

Without conscious thought they suddenly found themselves on the bed, buried in the soft mound of quilts and blankets. Morgan pulled off her shift, delighting in the silky warmth of her flesh. He stroked her curving hips, desperately trying to control his mounting passion. Together they pulled off his shirt and he impatiently kicked off his footed tights, wrestling with the garments inside the covers. Isobel seared her mouth with his. His kisses set her on fire until she sobbed deep in her throat with longing for him. Morgan's arms trembled with suppressed desire.

"Sweetheart, please," he whispered urgently, and she rejoiced in the raw passion in his voice.

They had been too long apart, there had been too much aching and longing, for him to wait any longer. She barely had time to caress his throbbing flesh, to reacquaint herself with his manhood, before she slid beneath him and spread her legs. In one swift, glorious movement, Morgan was inside her. They strove together, battling to get even closer. Now Isobel locked her legs about his lean hips, allowing her passion full rein. With one hot surge she was swept from this moonlit room to that place of mutual delight, wherein she forgot who she was, remembering only the insistent heat of his body and the splendor of his lovemaking.

"Oh, God, how much I love you," Morgan whispered

harshly, remembering to speak to her in English. Then, as the heat built and he was no longer aware of time and place, he forgot. Isobel delighted in the Welsh endearments that had always been part of their lovemaking. It did not matter that she did not understand every word, for they were part of Morgan's love for her.

Together they were swept away on a tide of mutual fulfillment. Soaring quickly to the pinnacle, they plunged over the top, and then, in a shuddering race, plummeted headlong back to earth, safe in each other's arms. Their mutual cries of pleasure were loud in the quiet room.

Bathed in moonlight, Isobel sighed in deep contentment as she nestled against him. This was as near to heaven as she could get here on earth. Morgan's mouth was soft with spent passion, though his kisses were still arousing. Even the throb of his blood was apparent as she lay against him, finding the steady rhythm of his heart an intoxicating song of love.

In this time of sheer bliss Isobel considered all the pain of the past months, deciding that maybe it had been worthwhile to bring about this glorious reunion. At last Morgan was back in her arms and they loved again. That pleasure made everything bearable.

Smiling in the shadowy room, she drifted to sleep in his arms, lulled by the comforting thud of his heart.

They woke a little later and made love again, this time more able to prolong the delight and savor the experience. When Isobel woke again closer to dawn, she found Morgan awake, watching her sleep, gently stroking her hair where it lay across the pillows. She wanted to weep for the pain of losing him again. This time when they made love there was a sad poignancy to their passion, and the depth of her emotion brought her to tears that trickled into her hair and ears. Morgan kissed away her tears and he held her close.

All too soon it was dawn. The noisy chorus of birdsong from the nearby trees told them the short summer night was past. With a heavy heart Morgan and Isobel broke their fast and went together to the manor's small chapel to pray for deliverance from whatever dangers lay ahead.

When all was ready for departure, Morgan came indoors from the stables, bringing Isobel a perfect peach he had picked for her out of the walled garden. When she wanted to keep the fruit to remember him by, he insisted she eat it now, laughing as rosy juice dripped off her chin. Then Morgan kissed her, savoring the fruit's sweet nectar on her mouth. And he knew, whenever he tasted peaches, it would always remind him of this summer morning.

The sun peeked in and out of clouds as the soldiers mounted up in the courtyard. Isobel had insisted they take supplies for their journey, providing a sumpter to carry them. Fear rocked through her when she looked at Morgan fully armed, looking like a stranger in his gleaming plate. The sight was a grim reminder that he could be going home to fight a battle. She might never see him again! Her hands shook as she thrust away the hateful thought, and she fervently prayed to God to send him safely back to her.

Morgan leaned down from the saddle to kiss her one last time. Standing on tiptoe, Isobel strained up to meet his mouth, aching to hold him against her and never let him go. But she knew that if she caused a scene, she would shame him before his men, so she smiled bravely and bid him good-bye. At the last she pressed a silver locket into his hand.

"To remind you of the moonlight," she whispered, and his smile told her he understood.

Morgan took his helmet off his saddle and put it on. Now she could not see his face, and he seemed even more a stranger. Isobel stepped back as the mounted troop moved forward, clattering over the cobbled yard. Morgan rode at the head of his men, leading them under the arch and along the broad drive to the highway, which would take them home to Wales.

For a long time Isobel watched them. Morgan turned to wave one final time and she fluttered her kerchief, hoping he could see her. Gradually the sounds of clopping hooves and jingling harness faded away as the mounted men disappeared in the trees.

Finally Isobel turned away, hot tears spilling down her cheeks. While Morgan could see her, she had not cried, keeping all her pain locked deep inside. Now there was no more reason to be brave. She turned her face to the wall. And, leaning against the chill masonry, she wept as if her heart would break.

Chapter Thirteen

Blodwen rode slowly along the track. Few people came this way, for grass and wildflowers were encroaching on the beaten earth. It was strange that she never saw hawks or kites on this hillside; neither were there any wild goats, or even hares. It was as if all living creatures were repelled by the brooding presence lurking here.

Dense birch and mountain ash grew wild amid a tangle of bracken and brambles heavy with purpling fruit. The mountain ash berries were already turning scarlet, heralding the changing season. And still Morgan had not come home.

Anger and sadness mingled in her heart. That Englishwoman was to blame, for until she had come into Morgan's life, there had been no discord between them. Because of Isobel De Lacy they had quarreled, and now Morgan had deserted his people to wander England in search of her.

Gripping the reins until her knuckles whitened, Blodwen was seized with a sudden wave of anger. She longed to wreak vengeance on that woman for causing so much strife. She could almost feel Isobel's smooth white neck yielding under her fingers. Shaken by the vivid image, Blodwen blinked. The intensity of her anger had made her contemplate murder! The unexpected strength of her emotion surprised her. Though since she had met Rhodri, she had found herself possessed by many strong emotions.

Smiling in pleasure as she pictured his darkly handsome face, Blodwen urged her horse to a faster pace, hardly able to wait until she could be with him again. In her mind's eye she pictured Rhodri striding toward her, strong arms outstretched in welcome. His eyes were dark as night. Bronzed skin stretched taut across his high cheekbones, a dark, pointed beard adding a sinister note to his strong, powerful face. It was the face of a fighter . . . but also of a lover. Blodwen shivered in delight as she recalled his caress, the feel of his mouth pressed against hers. Rhodri had whispered wonderful things she had never thought to hear spoken by any man, sweet, gentle and arousing things that reminded her she was a woman.

She neared the end of the track. Ahead lay the sacred oak grove. Rhodri should be here this afternoon, for this was the day he must make a sacrifice to the old gods. Not usually squeamish, Blodwen did not like seeing the slaughtered animals on that great slab of rock that served as an altar. Flanked by tall, slate gray pinnacles disappearing into the treetops, the altar was part of an ancient temple from pagan times. The oak grove's tangled undergrowth and towering trees kept a dark secret. Rhodri said it was not merely animals that had been sacrificed here—sometimes the sacrifice had been human!

The strange power this mysterious place exerted over her made the hair stand up on her arms. Whenever she neared this grove, Blodwen felt a palpable sense of evil she was helpless to resist. Yet maybe it was more the charms of the pagan temple's high priest she found hard to resist, for she was aware her heart started to race whenever she thought about him. Rhodri of the Mount was the first man who had ever treated her like a woman; he was also the first man she had ever kissed. Rhodri had not yet become her lover, though to her amazement she was greatly tempted. When Blodwen considered the emotions he aroused in her, she wondered afresh at the miracle. She had never expected to yield to a man of her own accord. In general she found men weak, unfaithful creatures. By contrast Rhodri was strong and powerful, a leader of men. But most important of all, Rhodri loved her!

The track ended at the trees and Blodwen's horse skidded to a stop. Impatiently she clicked to Penn, urging him forward, but he stubbornly refused to budge. Every time she came here he behaved like this, as if he was afraid to enter this place.

Dismounting, Blodwen looped the horse's reins about a nearby branch. She patted his neck reassuringly when his eyes rolled in fear.

Blodwen proceeded on foot, her soft-soled hide boots making little sound as she trod over the deep mast accumulated under these ancient oaks. Overhead, chance beams of light penetrated what had appeared to be a solid canopy, slanting over the path to eerily light pockets of mist lingering under the trees.

Blodwen shivered, not wholly from cold. She drew her cloak protectively about her body as she walked. Today she had not worn her leather jack, choosing instead a soft velvet garment of faded green. She had even plaited her mane of silver-gilt hair into a bun and secured it at the nape of her neck with bone pins. Her tall deerhide boots and the belt slung about her hips were both lavishly decorated with gold. Though she was reluctant to admit it, Blodwen had dressed to please Rhodri. Of course, she could have made the ultimate sacrifice and worn a gown. The thought of restricting skirts made her shudder. Someday it might come to that, but she had to take her transformation gradually.

She knew she was nearing the altar, for though she still could not see the standing stones, she felt that inexplicable presence. She shuddered, quickly crossing herself. Never overly religious, Blodwen felt the sudden need of divine protection to counteract whatever evil force inhabited this place.

There stood Rhodri before the altar, dressed in a flowing white robe. From the back he could have been any man, but in her heart Blodwen knew it was Rhodri. The sheer breadth of shoulder and his hard, compact body told her so. This was the first time she had seen him wearing the ceremonial robes of a high priest. The unfamiliar garments somehow alienated him from her.

As if he had eyes in the back of his head, Rhodri turned around before she took her next step. Blodwen drew in a sharp, startled breath, not prepared for what she saw. Around his neck was a glittering gold rope collar, and on his head was a circlet of the same design, studded with gems. But it was not the golden ornaments that riveted her attention: the front of his luminous white robe was spattered with blood.

Blodwen recoiled from the sight as he took a step toward her. Curiously, those shafts of light that had struggled to penetrate this dense grove pierced the canopy of leaves overhead to form twin beams, which met above the altar. Rhodri stood bathed in a supernatural glow that brought his blood-spattered robes into chilling focus. In his hand he still held a bloody ceremonial dagger. When he stepped out of those crossed beams of light, she noticed a gutted animal lying behind him on the altar. Its entrails had been cast on a smaller slab below. Sometimes ancient seers studied the entrails of an animal sacrifice to divine the future, and she assumed it must be this ceremony that Rhodri performed today.

"I was expecting you," Rhodri said in his rich, melodious voice. "Come, you mustn't hang back. There's nothing to fear."

Reluctant to move closer to that altar, Blodwen suddenly felt powerless to resist. Rhodri's eyes glowed with an unnatural light as he held her gaze, and she felt imprisoned by his will. She moved forward, each step a little easier, until she finally stood before him.

"I was hoping you'd still be here," she said, her deep voice husky with emotion. "Was it all right for me to come to the grove?" she asked belatedly.

"Of course, love, it is I who summoned you here," Rhodri said, a slight smile lifting his full lips. He reached out to stroke her face, blood from his hand smearing her cheek. "He's coming," he said simply.

"He?" she questioned, too distracted by his caress to puzzle over the statement.

"Your brother."

"Morgan! When?"

"Likely before the day's out. Then you'll have to decide what to do."

Blodwen was startled both by his unexpected news and by his last statement. "Do . . . what do you mean?"

Rhodri smiled as he laid the bloodstained dagger on the altar. "The gods reveal that a great evil is sweeping the land. There's no power on earth strong enough to stop it. I alone can keep it away. You'll have to trust me, Blodwen, *bach*."

"What evil? Do you mean an invading army?"

"Not that simple," Rhodri said as he took her arm. "Come here and let me show you."

Reluctantly she turned to the slimy gray and red mess spread out on the rock. Rhodri pointed to the entrails, explaining the great revelation he had seen there. He spoke in a low, hypnotic voice while he moved the heap about with the point of his sacred dagger, showing her the powerful portents that foretold great strife and death.

"You must trust what I tell you, Blodwen. It's the only way to avoid calamity. The gods have also revealed that I am the rightful ruler of all Powys. Your land of Nels should belong to me. And you will help me bring back that balance so our people can be saved."

Appalled by his suggestion, Blodwen drew back. "No! The land is *our* inheritance. It came to us through our mother. I can't betray Morgan. He and I rule together. *She's* the one. . . . Isobel has to go. Don't ask me to turn against him. He's my brother. I love him," she concluded earnestly, her eyes filling with tears at the thought of betrayal.

Rhodri stared at her contemptuously, his black eyes fathomless. "Then you're not ready," he said coldly. And he turned his back on her.

A chill gripped Blodwen's heart. Inwardly panicking at Rhodri's rejection, she grabbed the trailing sleeve of his robe.

Rhodri shook off her hand. "Go home to your beloved brother. As long as you defy me, Blodwen, there's no reason for us to see each other."

"No, Rhodri . . . please," she cried, trying to hold on to him and keep him with her. "I came to see you. Please, there has to be some other way. Maybe we could be allies. Without her, I know Morgan will come around. He loves this land and the people."

"Love can't save them. All of you have to return to the old ways. Don't you understand—your Christian god's forsaken you. Plague and famine are already stalking the land. You must do as I say."

"I can't." Blodwen gasped, appalled by his suggestion. "You would have me betray my own family."

"Look." Rhodri picked up a bunch of mistletoe from beside the altar, its white berries full and lush. Holding it out before her, he began to chant in an unfamiliar tongue. Staring in horror, Blodwen watched as each waxy white berry filled with blood. Then Rhodri took her hand and pressed a mistletoe sprig into her palm.

"Courage and devotion to the old ways, Blodwen. If

you'd be saved, you must stand with me against all others."

Viciously Rhodri crushed her hand about the mistletoe until her knuckles cracked. Blodwen winced at the unexpected pain, and when Rhodri finally let go of her hand, she stared at him in surprise. In all the time she had known him, he had never been anything but loving toward her. When she opened her hand, her palm ran red with blood. In revulsion she rubbed her hand against her clothing, but she could not get rid of the stain.

Eyes wide in disbelief, she saw Rhodri beginning to fade into the trees. Desperate to detain him, she stepped forward, reaching out to him. "Rhodri, don't leave me. What have I done to anger you? She's the cause of our trouble, it's not Morgan. Help me to get rid of *her.*"

"No, it's too late. The power's already at work. In time you'll learn to trust me. Until then—good-bye, Blodwen."

She blinked, startled to find herself suddenly alone in the oak grove with only the slaughtered beast for company. In horrid fascination, she watched as its big staring eyes began to weep in its disembodied head. In amazement she saw that it was a young bullock lying there, when moments before she had seen a much smaller creature. Surely no bigger than a kid, or even a hare . . .

Stumbling in terror, Blodwen plunged back through the undergrowth, unable to move fast enough. What had happened to the strength and courage of which she had always been so proud? Now she stumbled and fell, struggling up each time with great difficulty, as if unseen hands were pulling her back. Surely Rhodri wasn't casting her off so coldly. What of his words of love, his kisses and caresses? Today she had finally discovered what it was he demanded in exchange for his affection—it was a price she could not pay.

Despite his frightening talk of evil, of plague stalking the land, she doubted she would ever experience anything more evil than the presence that lurked in this grove. The more she dwelled on that terrible feeling, the harder it became to breathe, until Blodwen's breath tangled in her throat and she even began to have difficulty walking. In her head she could still hear Rhodri's voice urging her to betray her brother.

Shaken, Blodwen finally stumbled out into the light, emerging from the trees on the dusty track as thankful as if she had escaped from the gates of hell. She wanted to get away from this place as quickly as possible.

With trembling hands she unlooped the reins, surprised when Penn shrank from her touch. The horse must smell the blood on her hands. Desperately Blodwen scrubbed her palm against her clothing, spitting on it first, but the stain was still there.

Blodwen leaped into the saddle and wheeled about, moving down the track with lightning speed. Finally she slowed and turned around to look back at the forbidding black grove. She fancied she saw Rhodri's white robes gleam through the trees as if he stood watching her. Tears coursed down her cheeks as she rode. She had not cried in years. For the first time in her life Blodwen felt utterly defeated. She had never anticipated being faced with such a terrible ultimatum.

Rhodri watched the lone figure fleeing down the track, a triumphant smile on his face. Let her consider those odds for a while! This lady of Nels had expected things to be too easy. Behind him he heard a soft footfall and warily spun about.

He sighed in relief to find it was only Olwen, her green robes blending into the forest. Her pale hair shimmered loose to her waist, threaded with bright field flowers. His heart pitched at the sight of her, soft breasts barely hidden beneath her flowing draperies, rounded hips seductively swaying as she came toward him. There were only two creatures on earth he had ever loved in his life. One was Olwen—the other his pet goat, Bran.

"Olwen . . . how long have you been there?"

She smiled and reached up to stroke his face.

"Long enough. Has she gone? That was a masterful stroke, promising plague and destruction if she didn't do as she was told."

"How so, a masterful stroke . . . are you saying you doubt it's true?"

Olwen smiled knowingly. "Doubtless some of it's true. You forget how well I know you, Rhodri. Don't let ambition get in the way," she warned, tracing his mouth with her fingertip. "Be very careful with the power. Do you love her better than me?"

Surprised by her question, he smiled as he slowly shook his head. "What kind of man do you think I am to prefer that stick of a woman over you? And to answer your question, no—I don't love her at all. She serves a purpose, that is all," he assured her, sliding his hands over the prominence of her soft breasts. "Remember, you're to be mine forever. It is sworn."

She smiled at his reassuring words and leaned against him, whispering, "Yes . . . and don't ever forget it."

Hearing the warning in her voice, he held her near him.

"I won't. But I must still work on Blodwen. Until she cooperates, you'll have to be generous and share your man. Today only proves she's not ours yet. I miscalculated."

Olwen sighed, hating the truth. "All right, but only until she's ours."

"I promise. Who knows, likely she hasn't a hole between her legs—she's got no tits or arse."

Laughing at his observation, Olwen held on to him, not wanting Rhodri to return to the sacred altar. She did not want to exchange the Rhodri she loved for that other person who sometimes terrified her with his power and terrible knowledge.

* * *

Morgan rode uphill from the valley floor, alert for any sign of attack. All was peaceful. After the summer's heavy rainfall, the landscape was achingly green. Heavy-leafed trees stirred in the lazy breeze. Wildflowers starred the grass, and the tangled thickets were purple with blackberries. The lush meadow grass fattened the cattle, but the crops had not fared as well; beaten down by rain and drowned by standing water, the plants had yielded little.

Behind him he was aware of discontented muttering as his men surveyed their ruined fields. Some better-drained land had yielded a harvest, but the boggy bottoms had all been lost.

As he neared the first village, Morgan cautioned his men to be wary. They rode slowly through the settlement without incident, greeted joyously by assorted women and children. When questioned, these villagers said they had not been warned of an impending attack. All had been peaceful. They moved higher and received the same cheering news. Morgan's spirits rose. Overhead a hawk circled before dropping like a stone to its prey. Fresh, clean mountain air filled his lungs and lifted his spirits. He rejoiced to be home again.

Up to the gates of Llyswen they rode without hindrance. But Morgan reserved judgment until he could question his garrison. To his surprise, Blodwen raced out to greet him, tears coursing down her lean cheeks.

"Morgan, Morgan, oh, welcome home," she cried, racing alongside his horse as he rode inside the bailey. "You're here at last. We've all missed you."

Happy at her unexpected welcome, Morgan swung from the saddle and gathered Blodwen in his arms, struck by the unusual yielding of her body. It was a newfound softness to which he was unaccustomed.

"I'm glad to be home. The beauty of the valleys is enough to make a man weep," he said gruffly, pressing his cheek against her hair. He saw that it also was different, arranged in a more feminine fashion and perfumed with rosewater. Unease stirred in his breast. During his absence something had happened to change Blodwen, and her transformation seemed to confirm the tale he had been given that his sister had finally fallen in love. Generally that news would have overjoyed him: it was her choice of man that made all the difference.

Linking her arm in his, Blodwen led her brother into the cool interior of the old palace, striding alongside him, a little of her old vigor returning. "I see you're alone," she said at last. Maybe he had not found the woman.

"Isobel's in England at her own manor."

Her hopes shattered. "Is she not coming here?"

"Later. I'd heard there was unrest and I didn't want to endanger her," he explained carefully, unsure how much to reveal. If Blodwen was truly plotting against him, he had to be careful. Surely her joy at his arrival was not a deceitful ruse to lull him into complacency. With all his heart he wanted to banish his suspicions. The thought that his own sister could be plotting his demise was a painful truth Morgan did not want to face.

"Come . . . I've prepared a feast to welcome you home."

Morgan stopped in the corridor, where sunlight splashed a grid across the stone floor. "A feast! How could you know I was coming home today?" he asked uneasily.

Trapped by her own enthusiasm, Blodwen flushed. Now she rapidly searched for a plausible answer to his question.

"Oh, call it woman's intuition," she replied lamely. "After all, brother, don't forget, I'm a woman too, though usually you only have eyes for the Englishwoman."

After delivering that parting shot, Blodwen walked rapidly away.

Morgan leaned against the stone windowsill as he reviewed the possibilities. He had heard Rhodri of the Mount could divine the future. Was it from him that she had learned of his impending arrival? That explanation was quite plausible, and the possibility brought cold sweat prickling along his upper lip. It was also rumored that Rhodri could call down the wind and rain, and talk to trees and animals. If any of that were remotely true, this enemy was more formidable than any he had faced before, for Rhodri of the Mount was aided by powers from another world.

Morgan looked toward the west through the unglazed window. He could see Rhodri's land curving to the horizon, the upland heavily wooded. On that hill beyond the trees, at certain times, a huge fire blazed. Many rumors circulated about what took place at those ceremonial burnings, everything from pagan fertility rites to human sacrifice. It was also whispered that the devil himself presided over the festivities. Morgan's own people were Christian, though for many it was a tenuous belief. How easy it would be during this summer of incessant rain and crop failure to lure them back to the old ways. Was this what Rhodri hoped to achieve with Blodwen's help? If so, the coming fight would not be merely for his land; it would be for his people's very souls.

Morgan crossed himself, trying to shake off the cold chill moving down his spine. He turned in the other direction, heading for the keep. There he would assess the garrison's readiness to withstand an attack.

Later, at the loaded feast table, tears pricked Blodwen's eyes as she watched her brother eating. She despised the weakness that had arisen with the awakening of her more feminine nature. Pain tore at her heart when she considered betraying him. Without the Englishwoman's influence Morgan would govern well, just the way he had always done. It could be that now that he knew where Isobel was—and she had not cared enough to ask about his successful mission to find her—he would turn his attention back to his land. She breathed a sigh of relief, concluding that there would be no need to choose between Rhodri and Morgan after all. Everything could be as it was before that woman came to disrupt their lives.

Affectionately Blodwen patted his hand where it lay on the cloth beside her own. There were new lines in Morgan's face, making him look tired and drawn. Anger blazed whenever she considered that those changes were all Isobel's doing. Poor Morgan had ridden night and day in search of her, neglecting his land, his people, all for that cursed woman— She gasped, realizing just in time that her anger was rapidly accelerating to a frightening degree. In the back of her mind she fancied she could hear Rhodri's voice. Her heart thudded uneasily. People said Rhodri was a wizard, his power going far beyond that of a Druid high priest. Had he come to dwell inside her mind? Was it he who was arousing her anger in his effort to make her comply with his demands? She couldn't do as he asked—this land was their birthright, hers and Morgan's. Yet how she longed to have Rhodri smile at her again in that special, tender way. To feel his caress and taste his lips . . .

Blodwen picked up her ale cup and downed the brew. No, she cried inwardly, she would not allow him to dominate her soul. Her will was strong enough to combat whatever force he used in his effort to control her mind. Alarmed at the very idea of being powerless, she struggled to empty her mind of the disturbing thought, concentrating instead on what Morgan was saying about his travels. But while she listened, above his head, swirling in the smoke from the blazing torches, she saw Rhodri's face, his fathomless black eyes fixed on her.

Isobel found much to be done at Ambrey. Her steward apologized profusely when she outlined her long list of complaints. On Lord Hurley's orders he had suspended this activity and that, dismissed this servant, transferred that one . . . it was a never-ending litany of disaster. Anger made her tense her jaw, and her teeth gritted harder as the day wore on and she uncovered more evidence of Lionel's greed and stupidity.

First she ordered a thorough cleaning of the manor, which did not appear to have been done in a long time. Their food supplies were adequate, but she ordered more to be brought in. She toured the cellars, taking note of what was stored there. Not nearly as much as she would have liked to find with winter coming on. Now she realized that much of Ambrey's well-stocked cellars and granary had been siphoned off to sustain Lionel's own household. She was appalled to learn that Lionel had even sent some of her household staff into the fields, hoping that by having more workers, he could increase the crop's yield. Many of the manor's field serfs, denied adequate food and medical care, had succumbed to various ailments during the previous year. Those who survived were undernourished and dispirited.

Immediately Isobel opened the infirmary and sent word to the villages that all who had sickness in their families, or who needed teeth pulled, or wounds dressed, must come to the manor. Even she was not prepared for the line of limping, coughing patients who braved the drizzling rain. Fortunately, Lionel had not depleted her healing store of herbs, salves and tinctures. As he had denied her tenants treatment, none of it had been touched. Joined by several of her more skilled servants, Isobel donned a coarse linen apron and set to work, dispensing sympathy along with the treatment.

This frantic activity to return Ambrey Manor to its former glory filled her days. It was her nights that were long and lonely. How she ached to feel Morgan's arms about her, to have his pulsing, virile body pressed close to hers and taste his passionate kisses. Though it had been a little over a week, she felt as if it had been years since he made love to her and they had shared that secret world of lovers. So far there had been no news from Wales. Isobel began each day in the manor's chapel fervently praying for Morgan's continued safety.

After several more weeks of hard work, Ambrey began to look much as it had on that sad day when she was forced to ride away with Lionel to enforced exile at Stoneham Magna. Polished and swept, the gardens partially restored and the stables cleaned out, the old manor house had begun to hum along contentedly as it had done when she had sole charge of it. Now maids sang about their work, and Isobel heard the craftsmen whistling as they made much-needed repairs.

To her disappointment, she found the kennels empty. All her dogs had been taken away, first to Stoneham, then probably as gifts for the king. Fortunately she had left Sybil and Hector at Llyswen, where she trusted Morgan to care for them. It was unnaturally quiet without the dogs. As soon as she was able, she vowed to replenish her kennels.

There were so many charges mounting against Lionel, it would take a week to voice them all. Though she still wanted to vent her anger against him, she hoped he would never dare come to Ambrey again. The pleasure of telling him what she thought of him was worth forgoing if she need never look at his sly, scheming face for the rest of her days.

September was another rainy month. On rare sunny days Isobel rode about her manor, enjoying the warm laziness of this seasonal span between summer and autumn. In the meadows wild mushrooms spangled the grass, and dew-drenched honeysuckle trailed over the hedges where noisy blackbirds feasted on the last of the blackberries. Already russet hues overpowered the green leaves, and crimson sorrel stained the fields. In a few days it would be Michaelmas, the third quarter-day of the year. Then Isobel would set up a makeshift court to hear her tenants' complaints and settle their disputes. Also, Moffat, her steward, would sit at his table to collect the rents. This time she had hoped Morgan would be beside her to help dispense justice. Maybe at the Christmas quarter-day he would take his rightful place at her side. This Michaelmas, following such a soggy, chilly summer, she did not expect the manor's barns and coffers to be bursting with largesse.

Sometime during the night it began to rain in earnest, and water sluiced down the stonework. The wind blew a gale, rattling and creaking the shutters, and she could hear tree limbs shattering and crashing in the park. Later a noise downstairs, rising above the storm, disturbed her. It was as if a dozen horsemen clattered and banged through the stableyard. She glanced outside but saw no lights. When no one came to alert her, she assumed she had imagined the commotion. Tired after all her recent labors, Isobel burrowed into the soft feather bed and went back to sleep to dream longingly of Morgan.

Lightning cut a lurid swath across the sky, its brilliance flashing through her room. Isobel jumped, startled from her sleep by a clap of thunder.

She assumed a subsequent crash to be a second clap of thunder until an angry male voice growled, "Get up, you worthless bitch!"

Ice flowed through her veins. It was Lionel!

He stood in the doorway, his clothing soaked from the storm. Rain puddled about him on the rushes, running off his cloak and boots. Trickles from his velvet cap coursed down his face, and the bedraggled plumes were plastered against his cheek.

"How dare you come into my chamber?" Isobel demanded, trying to gather her wits.

Lionel glared at her, his anger palpable. Stepping forward, he crashed the door shut behind him. She could hear steps and voices outside in the corridor, but no one dared come into the room to protect her from the master's anger.

"I dare because this house belongs to me—you belong to me!" he snarled, ripping off his wet cloak and throwing it across a nearby chest.

"No! The manor is mine. And I am my own mistress," she corrected angrily, fighting to control the tremors shuddering through her frame. Isobel slid from the bed, quickly slipping her bedrobe over her shift. She did not want to be half-dressed in front of Lionel. His often hungry, lecherous appraisal of her body had warned her always to be careful where her stepbrother was concerned.

"What do you mean? Your wardship's mine; therefore Ambrey's mine," he ground out, going to the smoldering fire in the corner hearth. Viciously jabbing at the logs with a poker, he stirred them into a faltering blaze and held his hands to the meager warmth.

"The king gave me back my manor," Isobel lied boldly, wondering if he would know it was not true. For Lionel to be here instead of at court meant Edward was not pleased with him. If he had not actually been banished, he at least had not been made to feel welcome. She considered it well worth the gamble.

Lionel turned an angry face on her as he sneered. "Oh, so you bargained for your property inside his bedchamber, did you, you bitch? You were supposed to be spreading your legs, not negotiating a settlement!"

"What the king does is his own choice," she reminded him carefully, wondering where this conversation was headed.

"Fueled of course by you, embroidering the truth until he was beside himself with rage."

"I embroidered nothing. I told him why you brought me to court and the payment you demanded. All lies, I later found out, because Morgan was safe in Wales shortly after Christmas."

"That's another trick you'll pay dearly for—running away with a minstrel. For God's sake, Isobel, the humiliation . . ."

Could he not know? Was it possible Lionel actually thought she'd left Havering Bower with a stranger? "What do you mean, a minstrel?" she questioned warily.

"Aye, a minstrel, a Dragon Knight, a treacherous Welshman, they're all the same person," he said with a snarl, foam flecking his lips in his tirade. "When next I see him, I'll spit the treacherous bastard on my sword. You have my word on it, lady. Not like you who broke your word, after I'd spent a fortune decking you as fine as any princess. Worse than that, you betrayed me to the king!"

All the while as Lionel raged, Isobel was edging closer to the door. So angry was he, she hoped he had not noticed her movement. Suddenly he spun about and grabbed her arm, flinging her as hard as he could across the bed.

"Stop it! Don't you dare touch me, you liar!" she screamed, hitting out at him and catching his cheek.

"Because of you I'm over my head in debt. Edward's turned against me and you, you wanton little bitch, you're no use to me anymore. What man would want to marry you now? You wouldn't believe the tales going around court about you running off with a common minstrel."

"No man would marry me because I'm already betrothed to Morgan. From the start I told you I was satisfied with him. You forget, taking me to the king was all your idea, not mine."

Isobel grew uneasy as she realized Lionel was between her and the door. Black anger twisted his face as he glared at her. He lit a brace of candles and stuck the sputtering candelabra on the chest. Then, pulling off his wet doublet, he stood looking at her, his chest heaving with anger.

"You've ruined me! And I've nothing left to show for it. No favor. No alliance. Why did you have to tell Edward your pitiful tale? Couldn't you have just kept your mouth shut? He was hot for you. I had him just where I wanted him and you ruined it."

Beside the bed was the clothes chest where Isobel had

thrown her gown the night before, being too tired to put it away. Inside her sleeve in a false cuff was a small, jeweled dagger. It was a fashionable accessory, but it was also a practical one. Tonight it could prove useful. If she could work her way around to that side of the bed, she would at least have a little protection, for the snarling hatred and merciless condemnation in Lionel's face warned her to be careful.

"You're no good to me now," he cried, clenching his fists. "I should beat you to a pulp. Make you pay for ruining me," he threatened, though in reality, even now, he knew he could not mar her beauty. "Why?" he asked finally, his tone softening. "Why did you do it? Why did you ruin me?"

"I didn't want to be Edward's mistress. You knew that from the start. Only you wouldn't listen to me. You had to have your way. It was my last defense."

"You didn't think about me in your selfishness, did you? All the debt I'd entailed to launch you at court."

"I never asked for it. Besides, before you feel too sorry for yourself, remember you've stripped my manor to the bone to pay your living expenses. Why should I feel sympathetic? You've stolen right and left from me and this land. Likely what you've spent on me was my own money, after all."

Lionel glared at her, angry that she had presented such logic. Some of the fight was going out of him. He was tired, cold and wet. His belly rumbled from lack of food. He had raged inwardly halfway across England, contemplating beating her, bruising that famed beauty, until no man would have her. He had even pictured breaking her neck, then flinging her body into the moat, but that was all insanity. Now that he was actually here, face-to-face with her, he could not carry out those dire punishments. Isobel was too lovely. He still burned with thwarted desire for his stepsister.

At that point there came a thundering on the door, and

an agitated voice called for Lionel. Swearing beneath his breath, Lionel marched to the door and wrenched it open.

"What is it?"

"The Welsh prisoner, my lord, he's escaped."

"By God . . . all right, I'm coming. You," Lionel said with a snarl, rounding on Isobel, "dress and come downstairs to sup with me. I'm not finished with you yet."

With that he stormed out the door. His men were shouting to each other below in the yard, and horses' hooves clattered over the cobbles as they raced off in pursuit of their captive.

Isobel peered through the window but could make out little beyond bobbing torches and shadowy figures. Surely this Welsh prisoner could not be Morgan! Besides, had Lionel made such a coup, he could not have let it pass without gloating. And he certainly would not have kept it to himself.

Though she did not want to sup with him, Isobel supposed she had little choice. Chasing down a prisoner in the rain would not improve his mood. Determined not to make any special preparation, she pulled on the dress she had worn the night before and casually looped her hair inside a fret, which promptly fell off. Isobel finally decided to braid her hair under a short veil and chaplet. The dagger rested heavy and comforting inside her sleeve, and she patted it, making sure it was secure.

Sleepy-eyed servants made haste to prepare a meal, warming pottages, slicing meat, and whipping cream for a blackberry flummery. Wine and ale were brought up from the cellar. Soon the clatter outside revealed that the search party had returned, and by the cries of pain echoing inside the house, it also told her the prisoner had been captured.

Isobel turned to see who this Welsh prisoner might be. When a man stumbled inside the hall, arms bound and feet hobbled, she recognized him as one of Morgan's men.

"Why is this man your prisoner?" she demanded,

marching boldly up to Lionel when he came into the room.

"I've kept him prisoner since Shrewsbury. He was wounded in a skirmish and we cared for him, intending to send him home. But he's an ungrateful guest—he stabbed one of my men with a kitchen knife."

"Don't you suppose he was trying to escape? Few men relish being imprisoned in a foreign land," she said, going up to the man. She could see he recognized her, for a light of hope glimmered in his dark eyes. "Release him and let him go home."

"You don't give the orders here, lady," Lionel reminded sourly. "There's a serving wench too . . . the one you had in Shrewsbury."

"Mali's here!" Isobel cried, surprised and pleased by the news. "You've kept her prisoner too?"

"What else could I do with the woman? I intended to send them home together."

Isobel demanded that Mali be brought forward. When she finally appeared, Isobel saw by her dejected appearance and hollowed-eyed face, that Mali's stay had not been pleasant. Doubtless Lionel's men had used her as they pleased.

"Mali," she said gently, hand outstretched. To her dismay, Mali shrank from her as if she did not recognize her. She began to cry and waved her arms in defense, before sinking to the rushes, where she hid her face and wept. "Damn you, Lionel, what have you done to her?" Isobel demanded, rounding on him in anger. "She acts as if she's crazed."

Lionel shrugged and turned away. "Who knows? It's not any of my concern. I've far more important things to worry about than some serving slut."

At Isobel's request and with Lionel's grudging permission, the manor's steward arranged for the two prisoners to be taken out and fed. He assured Isobel the woman would be treated gently. Her heart sank as she watched

Mali shuffling away, head hanging down. It was her fault the poor woman had been reduced to a blubbering fool. Had she left her safe in Wales where she belonged, none of this would have happened.

"Oh, Lionel Hurley, that's just one more sin you've added to your list," she said angrily as she passed him on her way to the table. "If you live to be a hundred, you'll never be able to pay for all the damage you've done."

"You . . . shut up! I've heard all I want from you tonight," he ordered, throwing off his wet cloak. One of his men scurried forward to pick it up, warily eyeing his master. Lionel's rage was mounting, each incident accelerating the heat.

"You weren't invited here. This is my house and I'll say what I want in it," Isobel told him, aching to slap him as she slid into place at the high table. It was all she could do to sit there calmly and pretend to eat while he was in arm's reach.

To the casual observer it would have seemed as if the lord and lady of Ambrey supped with their retainers. All was quite civilized and congenial as they ladled the pottage, broke the bread and sliced the meat, when all the while Isobel longed to plunge her knife into Lionel, or to pour boiling soup over his head and kick him under the table. As she pictured that delicious revenge, she smiled. The expression was fleeting, but not so fleeting that Lionel did not see it.

"Ah, so your mood's sweetening, is it? Here, drink some more wine," he suggested, pouring syrupy Gascon wine, thick as blood, into her goblet.

"Now that you've ruined our chances of living at court, what plans have you for the future, my love?" Lionel asked her suddenly, the wine turning him morose.

"My plans haven't changed. You're the one who must make new plans, but then, plots and plans were always your specialty, weren't they, Lionel, dear?"

"I didn't come here to be insulted," he said in a growl, his hand tightening on the stem of his goblet. "If you can't be more congenial, then you'd best go back to bed."

"That will be my pleasure," she said, standing immediately. With head held high and shoulders back, she marched out of the hall, leaving Lionel sitting there stunned amid the remnants of his predawn feast.

On the way to her room Isobel stopped at the infirmary to check on Lionel's prisoners. The man, whose name she had remembered was Alun, had numerous cuts and bruises, and his knees were scraped raw where they had dragged him behind a horse. Moffat had already ordered his hurts cleansed and bandaged.

Mali's injuries were not as treatable.

Isobel crouched beside her where she sat next to the hearth, slumped on a bench. "Mali, it's Lady Isobel. Don't you remember me?"

Mali turned at the sound of her voice and, seeing it was a woman, she did not shrink away. But her pale eyes stayed glazed and uncomprehending. Even when Isobel took her hand and held it, soothing her, there was no response.

Alun spoke very few words of English, and Mali, who could have interpreted for him, was lost in her own world. With a sigh, Isobel stood up. It was pointless to try to do any more tonight.

She passed Alun's bench and patted his shoulder in reassurance. He smiled at her, his dark eyes puzzled at finding her here without his lord. Isobel did not know how to tell him in Welsh that this was her own manor, so she did not even try.

With a heavy heart Isobel went back to her room. It had started to rain again and Isobel went to the window to look out, watching the gray, slanting curtain sluicing down the stable wall. Saddled horses stood outside in the rain. *That fool!* Why didn't he send his men out to rub them down and stable them? Isobel paused, partway to the door to deal with the matter. No! Though she didn't like to see the horses suffer, the animals were Lionel's. Let him take care of them himself.

With her mouth set, Isobel pulled off her gown. She had not sent for a maid to help her dress and she did not need one to help her undress. Just to be on the safe side, she took the dagger from her sleeve and slid it under the pillow.

She felt too tense and angry for sleep. Her legs ached with the desire to get up, go downstairs, and physically abuse her stepbrother. Finally she began to drowse as the rain slackened, lulling her with its gentle patter. She lay on her back listening to the rain, wondering what Lionel would do next.

The click of the door latch alerted her. She had had the foresight to lock the door. The handle turned several times. Then she heard steps receding. Had Lionel come to pay her a visit? Grimly she smiled, plumped her pillow and turned over and went to sleep.

Something woke her. Isobel blinked, finding the room steely gray with morning light. It was no longer raining, and the fresh, damp wind coming through the window made her shiver. Isobel pulled the covers high around her chin. Then she heard a sound that made her tense beneath the quilts. Someone was in the room.

"Who's there?" she demanded, sitting up and trying to pierce the gloom.

"Only your loving brother."

Isobel's heart pounded in warning. Lionel must have used the master keys to let himself in while she slept. Her suspicion had been right. It was Lionel who had tried the door earlier.

"What are you doing here? That door was locked for a reason."

"Yes, to keep me out. I'm not that much of a fool," he said amiably, coming to stand beside the bed. He leaned over her, a foolish smile on his face, his expression revealing he had indulged far too freely in the honeyed Gascon wine.

"What do you want?"

"What any man wants when he looks at you."

A cold chill inched down her spine. "Get out!"

"You've successfully spoiled all our chances of pleasing Edward—God knows, no decent man would want you now. What am I to do with you, Isobel, love?"

"It's not for you to decide to do anything with me. Besides, you've had too much to drink and you need to sleep it off. Go back to your room and leave me in peace," she commanded, realizing she must rely on her own wit to save her. No one else would dare defy Lionel and risk losing his own life.

"We're both damned, Isobel. We belong together now. Think what that means. We've got to stop quarreling—there's no point to it. You've got to stop lashing out at me at every turn."

"All right, I'll stop. But in return you've got to leave me alone. Go home and let me live here in peace. It's not much to ask."

"You don't know how hard it is for me to leave you here," he began, sitting on the edge of the bed.

Isobel shrank from him, moving to the far side of the bed. "Go home to your wife and children. That's where you belong, Lionel, not trying to be a courtier, and certainly not here. Surely you've much to do at Stoneham. And you've got property in Ireland. This is an added responsibility you don't need," she suggested, feigning sympathy in the hope of appeasing him.

"You're right there," he readily agreed. As Lionel spoke he gathered the soft fabric of her bedrobe in his fist and brought it up to his face, breathing in its perfume. "Everything's too much responsibility . . . when there's really only one thing I want."

"And what's that?"

"You."

"Me!"

Appalled, Isobel stared at him, finding his face shadowed in the half light, which was slowly brightening as daylight crept through the unshuttered window.

"Yes, didn't you guess . . . all this time . . . oh, Isobel, Isobel, I was saving you for Edward. That doesn't matter now. None of it matters anymore. We can do as our hearts desire."

"Speak for yourself," she snapped, trying to slip out of the covers. She hoped it was just the drink talking. Lionel had drunk enough wine that he would be clumsy; if she was lucky he might even fall asleep if she could keep him talking long enough.

"There's no need to play hard to get, you silly woman. The chase is over. I'm here, in your bedchamber—we're alone," Lionel explained, smiling indulgently at her as if she were some silly child. "I've always wanted you. And now I intend to have you. But I'd prefer the desire to be mutual." When she failed to respond to his suggestion, Lionel cried petulantly, "Why are you always so cold to me? I'm a fine figure of a man. Other women find me attractive. Don't act so cold toward me, Isobel."

"You're my stepbrother!" she cried, appalled.

Lionel shrugged. "So? There's no blood tie between us. Laws of consanguinity apply only to marriage—I'm not going to marry you. Though, God knows, if I wasn't tied to that ugly stick of a wife, I'd not hesitate a moment."

As he spoke, Lionel was edging closer.

Isobel finally found herself pressed against the wall. To her alarm Lionel slid eagerly over the quilts. Suddenly he grabbed her and Isobel twisted out of his grasp. Now that the room was lighter, she saw that he was wearing only a bedrobe.

Holding her startled gaze, Lionel undid the sash of his bedrobe.

''There, woman! I challenge that cursed Welshman to better this,'' he boasted, indicating his towering erection. ''Am I not a better man than he ever thought about being . . . am I not?'' He was shouting now, his anger increasing.

''Lionel, you're a fine man, but I'm your stepsister and I won't ever want you like that.''

''Why not? God knows, all this time, I've wanted you . . . watching you . . . longing for you—damn it all, Isobel, I won't take no for an answer,'' he said with a snarl, his temper aroused. ''Now, lie back, damn you, and you won't get hurt.''

Lionel lunged for her. They fell together in a heap. Isobel gasped as he knocked the breath from her body. Desperately, she fought him but was alarmed to find that even when tipsy, Lionel was far too strong for her. Years of competing in tournaments had honed his muscles and made him taut and strong. The power he exerted over her only fueled his desire. Eyes gleaming in triumph, he reared above her.

''Now, tell me no, you ungrateful bitch,'' he said in a growl, positioning himself to mount her. With knees poised on either side of her thighs, he scrabbled to open her legs. In vain she thrashed and fought but could not dislodge him.

Isobel screamed for help and Lionel put his mouth over hers to stifle the sound. She bit his lips, tasting salty blood. With a yelp of pain, Lionel leaped back. While he tried to stanch the blood trickling down his chin, Isobel slid her hand under the pillow and her fingers closed around the hidden dagger.

''Damn you, that hurt! So you want to play rough, do you?'' he snarled, lunging for her, his punishing grip bruising her shoulders.

Isobel twisted and kicked, punching him with her free hand while she kept the other hand hidden on the dagger.

''You stupid bitch. I never wanted to hurt you,'' he

explained tearfully, "never wanted to bruise that white skin. But you give me no choice. Why couldn't you come to me as a lover? Why must you make me force you?"

"I've told you—I don't want you, Lionel. I never will!" she shouted. "Remember, you're the one who's set the terms of this combat."

Viciously Lionel wedged her legs apart until Isobel thought her hips would be dislocated. The feel of his wet organ sliding across her thigh made her gag. Going limp in the hope of catching him off guard, she lay unresisting. Surprised by her sudden acquiescence, Lionel let go of her wrist and started to fondle her breasts, exposed by her torn shift. Lionel's flesh surged as the added intimacy increased his desire. When he leaned down to kiss her, his suffocating mouth tasted of blood.

Isobel raised her arm, the dagger poised, and then she drove down, aiming for the side of his neck. The point slid home with surprising ease and she drove it to the hilt.

Lionel cried out, reaching for his neck, momentarily baffled. Isobel wrenched the blade free and leaped from the bed. Desperately she searched for something with which to defend herself. A long-handled warming pan hung on the wall. She grasped it and swung around just as Lionel half jumped, half fell, from the bed, clutching his neck. With all her strength, she brought the warming pan down on his head.

With a scream of pain and surprise, Lionel crumpled to his knees, then fell forward onto the rushes.

Isobel wasted no time checking his condition. She grabbed her boots and gown and struggled into them. Her hair was streaming wildly about her shoulders, and after she pulled on her cloak, she thrust her hair inside the hood. With the dagger back in her sleeve, she wrenched open the door. Lionel had not moved, but she didn't think he was dead, merely stunned. She did not know how much time she had before he would be up and doubly furious to have been outmaneuvered.

Taking the stairs two at a time, she headed for the stable. If those saddled horses still stood in the yard, she would take one and ride for open country. Before she reached the hall, that idea had been discarded. How would she survive alone without money? It would be better to head for Llyswen; the fact that she did not know the way failed to daunt her. Surely someone at a nearby inn would direct her to the Welsh border. Once she crossed over, she wondered how to make herself understood.

Then Isobel remembered the two prisoners in the infirmary. Alun would guide her to Llyswen! He could also speak for her. What a wonderful plan! Now she was almost glad Lionel had taken prisoners.

Flying now, her feet seeming barely to touch the flagstones, Isobel sped to the infirmary.

As soon as she burst through the door, Alun was up in a crouching position on his pallet, prepared to defend himself.

"Alun. Come," she cried, gesturing toward the door. He looked startled. She could not blame him, for she must look a wild sight with her hair flying loose, and splotched with Lionel's blood. "Go to Llyswen," she said slowly, hoping to make him understand. By the sudden light in his face, she saw she had succeeded.

He was up, hobbling because of his injuries and pointing to Mali. Isobel ran to rouse the woman, quieting her when she began to whimper. She took blankets from the pallets, giving one to Mali and one to Alun to use for a cloak. Aware that her time was running out, Isobel hurried them through the door, grateful that the infirmary led directly outside.

The cool gray dawn was alive with birdsong. The clattering of pans in the kitchens revealed that the manor was slowly coming to life. Isobel found the horses still patiently awaiting their masters. Though she was dubious about these horses' ability to carry them all the way to Wales, Isobel knew she had little choice. She indicated that Alun and Mali were each to mount a horse. At the last minute she changed her mind and raced to the stable to get Spartan.

With shaking hands she desperately fought to saddle him, finding the leather stiff and the buckles awkward. The gelding fidgeted with excitement. Finally, after what seemed like hours, she was ready for the road.

Out into the chill morning light she led Spartan, prancing and sidling, overjoyed to be taking this unexpected ride. Alun and Mali were already mounted, waiting for her. Signaling for them to follow, Isobel shot under the arch and down the drive, heading for the outside gate. So far no one had been alerted by the sound of hooves. As they had left their horses out in the rain, she assumed Lionel's men had probably spent the night drinking and wenching. The latter thought made her uneasy. She hoped her maids had not been mistreated, but she had no time to worry about their welfare now.

When they reached the highway, she pointed down the road. "Llyswen."

Alun looked around, and then rode to a rise of ground to get his bearings. When he galloped back to her, he pointed in the opposite direction.

"There," he said, grinning at his accomplishment in using an English word. The prospect of going home at last elated him. Grasping Mali's bridle, Alun took her along with him, telling her to hold on.

All three riders wheeled about and headed west toward Wales.

Chapter Fourteen

The sun slowly sank to its death beyond the mountains. Blodwen reined in to watch the painted sky deepen to a glorious, burning orange. Such beauty, but today it did not move her. All she could think about was Rhodri's abandonment. True to his word, he had not contacted her since that dreadful day in the oak grove.

Tightening her mouth, Blodwen pulled Siân's head about and plunged headlong downhill. It was in this wild spot she had met Rhodri all those months ago. Hope that he would be here again kept her coming back. That day she had not known who he was, merely someone who helped her when her horse went lame. Rhodri had pulled a stone from Penn's hoof, soothing him with some whispered rhyme, until, almost before her eyes, Siân was as good as new. The man's skill baffled her, for it was more like a magic spell than any actual knowledge of healing. Whatever his power, Rhodri held her in thrall. It was the first time she had ever been drawn to a man. The first time she did not want to outride him, outshoot him, or prove herself superior in any way. In fact, she longed for Rhodri to be her superior, though that was a hard truth to admit. If she was devastatingly honest she knew she wanted him to be her lover. Her heart ached when she considered that that wish could come true. Only the price she must pay for it was far too high.

Three figures on horseback straggled along the trail at the foot of the hill, heading her way. Eyes narrowed, Blodwen watched them. When they moved higher up the hill they would be challenged by a sentry, for men were posted on the hills to guard against surprise attack. But she wouldn't wait for the sentry's challenge; she would go down herself to find out who they were.

Kicking her heels into Siân's flanks, Blodwen careened down the hill. As she drew closer she could see a man and two women. They were a scurvy, wild bunch at that. The women's hair fluttered loose, flapping like banners in the wind. The man was bandaged and had wrapped himself in a blanket as a cloak. Only one of them even sat his mount well. And that gray was a superior beast.

Blodwen's heart lurched as she made the connection. Horses were a burning interest of hers. She never forgot a piece of good horseflesh, and that prancing gray looked painfully familiar. Surely it could not be—oh, dear God, no . . .

"Ho, there. We're bound for Llyswen."

The man hailed her from a distance. He was a Welshman. Why would Isobel De Lacy be traveling with a Welshman? Yet there was even something familiar about the man, with his dark beard and straggling hair. Then as he came closer she recognized him. "Alun?"

"Lady Blodwen, is it . . . oh, happy I am to see you. We're returned from the dead, God be praised."

Her heart was like stone as she looked at them. Alun, Mali—and that woman!

"Blodwen! How did you know we were coming?" Isobel asked in surprise, as she rode forward to greet her, face wreathed in smiles at finding a familiar face this far from Llyswen.

Blodwen looked at her unsmilingly, never before having seen the fine Lady Isobel looking quite this disheveled. Her tangled hair frothed about her shoulders like that of some gypsy wench, while her clothing was stained and her face grimy. Yet even looking like a beggar maid, she was still appealing, and Blodwen knew she could not fail to charm Morgan. Then, to her surprise, Blodwen noticed purpling bruises on Isobel's face, and the slender wrist jutting from her sleeve was encircled by a purple-and-yellow band.

"Well, this is a surprise. I didn't know you were coming," Blodwen mumbled at last, gathering her wits. "I was watching from the hill. Are there only three of you?"

"Yes, and all three of us are overjoyed to be home!"

Home! The shock of that word made her head pound. It was all beginning again. Rhodri's ultimatum lay like curdled milk in her stomach, throbbing with every heartbeat. The Englishwoman's unexpected arrival was forcing her hand. Almost as if Rhodri had planned the event himself. Morgan would again forsake his duties to please Isobel, who in turn would be set up as lady of the manor. And where would that leave Blodwen?

Choose, Blodwen. Trust me.

She spun about, hearing his voice as plainly as if Rhodri rode at her elbow. He was not there. Only the three bedraggled travelers plodded after her along the track. Somehow Rhodri's will was inside her, which was far worse than if he had been riding at her side.

Dusk lay heavy around him, long, gray shadows swallowing trees and bushes. Morgan had just finished a rigorous day of drilling his men. There was much grumbling in the ranks, for they did not see any wisdom to this intense training. The archery butts were in constant use as archers honed their skill. Swordplay and mounted combat were also being heavily emphasized. Many began to wonder if their lord intended to take them to battle.

Pulling off his helm, Morgan let the evening breeze blow refreshingly cool through his hair, which was wet with sweat. Over months of wandering he had let his hair grow, until now it brushed his shoulders. Before the week was out he must get a helm cut, for it was the only way drilling would be comfortable. In a way he was sorry, for he had grown used to the thick, curly mass spilling about his shoulders.

Morgan plunged his head in the trough of water in the courtyard, sluicing the cold water over his hot face and neck, shuddering as it snaked icily inside his jack. Hoofbeats sounded outside the wall and he heard Blodwen's voice answering the challenge. The creaking of the winch told him they were lowering the bridge. Why did she not come through the postern?

To his surprise he saw that Blodwen brought three riders with her. Because of his knowledge about Blodwen's weakness, Morgan tensed, his hand going to the knives at his belt.

"Oh, my lord, my lord," one of the riders was shouting as he galloped toward him. To his amazement, Morgan recognized Alun, who had been left for dead on the Ludlow road.

He broke into a loping run and was at Alun's stirrup in a moment, his face wreathed in smiles. "Alun, the saints be praised. I thought you were crow bait months ago."

Alun laughed and swung from the saddle, wincing because of his recent injuries. "See who I've brought with me. Safe and sound."

Morgan glanced at the other riders. Blodwen sat hunched and sullen, not even greeting him when she rode inside the court. The other two looked like serving women. Yet that gray gelding was familiar—his heart lurched and bumped. Surely it couldn't be . . . ?

"Morgan! Is that you?" Isobel asked, peering through the gloom at the long-haired, broad-shouldered stranger beside Alun's horse. His hair fell in wet ringlets about his face and shoulders, while drops of water gleamed on his cheeks and trickled down his neck.

"Isobel! By all that's holy! What do you here? Oh, my love—what's happened to you?"

Morgan swept her from the saddle, cradling her in his arms and showering her with kisses.

Blodwen watched, and the sickening familiarity of it all filled her with dread. Inside she was screaming out to him, *Don't make me do this, Morgan!* If only he knew. But she could not tell him and betray Rhodri. Fate must take its course. And the more she considered that fate, the more she wondered if it were being manipulated by the ancient gods of Rhodri of the Mount.

Morgan's face grew gray when he heard about Lionel's attempted rape of Isobel. When he saw Isobel's bruises, his anger mounted, until he longed to feel his fingers around Lionel's throat. Though she begged him not to act on his anger, Morgan refused to make any promises.

Isobel stretched on the soft bed amid the lambswool blankets and sighed with contentment. Her whole body felt as if it had been racked after the long ride following on the heels of Lionel's abuse. Though she tried to downplay her injuries, at times she could not help wincing when Morgan touched her.

"Promise you won't try to avenge me, Morgan. Let it go, sweet," she pleaded, leaning against his hard shoulder, feeling so bone weary she could hardly keep her eyes open.

"Are you afraid I'll kill him?"

She looked away. She wanted to say, "No, I'm afraid he'll kill you," but thought that would bruise his ego. "Lionel's vowed to kill you on sight. Don't give him the chance. We're together now. Isn't that all that matters?"

she soothed, stroking his mane of glossy hair and smiling at his altered appearance.

"Eat something, then rest until you feel stronger," was all Morgan said, as he gently laid her back against the mounded pillows. "There's some unfinished business I have to attend to."

Isobel caught his hand and kissed his fingers. "Will you be back soon?"

Morgan smiled and stroked her face. "Yes, soon."

She stretched out blissfully on the feather mattress. These past days had been a nightmare and, as a nightmare fades in the morning light, so they were slipping away now that she was with Morgan again. She sipped a warm milk drink guaranteed to cure her pains. Emptying the cup, she put it on the chest beside the bed and sighed, feeling warm and relaxed. Her eyelids were so heavy. After a few minutes she stopped fighting the drowsy feeling and let it carry her away.

Morgan soon found out all he wanted to know from Alun, who was only too pleased to relay all he knew about Lord Hurley's sins. He even enlightened Morgan about how he had been tricked at Shrewsbury. Hurley had bribed one of Martyn of Merioneth's soldiers to relay the false message, thereby luring them to the Ludlow road and into his ambush. Morgan felt responsible for Mali's pitiful state. Had she stayed safe in her village she would still be a functioning human being instead of this whimpering shell.

What made him even angrier was how close Isobel had come to becoming Hurley's victim also. She, too, could have been reduced to hopeless despair. The sight of Hurley's fingerprints imprinted on her flesh incensed him. *Damn Lionel Hurley to hell!* He would not get away with this! Lionel's threat to kill him on sight didn't matter, for he would have to be fast to accomplish that feat.

Within minutes Morgan had made up his mind.

Whether Isobel wished it or not, he was going to make Hurley pay for all he had done. If he left tonight he could take him by surprise while he lolled at Ambrey considering himself safe. Likely his men still caroused and lay around bloated and useless. They would strike quickly and stealthily, for Ambrey was not fortified. Whoever rode up to the door with sufficient force could become its conqueror.

One last time he questioned Huw at the keep, making sure his spies continued to report no further sign of hostilities. Apparently Rhodri's quest for power was temporarily over. Assuring his master Blodwen would be watched, Huw urged Morgan to make haste before his woman woke and put an end to his adventuring.

They laughed together about that probability, slapping each other on the shoulder, for Huw had been married many years and knew the persuasive ways of women. He also knew that Morgan's blood ran hot and that he could not live with himself if he did not avenge this crime.

Taking with him a small, handpicked force, Morgan was already riding over the drawbridge as the nearby parish clock struck midnight.

Blissfully unaware of his actions, Isobel slumbered on.

Bright sunlight flooded the room, shining over her face. Isobel blinked, surprised to find that Morgan's side of the bed had not been slept in. Where was he? She had not intended to sleep all night. That drink must have put her into a deep sleep. Uneasily she wondered if that had been Morgan's intention. Disappointment washed over her, for she had wanted to make love to him.

A rap sounded on the door and Isobel sat up.

"Come in," she called.

Instead of a maid, Blodwen herself strode into the room carrying a tray.

"Oh, Blodwen, how thoughtful of you," she said carefully, determined not to give his sister any cause for anger. "Is it late?"

"Aye, the morning's half gone."

Blodwen set the tray down on the bedside chest.

"Where's Morgan?"

"He's your man. Can't you keep track of him?" Blodwen snapped, glancing at the smooth side of the bed. She longed to tell Isobel he had spent the night with another woman; indeed, the lie was on the tip of her tongue, before she thought better of it.

Isobel picked at a slice of honey-covered bread and sipped from the cup of mead. "Where is he?" she persisted, sensing something hidden beneath Blodwen's hostility.

"I thought you'd tell me."

"He must be riding."

"All night? No one's seen him since last evening."

Isobel gasped in alarm as unease spread through her body. "Is his horse in the stable?"

"No . . . it's gone and so are a handful of his men. But no one will tell me a thing. Huw finally said you'd know. Do you?"

With a sinking feeling in the pit of her stomach, Isobel nodded. "He's gone to Ambrey to kill Lionel."

Blodwen drew in her breath. "Ambrey. Where's that?" she asked as she perched on the edge of the bed and helped herself to Isobel's breakfast.

"That's my manor in England. Blodwen, there's much you probably don't know. It's up to me to tell you." And reluctantly Isobel told her the whole story.

When she had finished, Blodwen jumped up and marched to the window. "Damn," she said, staring out over the countryside. "I wish he'd told me first. How long will he be gone?"

"I don't know," Isobel whispered tearfully. "There's always the chance we're wrong. He could have just gone to the nearby village."

"No. He took unmarried volunteers with him. That alone tells me he's on a dangerous journey. You know, it's all your fault. Before you came, we were happy. My brother was content to rule his land. He was even sorry when he had to go far afield to tournaments, but he always hurried back. He was a good lord to his people then."

"He's still a good lord. And how can you blame me for this? You know as well as I do that I couldn't have changed his mind. I never asked to come to Wales in the first place. It's only by a miracle that I fell in love with Morgan, for at first I thought I hated him. When you fall in love with someone, Blodwen, you'll understand what I mean."

Blodwen turned away, her back stiff and unrelenting. Oh, she understood, all right. Torn between pain and anger, she said nothing.

"I'm not asking you to love me, Blodwen. But we don't have to be enemies."

Blodwen turned to face her, pale eyes bleak as a winter sky. "We can never be anything else." Without another word, she marched from the room.

Isobel was left feeling shaken and afraid. Was it going to be like last time, when Blodwen turned everyone against her? Though she had only just arrived, she knew she could not endure weeks of that miserable treatment.

She got out of bed and went to the window. It was a rare sunny day with clouds scudding across the sky. A brisk wind stirred the trees, and she was surprised to see the branches bare. Autumn had already slipped into winter in these mountains. At Ambrey the weather was gentler, and she had so been looking forward to the approaching Christmas season. Her dream had been to share the festivities with Morgan and have him help oversee the Christmas court. Once again, unless Lionel had held a lord's court for her, Ambrey's tenants had gone another quarter without having their grievances addressed. Michaelmas had come and gone while she was on the road.

However, if Morgan had ousted Lionel from Ambrey, they could spend Christmas together there. The only flaw with that plan was that Morgan would already be on his way home to Llyswen . . . unless she met him on the road to Ambrey!

The startling idea made her heart leap in excitement. Alun had probably not gone with Morgan this time because of his injuries. She could ask him to guide her back to Ambrey. Of course, he would think her completely addled for wanting to return when she had been away only a week.

Twice Isobel talked herself out of the daring plan. Then, filled with determination, she dressed and went down to the hall, where she found Blodwen mending a piece of saddlery. At her approach, Morgan's sister glanced up and her face hardened.

"What do you want?"

"I came to tell you that you won't be inconvenienced by my presence, Lady Blodwen. I'm going back to Ambrey to join my husband. Likely we'll spend Christmas there." With that, Isobel turned on her heel.

Alun indeed wondered at her when he finally understood her request. But he was always ready for adventure and he had felt slighted when he was not picked to accompany his lord on this latest mission. He readily agreed to her proposal.

The following day, taking a loaded sumpter and two attendants, Isobel clattered over Llyswen's drawbridge and out into the bleak countryside. The north wind was cold and she pulled her fur-lined cloak high about her chin as they rode into the teeth of the wind.

Once she looked back, wondering if Blodwen watched her departure, but she saw no one. Leaving Llyswen had been so simple, it seemed unreal. Isobel half expected to wake in bed to find it was only a dream. But it was real, for Alun rode beside her, his cloak pulled tight, huddled against the elements. And the grains of sleet stinging her cheeks were real, too. For better or worse she was going to Ambrey; Isobel fervently prayed it would be for better.

Morgan and his men had ridden hard, and they'd made good time. His anger was still burning strong now as they reached Ambrey. Reining in on high ground, he looked down on the manor, reminded of the day Isobel had brought him here. When he had first seen her beloved manor, he had been amazed to find it was so orderly and placid, as different from Llyswen's rugged countryside as day and night. Now he felt a growing affinity for this manor because he knew how much Isobel loved it. It was her birthright and no one had the right to take it from her. Restoring Ambrey, however, was not what had sent him galloping, hell-bent for vengeance. Today Lionel Hurley would pay for trying to take by force that which Isobel gave readily to her lover. This time he would show the villain no mercy. Lord Hurley would forfeit his life!

With his mouth set in a determined line, Morgan signaled to his men that the manor was where they were headed. He would enter by the back road. At Ambrey there was no drawbridge to negotiate, no sentries either, from the look of it. The place was deserted.

They checked their weapons and adjusted the straps on their helmets. Then they were off, careening downhill, spreading out across the meadow. Below them the house slumbered placidly in the early morning light. Smoke curled from a chimney. Apart from that, the manor might have been uninhabited.

Around the farmyard they rode, spilling out of the meadow into the broad drive, headed for the gate leading into the courtyard. The gate stood open. They rode unchallenged into the heart of the manor house. Puzzled, Morgan reined in, wondering why none of Lionel's men had come out to offer resistance.

In the courtyard the Welsh horsemen milled about,

wondering what to do now. Several doors were padlocked. Finally, after pounding on the main door and rattling the ring on the small door cut into it, they heard the shuffle of approaching steps. A suspicious face peered through the hatch, the man's hair askew and his eyes bleary.

"What do you want with us?" the old servant asked.

"An audience with Lord Hurley. Tell him to come out to face me like a man instead of skulking inside like a coward."

Morgan had raised his voice, and the mocking challenge rang out, echoing back from the tall walls enclosing the court. His men glanced at one another, surprised when the challenge went unmet.

"Lord Hurley's gone to London to see the king," the old man explained. "Who be you?"

"Lady Isobel's husband."

"Ah." The old man nodded in understanding, then he quickly withdrew his head and shuffled away.

They waited, wondering what to do now. Morgan could not believe his misfortune at having missed his quarry. Of course, Hurley could be pretending not to be here to save his hide. Yet he doubted that, for in truth the place looked deserted. Though now, as he glanced about, he saw fleeting movement at the windows and could hear scurrying steps behind the door. Finally the door was opened, and the man he remembered as Isobel's steward stepped out to greet him.

Having hastily dressed, Moffat bowed formally and said, "Welcome to Ambrey, my lord. Will the Lady Isobel be joining you?"

"No. She's still in Wales. I came for Lord Hurley. How long since he left? Is there a chance I can catch him?"

"No. He's had several days' start. He left as soon as he was well enough to travel."

"Well enough . . . is he ill?"

Moffat tried to hide a smile, looking down at the cobbles.

"Not exactly ill, my lord; injured would be more accurate."

Morgan chuckled as he recalled Isobel's adventure with the warming pan. "Not injured enough, if you ask me," he said at last.

"Nay, nor me either. Will you come inside and sup, my lord?"

"Thank you, Moffat, a meal will be most welcome."

Sleet changed to light snow. The howling wind had followed Isobel all the way to the Welsh border and beyond, as if intentionally speeding her on her way. It was dawn of the following day when they finally arrived at Ambrey, chilled to the bone.

Isobel grew uneasy when she saw a number of horses in the stable. Surely Lionel could not still be here. There were no guards, but then Lionel was often lax about posting lookouts. What had happened to Morgan?

Yesterday evening she had taken shelter at an icy parish church and prayed for his safety, lighting a candle for that intention. The tiny flickering light in the gloomy church had given her hope. It was with renewed strength that she had walked out into the December day to begin this last leg of her journey.

Now she was here, and her heart was bumping unevenly as she dismounted in the stable yard. Then, to her relief, she spotted several familiar faces as men ran outside after recognizing Alun, greeting him heartily in their own tongue. These horses were Morgan's. Her prayers had been answered.

Ambrey's household staff were delighted to see her. Moffat, surprised by her unexpected arrival, wisely did not question her. Isobel was told Lord Morgan was still sleeping. She was not surprised by that news, for he had probably ridden through one night without sleeping.

She was relieved to learn that Lionel had already left

before Morgan arrived—though her relief changed to anger when she discovered that Lionel had stripped many of Ambrey's riches in a final bid for the king's acceptance. He had transported his loot to court by the wagonload. Anxious to impress the royal household with his own retinue, he had also taken some of her servants. How typical! Well, she wished him joy of them. No love was lost between Ambrey's servants and their erstwhile master. He would virtually have to beat them into serving him.

Only a skeleton staff remained. Wisely Isobel decided to leave her inventory of what Lionel had stolen from her for another day. She had the maids prepare her bath. Smiling as she contemplated what she intended to do, she began to tremble with anticipation. Though she wanted to luxuriate in the warm, scented water, Isobel did not want to waste time. If Morgan woke too soon, everything would be spoiled.

From her clothes chest Isobel took a fur-lined wine velvet bedrobe, quilted around the skirt in gold. When she moved, the scent of roses wafted from her glowing skin. The bed gown's soft fur lining made her shiver with pleasure as it brushed her body, whisper soft, silky smooth, its touch reminding her of his loving caress, the memory making her throb in anticipation.

Binding her hair with a ribbon, Isobel put on velvet slippers and walked out of her room. She had already asked which chamber Lord Morgan had chosen. Everything was ready.

Her heart thudded as she hurried along the chill corridor to what was known as the gold room because of the color of its furnishings. Runnels of ice had collected on the nearby gables, and a freezing wind blew through the row of unglazed windows as she hurried past. These windows overlooked the garden, and she could see some flowers in the border, and though sparse, there were still leaves on the trees. Beyond the manor grounds the ice-rimed fields lay cold, stark and bare. But inside she felt warm, and in a few minutes that warmth would be ignited into a blaze strong enough to warm the coldest day.

She saw that Morgan had posted a guard outside his door. Recognizing her, the man touched his forelock and stepped aside, assuming Lord Morgan was expecting her. Isobel lifted the latch and let herself into the room, making sure to close the door behind her and shoot the bolt. She didn't want any overanxious sentry disturbing them.

Tiptoeing to the bed, she virtually held her breath, not wanting to wake him. Ever alert to attack, Morgan usually slept lightly.

Isobel stood beside the bed, accustoming herself to the gloom, for the shutters were closed and the winter sun provided little light. Morgan lay on his back, his arm flung outside the covers. Though she had seen him recently, it was as if they had been apart for years. Her breath tangled in her chest and she swallowed nervously as she gazed at his beauty, recalling the first time she had admitted to herself that she loved him. His curly black hair made a dark pool on the pillow, glossy as an animal's pelt, the longer length softening his features and making him appear younger. His stern profile was not changed, however, nor his firm, sensual mouth, softly relaxed in sleep. A muscular forearm crumpled the velvet covers, his olive skin dark against the gold. The breadth of his shoulders made a discernible shadow against the linen pillows, deep scars puckering his skin, as a stark reminder of his profession. It was a reminder she did not welcome.

Turning away, Isobel took candles and lit them at the hearth, before placing them on the bedside chest. Now she could see him more clearly, though she was afraid the bright light would wake him. Morgan did stir, flinging his arm out and turning away from her.

Carefully, trying not to creak the bed, or dip the mattress, Isobel inched across the velvet cover. She had already discarded her bedrobe and she steeled herself not to shiver as the room's chill atmosphere surrounded her body like an unwelcome blanket. Isobel's heart pounded with excitement as she knelt astride him. Disturbed by the pressure, Morgan stirred again. Isobel leaned over him, letting her full breasts brush his face, willing him to open his eyes.

Slowly his thick fringe of black lashes fluttered, widened, and then she was looking into the winter blue softness she loved, that iridescent, luminous beauty, dark rimmed about the iris. Morgan blinked again in surprise and started to sit up, hardly able to believe what arousing treasures hung so invitingly within his reach.

"Good morning, my darling," Isobel breathed huskily. And she kissed him.

Awake now and thrilled beyond measure, he fondled her breasts, rejoicing in the pulsing throb of her flesh, smooth, full and terribly arousing. Morgan clasped Isobel in his arms, his hot mouth answering hers. Then he rolled her to her side, struggling to bring her against him inside the covers.

"Dear God, Isobel, 'tis the best awakening I've ever had," he breathed, covering her with kisses.

"Oh, Morgan, sweetheart, how much I've missed you."

Hot and trembling against her, he gripped her shoulders, holding her close, trying to decide by what miracle she was here. Morgan began to question her, but she would not let him speak, as she covered his mouth with her own. Their mouths opened, and as their questing tongues sought each other, he quickly lost interest in questions, finding his passion close to boiling.

Hungrily their mouths seared together in a deep, burning kiss. Isobel melted into his strength, softly yielding against his muscular body, feeling safe and loved in his arms. This was where she belonged. The ache of mounting passion became a physical pain as she unconsciously strained against him in primitive demand. The sweet fragrance of his mouth intoxicated her; the throb of his blood enslaved her.

"Oh, Morgan, love me, love me," she urged, sliding her hands over the hard, pulsing muscle and sinew that held her captive. Morgan's pounding heart echoed a throbbing drumbeat in her ear as he cradled her head against his chest.

Her nipples were hard and she purposely pressed them against his bare flesh, excited by the rasp of his crinkly black hair. Slipping her hand between them, she fingered his dark nipples, gently at first, then gradually increasing the pressure until he groaned with pleasure.

Against her thighs his steel-hard manhood burned and throbbed, clamoring for recognition. She fondled him, sliding her fingers slowly along the length and breadth of his flesh and encircling the throbbing tip. Tingling in every part of her body, Isobel leaned down to gently caress him with her tongue, slowly teasing his moist flesh until Morgan begged her to stop.

His strong hands moved along her spine, the fiery caress sliding over her hips until he finally encircled the firm lobes of her buttocks. Gently Morgan caressed her soft inner thigh. His tongue mimicked the caress and he moved higher, until she cried out in delight as he set fire to that throbbing ache between her legs. Gradually the passage of his tongue moved higher, up over her belly, until he finally reached her tingling breasts, where he encircled her nipples, the sensitive tips eager for his mouth.

At last, unable to endure the torment any longer, Isobel grasped his head; sinking her fingers into his luxuriant hair, she brought his face up to hers, her mouth searing his. Her hips strained to him, demanding release as she wordlessly begged him to end the torment.

Quickly Isobel positioned herself beneath him, and Morgan moved to cover her with his hard body. Poised above her, one final time he laved her swollen nipples with his hot tongue, making her sob with longing, desperate to feel the hot, hard thrust of his body deep inside her. She longed to release her pent-up desire in that most intimate of caresses. Opening her thighs wide, she lifted her hips in invitation, seeking him. She rejoiced as he suddenly filled her with heat, sliding home to the very core of her being.

Morgan moved inside her, making Isobel cry out in pleasure. She grasped his slim hips, trying to bring their bodies even closer. Though she wanted to prolong this ecstasy, the more he moved, the less able she was to hold out. At the last Morgan drove to the hilt, his thrusts becoming harder, more insistent, until she finally spiraled out of control.

Over and over, Isobel whispered in a litany of passion, ''Morgan, Morgan, I love you, I love you,'' until he smothered her cries with the heat of his mouth.

They came together in a long, shuddering climax, soothing all the want and longing born of separation. The loneliness, the grief, was forgotten. They were together at last, their mutual passion grandly consummated in this firelit room, where the winter wind stirred ice-frosted bushes beyond the window, and the cold December sun crept slowly across the land.

Chapter Fifteen

The frosty solitude of the winter day was broken by a bell tolling in some distant parish, the sound blown to them on the wind. The bell kept tolling. Aware that it marked a soul's passing, several among their party crossed themselves, freshly reminded of their own mortality.

The wind moaned in the trees, and soft flurries of snow blew down from the branches as they rode beneath. Here, at the fringe of the wood, the snow lay crisply undisturbed except for crisscrossing tracks of hare and fox.

These past weeks had been some of the happiest Isobel could remember. Morgan had chosen not to go home to Wales, neither had he left her to compete in a tourney, though the big Christmas events were just around the corner. She had him here, all to herself.

She had asked him not to compete in the Christmas tourneys this year, so that just once they could keep this special holytide together at her manor. This might be the only Christmas they would have at Ambrey, and she wanted at least one wonderful memory to cherish.

Today they had gone out to the woods to gather evergreens to decorate the manor house for the approaching season. Heaps of fresh-cut holly glistening with frost and bright with crimson berries, twining tendrils of ivy, and boughs of bay and evergreens all put out a pungent scent. Several large fir branches, asparkle with frost and splotched with snow, were being loaded on top of the heaped farm cart.

"Do you think this is enough?" Morgan shouted, riding around the cart and sending up a shower of powdery snow as his horse skidded to a halt.

Laughing, Isobel nodded. "More than enough—likely we can decorate all England with this."

He grinned at her before he wheeled about to continue his task.

She sat astride Spartan, watching as he directed the operation. At her request, Morgan had not cut his hair; a tangle of curls reached almost to his shoulders. There had been no need for a helm cut, as he was not competing. Today, beneath his feathered green hat, the shining mass of black hair looked quite dashing.

During these past weeks they had thoroughly inspected her lands and addressed many of her people's grievances. From a nearby market Morgan had brought back two fine falcons, and a pair of leggy black hounds to restock her kennel. He also sent for the rat catcher, with his ferret and terrier, to rid the granary and storehouses of vermin. Meat had been salted down for the winter, and fruits and vegetables were put by in the cold cellars. As a safeguard against a long winter, Morgan had purchased extra ale and grain, though those supplies had yet to arrive.

Together they had also inventoried Ambrey's losses as Isobel angrily determined just how much Lionel had stolen from her in his final effort to impress the king. Wall hangings, serving pieces, even candlesticks had been spirited away to mollify Edward's wrath.

There had also been time for play. They had ridden

races across the frosty meadows, flown the falcons and taught the pups basic commands. Morgan had also shown her how to improve her skill with her small hunting bow and taught her to play her favorite Welsh ballad on the lute.

And they made love. Isobel sighed with pleasure as she recalled all those wonderful, heated nights—and days, too, she must admit. Those times when no duty pressed and the fire was warm, when the soft lambence of arousing passion shone in his eyes and his voice grew husky with invitation—if only she could keep this season fresh forever. But she knew that was impossible, so she enjoyed each day as it came and was thankful.

Isobel watched Morgan galloping to the head of the party, his cloak blowing behind him like a sail. And her heart swelled with pride. He was authoritative with her servants, though today it was his own men he was directing as they dragged home a huge log for the yule hearth, using ropes and carthorses from a nearby farm. Morgan had quickly assumed his rightful position as lord here, and she marveled at his skill in dealing with the peasants, who tended to try to wheedle their way around their lady, but had never even attempted such tactics with this hardened knight.

The sweet, melodious song of a robin sounded from a nearby branch. Then the bird's song was abruptly halted as the two black hunting dogs bounded up, tongues lolling. A moment later they took off again, hard on the scent of a fox, noses glued to the snow.

When they were ready to head for home, the party set off, toiling back to the manor. Morgan took an elder whistle from his doublet and blew two long, shrill blasts to call the dogs. They came, falling and slithering through the brush, sending up cascading showers of snow as they raced to join their master.

Mist had collected in the hollows, and as she surveyed the countryside, a shiver passed over Isobel, for it seemed suddenly so bleak and dead. From this vantage point she usually saw peasants toiling in the villages, carrying wood, or leading livestock. After a snowfall children would normally be pelting each other with snowballs. She could not even see smoke coming from the chimneys, though on this cold and snowy day, the fires should be burning. Today everything was unnaturally quiet. No, not wholly quiet, for there was another tolling bell. It was not the same one she had heard earlier, for the wind had shifted to the west and now she could hear two separate bells tolling in succession. More deaths. This harsh winter was already taking its toll, and they were still in Advent.

It was pleasantly warm and welcoming inside the manor house. Isobel felt quite relieved to be safely indoors, away from the land that had suddenly turned lonely and inhospitable.

In the doorway Morgan paused and smiled down at her, drawing her close. Isobel's pulse quickened as she felt the warmth radiating from his body, reminding her of the pleasure of his embrace. He captured her face in his hands, his thumbs grazing her cheeks as he gazed down at her. He was not smiling now and his blue eyes were dark with emotion.

"You're the most precious thing I've ever known," he whispered, holding her slightly away from him. "You're all my life to me."

"Oh, Morgan, I love you so," she whispered, leaning against him. His doublet smelled of pine needles and was damp with melted snow, the fabric icy against her face. When she raised her head to receive his kiss, his lips felt chilled, but the warmth of his kiss, fueled by passion forever smoldering beneath the surface, quickly burned away the winter's cold.

"Come, sweet, let's go inside. There's much to do before dark."

She nodded agreement and tucked her arm companionably through his as they walked together into the manor's great hall. The servants were already struggling indoors with the morning's bounty. Two little maids giggled as they sorted through the branches for a mistletoe bough. There were none. When Isobel had pointed out some mistletoe to Morgan, suggesting they cut it for their kissing bough, his face had stiffened. Apparently mistletoe had a far more sinister reputation in his part of the world, being ever present in pagan ceremonies. Having mistletoe indoors made him uncomfortable. Isobel realized she had much to learn about the customs of his people. Sometimes their ways made her uneasy, for they smacked of some dark belief from long ago, its power undiminished by the Church.

They supped lightly while the decorating went on around them. Red bows and strings of silver bells were brought out of storage and were soon strung merrily around pine boughs and swags of bay and holly. Garlands of evergreen boughs all twined about with ivy and ribbons festooned the walls and topped doorways and mantels.

Isobel clapped her hands in delight as she looked around at the paneled hall, admiring its newly festive appearance. Special red cloths would be used on the tables, their gold fringes sweeping to the rushes, laid fresh for the holiday and sweetened with lavender and rosemary. As a special reward for the servants' splendid efforts today, she had ordered an extra ration of mead and ale to be served.

The short winter day was rapidly drawing to a close. Isobel still fancied she could hear tolling bells, yet it seemed too early for vespers and there would be no peasants to call in from the fields on this snowy day. She shivered as a strange feeling of foreboding passed over her. Across the meadows silver wisps of winter sunset brightened the clouds, and a faint gold haze settled over the distant hillside as day faded into night.

Unexpected movement from the road behind the hawthorne hedges caught her attention. Could this be their shipment of grain arriving so late in the day? As the shapes drew closer she could see two wagons, but there were far too many outriders for a grain shipment.

Isobel sped across the fresh rushes, finding them thick and uneven underfoot. She must tell Morgan about their visitors. He was perched on a ladder putting up a kissing bough, without mistletoe, but gay with holly and multi-colored ribbons that fluttered in the drafts from the windows.

"Morgan. There are riders coming up the drive."

Her news instantly wiped the smile from his face. Morgan descended quickly and strode to the nearest window to see for himself. He blinked and rubbed his eyes, for the most amazing sight met him, and he was afraid he was imagining it. Coming toward the archway was a magnificently dressed cleric in rich vestments, a bishop's mitre on his head. A handful of less important churchmen rode with him, all finely garbed, their fur-lined cloaks barely concealing their vestments, where gold and silver thread glinted in the fading light. It was as if they had turned from the altar during High Mass and mounted their horses. Behind them were a dozen servants and lesser officials, protecting two wagons loaded high with bags and boxes, barely covered with sheets of oiled canvas to keep out the wet.

"Dear Lord in heaven, why are we so blessed? Come, look, Isobel, can you believe it?"

She peered through the window in the gathering dusk, amazed to see a vested bishop being assisted from his horse. Flustered to be receiving such illustrious visitors, she sped to find Moffat and tell him to send servants to greet these important arrivals.

Astounded by this unexpected honor, Isobel was instantly aware of her smudged cheeks and resin-sticky fingers. Fir needles clung to her mulberry wool gown, caught in the fabric's threads. Hastily she pushed her wayward hair under a padded headdress. There was no time to change, for she already heard many feet thumping along the corridor. The door burst open and Moffat walked inside the hall, holding his staff of office, which he pounded on the floor for attention. Bowing, he introduced their guests.

"My lady Isobel, my lord Morgan, His Excellency, the Bishop of Carberry and his retinue," he announced importantly, drawing himself to his full height.

Isobel hurried forward with Morgan a half pace behind her.

"Welcome to Ambrey, Your Excellency," she said, awed by the bishop's magnificent presence. His gold mitre winked and glittered in the light from the sconces. She saw that his cope was of gold-embroidered brocade and scarlet velvet, and an ermine cape added dignity to his rotund figure.

Sinking to her knees in the rushes, she was aware of Morgan kneeling at her side. He lowered his head, ready to receive the bishop's blessing. When the blessing had been given, he stood and bowed formally to their guest.

"Welcome to Ambrey, Your Excellency. To what do we owe this honor?"

Though he spoke carefully, at first his Welsh accent defeated the balding bishop, who puzzled a moment before finally grasping what had been said.

"We're traveling from a distance, my lord, and were caught unaware by the early dark. There was nowhere close at hand to put up for the night, so we beg your indulgence. It would be our pleasure if we could spend this night with you. We'll be on our way in the morning."

Isobel thought it highly unusual that the bishop himself should request lodging. Generally those arrangements were made on his behalf by his chaplain or servants. The half dozen churchmen who accompanied him stepped up to the blazing hearth, shivering in pleasure at its welcome heat.

" 'Tis an unusually large party to be caught out so late

in the day, Bishop,'' Morgan said conversationally.

Isobel winced. She overheard him as she was ordering the servants to bring mulled wine to warm their guests. To her surprise, however, the great man merely smiled indulgently as he stretched his hands to the blaze, taking no offense at Morgan's informal address.

''To be sure,'' he agreed. ''We're on our way to say Christmas masses at . . . er . . . Hereford Cathedral,'' he finished, hesitating over the place. ''Some of my fellow servants of God are bound for Bristol. We're traveling together because larger numbers spell safety. We've treasure with us,'' he added in an undertone, as if he expected thieves to be listening behind the tapestries.

Morgan found the explanation strange, for surely Hereford had clergy enough of its own. ''Have you traveled much distance?'' he asked as the servants bustled inside the room carrying trays of ale and wine.

''Oh, yes, quite a distance. From the north. We'll pay handsomely for our board, my lord. We don't want to impose on you without any reward.''

''I thank you for your consideration,'' Morgan said with a slow smile as he passed the cups forward to be heated at the hearth. The sizzle of the hot pokers in the mulled wine cheered the travelers.

Isobel sped to the kitchens, desperately searching her mind for what she could provide that would be suitable for the bishop and his retinue. Though by ordinary standards Ambrey was well stocked, she was sure a bishop would be used to finer fare than she could provide at such short notice. There were spiced capons and jellied sturgeon, a brace of pheasants, jugged hares, a tureen of oxtail soup, fruit flummeries . . . her head spun as she mentally listed what she could serve. She made sure the cooks understood what a distinguished party they were hosting.

After making the kitchen arrangements, Isobel hurried to her chamber, where, with her maid's help, she dressed more appropriately. When she reentered the hall she wore cobalt blue velvet iced with silver brocade and topped by a short surcoat of lemon silk. On her head was a simple gold circlet anchoring a lemon gauze veil. Isobel was also wearing King Edward's emeralds. Though the color of the gems did not complement her dress, she felt such magnificence was well suited to the occasion.

Morgan's brows rose slightly in surprise when he saw her sweep grandly into the hall. Several of the bishop's party were already snoring, stretched out on the settles close to the hearth. The florid bishop had removed his mitre and unfastened his ermine-trimmed cope, and now he lolled at a nearby trestle playing chess with his host.

Isobel was still nervous as she curtsied before the churchman, informing him that a meal was being prepared for his party. The bishop smiled at her appreciatively, thoroughly appraising her beauty. Isobel thought that his eyes seemed somewhat clouded and distant. Likely he had already drunk too much mulled wine, she thought in alarm. The pale young cleric who served as the bishop's personal assistant asked if he might have a cup of cold ale, finding the mulled drinks too warm for his taste.

Isobel noticed the man was sweating and his eyes were bloodshot. He also coughed, though he turned away from her to splutter into a lace-edged kerchief. The soothing cup of ale was brought and he retreated to the far side of the hearth.

"There's been much sickness in the cities. That's why we are going to Hereford to replace indisposed clergy," the bishop explained smoothly in answer to his host's question. "This wet, bleak summer was a punishment from heaven. People aren't strong enough to face winter. The churchyards will be overflowing come spring, you mark my words."

After what seemed an embarrassingly long time, Isobel was told the meal was ready. The half dozen snoozing travelers were awakened; some time ago their servants had gone down to the kitchens to eat, their wants being served far quicker than those of their masters.

Isobel thought it was fortunate that the bishop's party had not arrived yesterday. The newly decorated hall looked magnificent. Fir and holly boughs decked with festive red ribbons and tinkling bells hid the imperfections in the woodwork. Ambrey's modest hall was warm and inviting. To add to the opulent mood they were using the red festival table covers and their best serving pieces.

When they were seated, the bishop said grace and then immediately began to eat. Isobel was pleasantly surprised by his lack of formality. Though by his girth she had already guessed he was a good trencherman who would not allow the food to go cold while he delivered a long, drawn-out prayer. In fact, had she not seen his vestments to remind her of his exalted status, she might have thought him an elderly neighbor dropping by uninvited to share a Christmas meal.

After munching his way through a heaped trencher of sauced capon, washed down with strong ale, the old bishop leaned on his elbow at the table and sighed in contentment. His sagging jowls were purple and mottled, revealing an intemperate life. His pudgy hands glinted with rings, his fingers so heavily encrusted with gold, rubies and emeralds, he could hardly bend them.

Despite his informal manner, Isobel still could not forget she was dining with a bishop. Morgan sat on his right, she on his left, with his entourage seated around them. One of Morgan's men played the harp and sang soft ballads while they ate. Isobel wished she could have provided grander entertainment for their guests, but she must be content with what they had.

When they had finished the first two courses, the bishop asked his assistant, Father Barnaby, to sing for them. His cough temporarily soothed, the young priest left his place at table to join Tomas, who was seated below the dais. Another member of the party brought a beribboned lute from their baggage wagon. The two young priests entertained them with songs of their own composition, reminiscent of ecclesiastical music, but still pleasing to the ear.

Finally Isobel began to relax. She knew if she could just forget that a bishop dined at her table, she would feel more at ease. Morgan still wore his green velvet doublet, his boots dark with moisture from the snow. Yet by his proud bearing he might have been wearing ermine and gold. He seemed not in the least in awe of their guest. In fact, as the night wore on and the wine flowed, Morgan told the bishop a ribald joke that made Isobel color and her unease deepen. To her amazement, far from being offended, the bishop laughed heartily and reciprocated with a bawdy joke of his own.

At last, stuffed until he could not eat another bite, the bishop leaned back in his chair and turned a leering smile on her. Isobel thought his expression most unholy. Her reaction went beyond surprise when the bishop began to stroke her cheek with a fat finger, slowly following its curve down to her neck, where he allowed his hand to rest.

"And you, Lady Isobel, I understand, are closely related to Lord Hurley. And you are also a dear friend of our king."

The latter was spoken with such a sly smile, Isobel quaked. The bishop must be familiar with the slanderous court gossip about her. She was thankful for the room's dim light, as her cheeks grew hot with embarrassment.

"Lionel's my stepbrother . . . we're not blood kin," she said stiffly, after clearing her throat.

"And are you and the Lord of Nels husband and wife?" the bishop asked next.

Again she swallowed, her face growing even hotter; she suspected he already knew they were still not united in the eyes of the church. How could a total stranger know all these things about her? Yet on second thought, she supposed Lionel's antics had been gossiped over and laughed about the length and breadth of the land.

Seeing her growing discomfort, Morgan answered instead.

"Lady Isobel and I are betrothed, though as yet we have not found a churchman to permanently unite us," he explained smoothly, a smile on his dark face and a challenge in his eye.

Not wanting to annoy his generous host, the bishop chose not to take up the gauntlet. "Search no more, my lord," said he, patting Isobel's shoulder, and then letting his hand slip so that it glanced off her breast.

She gasped in shock and moved away from the bishop. Tonight her faith in the Church was being sorely tested. Morgan grinned and winked at her, not nearly as discomfited as she by the revelation that the bishop was not as holy as she had expected.

"Are you volunteering to do the deed then, Bishop?" he asked, toying with the stem of his goblet.

"Most certainly. After all—it's the least I can do in payment for your hospitality."

"When do you suggest? My lady needs time to prepare."

"Tonight. Within the hour," the bishop concluded hastily, glancing toward his companions, who nodded their agreement.

"Get married within the hour! Nay, Your Excellency, it takes much preparation. I need more warning than this," Isobel protested in alarm. The entire subject made her uncomfortable, for she was sure the bishop already assumed she was the king's mistress as well as Morgan's.

"We must soon to bed, Lady Isobel, for we've a hard ride ahead of us tomorrow."

"Tomorrow is short notice enough."

"Out of the question. We must be on the road early in the morning. Come, my lady, what preparation does a beauty like you need? We've already eaten the wedding banquet, and I've brought you distinguished guests aplenty. We've music"—here he acknowledged Barnaby and the lute player, and he winked before adding suggestively, ''and the young groom looks well able to consummate his vows. Aye, beyond able, I'd say he's bursting to please.''

Isobel's eyes rounded in shock as the bishop burst into a gale of tipsy laughter. She looked at Morgan, who winked at her again and pushed back his chair.

''Whatever you say, Bishop. The chapel's at the back of the house.''

''Ah, so you've got a chapel. I'd thought we could perform the ceremony here before the fire. 'Tis very festive with the Christmas greenery.''

Morgan turned to Isobel, silently questioning.

''No, not here,'' she said quickly. ''In the chapel. But first I must change.''

''No.'' Morgan caught her arm and turned her about. She had jumped from her chair, flustered by the haste of these unexpected arrangements. ''You look lovely in that gown. Come, you silly goose, the bishop's going to make an honest woman of you.''

She smiled at him, but inside she felt less sure. A wedding was such a great event, coming only once in most women's lives. She had thought to have great banks of flowers, a new gown, attendants . . . not a tipsy bishop repaying a favor late of a winter night.

Father Barnaby began to sing a soft love song, his choice surprising because of its explicit words. The lute player accompanied him, and Morgan's harpist picked up the refrain. This lovely tribute brought her close to tears. Aware of Isobel's unexpected emotion, Morgan slid his arm comfortingly about her waist and hugged her against his side.

''Come, sweet,'' he whispered, ''how often do you have a bishop begging to perform your wedding ceremony?''

She had to agree it might never happen again. What was a new gown and flowers and guests? She had Morgan. There had been new gowns aplenty to go to court and none of them had ever made her happy.

When the song was over, Father Barnaby had a fit of coughing and Isobel sent one of the servants for a cool cup of ale to soothe him. This time the cooling drink did not make him better and he doubled over, spluttering, his sweating face scarlet.

Glancing from one to the other, the bishop abruptly stood and dismissed Father Barnaby. Isobel made arrangements for his care, ordering a posset to clear the congestion in his chest. When the sick man had left, they returned to the matter at hand. Their celebratory mood had subtly changed and she sensed new tension in the room as the churchmen glanced uneasily at each other. The bishop himself had lost a little of his high color.

Morgan took down a red-ribboned bunch of bay and holly from over the window and handed it to Isobel. "Here, sweet, this can be your bridal bouquet."

She breathed in the pungent fragrance of the evergreens, trying not to prick her fingers on the holly's spiky leaves.

"Yes, well, the sooner the better," muttered the bishop, quickly draining his goblet before he left the table.

"First I must make arrangements for the others," Isobel whispered to Morgan, beckoning to Moffat, with whom she hastily discussed the disposition of their guests, giving the bishop their best, most luxurious chamber. By putting several of their guests together in one room she was able to accommodate the large party.

At last, with the arrangements made, she could delay no longer. They were already man and wife in all but the eyes of the Church, for they had vowed to be soul mates for eternity.

She turned to Morgan and smiled at him. He looked darkly handsome in the firelight, and tears of happiness filled her eyes.

"Ready?" The warm clasp of his hand stirred her from

her thoughts, reminding her that time ticked away. With bleary eyes and stifled yawns, the bishop's attendants formed a solemn procession.

Placing his mitre on his balding head and refastening his cope, the bishop and his clergy solemnly processed toward the chapel.

The interior of the stone-floored chapel was icy. Isobel envied the bishop his ermine garment as she stood shivering in the darkness. Candles were lit, the two youngest clerics serving as acolytes. Then, leading the wedding party, the two young men advanced toward the altar. The chapel reeked of incense, metal polish and unwashed clothing. The churchmen must have ridden long and hard before reaching Ambrey, Isobel thought, wrinkling her nose.

Flickering candles illuminated the small altar. With Father Barnaby too ill to sing for them, and deeming his own men unsuited to a religious ceremony, Morgan chose to forgo music on his wedding night.

Bride and groom advanced to the steps, where they knelt before the altar. Isobel pulled her veil over her face in the manner of brides. The evergreen bouquet in her hands was a constant reminder of the approaching Christmas season. Absurdly she found herself close to laughter. The improbability of entertaining a bishop who would then preside over her wedding ceremony seemed more like the stuff of a confusing dream.

Reverting to a more holy demeanor before the altar, the bishop began the ceremony, the tipsy slurring gone from his voice. He dispensed with all but the most basic prayers of the nuptial mass, quickly moving to the wedding vows to which bride and groom made their required responses. Morgan took a ring from his own finger and placed it on Isobel's hand, where it hung large and heavy.

''Now you're man and wife,'' said the bishop, wiping his sweating brow with a pudgy hand.

Still moving as if in a dream, Isobel got to her feet.

Morgan put his arm around her shoulders with a reassuring squeeze. She thought he too was close to laughter as the bishop stumbled on the steps and hastily grabbed the altar rail, swaying there a moment before he recovered, his face red and bemused.

"Ah, it is well past time for bed," he remarked finally, holding up his head and rearranging his tilting mitre before he slowly led the procession back up the aisle, leaving bride and groom standing forgotten at the altar rail.

But the heavy warmth of Morgan's embrace, the tenderness of his mouth as he gently kissed her brow, made her feel far from abandoned. Trancelike, Isobel walked beside him, following the bishop's party from the chapel.

A few minutes later, when their guests had gone to their assigned chambers and herb possets had been provided for their impending hangovers, all that remained was for the bride and groom to go to bed.

On the way to their room Isobel began to giggle as she reviewed this whole amazing evening and fully appreciated the absurdity of it. When they were safely inside their chamber, they both began to laugh, until Isobel found tears trickling down her cheeks.

"This has been the most ridiculous night," Morgan gasped. "Having a tipsy—and I might add, randy—bishop marrying us in the middle of the night, galloping through the ceremony as if his life depended on it."

"You could have refused if you didn't want to wed me," she pointed out.

"Oh, no, sweet, I wouldn't have missed such a unique ceremony for the world. And I've wanted to marry you since first I laid eyes on you."

Isobel sighed as she said, a little wistfully, "I'd always thought our wedding would take place in Wales."

She took off her headdress and laid it on the chest.

"We can have one there too. There aren't any rules about how many ceremonies one may have."

She smiled and leaned against him. "I'd like that."

Morgan traced his mouth over her exposed neck, his breath warmly tantalizing on her skin. "You're my sweet wife at last in the eyes of the church, though in my eyes you've been that these many months."

She smiled as she slid her hand inside his doublet, feeling the warm, comforting beat of his heart. "Come, sweet, do you plan just to talk on our wedding night?"

"No." He grinned, pulling loose her thick black hair so that it tumbled about her shoulders. "I've other, much grander plans."

Isobel shivered as his mouth moved across her smooth shoulders, coming to rest beside the glittering emerald drop poised above the creamy swell of her breasts.

"You've made me the happiest woman alive," she whispered, sighing as she surrendered to the tender caress of his hands and mouth. Feeling languorous, as if she drifted on a cloud of happiness, Isobel traced his cheek with the tip of her tongue. "I want our wedding night to last a long time."

"You have my word on it, sweetheart," he vowed, lifting her in his arms and clasping her against his hard body. She felt soft, yielding and appealingly defenseless in contrast to his own strength. Overwhelming tenderness for the woman in his arms moved him until Morgan had to blink back moisture unexpectedly clouding his vision. "I'll make love to you till it be morrow, if that's what you want."

Isobel sighed happily and she turned her face into the warm comfort of his neck. "Oh, my love, that's exactly what I want. And if this night proves to be only a dream, after all, it'll be the most wonderful dream of my life."

During the night the thaw began, the warmer temperature brought by the westerly wind. Isobel awoke to the steady drip of icicles melting off the roof.

A great clattering came from the courtyard, soon followed by the thunder of many hooves. To her surprise, when she looked out the window, she saw the bishop's party galloping away, riding hard as if the devil himself were after them. Their wagons bounced and swayed as they were driven helter-skelter along the drive. As they recklessly rounded the bend on two wheels, several items tumbled from the wagon to lie neglected on the drive, for no one bothered to retrieve them.

Why were they in such haste? They must have left without even breaking their fast, for it was barely light. Gripped by unease, Isobel wondered if the sick chaplain rode with them, or if they had left him here for her to nurse.

As Isobel neared the bedchamber where Father Barnaby had slept, her feeling of foreboding increased. His door stood wide open. Peering inside the gloomy room, she was immediately struck by a peculiar, sickening odor, one she had not encountered before. Father Barnaby sprawled across the bed, lying outside the covers. He lay perfectly still, and his chest did not move. He either slept very soundly, or he was dead.

Moving closer to the bed, she no longer had to wonder if he slept. To her horror Isobel saw that his face was already dark, and blood congealed over the front of his habit and on the sheet. His lungs had hemorrhaged in the night.

A chill went over her. Had the priest died from plague? Yet she didn't see the telltale swellings she had always associated with plague, nor even purple patches on his skin from hemorrhaging under the surface.

Backing away, Isobel fled the sickroom.

In the full morning light servants pulled the dead man from the bed onto a door they were using for a stretcher. In horror, Isobel noticed the beginning of a swelling on his neck. It was not the grotesque, apple-sized lump she had heard described, rather a small nodule the size of an acorn. Perhaps Father Barnaby had died before there was time for the swelling to grow. They did not examine the body for further buboes out of fear of infection. But there was no need. Isobel was convinced their unexpected guests had brought with them the deadly gift of plague!

The body was taken by farm cart to the nearby parish church, where the local priest reluctantly gave the deceased a Christian burial. A group of villagers watched, standing well back from the grave site. The gravediggers swathed their faces with rags to keep out the plague's deadly humors.

It was a subdued household who took their simple noon meal. Today the bright Christmas garlands with their cheerfully festive message seemed a mockery. Now that the dreadful truth was out, the servants tiptoed about silently, the discovery too dreadful for gossip.

Morgan found a chest of treasure abandoned in the yard, and he assumed this was the payment promised for the bishop's lodging. A few puzzling mysteries about last night's guests fell right into place after this morning's hasty departure.

Likely these churchmen had turned directly from their altars to their saddles, an assumption he had found amusing last night. This morning he saw no humor in it. All this gold plate, the candlesticks and chalices, were treasures looted from a church, probably several churches, considering the number of bags and boxes heaped in their wagons.

He sent servants to retrieve the pieces that had fallen on the driveway during their hasty exit. They returned carrying a jewel-encrusted chalice, badly dented from its fall, and an elaborate monstrance, complete with host, which yesterday had probably graced some high altar.

There were similar pieces in the chest, also looted from some holy place. He had the treasure taken to the chapel, where it was placed in a more appropriate setting.

Morgan seethed with anger each time he considered that the fat bishop and his cronies must have been fleeing the plague. Instead they had merely carried it with them, unable to outride the specter of death. He supposed they were bound for Bristol with their looted treasure, probably intending to sail to safety in a foreign port.

Had he been as trusting of the clergy's holiness as Isobel appeared to be, his discovery would have been disillusioning. As it was, Morgan knew the Church seethed with corruption. Many priests dressed as fine as nobles, keeping women for their pleasure, or young boys, if that was their preference. Routinely enjoying fine wine and rich food, they ignored their vows of poverty, chastity and obedience. Corrupt though they were, he also knew these clergy were poor examples of the religion they espoused. These were the vices of ordinary men and had no place among those who professed to serve God.

By afternoon, Isobel's fear mounted as the two servants who had attended Father Barnaby began to feel unwell. Theirs was a vague malady with much sneezing and coughing, as if they had taken cold from the damp. But with her new understanding of this speedy and virulent form of illness, she was sure they too had contracted plague.

The sick were isolated in a sickroom off the infirmary in the hope of keeping the plague from spreading. The servants who stripped the chamber where Father Barnaby died wrapped linen cloths about their faces when they took the bedding outside to be burned. Isobel set bowls of herbs about the house, and on her wrist she carried the silver pomander Brother Andrew had given her, freshly filled with a pungent blend of herbs guaranteed to ward off the plague's ill humors.

By morning the two ailing servants were dead.

Isobel felt a chill of dread creeping along her arms and legs when she heard the news. So quickly! She had thought people lingered a long time with plague. She gave Moffat strict orders to report to her immediately when any other members of their household became ill.

Before noon, Moffat came to make his first grim report. Two more felt unwell, though this time the patients were flushed with fever and their skin burned hot and red. The sickroom had been thoroughly cleaned after the first two casualties. The new patients were brought there. Old Hilty offered to act as nurse to the sick, and Isobel was grateful for the servant's sacrifice.

''We have to find out how widespread this plague is,'' Morgan told Isobel as they broke their fast to the solemn accompaniment of the bell tolling from their own parish church. From time to time when the wind changed direction, the sporadic pealing of other church bells could be heard in the distance.

''To think they knew they were probably infected before they came here,'' she commented angrily, crushing a soft roll into a fistful of crumbs as she spoke. ''How dare they risk making us ill? And we, like fools, felt honored to have their company.''

''Speak for yourself.'' Morgan grinned at her, clasping her hand where it lay on the table. ''Remember, I wasn't nearly as impressed as you, my love. But it's done now. They're gone, thank God. By acting promptly perhaps we can contain it. We need to know if it's already in the surrounding villages. Maybe that's why the fields seemed so deserted the other day. People could be staying indoors because of the plague.'' Or maybe they are already dead, he added silently.

''Very well, but do be careful,'' Isobel cautioned uneasily, ''Please go to Ambrey Priory to make sure my aunt Blanche is well. She's prioress there.''

Morgan agreed he would.

After the noon meal, accompanied by several volunteers from among his own men, Morgan set out to review the situation.

He had already learned the plague had not reached Ambrey village, so he needed to go farther afield. When they approached the first village beyond the manor, he pulled a cloth up over his nose and mouth, instructing his men to do the same.

The melting snow had turned this narrow village street into a quagmire. They slid and squelched their way along. No one came out to see who they were, and Morgan found this in itself very ominous. There had been several sheep carcasses beside the road as they passed, so he surmised that this affliction affected animals too.

These cottages were little more than huts with a central hearth, all curiously cold on this blustery day. Inside the first hut he saw the family sprawled lifeless on their pallets. it was the same story in the next hovel, and the next. Outside the forge a yellow-haired woman lay in the mud, a rope tied around her body. At first he thought she had been hanged, but then he saw that the blacksmith's wife had been too heavy for her ill husband to carry, so he had tried to drag her to the churchyard. He had not gone far. He lay just inside the smithy door. Both bodies were grotesquely blackened, and Morgan backed away from them. There was no longer any reason to question the nature of this pestilence.

He ordered his men out of the plague-infested village. Grimly he selected a road leading east. In this village they found beasts aimlessly wandering untended amid the huts. A milk cow, seeing a human, came toward him, mooing plaintively, her udder distended with milk. Before he looked inside the first low-ceilinged dwelling, Morgan already knew what he would find.

To the west and the north, they found a similar story, though here there were enough people still alive to tell him things were far worse farther south. They also warned him to stay away from the priory, where all souls had already perished, infected by wandering beggars. They had also heard that in the cities there were not enough priests to bury the dead and that grass was growing in the streets. Huge communal burial pits had been opened to contain the plague-dead, for the digging of individual graves had been abandoned long ago.

Morgan's face tightened as he learned of the widespread reach of this terrible plague. Living their idyllic life at Ambrey, isolated from the rest of the world, he and Isobel had remained blissfully unaware of the horror creeping across the land.

Now he was concerned for the safety of his own people, who were also unaware of the danger relentlessly moving their way. He must go home to warn them. If they kept all strangers away from the villages and had enough food and water put by to make them self-sufficient, there was hope. Any sickness would have to be reported at once and that person isolated to stop the spread of the disease.

What of Isobel? His heart lurched in shock, before thundering back to life. She had been in contact with the dying priest, who had sung so sweetly for them during his final hours. If she was not already infected, there was hope. He had to get her away from Ambrey. Praying, his lips moving soundlessly, Morgan turned about and headed for the manor. He already knew what he must do.

"Sweet, this is best for you. At Stoneham you can pull up the bridge and keep people out. If they're still plague-free, you'll be safe. Think of it as a seige. You'll have to stay inside until the sickness has burned itself out."

"I can't go back to Stoneham, not to Lionel. I want to stay with you. Oh, Morgan, it won't be any safer there than here."

"You can't stay here," he said firmly.

"Why can't I come with you?" she asked, stubbornly refusing to accept his plan.

"Because I don't know what to expect there. The plague's moving this way, but it might not be in Wales yet. If I were sure of that, you could come with me, but I'm not. I have to warn my people to take precautions. That way we might be able to ward off the worst of it."

"How can you say Stoneham's safer than here, especially with Lionel there? We don't have to entertain any more holy visitors," she said with a wan little smile, trying to lighten the horror of this dread illness.

"Even without visitors, the plague's already in the house. We're leaving today before it's too late. At Stoneham you can isolate yourself. Lionel's probably still at court trying to impress the king. You can pull up the bridge and shut everyone out. Here you can't do that. Before long some of the survivors will come begging for food. I already saw ragged travelers on the roads."

Finding his argument unpleasant, but logical, Isobel reluctantly packed her trunk and caged the dogs and falcons for travel. She picked a few servants to accompany them. Morgan's men were as anxious as he to get home to learn the worst.

It was a downcast party that braved the brisk wind and muddy roads heading south to Stoneham.

Though he had not told Isobel, Morgan had already decided that if Lord Hurley was at the castle, he would challenge him to a fight. Giving him the chance to defend himself would be more chivalrous than murdering him, though it would have given him great satisfaction to plunge his dagger to the hilt in Lionel Hurley's black heart!

The countryside about Stoneham Magna was gray and deserted. When they neared a settlement they always covered their faces as a safeguard against infection. Isobel's heart grew heavy as they drew closer to their destination. Here the neglect of the surrounding villages with their overgrown fields and gardens all told the same story. She had hoped to find things unchanged, the plague far away. On their journey their constant companion had been the tolling church bells. Better than anything else these church bells had eloquently told the story of the sheer magnitude of the disaster sweeping across the land. Each parish they entered tolled ceaselessly for its dead, until Isobel began to wonder if anywhere on earth was safe from the relentless spread of plague.

They spent nights in the wagon, fearing contact with infected travelers at inns and taverns. Though she felt sad and dispirited, Isobel slept safely in Morgan's arms, drawing a modicum of comfort from his strength. Aware of her sadness, he did not suggest making love, nor did she initiate it. They clung together in the darkness, as if by the power of their love alone they would be protected from danger.

So far none among their party had sickened. As each day passed and still no one became ill, Morgan began to breathe a little easier; somehow they had miraculously escaped infection from the bishop's plague-ridden party.

Stoneham Magna Castle loomed before them, gray and forbidding in the morning mist. The surrounding countryside was unnaturally quiet, as if already dead. No bells tolled here. Mist collected in hollows and under trees. The sodden December landscape was locked in slumber. Dead sheep dotted the meadow below the castle, warning them that here also the plague had been at work.

To his surprise, when they neared the moat, Morgan saw that the bridge was down. There were no visible sentries at the towers. He reined in, shouting to alert someone, but there was no response. It was not until they had clattered across the wooden bridge into the outer bailey that a man finally came outside.

The castle gate stood open; the portcullis was up.

"Ho, there, Lady Isobel and the Lord of Nels seek admittance."

The man leaned weakly against a wooden post and shook his head.

"Nay, my lord, you don't want to come inside this charnel house."

Isobel gasped at his choice of words.

"What do you mean?" she demanded, not recognizing

the man and assuming he must be one of Lionel's soldiers. "Where's your master? Is he still in London? And why is the bridge down? We rode across it and weren't even challenged."

The man shrugged. "No one wants to come here. We're safe. We have a champion to protect us far more powerful than any living man. Brought back from London by our generous master. If I were you, lady, I'd turn around and go back the way I came."

Ignoring his advice, their party rode on to the inner bailey. Here grass grew amid the cobbles, and the stone slabs of the castle wall were draped with moss and ivy. Several scrawny dogs scavenged amid the heaps of refuse, while a pig and a cow wandered unchecked through the derelict kitchen garden.

Glancing around uneasily, the riders dismounted. Morgan took three men with him and asked Isobel to wait outside in the bailey until he learned the conditions inside the castle.

Beckoning to his men, Morgan ducked beneath the low stone arch leading into the castle. Immediately their nostrils were assaulted by an overwhelming smell, a mingling of foulness from many sources, none of them pleasant. To a man they pulled the cloths into place over their noses and mouths. From close at hand came the sound of singing and laughter. They stopped, looking at each other in surprise, for they had been expecting nothing but sickness and gloom. These revelers sounded drunk. A lively tune was being played, replete with many false notes. More gales of laughter echoed along the stone corridors.

By chance they had taken the circuitous route that led into the great hall from a narrow passage out of the buttery. As they approached the heart of the castle, the sounds of revelry grew louder. The travelers stepped through an arch into the hall, coming out just below the dais, where the lord's table stood before a blazing hearth.

They were met by the most amazing sight.

Half-dressed peasants danced a country round, laughing and stumbling, some holding jugs of ale to their mouths as they danced. A few soldiers and servants lolled at a nearby trestle, the table heaped with rotting food and debris. Slack mouthed, the raucous peasants kept at their round, grabbing bare breasts and bestowing wet kisses. Movement from the filthy rushes revealed others openly fornicating. With shrieks of drunken laughter, the dancers finally collapsed into a sweating heap. The thirsty musicians staggered toward the ale butt, where they drew themselves refills from the flowing spigot.

Someone finally noticed the new arrivals, and a wild-haired slattern weaved toward them, a welcoming smile on her blowsy face.

"Come in, my lovelies. We've need of new blood." She cackled, pulling down her bodice to expose her breasts. She turned a hopefully inviting smile on Morgan, who was nearest. "See what I've got for 'ee."

"Where's your lord?" Morgan asked, stepping back a pace as the seductress advanced.

She vaguely waved her hand toward the dais.

He turned and was surprised to see a lone figure sprawled at the table before the roaring fire.

"Lord Hurley?"

Lionel raised his head, eyes bloodshot.

"Aye, come in. Join the merrymakers. None of us will likely live out the week. But we promise you safe passage to hell."

Guffaws of laughter met his invitation, and a woman crawled drunkenly up the steps to the dais, openly offering herself to him. First Lionel ignored her, but, when she persisted, he finally pushed her away with his booted foot, and she toppled giggling onto the rushes.

"What's the meaning of all this?" Morgan asked, stepping up one step of the dais, but going no closer.

"Meaning?" Lionel asked curiously. "There is none.

No meaning to anything. For a while we live, and soon we die. You too. No one escapes."

"Who are all these people? They don't live here at the castle. Why are they here?"

Lionel shrugged. "They're my guests. Here they eat and drink . . . they rut . . . and they die. That's the way of all flesh."

"Have you the sickness too?" Morgan asked him then, finding his rambling discourse suggestive of an addled brain. "What of your lady wife? And your children?"

Lionel looked up at him, peering through the gloom in an effort to identify the speaker. He ran his hand across his sweating face. "Dead. All dead. Me too. This isn't the real me. This is just a cruel parody of Lionel Hurley. Soon the worms will devour every last soul at Stoneham. And then the world will end. Do you believe that, traveler?"

"Possibly," Morgan allowed, glancing around the great hall. Now that his eyes had become accustomed to the dim light, he discovered corpses lying at the sides of the room where they had been dragged. There, amid the fouled rushes, all smeared with waste and spoiled food, these poor souls would eventually decompose. A shudder of revulsion went through him.

"Why don't you have your people clear out this drunken rabble? Bury the dead. You're all going to perish living this way."

"What's the point? We'll all perish anyway. There aren't any priests left to bury the dead," Lionel said, bursting into a fit of coughing. He stood, lurching from his seat, and he held on to the edge of the table for support. "I'm ruined anyway. That bitch of a sister ruined me. I've no reason left to live."

Again he began to cough, holding a soiled napkin to his mouth to stifle the cough. When next he looked at him, Morgan could see blood on his lips. Lionel's clothes were rumpled and stained, his graying hair shaggy and falling over his face in greasy strands. Morgan had never seen him look so unkempt. This man was a stranger!

"You're ill. You should be in your bed."

"No . . . no . . . can't go there. That dead bitch lies in my bed," Lionel said with a feeble grin. "Come to think of it, she's always been dead in my bed." He began to chuckle at his own wit until he was seized with another fit of coughing.

As Morgan looked at his former adversary, he realized his hatred had slipped away. Now that he had finally come face-to-face with Lionel Hurley, he could not kill him. This sick remnant of the man he'd known was more deserving of his pity than his rage.

He turned away, taking a step toward the arch. There was nothing for them here. In fact, he longed to race out of this hell on earth. How glad he was that Isobel had stayed outside in the bailey, that she had not witnessed the desecration of her former home. . . .

"Dear God! Lionel! Is that you?"

Morgan spun about in surprise at her unexpected voice. There she stood, her hands to her face. She had followed him after all. He would have given anything for her not to have seen this depravity.

"Isobel, get back. Don't come any closer," he warned gruffly, holding out his arm to bar her way.

"Isobel," Lionel repeated, catching the familiar name. "That's my sister's name. That treacherous bitch betrayed me. She's the cause of all this, you know—wouldn't have happened without her."

"Go back outside," Morgan commanded grimly, pushing her back into the corridor. He knew it was already too late, for she had seen and smelled the foulness of the hall, the slack abandon of these drunken peasants, who stared curiously at her. One of the men, noticing a new female, lurched toward them, making suggestive motions as he called out for her to stop.

At his command, Morgan's men caught Isobel's arms and forcibly propelled her back outside.

Lionel was shouting for ale, cursing the servants and villagers who ignored him. Morgan stood there, torn between aiding his former enemy and saving his own hide. There was nothing he could do for Lionel Hurley, for the mark of death was already on him. If he went any closer, he might catch the infection and take it home to his own people. He would be lucky if he had not already been corrupted by this place of death.

The decision made, he spun about and strode as quickly as he could into the fresh air, trying not to breathe the foulness, though it crept inside his nostrils, penetrating the kerchief tied around his face.

Behind him Morgan could hear Lionel still ranting and raving, his voice echoing along the corridor. Uncaring, the peasants again struck up a tune, and someone sang a ribald song accompanied by much hiccuping and laughter, until he finally fell over on the rushes and the song stopped. Morgan heard the thud as he fell, not knowing whether the fellow was drunk or dead.

Grimly Morgan remounted his horse. Isobel wept quietly in the saddle, and she turned away from him when he asked her why she had not stayed outside. It did not really matter. It was done now. He knew in her mind she would forever carry the hateful picture of the drunken revels in Stoneham's great hall. Of those villagers whirling desperately toward their own end, abandoning all sense of decency. This was the first time he had ever witnessed such a scene, though he had been told it was not uncommon among plague survivors as their numbers dwindled along with their faith.

For a long time they rode in silence, sobered by that ghoulish scene. There was nothing to do now but to head home to Wales and pray they were fast enough to outride the plague.

Chapter Sixteen

Blodwen stretched and smiled with pleasure. In the quiet room she could hear Rhodri's even breathing as he slept beside her. Outside, the winter morn was gradually stirring to life. Cocks crowed and there was clattering from the bailey. Startled curlews screeched eerily about the battlements before fleeing to join their flock at the nearby estuary.

Life continued as if nothing had changed. But it had changed! She hugged herself in delight, taking strands of her glittering hair and winding them seductively around her small breasts. Rhodri had awakened her as a woman. He loved her! She kept repeating the words to herself, bemused and disbelieving. In those weeks since Morgan had left to defend his woman's honor she had thought long and hard about the future. Though it was a difficult decision, she finally knew what she must do.

Humble and penitent, she had ridden to Rhodri's small stronghold, begging entrance. At first she had thought he was going to deny her, for he came and stood unwelcoming at the gate. Powerful and broad shouldered in his boiled leather jack, his black hair fluttering in the wind, he made her heart lurch with love. At that moment she could have denied him nothing. Rhodri was the perfect soldier prince. Above and beyond his mystical powers, he had the ability to lead people, to carve an empire from this rugged land.

When he finally strode through the gate, she had dismounted to kneel before him. In her hand she carried the ancient seal of Nels, a golden disk embossed with a dragon, handed down over the generations to the hereditary lord of the land.

"It is yours," she said softly.

And when he raised her up, they gazed into each other's eyes, standing shoulder to shoulder as equal rulers of this place.

Even now Blodwen shivered with delight as she relived the excitement of that day. Later Rhodri had come to Lyswen to inspect the palace and its defenses, but he had not stayed. Blodwen found it hard to hide her disappointment, for she had thought he would come to live here with her. Not yet, he had said: the time was not right.

Now she turned and traced her finger down the hard bridge of his nose, before bending to kiss his mouth.

Rhodri's eyes opened and he was instantly alert.

"Oh, Blodwen," he said, as if surprised. "Is it already light?" he demanded, moving from her caress, not sparing a glance at her artfully seductive pose.

Disappointed and feeling foolish, she quickly pulled up the sheet to cover her nakedness. "Yes, it's time to get up," she agreed, swallowing her emotion. Angrily she realized she was close to tears. Though she enjoyed being a woman in Rhodri's arms, she hated the newfound weakness that came with it. She was not used to tears and sighs and she did not like them.

She lay back against the pillows, eagerly anticipating the thrilling sight of his powerful body with its mat of black hair. Rhodri was barrel chested with sturdy legs, a born fighter. Huge sinews swelled like gnarled tree trunks in his arms and legs. But it was that other part of him she was most curious about. Though once she had glimpsed him completely naked, he did not encourage her in that respect. Always he came to her in darkness and haste. Perhaps this was the way of men and women. She did not know, as she had nothing with which to compare. In her heart of hearts, she loved him desperately, despite his sometimes callous disregard for her feelings. Rhodri meant more to her than anything on this earth, her love for him going beyond loyalty, beyond family, almost beyond life, she decided, finding tears pricking her eyes. Damn it, there it was again, that puling weakness she despised.

"Why didn't you wake me earlier? I'm going to be late," Rhodri snarled, sliding out of bed, his back to her.

Once again Blodwen was disappointed. She slid across the bed and reached out to stroke his back where his long hair tangled between his shoulder blades. He was a magnificent beast of a man, wild, primitive . . . and hers.

Rhodri moved away from her caress and pulled his clothing on.

"You don't have to leave yet. We haven't broken our fast."

"Yes, I do. I've urgent business with my neighbor."

"Which neighbor is that?"

"Ivar Wolfbane."

Blodwen shuddered and crossed herself at the mention of that name. She did not like Rhodri to associate with the reputed wizard. "What do you need him for?"

"He's helping me determine the right time."

"For what?"

Rhodri turned and grinned at her. Then, leaning across the bed, he lifted strands of hair off her breast and bent to kiss the small, apple-hard mound. Blodwen shivered in delight, but when she would have held him to her, keeping him there just a little longer, Rhodri pulled away.

"You'll see. Trust me, Blodwen, and don't ask too many questions."

And with that abrupt answer, she had to be content.

Later Blodwen watched him ride away, accompanied by his six men at arms. All traces of Rhodri of the Mount had been erased from Llyswen, for he would leave no possessions here that could be used in a witch's spell to harm him. When she had laughed at his reasoning, he grew dark with anger. Each time he left, she felt bereft. It was as if he had never really been here, as if that stolen, rapturous time had taken place only in her imagination.

Uneasily Blodwen wondered what right time he sought. There had been no hostilities, yet she had been told he was building his military strength. This puzzled her. Rhodri had no need of soldiers to use against Llyswen, for if she willed it, the garrison would accept him as lord. Of course, Huw, Morgan's second in command, would have to be killed: he would never accept Rhodri as his lord. The steward, Mervyn, could be persuaded. Already she had planted the seeds, telling him Morgan's absentee lordship endangered their people. Mervyn had seen the sense of her argument. Everything was falling into place, just the way she had hoped it would. In desperation she had bargained to regain Rhodri's love using the only power she possessed, the control of the ancient princedom of Nels. Though some might call it treachery, she had bought their people a powerful lord who could even summon the elements of nature to his bidding.

Out of the noonday sun she saw the riders. From this distance she could not identify their banner, or even if they carried one. There was a wagon and mounted men. . . .

Blodwen spun from the window, her heart thudding in dread. It was Morgan! It had to be Morgan coming home. Like a naughty child, she suddenly feared his wrath when he learned of her love for Rhodri. She was a grown woman. Why should she not have a lover? Yet somehow she knew that argument would have little validity where her brother was concerned. Rhodri had always been his enemy. Nothing she could say would change that.

Morgan reached out to clasp Isobel's hand as they toiled up the steep track. He felt a great wave of relief wash over him to find his lands undisturbed. Here cattle and horses flourished, and there was no stink of death, nor tolling chimes for the dead.

"Things look well enough, don't you think?" he asked, looking down into the valley, where a shepherd moved among his sheep.

"So far," she agreed, following his gaze.

He wanted to dispute her gloomy observation, but he knew she was right. So far. What tomorrow brought could change the entire picture. Ever since they'd left Stoneham Magna he had worried constantly that they had been infected. Miraculously no one had complained of illness. Morgan had grown to believe there were two distinct forms of plague. The first made men swell with terrible boils, grotesquely disfiguring their bodies. With this malady people lingered more than a week. The second form, which was probably more virulent, he supposed was borne in the air, spread by coughs and sneezes. Striking almost overnight, this plague brought about a speedy death from fever and rotting lungs.

Morgan fervently prayed the people of Nels could miraculously escape both kinds.

Lately, as he'd traveled over the land ravaged by pestilence, he had even begun to question his own faith. Had prayer any value as a protection against the sickness, the worst hit would not be priests and monks. Yet on second thought, Morgan realized that they must perform the last rites of the dying, catching the sickness from their own congregations. This conclusion eased his conscience. He did not want to accept the oft-repeated charge that God had forsaken them.

Morgan straightened in the saddle and breathed deeply of the sharp, fresh air; here, it smelled only of growing things and the sea. He looked around the wintery landscape with pleasure, feeling that old contentment at being home again. A cottager stood at his door, watching the riders.

Morgan hailed him. With a grin of delight, the man stumbled forward to greet his lord. His small rock dwelling stood in the lee of the hillside, its well-tended garden boasting rows of winter cabbage and orderly patches of herbs.

"Prys, isn't it?" Morgan called.

"Aye, my lord, that's right. Welcome home. You're sore needed here."

Uneasily Morgan drew rein. "How's that?"

"Word is your lady sister's forming an unholy alliance with Rhodri of the Mount. For the most part our crops failed, and there's bad sickness in some of the villages—"

"Sickness?" Morgan interrupted, the ominous word hitting him like a thunderbolt.

"My woman's been took bad ever since she come back from her sister's these three days past. Terrible bad, she is, Lord Morgan."

"Where does her sister live?"

"A long way from here. Across the river, near the border."

Morgan and Isobel exchanged stricken looks. They knew they were too late. The plague had arrived before them.

"What's this I hear, Blodwen, about you bedding Rhodri of the Mount?" Morgan thundered, not mincing words with his sister.

Isobel sat quietly beside the hearth, staying out of the

fight. Much of what was being said in Welsh escaped her, but the gist of it was clear.

Blodwen drew herself up to her full height and tossed back her flowing silver-gilt hair. "Why is it any different from you bedding the Englishwoman?" she demanded hostilely.

Morgan grasped her wrist, his face dark with anger. Though his fingers bit into her flesh, she would not twist away. "I trusted you to rule in my absence. He's our sworn enemy! God knows, if you needed servicing, there are a dozen good men inside these walls you could have chosen."

"Servicing . . . is that what you think it is? Rhodri loves me! You wouldn't understand that, for you've never seen him as a man—only as a threat."

"Exactly, and now he's a worse threat than ever. Well, he'll never enter these walls again."

She gasped in shock at his pronouncement. "Then I'll go to him."

Morgan pushed her away. "No! For the time being you're under guard for your own safety."

"You can't keep me prisoner here," she shouted, glaring at him. Blodwen reached out, trying to grab his hair. "You shan't rule my life!"

"I'm lord here. You'll do as I say."

With that, Morgan spun on his heel, leaving Blodwen slumped against the table, weeping softly.

Isobel stared at her stricken sister-in-law, hardly able to believe what she saw. Tears! She had never even supposed Blodwen to be capable of tears. Though much of their argument had eluded her, she assumed it was about Blodwen choosing Morgan's hated enemy as her lover. She had heard that Rhodri was a pagan high priest, able to cast spells and control the elements—and probably a woman's heart.

With an uneasy sigh, she went to comfort Blodwen.

Blodwen refused to accept the hand she offered. She

glared angrily at Isobel and flung the hand away from her. "Get away from me. This is all your fault," she snarled.

"According to you, everything in the world is my fault. I suppose you blame me for the plague as well."

"What plague?"

"There's a dreadful plague across the border. It'll soon be here at Llyswen unless Morgan can stop its spread. That's why you mustn't leave the castle. No one can come in, and no one goes out. Even the villages will have to become self-sufficient. It's the only way Morgan knows to control the plague."

Blodwen paled at the dire news. Was this the terrible calamity Rhodri had warned her about? The disaster that only he could overcome? "Is it that bad?"

"Terrible. Worse than you could ever imagine."

"Are they not offering prayers for deliverance?"

Isobel smiled sadly. "Of course, but it's to no avail. Priests and monks have been hit hard. Some entire villages are wiped out. That's why you must do as Morgan asks. It's the only hope he has of keeping your people alive."

Blodwen looked at her with a chilling gaze. "No. There's only one who can do that."

As Isobel watched Blodwen stride from the hall, she felt a chill of foreboding. It was not going to be easy to isolate these people. She had the feeling Blodwen would not be of any help.

Before the day was out Morgan had sent messengers to all the villages under his jurisdiction, telling them about his quarantine. He also wanted to know if they had sickness in the village.

The ensuing report was grim.

"Four villages already report sickness," Morgan told Isobel. "It could be plague, or just winter ills. We don't know yet. My people are used to their freedom. They don't understand how the plague works, putting too much trust in charms and spells. Have you seen Blodwen?"

"Not since this afternoon. Is she not in her chamber?"

Morgan sighed wearily and shook his head. "No, but her horse is still in the stable. I've given orders that he's not to be ridden. So, unless she left on foot, she must still be here somewhere."

Morgan absently crumbled bread on his trencher, his mind a million miles away as he sorted through plans to protect his people. He could threaten them with dire consequences if they disobeyed. But he didn't want to do that. He decided he must ride through the villages himself in an effort to impress upon them the importance of not moving from place to place. In those places already stricken, his men could leave food at the village boundary.

"How bad is it?" Isobel asked, smiling at him, her hand gentle on his arm.

Morgan covered her small white hand with his own.

"No deaths yet," he said reassuringly.

"Eat your supper. Fasting won't help anything," she said with wifely concern.

Obediently he speared a chunk of meat on his hunting knife and bit into it, tearing it apart with strong, white teeth.

Isobel smiled. "There, you see, you're becoming far more obedient now that we're really married," she teased.

A great clamor from outside startled them. Morgan leaped to his feet, running from the hall to see what was happening. Isobel followed swiftly on his heels, tripping over her skirts in her haste to keep up with him. She hoisted her trailing skirts high above her ankles and kept on running.

The cold night wind set the torch flames leaping on the battlements. Below the walls a hundred more torches flickered in the darkness, held by mounted men gathered in the meadow across the moat.

Morgan cursed under his breath when he saw them. It took no great imagination to know whose men they were.

He put his arm protectively around Isobel's shoulders, wanting to reassure her they were in no danger.

A few minutes later, Huw came to make his report.

"The bridge is secure. And extra sentries have been posted. It seems the Lord of the Mount is just a little late," Huw commented, chest thrown out in pride at his own efficiency.

"You've done well, Huw. I've complete faith in your judgment. How else could I leave the castle in your charge?" Morgan said, clapping him on the shoulder as they walked to the edge of the battlements to confront the enemy.

A lone horseman detached himself from the others and rode forward. He wore flowing white robes, and on his head a golden circlet glinted in the torchlight.

"What do you want with me, Rhodri?" Morgan shouted, aware of his antagonist's identity, even in the fanciful garb of Druid priest.

"How clever you are, Lord Morgan, and such good timing. Another day and this castle would have been mine," Rhodri shouted back in reply.

"Well, as you are a day late, you can march your troops back home again and put up your swords."

"These are only a handful of my men," Rhodri boasted, his deep voice carrying across the battlements. "We've a whole legion of soldiers."

"So do I."

"Your people have the pestilence."

Morgan drew in his breath. "What makes you think yours don't?"

"Because, my brave lord, we're well protected by our gods. Your puny Christian god hasn't the power to stop this disaster. Only by following me can your people live. Tell them that instead of giving them useless rules. If they choose your way, they'll stay home to die in their beds. I can protect them. If they follow me, they'll live. Once they're given that simple choice, you'll see whose word they accept. I am all-powerful."

Morgan grew aware of a dull rumbling of dissent from his own men as Rhodri's chilling words hit home. The men who had gone to England with him had already regaled their fellows with hideous stories of the devastation they had seen.

"What power's that, Rhodri? I don't call seducing women with lies of love *power,*" he shouted. "You thought to walk in here with my sister's blessing. You've deceived her with your lies. Likely you'd deceive my people the same way."

Angrily, Rhodri drew himself up, sitting ramrod straight in the saddle.

"What do you mean? What lies? Your sister loves me. It's with her help I'll conquer you."

"I don't dispute *her* feelings—it's your lies I take issue with." Morgan heard a movement behind him, and he felt Blodwen's presence by the sheer excitement radiating from her body as she looked down on her lover. Yesterday on his journey through the villages he had learned some condemning news about Rhodri, a secret he was sure Blodwen did not know. Morgan contemplated what he was going to say next, aware it would wound his sister, but also aware it was his best line of defense. Maybe when she knew the truth about her lover she would not be so eager to join him.

"What are you talking about?" Rhodri demanded, sneering at his opponent, aware that Blodwen stood behind Morgan on the battlements. "She's there now, mighty Dragon Knight. Why don't you ask her how she feels about me, and while you're at it, ask her who keeps the seal of Nels."

Morgan's face tightened and his heart lurched in shock at that last challenge. Dear God, had she given away their sacred token? Shaking his head to clear his thoughts, Morgan was freshly determined not to allow his advantage to slip away.

"And I'll also ask her if she minds sharing you with Olwen Gwyn," Morgan snarled angrily, his voice turned rough with emotion. "Tell her whose child Olwen carries."

Behind him Morgan was aware of Blodwen's protesting cry. Remorse for causing her pain coursed through him and he turned to comfort her. Blodwen crumpled against the wall.

"I'm sorry," Morgan whispered remorsefully, trying to bring her to her feet. "It's true. You had to know."

"No, it's not true," she screamed at him. "Rhodri loves *me.* Why, only this morning he left Llyswen. He's my lover and it's to him I pledge my loyalty."

Her words wounded him intensely. Morgan tried to take her hand, but she snatched it away. "Listen to me, Blodwen: he only pretends to care for you to win your confidence. It's a ruse to gain control here. He's deceiving you. What reason do I have to lie?"

Tears glittered on her cheeks. "I love you, Morgan, because you're my brother. But unless you accept Rhodri's command, you'll die. We'll all die. He has special powers. He alone can save us from the plague. You have to trust him."

"Trust that treacherous devil—you must be mad! Or likely he's bewitched you with his evil spells." Morgan spat, angrily thrusting her aside when she clung to his arm.

"All you ever think about is *her.* You've neglected your people and now they're going to die," Blodwen replied angrily, backing away. "I warn you, brother, that woman will be your death."

Blodwen went to the edge of the battlements and leaned out. "Rhodri, can you hear me?" she shouted. "I'll come with you tonight, if you'll have me."

A buzz of shocked surprise came from Rhodri's men,

the noise echoed by the listening soldiers on Llyswen's battlements.

"Aye, my love, of a certainty. I knew you were too clever to listen to his lies."

"Let her go," Morgan snarled to Huw, who tried to hold Blodwen back. "I'll not stop you, Blodwen, but I warn you, if you leave tonight, you can never come back."

She inclined her head to him in farewell, and then she swept majestically from the battlements. Morgan leaned against the cold stonework, catching his breath, feeling as if he had been dealt a great blow in the chest. Tonight he found betrayal a bitter herb to swallow.

Isobel ran to his side, aware of his devastation. She did not speak, merely slipped her arm about his waist and leaned in to him, hugging his body against hers, letting him know she was there to support him.

Soon a torch bobbed from the postern across the meadow as Blodwen and a handful of her servants crossed the moat and left Llyswen.

Before she joined her lover, Blodwen reined in and turned about for one last look at her home. There, on the battlements, stood her handsome brother, so young to have the pall of certain death hanging over him. A flicker of regret made her pause, until she saw that evil woman standing close beside him, the cause of all the ill will between them.

Strengthened by the reminder that she had no choice but to change loyalties, Blodwen also accepted that this was probably the last time she would see her brother. Morgan had given Rhodri no option. Rhodri must kill him to gain control of Llyswen. She also believed that Rhodri alone was capable of saving them, for she had heard the hideous tales of pestilence, a coming disaster Rhodri had foretold months before.

Purposely Blodwen turned her back on the sprawling, glistening white palace where she had been born, and she galloped to Rhodri's side. There had been a moment's doubt, when she wondered if Morgan's accusations about a woman called Olwen Gwyn could be true. She knew they weren't. They were desperate lies designed to turn her against Rhodri. Sometimes she had wondered what he did on those days and nights he didn't spend with her. And his impatience during lovemaking had also made her wonder how selfless was his love. . . . *No!* Blodwen gripped the reins as she forcefully drove out those painful thoughts. She had cast her lot with Rhodri. There was no turning back now.

"Ah, Blodwen, my brave love, you're welcome to come home with me," he said, his deep voice a seductive whisper in her ear.

Not even sure he had actually spoken, Blodwen smiled up at him, her face wet with tears.

"Tonight I've chosen life over death," she said.

In the weeks that followed, their worst fears were confirmed. Reports of the first deaths came from the surrounding villages, panicking Morgan's tenants. All his appeals to them went unheeded. Even from inside the castle, at night, and secretly, people began to slip away to join Rhodri of the Mount, who had promised to save them from the plague.

Isobel was alarmed by the growing defection. A dozen servants were unswervingly loyal and she was grateful to them; a growing appreciation of these once-hostile people warmed her heart. Huw, the captain of the garrison, would give his last breath for his master. Thirty men at arms were loyal—the rest fled. Much of Morgan's great fighting strength had traditionally come from the villages, whose men were called to arms when needed. Never before had Morgan questioned their allegiance.

Morgan's face tightened and grew gray to hear of his people's mass exodus to Rhodri's side, as cottages emptied the length and breadth of his territory. Rhodri had convinced them that if they stayed to obey the edict of their lord, they signed their own death warrants. Superstition and fear drew them away.

"I've heard Rhodri of the Mount has set up altars in the grove, and now they worship en masse, my lord," Huw told them at supper one evening.

Iestyn, horrified by this return to paganism, crossed himself and turned appealing eyes to his lord.

Morgan smiled sympathetically at his young squire. "Don't fear for their souls, lad; just tend to your own."

They were brave words, but he inwardly quailed at this alarming news. He had already heard fanciful tales of disembodied spirits hovering over the woods, and of terrifying claps of thunder, called down by the powerful Rhodri to demonstrate his union with the old gods.

All these tales had supposedly been shouted to the Lyswen inhabitants from outside the walls, but Morgan had his doubts about this. Desperate for news of loved ones, he suspected that either some servant, or one of his soldiers, slipped outside to spy. So far he had not been able to catch the culprit, but when he did, he would have no recourse but to punish him severely. Their only chance of survival lay in assuming siege conditions.

Nowadays, Isobel helped bring the food to the table, finding the kitchens a welcome refuge. With many servants gone, she was needed to oversee the meals for those who were left. Fortunately, now that they had not so many mouths to feed, their supplies would stretch well beyond a year. Surely, by then, the plague would have finally burned itself out.

That night in their bedchamber, she longed to comfort Morgan, to take the pain from his face and erase the new lines deepening by the week. Though he did not speak about it, she knew Blodwen's betrayal had wounded him to the quick. It also pained him to abandon his tenants while hiding inside the castle walls with the bridge drawn up. It was so contrary to his nature, she sometimes wondered if he was on the verge of breaking his own quarantine in an effort to bring his people back and save them from Rhodri's evil influence.

"Sweet, it's been over two weeks since we heard about any deaths. Do you suppose the danger's over?" she asked hopefully, smoothing a tangle of hair off his brow as he sat brooding beside the hearth.

"What do you think?" he asked sharply, but he took her hand and raised it to his lips. "Fortunately those who've gone to Rhodri will be fed. With me skulking in here like some animal gone to ground, they'll think I've abandoned them. God knows how the sick are faring without food."

Morgan rubbed his hands across his face in a weary gesture, heartsick when he considered the losses Nels had suffered.

"We could send food and leave it outside the villages, as you proposed in the beginning. We've enough to share."

Her suggestion was good, and together they planned their strategy. They would use volunteers to drive a wagon of supplies on this mission of mercy. The villagers could retrieve the food when the wagon had left. At least that way people would not have to join Rhodri's ranks to eat.

Now when they made love, it was less from burning desire than from a need to comfort each other, to assure one another that their love, at least, remained constant in this changing world. Isobel sensed Morgan's deep need of support, and though this change in him surprised her, she cherished him and held him close. These days her only reality was Morgan's love. They strengthened each other, feeling that as long as they were together, they would endure.

At Rhodri's stronghold, Blodwen helped her lover keep track of the incoming recruits. It was amazing how many men came from Morgan's territories. These people brought their beasts and families with them in the hope of being spared from certain death. Eventually, what had at first seemed to be a blessing had turned into a curse.

"By God, how will we feed this horde?" Rhodri asked angrily as he surveyed the straggling camp sprawling across the open fields surrounding his fortress.

Blodwen looked at him in surprise. "You can do it," she assured him adoringly. "You can call on the gods to help you."

His lip curled scornfully. "The gods offer only so much aid," he said with a snarl, and when she would have embraced him, he turned away. "We cannot go on like this. We must make a move. Soon it will be spring."

"What kind of move?"

"As long as your brother sits in his stronghold, nothing will be resolved. I have to take Llyswen. I've more than enough men, especially since many of his soldiers have come over to me. He can't have more than a skeleton force. But I'll be damned if that has made him surrender. They'll stay inside the castle for ten years at this rate. There has to be a way to get inside. You know it like the back of your hand . . . tell me."

Blodwen gulped, not prepared for his question. She knew about a tunnel, though by now it had probably been sealed by falling rock. She had explored it as a child, when she and Morgan had hidden there once to escape punishment. The tunnel ran from the hillside into the very bowels of the castle, coming out in the cellars. For some strange reason, she was reluctant to tell Rhodri of this secret entrance. To reveal Llyswen's weakness would be the ultimate betrayal.

"Well?"

"No . . . nothing," she mumbled, glancing away from him.

Rhodri's dark eyes flashed. Angry, he seized a fistful of her glittering hair and drew her to him. "Don't lie to me, Blodwen, *bach*. You know I can read your mind."

He thrust her from him and she stumbled against the

table, painfully turning her ankle. She sat down suddenly on the rushes. Numb with shock, she watched him storm out of the room.

Where did he go when he stalked away from her in anger? She knew he sometimes spent time with his men. Or he went to the sacred grove to commune with his gods. And sometimes he went elsewhere. It was that mystery location that tore at her heart. As time passed, she had begun to wonder if Morgan had been right about that other woman. When she had asked Rhodri about Olwen Gwyn, he had grown so violently angry, she shuddered beneath his wrath. Blodwen knew she could have asked the servants. There would be someone here only too eager to spread gossip, to break her pride, for she was aware they did not like her. Not overly sensitive, even she could tell she was deeply resented here. She could ask them . . . but her towering pride kept her silent.

Rhodri finished his nightly inspection of the garrison, anxious to be on his way. Olwen was waiting, and she did not suffer his tardiness with good grace. The coming baby made her moody.

One man was still unaccounted for. In annoyance, he discovered the lazy dolt lying abed. Raising him up for a tongue-lashing, Rhodri went rigid with shock as he saw a huge swelling in the lad's armpit. No, it couldn't be! He had offered many sacrifices to buy their protection. For all this time the magic had held. There had been no breath of pestilence here. Buoyed up with confidence, he had reveled in his own power. And now this. *No! No!*

In a rage, he yanked the sick youth from his bed.

"What mean you, lying here, you lazy bastard! You should be drilling with the rest."

Too ill to care, the lad stared up at him through watery eyes, his flushed face hot with fever. Rhodri glared at him, and in that instant he knew. The glow of death hovered over the lad, momentarily illuminating his body before it vanished.

Staggering back, Rhodri looked down at him, appalled. This one weak creature threatened to bring down his empire. This one sick bastard would undermine everything he had built.

Beside himself with rage, Rhodri seized the lad's collar and dragged him up, ignoring his pleas, trying not to touch his burning flesh. "Come with me, you slacker," he said with a snarl, propelling him forward on wobbling legs. Out of the room they went. The other men were singing and eating their evening meal, so the corridor outside the guardroom was deserted. Protesting, weeping in fear, the doomed lad tried to save himself by holding on to doors as they passed. It was to no avail. They continued their relentless journey to the kitchens.

At the chute to the yawning refuse pit, Rhodri halted, the miserable creature in his grasp openly weeping now as he understood his fate. With a mighty heave, Rhodri pushed him into the yawning cavern. He cried out one time as he fell. Then nothing.

Satisfied he had mended the fateful flaw in his armor, Rhodri went to the water butt and scrubbed his hands.

It was more important than ever that Blodwen reveal Llyswen's secret. His ability to read her mind came and went. Tonight he had been unable to see past the barrier she erected against him, so he had not learned her secret. He knew only that she was hiding something from him, something he needed to know to save their lives. If word got out that plague was in his own ranks, that even he was powerless to protect them, he was finished.

Rhodri went out into the cold winter night. Across the spreading grasslands cookfires flickered like fireflies in the dark. All these people had come to his command, believing in his invincibility. How many more among this rabble sickened? How many other weaklings would succumb to the pestilence and thereby destroy all he had striven for? There was no time to lose. He had to make a move without delay.

He did not ride to Olwen's cottage beyond the wood as he had intended, though he knew she waited for him. He ached for her. All this time spent appeasing Blodwen had worn him down. He needed an hour in sweet Olwen's arms, an hour when he had no need to pretend emotion he did not feel, an hour when the liquid delight flowed in his veins, hot as blood. . . .

Rhodri turned aside. Though he hoped that the sick lad was an isolated incident, that the magic still held, there was one thing left to do to assure their success. He stopped, his heart pounding as he contemplated it. Bran would have to be sacrificed! Inside he screamed out against the idea, for he loved Bran as a child. It was strange that he could feel such tenderness toward an animal.

At the goat's pen, he stopped, and Bran ran up to him, eager to greet its master. The pure white goat was a holy creature, saved for some ultimate sacrifice to the gods, the sacrifice of all sacrifices, which he had fervently hoped need never be made. Warm animal breath fanned his hand as the little goat nuzzled his palm, looking for treats. Rhodri ruffled its head, the hair silky and soft, not rough like the coats of the others. Bran was his darling. His love. Rhodri stroked the velvet-soft neck, his pain mounting as he visualized what he must do. . . .

"Here, *bach,* come to me," he called, his voice thick with tears. The little goat kicked up its heels; it bucked, it danced, and each pretty movement tore Rhodri's heart in two. There was no need to rope the animal, for it trotted obediently at his heels in perfect trust.

Every step was a torment and he wanted to turn back, almost did a dozen times, but he knew he must go on. To save an empire, to save his own life, he must sacrifice the goat to the hungry gods to appease the anger that had weakened the spell he had cast for protection.

Into the silent oak grove they went. Bran stopped, nosing in the undergrowth, and Rhodri called sharply to it. He held up his lantern and saw the goat coming, a piece of vegetation dangling from its soft lip as Bran trotted toward him. Slowly they walked to the altar. The sky was cloudy. There was no moon tonight.

Rhodri caught the little animal to him, his arms wrapped tight about the warm, furry body. He kissed the goat, his tears falling on Bran's head. Then he drew his ceremonial dagger and swiftly slit Bran's throat. The goat's large brown eyes seemed to reproach him even as he slit its snow white gullet, now rapidly turning scarlet. On the altar he laid his terrible sacrifice and he knelt before it to pray. But tears choked out the words of the prayers and he laid his head against Bran's still-warm side and wept.

Blodwen decided she could hold out against Rhodri no longer. She wanted him beside her, wanted to be in his favor again. When he was angry with her every day was torment. She was fully aware of the price she must pay for that gift, the bargain unspoken between them.

Slowly she walked to his chamber. Never before had she gone to Rhodri, always waiting for him to come to her. Timidly she knocked on the iron-banded door. There was no answer. Maybe he wasn't here. But she was sure she could hear a noise inside, almost like weeping.

She pushed open the door. The room was lit by a lone candle and the glow from a small fire. Rhodri knelt before a marble altar, his head in his hands, shoulders heaving even as she watched. Startled by his unexpected emotion, she stopped. Never before had she seen Rhodri unmanned. Curiously, instead of repelling her, this new insight into his character charmed her. Beneath that tough exterior, his heart beat tender and true. Tears pricked her eyes and she went to comfort him, her footfalls soft on the rushes.

Immediately sensing a presence, Rhodri turned and was startled to find Blodwen there.

"Rhodri."

"What do you want?" he asked, his voice ragged.

She was somewhat repelled by the bloodstains on his hands as he reached out to her, by the splatters staining his yellow tunic. He must have gone to the grove tonight to make a sacrifice. Relief spread through her. Anything was better than his spending the night in another woman's bed.

"I remembered—there's a way inside Llyswen."

Rhodri's face was transformed. Already the power was working, assuring him his darling had not died in vain.

"Tell me, Blodwen, love. Come, tell me."

He crouched on the floor before the hearth, patting the place beside him. She sat on the rushes and told him about the secret passage, how to find its entrance on the hillside, and where it came out inside Llyswen. "It's so narrow there's only room for a single file. It wouldn't work for an army."

He digested the information, thinking how best to use it. Just now, as he prayed, he had seen a huge conflagration, hungry flames leaping heavenward. "I'll smoke them out," he decided suddenly, knowing it was Llyswen he had seen burning. "Some of their own men who've changed sides can go back and, once they're inside, lay the fires. At a given signal, we'll torch it—the whole place will go up like an inferno with all that timber and those fanciful draperies. I've no use for it. It'll be good riddance."

Appalled by his startling plan, Blodwen stared at him in horror.

"Torch it—you can't mean that! You said we'd live there together."

"I've different plans now."

"But, Rhodri—Llyswen's my home. It's my birthright. I want us to rule equally there. That's what we agreed."

He stood looking down at her impassively. "If you want me to love you, Blodwen, you'll have to trust and not keep trying to change things to suit yourself. Remember, I always know what's best. Just now in a vision it was revealed to me. It is what will be."

"I love the palace. . . . I don't want it destroyed. Why can't we just slip inside and overrun them instead? You said yourself they've only a skeleton force. Oh, please, Rhodri, please," she begged, devastated by his unyielding stance. Blodwen tried to hold on to his hand, but he pulled away.

He stood looking down at her, dark eyes smoldering like coals. "Earlier tonight you complained that there was never any time for lovemaking between us. This is a perfect time—or would you rather whine about Llyswen?"

Blodwen swallowed, torn between needing to argue him out of his rash plan, and taking advantage of what was being offered. Gently he stroked her face and pulled down her knotted hair so that it spilled in a silver-gilt fall down her back.

"If you'd rule beside me, Blodwen, first you must learn obedience," he said, his rich voice warm and low. "You're a very powerful woman. It's beneath your dignity to beg."

She smiled at him, blinking back her tears. Taking his hand, she pressed it against her lips, ignoring the rank taste of blood. To win Rhodri's love, she would sacrifice anything—even her birthright.

Chapter Seventeen

Out of the gray morning light appeared four of Llyswen's former garrison, standing on the far side of the moat, seeking admission to the stronghold. Morgan was brought from his meal to speak to them. He heard them out, his face set. They had had a change of heart, they said, and were sorry for deserting him and hoped he would forgive them and allow them to come back.

Morgan refused. Even Huw found his reaction harsh.

"Don't you see, they could already be infected," Morgan explained patiently, not expecting to have to defend his actions to his captain.

Huw nodded, but by his set face, Morgan knew he was not in agreement. To Huw the return of four men was a triumph, an indication that the tide was turning in their favor. Why else would the men have come back unless they were disillusioned with Rhodri's promises?

Morgan was not as sure. He discussed the situation with Isobel, and though she did not know why, the men's unexpected return made her uneasy. These men could be infected; it could even be Rhodri's intention to spread the disease inside Llyswen. Just in case the men's regrets were genuine, Morgan did not want to cast them off. There was a fodder shed across the meadow. Morgan decided to let them use that as a shelter: food and water would be let down to them over the wall. But he stayed firm in his refusal to let them inside.

When Rhodri heard this unexpected news, he was furious. He had to get them inside. There was no other way. The men would have to go through the tunnel in secret to lay the fires. And it must be today.

The soldiers were not enthusiastic about betraying their former master. They were even tempted to take up his offer of shelter in the fodder shed until the danger was past. But they knew it was not wise to defy Rhodri of the Mount; if they did they would not last a night, for Lord Morgan could not protect them from Rhodri's unholy power. Several among their number had mysteriously disappeared these past few days. Though Rhodri suggested they were traitors who had returned to Llyswen, Lord Morgan's refusal to admit anyone made a lie of the tale. Possibly their comrades had refused to obey an order and were spirited away to the underworld. Uneasily all four men agreed to Rhodri's plan.

They were to carry tinder and flammables on their backs. The mass attack was to take place the following day at dawn. Rhodri's oracles forecast dry, windy and sunny weather, nearly perfect conditions for his purpose. In fact, the weather would be suitable for the next three days, but he could not afford to wait any longer.

During these past couple of days three soldiers had already succumbed to the plague. This morning Rhodri had learned that some women and children had sickened in the camp. They must move now before it was too late. If word leaked out that people were dying from the plague, there would be mass panic. He had cleverly concealed the dying from the others, but he could not go on like this.

There was no room for more. Soon the refuse pit would begin to betray its secret. Time was running out.

The garrison at Llyswen was put on heightened alert. Morgan sensed a change in Rhodri's tactics. There was much movement in the hills as Rhodri's troops moved closer. Now, more than ever, he suspected the deserters' timely change of heart had been orchestrated by his enemy, but for what purpose he did not know.

From the battlements Morgan and Isobel watched the twisting, glittering columns moving on the hillside, going down, then up, until they finally reached the flat plain, where they pitched camp. Fearing an imminent attack, Morgan ordered weapons handed out to all able-bodied souls inside the fortress. Even the servants were issued swords or halberds, women also being armed. Rhodri's massed forces suggested that they would soon have to make a stand.

Morgan had a dozen loyal archers and plenty of arrows. For a while, they could pick off the enemy as they advanced. After dark the defense of Llyswen would be harder. Their small force could not man every entrance, and they would have to sleep. Morgan worked out a rotating schedule of two hours on, two hours off, for their thin force, trying to deploy his men to maximum advantage. Then they waited for Rhodri to make his next move.

Glumly Isobel watched the enemy troops massed below. How could so many have escaped the plague? Could it be true, as Rhodri claimed, that the power of his ancient gods could turn away the plague? Christian prayers had not helped the thousands of poor souls who had already succumbed. She voiced her observation to Morgan.

"How can you say that? We're alive. We have each other. When you consider how many chances we've had to come down with plague, you must agree, a divine force has brought us safely to this day."

"You're right," she agreed guiltily. "Somehow my

faith isn't as strong as it used to be. Maybe I should light a candle in the chapel and offer prayers for our deliverance."

"Likely Rhodri's doing the same thing, all decked out in his robes and gold necklace. I don't have much faith in the power he's calling on. We'll go to the chapel after supper together."

When their evening meal was over they went to Llyswen's cold, dark chapel. Immediately they were struck by the sense of holiness inside these ancient, hallowed walls. After lighting their candles and offering prayers, they clasped hands before the altar. Here Morgan lit the altar tapers and together they knelt before the holy rood, the crucified figure of Christ, flanked by St. John and the Blessed Mother.

The gold altar candlesticks rippled fire from the flames, each sconce upheld by the hereditary dragon of Nels. It still pained Morgan when he thought about Rhodri possessing their sacred seal, handed to him by his own treacherous sister. What fools women could sometimes become when they were blinded by love.

Then Morgan glanced at Isobel kneeling beside him, gazing reverently at the crucified Christ as she prayed. At this moment she was more lovely than ever, and his heart pitched with love for her. As he considered what she had done and suffered out of love for him, he was suddenly grateful for this necessary affliction of women. Unexpectedly he hugged her against him, and when she asked what he was smiling about, he would not tell her.

Before dawn a great outcry sounded the length and breadth of Rhodri's camp as panic assailed his followers. Plague was in the camp! It had crept silently through tents and makeshift hovels, turning trusting disciples into hysterical accusers.

At first Rhodri was unaware of the change. In the chill hours before first light, he supervised the deployment of his troops, riding from his tent in full battle array.

Dressed in a leather jack and men's hose and boots, Blodwen rode beside him. She wore a helmet over her silvery hair, which blew loose across her shoulders. Riding straight and proud, together they reviewed their troops.

The thrill of impending conflict quickened Rhodri's blood, a phenomenon that always turned his thoughts to Olwen. He wondered how she fared, for he had not dared visit her. They were too close to victory for him to risk angering Blodwen. He was afraid she would betray him and warn the garrison at Llyswen. So, around the clock, he had feigned passion and affection for her, until he came close to retching at the need to constantly romance this hard woman. With him she had come as close to female as she could ever be—for Rhodri's taste, it was not near enough.

"Before the day's out we'll command all the land as far as we can see," she said in excitement, stopping on a rise of ground to look down on Llyswen, where lights pricked the darkness and shone in puddles on the moat. Her heart lurched at the sight of her childhood home so close, so dear. Blodwen shuddered at the thought of the palace being consumed by flames. All along she had intended to come up with some brilliant counterplan to save Llyswen from its fate. But she had not. In fact, this morning her head felt muzzy and her eyes burned. Not enough sleep, or too much wine last night, she quickly dismissed, wiping sweat from her brow. It was the sweat of excitement, for she could not wait to ride into battle beside her beloved.

Rhodri smiled at her and he clicked to his horse and raced back down the hillock. A deputation of men were coming toward him through the gloom, hurrying in obvious distress.

"My lord, my lord—there's plague in the ranks! Men are deserting by the droves."

"What! This can't be," Rhodri cried, his face blanching. Spurring his horse to a gallop, he raced through the gathering, scattering men as he went.

Shocked by the alarming news, Blodwen spurred her horse after him, trying to catch up, though he already shot ahead in the distance. She seemed unable to match his pace this morning. Damn, of all mornings to have the woman's ailment coming on, for surely that was what it was, this vague feeling of being unwell, a heavy, hot head and burning eyes, pains in her body. . . . Appalled by a sudden thought, Blodwen allowed her horse to slack off until they were barely moving.

Dear God, no, surely she could not be sickening with the plague! Faltering, she put her hand to her brow, which ran with sweat and felt hot to the touch. Her throat rasped and her chest ached. In fact, she suddenly felt so nauseated, she found sitting in the saddle an effort in itself. Slowly she slid to the ground, where she leaned against her mount's sweating flank. If she didn't lie down soon, she was going to vomit. Dragging the horse aside with her, she moved off the path and dropped down on the damp grass beside a tent. There she drew up her knees, resting her head against them. She wept out of sickness and defeat.

On all sides men were leaving the camp, fleeing like rats from a sinking ship. Rhodri slapped them with the flat of his sword, trying to stop the panic. He elicited cries of pain but could not stem the tide. Men, women and children streamed away from his magnificent army, running back to their villages in a desperate bid to escape the plague.

"Stop! Stop!" he screamed at them. "Only I can save you. Listen to me, you fools. You're taking the plague back with you. You're doomed."

Finally he stopped trying, for they were deaf to his pleas. Defeated, he dropped back, slumping in the saddle as he watched them leave. His own men stayed with him, but compared to his glorious army, they were a pitiful few. How could so grand an army be dissolving before his eyes? They could still fire Llyswen and smoke them out. He had more than enough men for that strategy.

Rhodri ordered his soldiers into position on the flatland facing Llyswen, reminding them to keep out of range of Lord Morgan's archers. Taking a half dozen men with him, Rhodri scrambled on foot up the hillside, keeping low, not wanting to attract attention. It was already getting light, and as they moved uphill, the burning rim of the sun crept over the horizon, spilling golden light across the hillside.

He had no idea what had happened to the four deserters from Llyswen's garrison; he would have to trust that they had followed his written plans of where best to set the fires. He had chosen a half dozen sites where they could do the most damage. The garrison would be so busy trying to man their defenses, the piles of brush and dry tinder had probably been overlooked.

This narrow tunnel was musty and the bad air made him gag. In fact, several of the men behind him vomited in the darkness, and Rhodri wondered uneasily if it was merely the poor air in the passage that made them lose their guts, or the more insidious work of the plague. Under his clothes he wore a sacred amulet, and he nervously fingered the precious metal as he hurried along the passage. In a few places rocks had fallen and they had to scramble over the rubble, but in all, this tunnel had weathered the years without mishap. Undoubtedly this good fortune was the work of the gods, reassuring him that they still smiled on him.

Rhodri began to feel more confident when the entrance leading out into Llyswen's cellars came in sight. Taking a deep breath, he tentatively tried the door, which had been hidden by casks and boxes. It slid open easily on freshly oiled hinges, and his confidence increased. At least his advance party had taken care of this important detail. It was so dark down here he had trouble seeing the strategic spots he had sketched for them on the map.

They left the castle cellars and came up into the corridors without seeing anyone. Likely the inhabitants were all on the battlements, baring their teeth and flexing their muscles in a futile attempt to intimidate his troops. So ridiculous was the picture forming in his mind's eye, Rhodri began to chuckle before he forced down his humor, aware that his action could spell disaster.

They fanned out, three to the main floor, two to the stairwell. He would personally take the lord's wing, for he wanted the pleasure of killing the arrogant Dragon Knight himself, eager to show him who was champion now.

Stealthily they moved along the corridors. Rhodri had arranged with his troops to wait a half hour past sunup before blowing a bugle. The bugle would bring all Lyswen's garrison to the battlements to see what action was impending. That would give them uninterrupted time to light the fires.

It must be time. Rhodri peered through an arrow slit at the brightening sky. From here he could see his men sitting proudly in formation, the loyal core of his forces. He didn't need those plague-ridden peasants to conquer Lyswen. He would soon be supreme lord of Nels and all its surrounding territory.

Clutching his amulet and silently mouthing a prayer, Rhodri cocked his head. There it was—a shrill bugle blast. Overhead he could hear running feet, and he smiled. Just as he had expected, they were running onto the battlements to see what was happening.

To a man, his secret force struck the tinder. At first his fire did not catch and Rhodri swore under his breath, knowing a moment's panic until the flame grew, pushing out a puff of smoke, before beginning to crackle pleasantly as it snaked along its trail of dry bracken to the flammables behind the door.

Rhodri was safely down the corridor when he heard the whoosh, the roar, as it all went up. He knew he must be close to the lord's chamber, but he doubted Lord Morgan still lounged abed with his Englishwoman. Doubtless he stood on the battlements with the rest, puzzling over the battle plan of the troops massed below. Now all that remained was to offer a challenge to his archenemy, then escape before the fire cut off all routes.

Rhodri smiled. It was simple to say. Again he rubbed the gold amulet. Now more than ever he needed the cooperation of the gods to make the task equally as simple to carry out.

Though as yet no enemy archers had appeared, Morgan placed Isobel in an angle of the tower to shelter her from arrows. His own men crouched behind their arrow slits, ready to pick off the enemy as soon as they came into range. Heating pots of pitch were being tended by two kitchen scullions. If Rhodri used scaling ladders, the pitch would be poured over the invaders as they came up the ladders. Though Llyswen had few troops, Morgan intended to make full use of all he had.

Isobel's task was to bundle and sort sheaves of arrows to feed to their archers; a kitchen lad was assigned to distribute them when needed. She was also to oversee a bucket chain if flaming arrows were shot over the walls. Having these tasks made her feel part of the defense, though she suspected Morgan mainly wanted to keep her busy.

Young Iestyn stood proudly beside his lord, squaring his shoulders and looking stern. Huw, the captain of the guard, and a handful of loyal men, had helped Morgan organize their thin defenses. They found it strange that after the bugle was blown, the enemy still did not advance. The defenders watched tensely in the bright morning light, waiting for their opponents to make a move.

What were Rhodri's men waiting for? Morgan leaned against the battlements. If the plan was to make him nervous, it was succeeding. Earlier he had watched Rhodri's camp disbanding, many of them fleeing as if in a rout. That had also seemed a strange tactic, yet now, in the face of the inaction of Rhodri's mounted elite, he began to wonder if it was not all part of some grand plan.

The wind whipped across the battlements, picking up briskly. Below, the enemy's flags and banners flapped like sails while they waited astride their shaggy mounts.

A sudden cry of alarm came from the west tower. When Morgan looked back, he froze at what he saw. Billowing black smoke poured out of the tower, spreading in the wind. A second cry of alarm sounded as smoke came from the northern defense. Men panicked, racing with buckets of water to put out the flames.

Thundering down from the battlements, Llyswen's defenders spread in all directions. The extent of the blaze was unbelievable! Fire seemed to have spread to every part of the structure. The main staircase was already alight, and despite his men's valiant efforts, the fire rapidly gained hold.

Desperately trying to smother the flames, they finally abandoned the west tower, and the firefighters pulled back to concentrate their efforts on the main staircase. Isobel joined the others, trying to beat out the fire with pieces of canvas. Smoke choked them and blackened their hands and faces.

Morgan decided it was time to move Isobel to safety. Ignoring her protests, he hurried her to a section of the sprawling dwelling as yet untouched by flames, sending her to sit outside in the fresh air. Though she argued with him about his own safety, Morgan ran back to salvage what he could.

The last of the defenders had come down from the battlements, not knowing whether to stay to resist the enemy, try to put out the fire, or flee for their lives. In most cases they ran for safety.

Pulling his hood over his nose against the smoke, Morgan plunged back inside. There was only one explanation for so intense a blaze: these fires had been intentionally set. Now he knew what Rhodri's troops had been waiting for. He need not look below to know the mounted men moved closer, prepared to slaughter Llyswen's garrison when they ran outside to escape the blaze. Angrily Morgan shouted to his fleeing people, telling them where they could be safe without heedlessly risking their lives. There was no need to run into enemy swords. Some listened. Most did not.

Next he turned his attention to saving those closest to him. Huw was safe, for he had seen him outside. Now he must find Iestyn, who had been standing beside him on the battlements. He had not seen the squire since the fire began. Flames had already consumed the ornamental wooden staircase in the center of the house. At least these stairs leading onto the battlements were made of stone. Llyswen's unique timbered gables, its flowing draperies and carvings, had all helped feed the blaze. Whoever had set fire to Llyswen knew exactly what they were doing.

Morgan began to cough in the thickening smoke and he leaned against an arrow slit, gulping fresh air. It took little imagination to solve the puzzle. Blodwen had brought Rhodri of the Mount inside Llyswen, giving him ample time to learn its most vulnerable points. That still did not explain how these fires had been set.

Then Morgan suddenly had the answer. In shock he realized there was one great forgotten chink in their armor, a secret known only to the family. And Blodwen knew it! That old passage from the hillside! Dear God! That made her betrayal of him complete! They must have come through there today while he was on the battlements.

The pain of Blodwen's betrayal went deep. Out of love,

she had defected to the enemy: fear of plague had kept her there. Those were flaws he could forgive. It was this final act of betrayal he found hardest to bear.

Anger hardened his face as he began the final ascent to the battlements. Smoke billowed down the stairs, suggesting that the higher levels were already on fire. Morgan sprinted up the stone steps, holding his breath as he plunged into a cloud of smoke. He rounded the bend, and a figure loomed out of the smoke to block his way. Morgan automatically reached for his sword, but because of the way the tower was constructed, the advantage was with his opponent. He barely had room to draw his sword, let alone wield it, his sword arm confined by the central stone pillar. A gust of wind blowing through the arrow slit dissipated the smoke to reveal the identity of his attacker.

Rhodri of the Mount stood before him, white teeth gleaming in a face blackened by smoke. A malicious grin suffused his features as he faced the Lord of Nels.

"So, Dragon Knight, you've finally met your match. Now who has the power?"

Billowing smoke swirled downstairs to engulf them both. Rhodri doubled over coughing, giving Morgan a temporary advantage. He leaped up the steps, until he was level with Rhodri, and he smashed him against the wall. Then he moved higher on the stairs. Now it was Rhodri who was at a disadvantage against the confining masonry. Undaunted, he promptly sheathed his sword and pulled twin daggers from his belt.

Morgan jumped away and virtually fell through the door onto the battlements. Here he gulped deeply of the fresh air. Rhodri tumbled after him, rolling across the masonry to come up in a fighting crouch, daggers at the ready.

The lifelong enemies faced each other on the narrow walkway. Morgan slashed and Rhodri ducked. Again and again they repeated the maneuver, dancing a macabre dance amid the smoke and flames. Morgan pierced Rhodri's shoulder before he wrenched away. Unfortunately his sword wedged in a metal fitting on his enemy's armor and was torn from his hand. Now Morgan drew his own daggers to defend himself as they moved in closer for hand-to-hand combat. To Morgan's surprise, as Rhodri lashed out at him he felt a cold slash of steel. Blood trickled down his arm, washing through the soot and grime. The wound, though deep, was narrow, for Rhodri had not had time to twist or slash.

Rhodri crouched before him, teeth bared like a ferocious animal as he concentrated on defeating his opponent. Suddenly Morgan got inside his guard. Catching the bottom of Rhodri's jack, he thrust upward. Rhodri grunted in pain and Morgan felt the hot trickle of blood running over his hand before Rhodri leaped at him and bore him backward. They crashed together on the stone walkway, momentarily knocking the breath from their bodies. Grappling together, legs wrapped around each other, they rolled to the edge of the battlements, strength against strength. Once again Rhodri drove home. Morgan cried out in pain as cold steel tore into his side through a weak point in his jack.

The taste of victory made Rhodri careless. He pulled away, preparing to jump on his enemy and slash his throat. Fighting against the pain, Morgan awaited the move, and, as Rhodri leaped, he raised his arm, trying to hold it against the other man's weight. The force was too much. Morgan's arm went to the side on impact. But his dagger plunged deep into Rhodri's gut.

Dark eyes widening in shock, Rhodri opened his mouth to speak and blood frothed out. Still fighting, Rhodri fell hard against Morgan, whose body cushioned his fall. With a mighty effort, Morgan finally thrust the other man off him, feeling the strength of his arms ebbing away. It was all he could do to roll clear of Rhodri's bulk. Their blood flowed together across the stonework.

Morgan felt a strange pumping sensation under his jack, like the throb and ebb of blood. Startled by the discovery, he saw that it was his own lifeblood running over the stones. He desperately tried to stop the flow. His hands were too weak to respond. They were all bloodied and still, as if they belonged to another, refusing to obey his will.

Orange flames formed a garish halo overhead as thick black smoke streamed heavenward, billowing and gaining strength until a mighty cloud stretched far into the horizon. Llyswen burned beyond salvation. Before his eyes his beloved home was being reduced to ash and rubble while he lay there helpless to prevent it. Then he thought about Isobel. Where was she? Had she gotten out safely or had she run back inside the building? Feebly he called her name, but his only answer was the roar of the fire.

Morgan drew up his knees, trying to stand. The stonework swam crazily around him and he fell back. He had to save Isobel—it was already too late to save his home. Llyswen was dying around him. Later, despite the heat from the flames, a deep chill began to settle in his bones, making him aware that he was dying with it.

''Oh, my lady, my lady, come quick. Hurry.''

Iestyn tugged Isobel's arm, trying to get her to go with him. Through the billowing smoke she finally identified Morgan's squire, though his fair hair was singed, his clothes scorched, his face dark as a blackamoor's.

''What is it?''

''Lord Morgan's hurt. . . . Come, you have to help me, lady.''

Panicking at the news, Isobel raced after him inside the building, drawing her skirt over her head to try to keep out the smoke. In this spot the fire had lessened, leaving blackened beams and smoldering fabrics in its wake.

Iestyn led her along a corridor to the tower stairs. As she stumbled up the twisting stairs, Isobel found the stone pillars warm to the touch. The fire had flashed through this tower, devouring all flammables in its path before finally shooting out through the roof. Now, between charred beams, she could see blue sky and sunlight.

Below there was shouting and the clang of weapons as Llyswen's defenders fought for their lives against Rhodri's troops. Men had jumped into the moat to try to escape the flames and were being cut down as they scrambled up the other side.

"Over here."

Isobel stumbled over a body as she followed Iestyn, who was now crouched beside his master. Appalled by what she saw, Isobel fought back tears. Morgan was deathly pale under his sooty overlay, and by his very stillness, Isobel thought him already dead. There was so much blood! Isobel prayed that some of it belonged to the other man.

Between them they struggled to pull open his jack and saw the huge, gaping slit. Isobel ripped strips from her smoky, begrimed shift, and pushed a wad of fabric into the wound to try to stop the bleeding. She bound another strip around his chest to hold the compress in place and pinned the bandage with a brooch from her dress.

"That's Rhodri of the Mount." Iestyn spat as he pushed the body over with his foot.

Isobel looked at the dead man. She shuddered as she realized she was looking at their much-feared enemy. In death Rhodri seemed smaller and less formidable than she had expected. This must have been a duel to the death. She thanked God it was Morgan who was the victor.

"He's too heavy for us to move him," Isobel said, looking around for someone to help but seeing no one.

Iestyn wrestled a half-burned door off its hinge to use as a stretcher. Between them they rolled Morgan onto the door, trying not to jar him too much and make his wound bleed. Now that he was moved, Isobel saw that blood also oozed from his arm, and the back of his shirt was sodden and red.

Though they tried until they staggered to their knees, they could not carry his weight. Isobel suggested they slide the door down the steps, with one pushing, the other guiding. The squire agreed, though he argued he should go first, as more weight would come to him and he was best able to bear it. Any other time she would have laughed at the lad's conceit; today she nodded and set to work.

It was hard to guide the makeshift stretcher, for it stopped at every bend, wedging against the stonework. Fragments of burning wood fell around them, and they dodged a rain of debris as they bumped and slid down each level until they finally reached the bailey.

Leaning against the wall, they rested, gulping for breath. Isobel's lungs burned and she did not know if it was from exertion or from breathing the smoke. Morgan had moaned pitifully as they bumped and jarred him down the tower. By those sounds Isobel knew he still lived. She knelt beside him and kissed his face, whispering encouragement. He did not seem to hear her.

After a few minutes' rest it was time to venture outside. Isobel peered around the burned doorjamb, looking for enemy soldiers. They surely had breached the walls by now. She saw several bodies, but those men seemed to have been killed by falling timbers. There was no sign of Rhodri's troops.

She signaled Iestyn that it was clear, and they pushed and pulled Morgan out into the fresh air. Iestyn found a length of rope, which he ran around Morgan's body to lash him to the door, leaving two long ends to pull. They dragged Morgan across the bailey, using the door as a sled.

They rested again in the shadow of the wall. Sounds of battle still came from the other side. Their next dilemma was how to get Morgan out of Llyswen without being captured.

Isobel moved Morgan's hand off the ground and tucked it safely at his side. She held his blood-caked fingers against her cheek, alarmed when he gave no response. Iestyn had gone to reconnoiter. As she waited, the din beyond the walls seemed to move away. Isobel leaned back wearily against the stone, aware that the building still smoked behind her. Sweat trickled down her face and she could feel it snaking down her back between her shoulder blades. The flames created such heat, her throat was parched.

After what seemed like hours, Iestyn reappeared with a bag slung over his shoulder and several daggers thrust in his belt. He gave a dagger to Isobel and she slipped it through the lacing of her surcoat. Iestyn had also found a couple of cloaks, which he spread over his master.

"The postern's clear," he said slowly, carefully choosing his English words. "We can cross at the shallows."

Appalled by his suggestion, Isobel suddenly felt defeated by the momentous task ahead. How could they get Morgan across the moat without being seen? Even if they were successful, how could they move him across country? It was hopeless. Tears trickled down her cheeks, making rivers through the grime.

"Don't cry." Iestyn patted her bowed head. "There's a donkey in the smithy."

Reluctantly Isobel got to her feet. Iestyn slung the bag of supplies over his shoulder and they dragged the door to the blacksmith's shed. Carcasses littered the stables. The horses had panicked and kicked down their stall doors but had still been unable to get out. The stable's thatched roof still smoldered, blackened pieces fluttering down in the wind. Spartan had been inside. Pain stabbed Isobel at the realization that he was dead. Yet she was somehow numbed to this new grief. There had already been so much to weep about.

Inside the blacksmith's forge a donkey was tethered to an iron ring. Miraculously much of the smithy was intact. Iestyn found a saddle for the beast and they debated how best to get Morgan on its back. Tilting the door against the mounting block, they pushed and pulled until they had Morgan in the saddle. It was a terrible struggle, and he groaned and cried out in pain during the ordeal. Isobel wept out of fatigue and for the hopelessness of their task, and finally out of pity for his pain. Morgan was finally in the saddle, slumped across the donkey's neck. Iestyn bound him in place and they went back outside.

The postern was still unguarded. The gate gave onto a grassy mound, which sloped down to the moat. Here, on the back side of the fortress, it was deserted. Isobel could not believe her eyes. She blinked, sure she must have overlooked some waiting marksman. When she opened them again, they were still alone. Debris and bodies were scattered across the open ground on the other side of the moat. They waited and watched. Nothing moved.

Keeping close to the stonework to avoid detection, they headed for the shallows. The donkey was docile, which was a blessing. Iestyn flattened himself against the wall, sidling around the curve. It was still safe. Below lay the most passable part of the moat. All the remaining action was confined to the front of the structure, where shouts and the clash of swords could still be heard.

They set out warily, alert for enemy soldiers. Iestyn showed her where the moat was shallowest, but even so Isobel plunged up to her hips in icy water. In the middle of the moat, the donkey balked. Isobel prayed it was not going to throw back its head and bray in protest.

Stroking its head, coaxing sweetly, Isobel finally persuaded the donkey to walk a few steps, until they were on the move again. It seemed an eternity before they were scrambling up the far bank. From this distance Llyswen was a pitiful, blackened sight. When she recalled how much Morgan loved his home and how proud he had been of each improvement, pain tugged at her heart. There was little remaining beyond a stone hull. It was hard to believe it had burned so quickly. Perhaps Rhodri had used his famous black magic to speed the fire. But she could not waste energy worrying about the how and why—the reality was that Llyswen was destroyed.

Iestyn hurried her over the rough ground, pulling her down into a hollow amid a tangle of gorse and brambles. He had chosen this route in hopes of hiding the donkey from troops on the battlements, or even worse, those still on this side of the moat.

Virtually running now, Isobel sobbed with fatigue as she tried to keep up with the lithe squire. The donkey, however, seemed to enjoy this pace, and it kicked up its heels in pleasure, until they had to slow down, or risk Morgan being thrown from the saddle.

Iestyn led them deep into the hills. The track they walked was barely wide enough for the donkey.

"Where are we going?" Isobel asked, tugging his arm in hopes of slowing him down.

"Only a few more minutes," Iestyn assured her breathlessly, plunging ahead on an ever narrowing track. Clumps of brush and bushes choked the path, forcing Isobel to pick her way. Finally, with a shout of triumph, Iestyn jumped forward to drag back a tangle of brush. Rusty bracken grew amid a thicket of mountain ash to conceal the mouth of a cave.

"Oh, Iestyn, thank you. This is perfect." Isobel gasped in relief.

Smiling proudly, he coaxed the donkey inside the cave. Once they were all safely inside, he rearranged the camouflage. To the casual observer, the cave had ceased to exist.

"How did you find this?"

"As a lad I played soldier in these hills," he explained.

Together they struggled to lift Morgan from the saddle, staggering under his weight as they laid him on a heap of dried bracken on the cave floor. Then Isobel grabbed the donkey's reins as the animal tried to go back outside. Under the animal's great protest she fastened its reins around a protruding spur of rock.

From his bag Iestyn produced a pot of salve, linen bandages, needle and thread, tinder, a rushlight, a skin of wine, and some bread and cheese.

They wedged the rushlight in a crevice in the rock and began the formidable task of cleaning Morgan's wounds. Isobel was appalled by the severity of his injuries. Her heart fluttered in fear as she wondered if they were already too late to save him. He was deathly white, his pallor reminding her about the pool of blood she had seen congealing on the battlements. Not familiar with dressing battle wounds, she took instructions from Iestyn, who could not keep from gasping himself when he saw the extent of his master's wound.

They cleaned the flesh by pouring wine over it. The slash still oozed blood and lay deep and wide. Iestyn knew they needed to pull the edges together to help it heal. Isobel shuddered as he used the needle and thread to sew a clumsy seam. Beads of sweat dripped from her brow and nausea rose in her throat as she watched. At last it was finished and they put salve over the repair and wrapped it with a clean bandage.

Morgan had lapsed into unconsciousness during the ordeal, which was a blessing. Now they could not rouse him to eat, so Isobel saved his portion of food for later. They were able to pour a trickle of wine down his throat, holding his head so he would not choke and massaging his neck to make him swallow.

Worn out from the day's terrible events, Isobel wrapped her cloak around herself and leaned back against the cave's stone surface. So exhausted was she, the rock might have been a feather bed. In a few minutes she was asleep.

Chapter Eighteen

The next day Morgan was delirious. He tossed and moaned, burning with fever. Isobel prayed that this fever was caused by the wound, thrusting away the terrifying thought that he had caught the plague. Iestyn assured her that fever was the natural outcome of battle wounds, but she did not know if he meant it, or was trying to cheer her up.

There was a mountain stream close by, and there she soaked a piece from her skirt and laid the cold cloth over Morgan's face to reduce his fever.

From her vantage point on the hillside, Isobel saw that Rhodri's men had pitched camp outside Llyswen's walls. From here she watched as they carried bags and boxes out of the ruin. Everything had not burned, and these fierce looters were salvaging what they could.

Eventually the brief spell of fine weather broke and the rain came down in sheets.

On one of his forays outside the cave, Iestyn found a pot of healing salve in an abandoned hut, and though Isobel quailed at the thought that it could carry the plague, she had to use it on Morgan's wound to save his life. Each day Iestyn set rabbit snares. He skinned and cooked his catch in a battered pot he had also retrieved from the hut. There were turnips and parsnips scavenged from an abandoned garden. These they cooked together to make a tasty rabbit stew.

Painstakingly Isobel spooned broth into Morgan's mouth. For the most part he was unresponsive, but if she held his head up and massaged his throat, he would swallow.

Some days Iestyn scavenged further afield, and one time he returned with a skin of wine, some goat cheese and flour. On the flat cook stone at the cave's hearth, Isobel cooked cakes made from flour, water and hoarded rabbit grease.

After the first few days the donkey ran away. Isobel woke one morning to find it gone. Though Iestyn went to look for it, he never found the donkey.

Morgan's side festered and his fever raged. He grew thinner. But he lived. Isobel bathed his hot face and poured the last of the wine over his wound in hope of combating the infection. With his dagger, Iestyn cleaned away some of the putrefying flesh. They repacked the wound with linen washed in the mountain stream and bleached in the sun. And they prayed.

During this time together in the cave, Iestyn became like a brother to Isobel. They laughed as she tried to teach him English, and he reciprocated by teaching her Welsh. She thanked him sincerely for his help in caring for Morgan and for providing their meals. Iestyn told her the enemy camp was deserted now, though many of Rhodri's men had not gone home: they lay dead in their tents, all victims of the plague.

Isobel listened in horror to his story, not out of concern for the enemy, but because Iestyn had gone back and forth pilfering from that camp to add to their comfort in the cave. She told him he must not go back there, nor enter any more abandoned dwellings. Reluctantly he agreed and went back to snaring rabbits and catching fish from the stream, using the pin from her brooch and string salvaged from some sacking he had scavenged for their beds.

Finally the rain stopped. Such a constant sound had it become, it was disturbingly quiet without it.

The return of sunshine excited Iestyn, who couldn't wait to be out and about. Reminding him not to venture into the deserted camp, Isobel took the first shift of caring for Morgan, freeing Iestyn to go foraging.

It was well into the afternoon and the sun was dropping. Iestyn had not returned. Isobel wondered uneasily why he was so late. She went outside the cave, shielding her eyes from the glare as she scanned the hillside. Nothing moved.

The previous day they had cooked several rabbits, and there was already a bucket of water drawn from the stream. She went back inside the cave to begin the monotonous tasks of sponging Morgan's body in an effort to bring down his fever, and then trying to spoon broth into his mouth.

Days passed and Iestyn did not come back. Isobel gradually gave up hope of ever seeing him again. Had he caught the plague? Or had one of Rhodri's men killed him? He could have fallen and injured himself. Her loss and the task of now caring for Morgan alone brought her close to despair. Isobel wept for all she had lost. When she finally dried her eyes, she felt empty of grief. And she vowed not to succumb to weakness again. Tears solved nothing. Everything depended on her own ability to survive, for without her Morgan was doomed.

After she had made him comfortable she decided to search the nearby trails in case Iestyn had fallen, or been attacked and lay wounded. Today Morgan's wound was not suppurating and his fever was down. This was the first time his sleep had been normal. She found this improvement encouraging, and it bolstered her determination to go on.

Isobel stayed close to the rocks to avoid being seen. And though she spent several hours searching, there was no sign of Iestyn. She did meet a limping pup who was overjoyed to see her.

Taking pity on the dog, she coaxed him back to the cave and gave him some rabbit offal from their last kill. Without Iestyn they had no supply of food. It would be up to her to provide food. With a heavy heart, Isobel wondered how she would manage.

Driven by hunger, she finally had to forage for herself. Though the danger of catching the plague was still very real, the specter of starvation loomed closer still.

To her surprise Isobel discovered spring had come to the valley. She leaned against the rock and surveyed the green land. Up here the trees were softened with green along their winter-bare branches, but below, in the valley, trees and bushes were covered with leaves. She gasped in delight at the misty blue carpet of bluebells spreading under the trees of a nearby wood, the blue haze stretching as far as the eye could see.

Though she had intended for him to guard Morgan, the dog decided to come exploring with her. She didn't scold him, because she was glad of his company. Isobel still saw no sign of life in the surrounding countryside. It was as if they were alone in the world. If enemy soldiers were nearby, she did not see them. It appeared safe now to explore further, so she took a saddlebag and went to scavenge for food inside Llyswen. Morgan needed fresh bandages and salve; she would also get wine to cleanse the wound, if she could find it. Most of all, they needed food.

Iestyn had shown Isobel how to make a snare, but she had never caught anything. The thought of food made her stomach protest, and it growled loudly as she picked her way down the hillside, headed for Llyswen.

With the dog swimming beside her, they crossed the

moat. After this spell of dry weather, the water level was low, making today the perfect day to cross before it rained again. After first plunging into a hole up to her waist, Isobel finally located the shingled bar Iestyn had shown her.

Uneasily Isobel edged through the postern. She gagged at the stench that met her, wrapping her skirt around her mouth and nose. The noxious stink of burn and decay hung in the air. Uneasy, the pup hugged close to her legs and she patted his sleek black head, grateful for his company.

The granary had already been broken into. But she found some spilled grain she could parch over the fire. And rats. They must have feasted well on the bodies. Many of them had also succumbed to the plague, for their bodies were as numerous as those of the human victims.

Into her saddlebag she put her treasured grain, and a skin of some strong liquor. In the infirmary she found a pot of comfrey and primrose-leaf ointment, some linen bandages and a jar of sallow willow. From the kitchens came a pot of salted meat paste, overlooked during the looting, a crock of blackberries in honey, and some flour. Wondering how to haul her find, she put the saddlebag over the hound's back. He protested, but was finally coaxed into moving under his burden. On a yoke around her neck Isobel carried two buckets filled with supplies. Crossing the moat was going to be difficult, and she thought to balance the bags on her head in hopes of keeping them dry.

As they moved across the bailey, a strange sound startled her. It was the donkey braying! There stood the runaway donkey waiting docilely inside its old home, eagerly welcoming her. The pup growled as they entered the smithy, snapping at the donkey's hooves until Isobel scolded him. Shedding tears of sheer joy, she put her arms around the donkey's neck and hugged it in delight. It was very bony and she doubted it had found much to eat here.

She had always picked forage for the beast. Much to the dog's relief, she transferred the saddlebag to the donkey's back. They set out for the cave.

Having the donkey made crossing the moat far easier, though she still had to coax it across. Toiling back up the hillside, Isobel frequently stopped to rest, marveling again how green everything was. The breeze was fragrant with spring vegetation. That offensive smell from Llyswen came to her only when the wind blew from the west. Today she could fill her lungs with pure mountain air, and rid her nostrils of those noxious smells. Something moved on the distant hillside, and she saw a family of feral goats going down the track.

She was beginning to hope the plague had burned itself out. If only Morgan could get his strength back. Uneasily she counted the days he had been tossing in fever. Many men would have been dead by now. It was only his strong constitution that had kept him alive this long. She also liked to think her deep love for him had helped.

When Isobel returned to the cave, the last golden rays of sunshine spilled across the entrance. She held aside the curtain of foliage, allowing light to enter, bringing the subterranean gloom instantly to life. She could see the depth and breadth of the cave, its craggy gray walls and smoke-blackened roof. She also noticed that Morgan had changed position since she left, moving to the edge of the bracken bed and pulling the blanket over himself as if he felt the cold.

The dog bounded ahead of her and began to lick Morgan's face. Isobel thought she must be dreaming when she heard his rasping voice admonishing the dog before he began to chuckle and fondle the animal's head.

"Morgan," she cried in delight, dropping to her knees beside him. "Oh, Morgan, sweetheart, you're awake."

He blinked, struggling to focus as the shaft of golden light flooded his face. "Isobel—is that you?"

"Oh, yes, it's me. You're better," she cried, weeping in joy as she laid her face against his.

She helped him sit up, propping him against the cave's wall for support. The dog came to lie down beside him and the donkey brayed outside for attention.

After she had given Morgan food, which for the first time he was able to eat by himself, Isobel helped him stand. It was a struggle. Morgan was so weak, Isobel had to take much of his weight against her. His face looked gaunt and white, the lower half obscured by a bushy black beard.

"God, I must look like a hermit," Morgan said, touching his shaggy, unkempt hair and beard. "How long have I been here? And where exactly is here?"

"I've lost count of the days. We're in a cave on the hill."

"Why?" he asked, puzzled. "Has Rhodri captured Llyswen?"

Isobel shook her head, realizing he did not remember.

Morgan winced with each step, the pain from his wound making him gasp. "I gather I'm wounded too. Is it serious?" he asked next, reaching under his clothing to explore the bandage.

"Yes—but you're on the mend now. Maybe when you're feeling better you can tell me how to care for you properly. Iestyn sewed the cut together with thread and it's grown into the flesh. I was afraid to try to pull it out."

"Iestyn's here?"

She glanced away and shook her head. "He was . . . but one day he didn't come back. I don't know what happened."

Morgan had stumbled through the opening of the cave and was looking about, trying to get his bearings. He was amazed to find the season changed and the trees in leaf. It was already close to dusk. He turned about to see Llyswen. From inside the cave Isobel heard his exclamation of horror as he leaned back against the rock for support.

"It's gone," he croaked in disbelief, swallowing, blinking rapidly in the hope that weakness alone played tricks on his eyes.

"Yes. Much of it. Do you remember what happened?"

"Some of it's coming back. I thought it was all part of some terrible, delirious dream. . . . I only wish it were. Where is everyone?"

"Dead maybe. I don't know. Today I saw wild goats. And the donkey and the dog are still alive. I've not seen any people since Rhodri's troops looted Llyswen. There are a lot of bodies inside."

"Plague?"

"Yes. That could be what happened to Iestyn. He kept going into the camp and the cottages."

"Have you been well?"

"Yes, thank God. And now that you're better, I thank him even more."

"Better—weak as a kitten, but I pray that'll remedy itself. Let's look at the wound before the light's gone."

Isobel painstakingly unwound his bandage, and Morgan gasped in surprise to see a livid gash grooved out of his side. The putrefying aftermath had sloughed off, and healthy pink flesh formed along the crudely sewn scar, all gaily laced with threads of blue. Morgan shook his head. "The lad probably saved my life, but that'll be hell to pull out. We'll do it tomorrow when the sun's high. Have we food?"

"Some. I went scavaging today at Llyswen. It's in the saddlebags and the buckets," she said.

Though of little help, Morgan tried to carry the bags. Together they dragged them into the cave.

She produced each treasure like a splendid gift from her bags. Morgan eagerly seized the meat paste and stuck his finger in it, sucking in delight. Isobel did the same. It tasted heavenly. And to think there had been times in the past when she had scorned ordinary salted paste. The honeyed fruit came next, and they took turns eating that with a purloined spoon from the kitchen. The wineskin Morgan greeted joyously and they passed it back and forth. Isobel found this fiery liquid much stronger than wine and it burned her throat as it went down. But later she found it created a peaceful, relaxing mood.

They lay close on the bracken bed and kissed for the first time since the battle. Morgan's rough beard tickled Isobel's face. To have him in her arms, the crisis over, was the most wonderful gift of all. She even began to wonder if it was an illusion produced by that fiery liquid, as they kissed and caressed, holding each other close. They clung together like two survivors from the shipwreck of dreams.

When it was time to sleep, they lay in each other's arms. A patch of star-sprinkled sky was visible through the cave's opening, and Isobel lay there counting the stars. The dog nuzzled her side, and behind them she could hear the donkey rustling. Far closer, she was aware of Morgan's even breathing. His skin felt cool to the touch. The fever had finally burned itself out. Like the rebirth of life spreading over the land, now they, too, had hope for the future.

Morgan steadily gained strength. He began to chafe for the day he was strong enough to go back to Llyswen and discover what was left of his grand white palace.

Though Morgan eagerly awaited that day, Isobel was apprehensive of it. She did not know if he could accept the utter devastation inside those walls. Had she been able, she would have kept him away indefinitely.

The day finally arrived. Their small party forded the moat and slipped through the postern into another world. By the grim set of his face, Isobel knew the sight was hard for Morgan to bear. All he had loved here was destroyed.

They tied cloths over their faces to fight the smell of death, though buzzards, kites and carrion crows had done their best to erase the reminders of plague and battle.

Leading the donkey with them, and keeping the dog at their side, Morgan and Isobel moved through the ruin. To Isobel's surprise, she found that whole portions of Llyswen had escaped the flames. On that terrible day when she'd fled the burning building, she had assumed everything would be consumed. The beauty was gone, the murals, the carvings, those treasured touches of luxury so hard-won. For the most part the furniture had been either destroyed or looted by Rhodri's troops, though Isobel had seen some of it standing outside forlornly in the weather, abandoned by looters who were too ill to carry it farther.

They gathered what food they could find. Much of the north wing was intact. Even some of the overhanging timberwork had survived, though it was blackened by smoke. There were tables, chairs, a bed. . . .

They stopped, aware that this furniture placement was not by chance. These items had been methodically gathered by someone. A friend, for as they scouted unaware through the ruin, they made perfect targets for an enemy.

Morgan shouted for the squatter to make himself seen, his voice echoing around the stonework, eerily going the length and breadth of the masonry shell. Nothing. He shouted again. And they waited. Suddenly the dog growled a warning and they turned to find a half dozen gaunt, ragged men slipping out of the ruins.

They were men from Llyswen's garrison! Morgan shouted a greeting to them, and they fell at his feet, weeping for joy. They had thought him dead in the fire. Over the weeks, one by one, these men had crept from their hiding places until they were all reunited inside this burned-out hull.

"There are others, my lord. Even some who survived the plague. They're living down by the estuary."

"Men from Llyswen?"

"For the most part." The men glanced from one to the other as if debating some action, and then, finally, the decision made, Tomas was chosen as spokesman.

"Will you rebuild Llyswen and lead us again, Lord Morgan?"

"It's my intention. There's much to be done before the building's safe. It's a big task."

"Everyone who's left will help. We'll tell the others we've seen you."

"First thing, we have to clear away the bodies," Morgan said, gesturing toward the abandoned camp outside the walls. "I'm not sure how to do it without risking lives. They must be burned."

"Plague survivors, my lord. They'd be best to clear away. Reckon they won't catch the sickness twice."

Morgan agreed to the suggestion. "Have we any animals left?"

"Two cows, a couple of goats. Owen's seen chickens over the hill," offered one man with a grin. "Reckon we're well away."

It was hard to believe these men had survived with their untreated wounds wrapped in filthy bandages. They were a gaunt, bearded rabble, bearing little resemblance to their former selves. Then Isobel glanced at Morgan and she began to laugh. He made a perfect leader, for he looked just like them.

With lifting spirits they made their way back to the cave. Isobel encouraged Morgan's plans for rebuilding Llyswen, however far-fetched they might seem today. The drive to succeed would act as a far stronger tonic than any she could concoct from herbs. They discussed moving back to the palace once it had been cleared and the roof patched. As it was the least damaged, the north wing would be best suited to rebuild.

After they struggled back up the mountain track, Morgan was very tired and his side had begun to ooze. Alarmed that he had overdone things, Isobel made him lie down. He pulled her down beside him and held her close, cherishing her for all she meant to him. Careful not to press against his wound, Isobel kissed his face and neck. As she nuzzled against him, his beard rasped her face and she said with conviction, "On our next voyage of discovery, I won't rest until we find a razor. I don't know this old man of the woods."

"How so? You were the one who wanted me to let my hair grow," he reminded her with a chuckle, stroking her face, seeing her again as if for the first time. Isobel's hair was straggling untidily about her face and her clothing was ragged; she was virtually barefoot, for her shoes were worn through and were tied around her ankles with rags. Her legs were scratched and her once lovely nails were broken. Yet today he thought her the most beautiful creature he had ever seen. Not even her most sumptuous court gown could have made her any more lovely to him than she was at this moment, seen through eyes clear of fever and delirium for the first time in weeks.

Morgan reached up to trace gently the dimple beside her mouth, the dark mole on her cheek. "Yes, you really are my Isobel," he whispered with a sigh of happiness.

"Did you ever doubt it?" she asked, kissing his eyelids, tracing her tongue across his gaunt cheekbone. "Though I realize my clothing's shabby, I'm the same inside. Out of love for you, sweetheart, I sank to this depth. You know I couldn't ever leave you. We belong together."

"Thank you, darling," he whispered, tears filling his eyes. They were tears of love and gratitude for all she had done for him.

Presently he drifted to sleep and Isobel got up. She went outside to fill the bucket at the spring. They had brought back scavenged supplies from Llyswen's kitchens, though now that they must share with the squatters, what little remained would not last long. She had faith that once his strength returned, Morgan could trap and catch enough to keep them alive. With her hope restored, Isobel's heart soared with joy.

Spring revived the winter-bare landscape, and that same transformation was taking place inside her heart.

As she filled the leather bucket, Isobel noticed a figure trudging up the hill. Apart from the men they had talked to today, this was the first living soul she had seen since the fire.

"Hello," she called out, not sure if her English would be understood.

The ragged creature was tall, but she could not tell if it was male or female, for the garments hung in tatters, revealing bare calves and broken-down leather boots. The men at Llyswen must have told someone else their lord was alive, and he had come to see for himself.

"I am Lady Isobel," she said loudly and carefully as the ragged form halted a few feet away.

"I know who you are."

Recognizing Blodwen's voice, Isobel gasped in shock and took a protective step backward. "You!"

"Aye, it's me, straight from the jaws of hell." Blodwen shook off her dirty hood, and her abundant hair spilled around her shoulders. To Isobel's surprise, it was no longer shining silver gilt, but an old woman's raddled gray. "You need not fear me, Isobel. I know I can't repair what's been done, but I want to tell you, from the bottom of my heart, I'm sorry for it."

Blodwen extended her clawlike hand in friendship. At first Isobel hesitated, remembering all the reasons she had to dislike this woman, but then she took Blodwen's hand in her own. Tears coursed down Blodwen's lined cheeks, and Isobel saw that her remorse was genuine.

"Why did you do it?" she asked her simply, still clasping her hand.

"A question I've asked myself many times. I suppose because I loved him. And oh, God, did he betray me. If Morgan will accept me back, I'll never give him cause to doubt again."

"I don't know if he's ready yet."

Blodwen's smile was faint and she nodded in understanding.

"Let him know I still love him. What I did I thought was best for our people. Too late I found out I was wrong. They tell me you nursed him back from death's door. I'll never forget that, Isobel. I'll be forever in your debt."

Looking closely into that ravaged face, Isobel saw that Blodwen's pale eyes were glassy with tears. She knew what it was like to love so desperately that little else mattered.

"See," Blodwen said, "I've picked these primroses for you. I remembered how much you like flowers. Go on, take them, it's a peace offering," she added, as Isobel hesitated.

"Thank you, they're pretty," Isobel said, not sure what to say. In all the times she had anticipated meeting Blodwen again, their conversation had never been like this.

"I'm a plague survivor myself. One of the fortunate ones. There are six of us down by the estuary. We can help you clean out, if you'll let us. They say once you've recovered, it's safe."

The sun was sinking and the soft spring light was slowly fading from the hillside. Isobel heard birds twittering in the trees. The unexpected sound pleased her. It was the first time she had heard birds, except for the cawing of the carrion birds as they feasted on their spoils. Across the hill she saw the family of goats treking along the hillside. The birds were back; the goats were on the hills; the nightmare was over. They had come through the valley of the shadow and survived.

She held out her hand to Blodwen. "Come with me. I'll tell Morgan you're here."

Isobel hurried ahead along the trail. Morgan waited for her at the cave entrance. He had watched her coming uphill and wondered who was following her. The dog did not growl at the stranger, so he felt reassured that there was no danger.

''Sweetheart, someone's here to see you,'' Isobel began, her heart fluttering uneasily as she prepared him. Would the sight of his sister set back his healing? She knew how deeply wounded he had been by Blodwen's betrayal.

''Who is it?'' he asked curiously, leaning against the rock entrance for support. He was weary after today's long journey, finding he was not nearly as strong as he liked to think.

Blodwen came closer, her frizzy gray hair fluttering wildly about her shoulders. He peered at her through the gloom, for her back was to the fading daylight.

''Will you still be my brother?'' she asked him gruffly.

Morgan gasped and his face instantly hardened. ''Blodwen!''

''Yes, it's me. I won't ask your forgiveness for what I've done. Only that you'll accept my apologies and allow me to live on the land again.''

He tossed many thoughts about in his mind. All his preconceived vows of vengeance against their betrayer were somehow meaningless in the face of all that had happened since. Silence stretched on. The sun dropped lower to rest on the distant hills.

Finally Morgan said gruffly, ''I accept your apology.''

Blodwen's face broke into a smile of relief, making her look more like the sister he remembered.

''Thank you,'' she said simply.

They embraced in forgiveness and tears glistened in their eyes. ''Will you rebuild?'' she asked after she had stepped back.

''That's what we intend,'' Isobel said quickly as she understood the question. She came to stand beside Morgan and slid her arm around him.

Surprised and pleased by her answer, Morgan gave Isobel a grateful smile. ''Thank you,'' he whispered.

''I'm glad to hear that,'' Blodwen said, straightening

up and regaining a little of her old vigor. "In that case you'll need this."

Blodwen held out her hand, and the golden seal of Nels caught fire in the rays of the fading sun.

"I've kept this safe for you."

Moved beyond measure, Morgan accepted the ancient symbol of the sovereignty of Nels, this reminder of his ancient bloodline, stretching back to the mists of time when this land was first inhabited. The lordship of Nels was his birthright. And as long as he lived, it would not die.

"Thank you, Blodwen."

"Yes, Blodwen, thank you from both of us," Isobel said, struggling to bury the last of her animosity toward this woman. She held out her hand and Blodwen gripped it thankfully. "We'll work together to rebuild what we've lost."

As one they turned toward the smoke-blackened ruin of Morgan's beloved white palace, its pale masonry gleaming in the fading light. Birds fluttered around the turrets, and woodland creatures moved stealthily through its long shadows. Though it was scarred and battle-weary, Llyswen lived on in their hearts. Someday it would rise again from the ashes, and their love would breathe life into its embers.

AUTHOR'S NOTE

In 1345, bubonic plague, known as the Black Death, spread from Asia into Europe. Spread by fleas from rats, the plague arrived in England aboard ship from France in the summer of 1348. The year was unusually wet. Crops rotted in the fields. People spent much time indoors, hastening the spread of the disease. By the time the plague was over, a third of England's population had died.

Sandra Hill's romances are "delicious, witty, and funny!"
—Romantic Times

Banished from polite society for bearing a child out of wedlock, Lady Eadyth of Hawks' Lair spends her days hidden under a voluminous veil, tending her bees. But when her son's detested father threatens to reveal the boy's true paternity and seize her beloved lands, Lady Eadyth seeks a husband who will claim the child as his own.

Notorious for loving—and leaving—the most beautiful damsels in the land, Eirik of Ravenshire is England's most virile bachelor. Yet when a mysterious beekeeper offers him a vow of chaste matrimony in exchange for revenge against his most hated enemy, Eirik can't refuse. But the lucky knight's plans go awry when he succumbs to the sweet sting of the tarnished lady's love.

_3834-X $5.50 US/$7.50 CAN

Dorchester Publishing Co., Inc.
P.O. Box 6640
Wayne, PA 19087-8640

Please add $1.75 for shipping and handling for the first book and $.50 for each book thereafter. NY, NYC, and PA residents, please add appropriate sales tax. No cash, stamps, or C.O.D.s. All orders shipped within 6 weeks via postal service book rate. Canadian orders require $2.00 extra postage and must be paid in U.S. dollars through a U.S. banking facility.

Name____
Address____
City_________________________State________Zip__________
I have enclosed $__________ in payment for the checked book(s).
Payment must accompany all orders. ☐ Please send a free catalog.